About th

Louise Fuller was a tomboy
wanted to be the prince. Not .... creating heroines who aren't pretty pushovers but strong, believable women. Before writing for Mills & Boon, she studied literature and philosophy at university and then worked as a reporter on her local newspaper. She lives in Tunbridge Wells with her impossibly handsome husband, Patrick and their six children.

Amanda Cinelli was born into a large Irish-Italian family and raised in the leafy green suburbs of County Dublin, Ireland. After dabbling in a few different career paths, she finally found her calling as an author after winning an online writing competition with her first finished novel. Her days are usually spent trying to find time to write in between the school runs and playing chef/chauffeur and referee to four young children.

USA Today bestselling author **Heidi Rice** used to work as a film journalist until she found a new dream job writing romance for Mills & Boon in 2007. She adores getting swept up in a world of high emotions, sensual excitement, funny feisty women, sexy tortured men and glamourous locations where laundry doesn't exist. She lives in London, England with her husband, two sons and lots of other gorgeous men who exist entirely in her imagination (unlike the laundry, unfortunately!).

Second Chance

Second Chance:

His Unexpected Heir

LOUISE FULLER

AMANDA CINELLI

HEIDI RICE

MILLS & BOON

First Published in Great Britain 2025
by Mills & Boon, an imprint of HarperCollins*Publishers* Ltd
1 London Bridge Street, London, SE1 9GF

www.harpercollins.co.uk

HarperCollins*Publishers*
Macken House, 39/40 Mayor Street Upper,
Dublin 1, D01 C9W8, Ireland

ISBN: 978-0-263-41740-1

MIX
Paper | Supporting
responsible forestry
FSC™ C007454

This book contains FSC™ certified paper and other controlled sources to ensure responsible forest management.

For more information visit: www.harpercollins.co.uk/green

Printed and Bound in the UK using 100% Renewable Electricity at CPI Group (UK) Ltd, Croydon, CR0 4YY

DEMANDING HIS SECRET SON

LOUISE FULLER

For Archie: for sticking at the hard stuff,
and making life easier for everyone
around you, especially me.

CHAPTER ONE

LEANING FORWARD, TEDDIE TAYLOR spread the three playing cards out swiftly, then quickly flipped them over, covering them with her hand and rearranging them. Her green eyes gave away none of her excitement, nor the jump of her heart as the man sitting opposite her pointed confidently at the middle card.

He groaned as she turned it over, holding his hands up in defeat. 'Incredible,' he murmured.

Rising to his feet, Edward Claiborne held out his hand, a satisfied smile creasing his smooth patrician features.

'I can't tell you how happy I am that you're on board.' His blue eyes fixed on Teddie's face. 'I'm looking forward to having a little magic in my life.'

Teddie smiled. From another, younger, less urbane man, the remark might have sounded a little cheesy. But she knew Claiborne was far too well-bred to do anything as crass and inappropriate as flirt with a woman half his age to whom he had just given a job at his new prestigious private members' club.

'I'm looking forward to it too, Mr Claiborne—no, please—' she stopped him as he reached into the pocket of his jacket '—let me get these.' She gestured towards the coffee. 'You're a client now.'

Watching him walk away to talk to someone in the hotel lounge, she took a deep breath and sat down, resisting the urge to pump the air with her fist in time to the victory chant inside her head. She'd done it! Finally she'd netted a client who saw magic as more than just an amusing diversion at a party.

Across the lounge, Edward Claiborne was shaking hands, smiling smoothly and, leaning back in her armchair, she let elation wash over her. This was what she and Elliot had been chasing, but this new contract was worth more to them than a paycheque. Claiborne was fifth generation New York money and a recommendation from him would give their business the kind of publicity they couldn't buy.

Pulling out her phone, she punched in Elliot's number. He answered immediately, almost as though he'd been waiting for her to call—which, of course, he had.

'That was quick. How did it go?'

He sounded as he always did, speaking with that casual west-coast drawl that people sometimes mistook for slowness or lack of comprehension. But to Teddie, who had known him since she was thirteen, there was a tension to his voice—understandably. A three-nights-a-week job of bringing magic and illusion to the brand-new Castine Club would not only boost their income, it would mean they could employ someone to do the day-to-day admin. And that would mean they wouldn't end up with a repeat of today's last-minute panic when Elliot had realised he'd double-booked himself.

For a moment, she considered making him sweat, but she was too happy and relieved. 'He's in!'

Hearing Elliot's triumphant 'Surf's up, baby!' she laughed.

It was one of the things she loved most about her business partner and best friend—the way he reverted to his Californian roots when he was excited. Her heart swelled. That and the fact that, no matter how unjustified it was, he always had complete faith in her.

'I'm not saying I thought it was guaranteed, but honestly—I don't think I've ever met anyone who loves magic so much.'

'So what clinched it? No, let me guess. The three-card Monte. I'm right, aren't I?'

Teddie could practically picture the familiar wicked grin on Elliot's face.

'Yes! But that doesn't mean I forgive you for throwing me in at the deep end.'

He laughed. 'So how about I take you and George to Pete's Grill at the weekend? To make amends and celebrate?'

'You're on.' She frowned. 'How come you're talking to me, anyway? I thought the whole reason I had to do this was because you had a meeting.'

'I do—I'm waiting to go in. Actually, I'm going to have to go—okay, babe? But I'll drop round later.' He whooped. 'I love this job!'

He hung up, and Teddie grinned. She loved her job too, and Elliot was right: they should celebrate. And George loved Pete's.

Thinking about her son, Teddie felt her heart tighten. She did love her job, but her love for George was fierce and absolute. From the moment she'd held him in her arms after his birth, her heart had been enslaved by his huge dark eyes.

He was perfect, and he was hers. And maybe, if this job went well, in a couple of years they'd be celebrating here.

Leaning back against the smooth leather upholstery of a chair that probably cost more than her car, Teddie glanced around the hotel lounge. Well, maybe not here. The Kildare Hotel was new, and completely beyond her pay grade, oozing a mixture of old-school comfort and avant-garde design that she might have found intimidating if she hadn't been feeling so euphoric.

It was clearly the place to be seen, judging by the mix of hip, moneyed guests, although—she stared critically at the two huge Warhol prints that dwarfed one wall—wasn't it a bit corny to have all these copies of famous paintings hanging everywhere. Why not use originals by local artists?

Glancing over to where Claiborne was still chatting, she felt her pulse skitter forward. Really, she should be over there too, networking. It didn't have to be too obvious. All she had to do was smile as she passed by and her new boss would definitely call her over to introduce her to his companion.

She couldn't see the man's face, but even at a distance his glamour and self-assurance were tangible. Silhouetted against the industrial-sized window, with sunlight fanning around him like a sunburst, he looked almost mythical. The effect was mesmerising, irresistible—and, catching sight of the furtive glances of the other guests, she realised that it wasn't only she who thought so.

She wondered idly if he was aware of the effect he was having or if he was worthy of all the attention. Maybe she should just go and see for herself, she thought, emboldened by her business triumph.

And then, as she began picking up the cards that were still strewn all over the table, she noticed that Claiborne was gesturing in her direction. Automatically her lips started to curve upwards as the man standing beside him turned towards her.

The welcoming smile froze on her face.

She swallowed thickly. Her heart felt hard and heavy—in fact, her whole body seemed to be slowly turning to stone. Her euphoria of just moments earlier felt like a muddied memory.

No—no way! This couldn't be happening. He couldn't be here. Not here, not now.

But he was. Worse, having shaken hands with Claiborne, he was excusing himself and walking—no, *swaggering* towards her, his familiar dark gaze locked with hers. And, despite the alarm shrieking inside her head, she couldn't drag her eyes away from his cold, staggeringly handsome face and lean, muscular body.

For just a split second she watched him make his way across the room, and then her heart began pounding like a jackhammer and she knew that she had to move, to run, to flee. It might not be dignified, but frankly she didn't care. Her ex-husband, Aristotle Leonidas, was the last person on earth she wanted to see, much less talk to. There was too much history between them—not just a failed marriage, but a three-year-old son he knew nothing about.

Snatching at the rest of the cards, she tried to force them into the box. Only, panic made her clumsier than usual and they slipped out of her hands, spilling onto the floor in every direction.

'Allow me.'

If it had been a shock seeing him across the room, seeing him up close was like being struck by lightning. It would have been easier if he'd developed a paunch, but he hadn't changed at all. If anything, he was more devastating than ever, and it was clear that he had risen to such a point of power and wealth that he was immune to such earthly concerns as appearances.

But, to Teddie, his beauty was still hypnotic—the knife-sharp bone structure and obsidian-dark eyes still too perfect to be human.

Feeling her pulse accelerate, Teddie steeled herself to meet his gaze.

It had been four years since he'd broken her heart and turned his back on the gift of her love, but she had never forgotten him nor forgiven him for deleting her—and by default George—from his life like some unsolicited junk email. But evidently she had underestimated the impact of his husky, seductive voice—or why else was her pulse shying sideways like a startled pony?

It was just shock, she reassured herself. After four years she was obviously not expecting to see him.

Pushing aside the memory of that moment when he'd dismissed her like some underperforming junior member of his staff, she frowned. 'I'm fine. Just leave it.'

He ignored her, crouching down and calmly and methodically picking up each and every card.

'Here.' Standing up, he held out the pack, but she stared at him tensely, reluctant to risk even the slightest physical contact between them.

Her body's irrational response to hearing him speak again had made her realise that despite everything he'd done—and not done—there was still a connection between them, a memory of what had once been, how good it had been—

Ignoring both that unsettling thought, and the tug of his gaze, she sat down. She wanted to leave, but she would have to push past him to do so, and sitting seemed like the lesser of two evils. He watched her for a moment, as though gauging the likelihood of her trying to escape, and then she felt her pulse jolt forward as he settled into the chair recently vacated by Claiborne.

'What are you doing here?' she said stiffly.

After they'd split up he'd moved to London—or that was what Elliot had been told when he'd gone to collect her things. The apartment hadn't been part of the divorce settlement, and she'd always assumed he'd sold it. But then, he had no need of money, and it probably had no bad memories for him as he'd hardly ever been there.

His level gaze swept over her face. 'In New York?' He shrugged. 'I'm living here. Again,' he added softly.

She swallowed, stung at the thought of him returning to their home and simply picking up where he'd left off. She wished she could think of something devastating to say back to him. But to do so would only suggest that she cared—which she obviously didn't.

She watched warily as he slid the pack across the table towards her.

Catching sight of her expression, he tutted under his breath, his dark brown eyes narrowing. 'I don't know why you're looking at me like that,' he said coolly. 'It's me who should be worried. Or at least checking my wrist.'

His gaze hovered on her face and she blinked. She'd thought her body's unintended and unwelcome response to his was a by-product of shock, but now, beneath the politeness, further down than the hostility, she could feel it still—a thread of heat that was undiminished by time or reason. It made no sense—she doubted that he'd given her as much as a passing thought in the last four years—but that didn't seem to stop her skin from tingling beneath his gaze.

Watching the fury flare in her fabulous green eyes, Aristo gritted his teeth. She was still as stubborn as ever, but he was grateful she hadn't taken the cards from him. If both his hands had been free he might have been tempted to strangle her.

He hadn't spotted Teddie when he'd first walked into the lounge, partly because her dark brown hair was not falling loosely to her shoulders, as it had done when he'd last seen her, but was folded neatly at the back of her head.

In the main, though, he hadn't spotted her because, frankly, he hadn't ever expected to see his ex-wife again. He felt a tiny stab of pain in his heart like a splinter of ice.

But then, why would he?

Four years ago Theodora Taylor had ensnared him with her green eyes, her long legs and her diffident manner. She had breezed into his life like the Sirocco, interrupting his calm and ordered ascent into the financial stratosphere, and then just as quickly she had gone, an emptied bank account and his lacerated heart the only reminders of their six-month marriage.

He gave her a long, implacable stare. Teddie had taken more than his money. She had stolen the beat from his heart and taken what little trust he'd had for women and trampled it into the ground. It had been the first time he'd let down his guard, even going so far as to honour her with his name, but she had only married him in the hope that his money and connections would act as a stepping stone to a better life.

Of course he hadn't realised the truth until he'd returned from a business trip to find her gone. Hurt and humiliated, he had thrown himself into his job and put the whole disastrous episode behind him.

Until he'd bumped into Edward Claiborne a moment ago. He knew Edward socially, and liked him for his quiet self-assurance and old-school courtesy.

Walking into the hotel lounge, he'd noticed him laughing and chatting with uncharacteristic animation to a female companion. But it had only been when Edward had invited him to the new regular magic slot at his club, and then mentioned that he'd just finished having coffee with the woman who'd be running the shows, that he had turned and seen Teddie.

The muscle in his jaw had flexed, kick-starting a chain reaction through his body so that suddenly his heart had been pounding so hard and fast that he'd felt almost dizzy.

He studied her silently now, safe in the knowledge that his external composure gave no hint of the battle raging inside him. His head was telling him there was only one course of action. That a sensible, sane man would get up and walk away. But sense and sanity had never played that much of a part in his relationship with Theodora Taylor, and clearly nothing had changed—because despite knowing that she was the biggest mistake he had ever made, he stayed sitting.

His lip curled as he glanced down at his wrist. 'No, still there. But maybe I should double-check my wallet. Or perhaps I should give Edward Claiborne a call…make sure he still has his. I know you were only having coffee, but you were always a quick worker. I should know.'

Teddie felt her cheeks grow warm. His face was impenetrable, but the derision in his voice as much as his words was insultingly obvious.

How dare he talk to her like that? As though she was the bad guy when he was the one who had cut her out of his life without so much as a word.

Not that she'd ever been high on his list of priorities. Six months of married life had made it clear that Aristo had no time in his life for a wife. Even when she'd moved out and they'd begun divorce proceedings, he'd carried on working as though nothing had happened. Although no amount of his neglect and indifference could have prepared her for how he'd behaved at the end.

It had been a mistake, sleeping together that last time.

With emotions running high after a meeting to discuss their divorce, they'd ended up in bed and she'd ended up pregnant. Only, by the time she'd realised that her tiredness and nausea weren't just symptoms of stress, the divorce had been finalised, and Aristo had been on the other side of the world, building his European operations.

Although he might just as well have been in outer space.

Remembering her repeated, increasingly desperate and unsuccessful attempts to get in touch, she felt her back stiffen. She'd been frantic to tell him she was pregnant, but his complete radio silence had made it clear—horribly, humiliatingly clear—not only that he didn't want to talk to her, but that he didn't want to listen to *anything* she had to say.

It had been during a call to his London office, when an over-officious PA had cut short her stumbling and not very coherent attempt to speak to him, that she had decided doing the right thing was not going to work.

It certainly hadn't worked for her parents.

Sometimes it was better to face the truth, even if it was painful—and, truthfully, she and Aristo's relationship had had pretty flimsy foundations. Judging by the mess they'd made of their marriage, it certainly wasn't strong enough to cope with an unplanned pregnancy.

But it had been hard.

Aristo's rejection had broken her heart, and the repercussions of their brief and ill-fated marriage had lasted longer than her tears. Even now, she was still so wary of men that she'd barely gone out with anyone since they'd parted ways. Thanks to her father's casual, cursory attitude to parenting, she found it hard to believe that she would ever be anything more than an afterthought to any man. Aristo's casual, cruel rejection had confirmed that deep-seated privately held fear.

Much as she cared for Elliot, it was as a sister. Aristo was still the only man she'd ever loved. He had been her first love—not her first lover, but he had taught her everything about pleasure.

Her green eyes lifted to his. And not just pleasure. Because of him she'd become an authority on heartache and regret too.

So what exactly gave *him* the right to stand there with a sneer on that irritatingly handsome face?

Suddenly she was glad she hadn't turned tail. Fingers curling into fists, she glared at him. 'I think your memory must be playing tricks on you, Aristo. Work was always your thing—not mine. And, not that it's any of your concern, but Edward Claiborne is a very generous man. He was more than happy to pay the bill.'

She knew how she was making it sound, but it wasn't quite a lie. He *had* offered to pay. And besides, if it made Aristo feel even a fraction of her pain, then why not rub it in? He might not have thought her worthy of his attention and commitment, but Edward had been happy to give her his time and his company.

'And that's what matters to you, isn't it, Theodora? Getting your bills paid. Even if it means taking what isn't yours.'

He didn't really care about the money—even before his ruthless onwards-and-upwards rise to global domination, the amount she'd taken had been a negligible amount. Now it would barely make a dent in the Leonidas billions. At the time, though, it had stung—particularly as it had been down to his own stupidity.

For some unknown reason he hadn't closed their shared accounts immediately after the divorce was finalised, and Teddie had wasted no time taking advantage. Not that he should have been surprised. No matter how pampered they were, women were never satisfied with what they had. He'd learned that aged six, when his mother had found a titled, wealthier replacement for his father.

But knowing Teddie had worked her 'magic' on Edward hurt—and, childish though it was, he wanted to hurt her back.

Her eyes narrowed. 'It was mine,' she said hotly. '*It was ours*. That's what marriage is about, Aristo— it's called sharing.'

He stared at her disparagingly. The briefness of their marriage and the ruthless determination of his legal team had ensured that her financial settlement had been minimal, but it was more than she deserved.

'Is that what you tell yourself?'

She felt the hairs stand up on the back of her neck as he shook his head slowly.

'Just because it was still a joint account that didn't mean you had the right to empty it.'

'If it bothered you that much you could have *talked* to me,' she snarled. 'But I was only your wife—why would you want to talk to me?'

'Don't give me that,' he said sharply. 'I talked to you.'

'You talked at me about work. Never about us.'

Never about the fact that they were basically living separate lives—two strangers sharing a bed but never a meal or a joke.

Hearing the emotion in her voice, she stopped abruptly. What was the point of having this conversation? It was four years too late, and their marriage couldn't have mattered that much to him if all he wanted to discuss now was their bank account.

And was it really that surprising? His whole life had been dedicated to making money.

She breathed in unsteadily. 'And, as for the money, I took what I needed to live.'

To look after our son, she thought with a sudden flare of anger. A son who even before his birth had been relegated to second place.

'I'm not going to apologise for that, and if it was a problem then you should have said something at the time, but you made it quite clear that you didn't want to talk to me.'

Aristo stared at her, anger pulsing beneath his skin. At the time he had seen her behaviour as just more evidence of his poor judgement. More proof that the women in his life would inevitably turn their backs on him.

But he was not about to reveal his reasons for staying silent—why should he? He wasn't the one who'd walked out on their marriage. He didn't need to explain himself.

His heart began to thump rhythmically inside his chest, and an old, familiar feeling of bitter, impotent fury formed a knot in his stomach. She was right. He should have dealt

with this years ago—because even though he had succeeded in erasing her from his heart and his home, he had
never quite managed to wipe her betrayal from his memory.

How could he, though? Their relationship had been over
so quickly and had ended with such finality that there had
been no time to confront her properly.

Until now.

Teddie stared at him in appalled silence as, leaning back,
he stretched out his legs. Moments earlier she had wanted
to throw George's existence in his face. Now, though,
she could feel spidery panic scuttling over her skin at the
thought of how close she'd come to revealing the truth.

'So let's talk now,' he said, turning to nod curtly at a
passing waiter, who hurried over with almost comical haste.

She nearly laughed, only it was more sad than funny. He
didn't want to talk now any more than he had four years
ago, but he knew that she wanted to leave so he wanted to
make her stay. Nothing had changed. He hadn't changed.
He just wanted to get his own way.

'An espresso, please, and an Americano.' He gave the
order without so much as looking at her, and the fact that
he could still remember her favourite drink, as much as his
arrogant assumption that she would be joining him, made
her want to scream.

'I'm not staying,' she said coldly. She knew from past
experience that his powers of persuasion were incomparable, but in the past she had loved him to distraction. Here,
in the present, she wasn't going to let him push her into a
corner. 'And I don't want to speak to you,' she said, glancing pointedly past him.

He shrugged, a mocking smile curving his mouth. 'Then
I'll talk and you can listen.'

Cheeks darkening with angry colour, she sat mutinously
as the waiter reappeared and, with a swift, nervous glance
at Aristo, deposited the drinks in front of them.

'Is there anything else, Mr Leonidas?'

Aristo shook his head. 'No, thank you.'

Teddie stared at him, a beat of irritation jumping in her chest. It was always the same, this effect that Aristo had on people. When they'd first met she'd teased him about it: as a magician, *she* was supposed to be the centre of attention. But even when his wealth had been visible but not daunting, he'd had something that set him apart from all the other beautiful rich people—a potent mix of power and beauty and vitality that created an irresistible gravitational pull around him.

She could hardly blame the poor waiter for being like a cat on hot bricks when she had been just as susceptible. It was still maddening, though.

Some of her feelings must be showing on her face, for as he reached to pick up his cup, he paused. 'Is there a problem?'

She raised her eyebrows. 'Other than you, you mean?'

He sighed. 'I meant with your drink. I can send it back.'

'Could you just stop throwing your weight around?' She shook her head in exasperation. 'I know it must be difficult for you to switch off from work, but this isn't one of your hotels.'

Leaning back, he raised the cup to his mouth, his eyes never leaving her face. 'Actually it is,' he said mildly. 'It's the first in a new line we're trying out—traditional elegance and luxury with impeccable sustainability.' He smiled at the look of frozen horror on her face. 'And a constantly rotating collection of contemporary art.'

She felt her breathing jerk as out of the corner of her eye she noticed the tiny lion's head logo on the coaster. Cheeks burning, she glanced furtively over at the Warhols.

Damn it, but of course they were real. Aristo Leonidas would never have anything in his life that wasn't one hundred per cent perfect—it was why he'd found it so devastatingly easy to abandon her.

Her heartbeat stumbled in her chest. No doubt he'd only wanted her to stay here so he could point out this latest addition to his empire.

Cursing herself, and Aristo, and Elliot for being so useless at managing their schedule, she half rose.

'Sit down,' he said softly.

Their eyes clashed. 'I don't want to.'

'Why? Are you scared of what will happen if you do?

Was she scared?

She felt her insides flip over, and she suddenly felt hot and dizzy.

Once she had been in thrall to him. He'd been everything she'd wanted in a lover and in a man. Caught in the dark shimmering intensity of his gaze, she had felt warm and wanted.

And now, as the heat spread outwards, she was forced to accept again that, even hating him as she did, her body was still reacting in the same way, unconstrained by logic or even the most basic sense of self-preservation.

Horrified by this revelation of her continuing vulnerability—or maybe stupidity—she lifted her chin, her eyes narrowing, muscles tensing as though for combat.

'I'm not, no. But *you* should be. Or maybe you like your suits with coffee stains?'

His dark eyes flickered with amusement. 'If you want me to get undressed, you could just ask.'

He was unbelievable and unfair, making such a blatant reference to their sexual past. But, despite her outrage, she felt the kick of desire. Just as she had that night four years ago, when her body had betrayed her.

Her heart thudded. How could she have let it happen? Just hours earlier they'd been thrashing out their divorce.

She'd known he didn't love her, and yet she'd still slept with him.

But she could never fully regret her stupidity for that was the night she'd conceived George.

She glowered at him. 'I don't want you at all,' she lied. 'And I don't want to have some stupid conversation about coffee or art.'

He held up his hands in mock surrender. 'Okay, okay. Look, this is hard for both us, but we share a history. Surely if fate has chosen to throw us together we can put our differences behind us for old times' sake,' he said smoothly. 'Surely you can spare a couple of minutes to catch up.'

Teddie felt her heart start to pound. If only if was just the past they shared. But it wasn't, and hiding that fact from Aristo was proving harder than she'd ever imagined.

But how could she tell him the truth? That he had a three-year-old son called George he'd never met. She caught her breath, trying to imagine how that conversation would start, much less end.

More importantly, though, why would she tell him? Their marriage might have been short-lived, but it had been long enough for her to know that there was no room in her ex-husband's life for anything but his career. And, having been on the receiving end of her father's intermittent attention, she knew exactly what it felt like to be a side dish to the main meal, and she was not about to let her son suffer the same fate.

'I just told you. I don't want to stay.' But, glancing up into his dark eyes, she felt a flare of panic, for they were cold and flat like slate, and they matched the uncompromising expression on his face.

'I wasn't actually giving you an option.'

She felt the colour leave her face. Had he really just said what she thought he had?

'What is that supposed to mean?' Instantly her panic

was forgotten, obliterated in a white-out of fury. 'Just because this is your hotel, Aristo, it doesn't mean you can act like some despot,' she snapped.' If I want to leave, I will, thank you very much, and there's nothing you can do about it.'

Aristo stared at her in silence. Was this why he had sought out her company instead of simply retreating? To force a confrontation so that, unlike in their marriage, he would be the one to dictate when she left? Would that heal the still festering wound of her betrayal? Quiet the suspicion, the knowledge, that he had been used like a plaything to pass the time until something, or more likely *someone*, better came along?

He shrugged dismissively. 'That would depend, I suppose, on how you leave and whether you value your reputation. Being removed by Security in front of a room full of people could be quite damaging.' Leaning back in his seat, he raised an eyebrow. 'I can't imagine what your new boss would think if he heard about it.'

'You wouldn't dare,' she said softly.

His eyes didn't leave her face. 'Try me!'

He could see the conflict in her eyes—frustration and resentment battling with logic and resignation—but he knew the battle was already won. If she was going to leave she would already be on her feet.

With immense satisfaction he watched her sit back stiffly in her seat. This wasn't about revenge, but even so he couldn't help letting a small, triumphant smile curve his mouth.

'So...' He gestured towards the pack of cards. 'You're still a magician, then.'

Teddie stared at the cards. To anyone else his remark would have sounded innocuous, nothing more than a polite show of interest in an ex's current means of employment. But she wasn't anyone. She had been his wife, and she could hear the resentment in his voice for she had heard it before.

It was another reminder of why their marriage had failed. And why she should have confronted the past head-on instead of pretending her marriage had never happened. She might have been strong for her son, but she'd been a coward when it came to facing Aristo.

Only, she'd had good reason not to want to face him. Lots of good reasons, actually.

In the aftermath of their marriage he'd been cold and unapproachable, and later she'd been so sick with her pregnancy, and then, by the time she'd felt well again, George had been born—and that was a whole other conversation.

She was suddenly conscious of Aristo's steady, dark gaze and her heart gave a thump. She had to stop thinking about George or something was going to slip out.

'Yes,' she said curtly. 'I'm still a magician, Aristo. And you're still in hotels.'

Her heart was thumping hard against her chest. Did he really want to sit here with her while they politely pretended to be on speaking terms? Her hands felt suddenly damp and she pressed them against the cooling leather. Clearly he did. But then, he didn't have a secret to keep.

He nodded. 'Mostly, but I've diversified my interests.'

She gritted her teeth. So even less time for anything other than work. For some reason that thought made her feel sad rather than angry and, caught off-guard, she picked up her coffee and took a sip.

Aristo looked at her, his gaze impassive. 'You must have done well. Edward Claiborne doesn't often go out of his comfort zone. So how did you two meet?'

His eyes tangled with hers and he felt a stab of anger, remembering Edward Claiborne's proprietorial manner as he'd turned and gestured across the room towards Teddie.

She shrugged. 'Elliot and I did some magic showcases at a couple of charity balls last year and he was there.'

Aristo stared at her coldly. 'You work with Elliot?'

For some reason her defiant nod made a primitive jealousy rip through him like a box-cutter. In his head—if he'd allowed himself to picture her at all—she had been alone, suffering as he was. Only, now it appeared that not only had she survived, she was prospering with Elliot.

'We set up a business together. He does the admin, front of house and accountancy. I do the magic.'

He felt another spasm of irritation—pain, almost. He knew Teddie had never been romantically or sexually involved with Elliot, but he had supported her, and once that had been *his* job. It was bad enough that his half-brother, Oliver, had displaced him in his mother's affections—now it appeared that Elliot had usurped him in Teddie's.

'From memory, he wasn't much of a businessman,' he said coolly.

For the first time since she'd sat down Teddie smiled and, watching her eyes soften, he had to fight an overwhelming urge to reach out and stroke her cheek, for once her eyes had used to soften for him in that way.

'He's not, but he's my best friend and I trust him,' she said simply. 'And that's what matters.'

It was tempting to lie, to tell him that she'd found love and unimaginable passion in Elliot's arms, but it would only end up making her look sad and desperate.

He raised an eyebrow. 'Surely what matters is profit?'

She'd always known he felt like that, but somehow his remark hurt more than it should, for it was the reason her son would grow up without a father.

Her fingers curled. 'Some things are more important than money, Aristo.'

'Not in business,' he said dismissively.

She glared at him, hating him and his stupid, blinkered

view of life, but hating herself more for still caring what he thought.

'But there's more to life than business. There's feelings and people—friends, family—'

She broke off, the emotion in her voice echoing inside her head. Glancing up, she found him watching her, his gaze darkly impassive, and it was hard not to turn away, for the heartbreakingly familiar masculine beauty of his face seemed so at odds with the distance in his eyes.

'You don't have a family,' he said.

It was one of the few facts she'd shared with him about her life—that she was an orphan. Dazed, Teddie blinked. She was about to retort that she was a mother to his son, when abruptly her brain came back online and she bit back her words. Given how he'd behaved, and was still behaving, she certainly didn't owe him the truth.

But George was his child. Didn't he deserve to know that?

Her heartbeat stalled, and for a moment she couldn't breathe. Her stomach seemed to be turning in on itself. Wishing that she could make herself disappear as effortlessly as she could make watches and wallets vanish, she forced herself to meet his gaze.

'No, I don't,' she lied.

And suddenly she knew that she had to leave right there and then, for to stay would mean more lies, and she couldn't do it—she didn't want to lie about her son.

Neither could she carry on lying to herself.

Up until today she had wanted to believe that she was over Aristo. But as she stared into his dark, distant eyes, the pain of pretending erupted inside of her, and suddenly she needed to make certain this *never* happened again.

She'd made the mistake of letting him back into her life before—made the mistake of following her heart, not her head. And although she didn't regret it—for that would mean regretting having her son—after that one-night stand she'd accepted not only that their marriage was over, but that it was the best possible outcome.

Only by staying out of his orbit would she be safe—not just from him, but from herself.

She lifted her chin. This meeting would be their last.

Ignoring the intensity of his dark gaze, and the full, sensuous mouth that had so often kissed her into a state of helpless bliss, she cleared her throat. 'Fascinating though this is, Aristo, I don't really think there's any point in us carrying on with this conversation,' she said. 'Small talk—any kind of talk, really—wasn't ever your strong point, and we got divorced for a reason—several, actually.'

He held her gaze. 'Are you refusing to talk to me?'

'Yes, I am.'

But she didn't want to explain why. Didn't want to explain the complex and conflicting emotions swirling inside her.

Her heart was banging against her ribs and, breathing in deeply, she steadied herself. Reaching into her bag, she pulled out a pen and a notebook and scrawled something on a page inside it. Tearing the page free, she folded it in half and slid it onto the table.

'I don't expect to hear from you again, but if you have to get in touch this is my lawyer's number. Goodbye, Aristotle.'

And then, before he'd even had a chance to react, let alone respond, she turned and almost ran out of the hotel lounge.

Left alone, Aristo stared at the empty seat, a mass of emotions churning inside him. His heart was beating out of time. Teddie's words had shocked him. But, although she had no doubt intended her curt goodbye to be a slap in the face, to him it felt as though she'd thrown down a gauntlet at his feet.

And in doing so she'd sealed her fate. Four years ago she had waltzed out of their marriage and his life and he'd spent the intervening years suppressing hurt and disappointment. Now, though, he was ready to confront his past—*and* his ex-wife.

But he would do so on his terms, he thought coldly. And, reaching into his jacket, he pulled out his phone.

Three hours later, having fed and bathed George and tidied away his toys, Teddie leaned back against the faded cushions of her sofa and let out a long, slow breath. She felt exhausted. Her apartment—her wonderful apartment—with its bright walls and wooden floors, which was usually a place of sanctuary, looked shabby after the high gloss of the Kildare Hotel. And, although her son was usually a sweet-tempered and easy-going toddler, he must have picked up on her tension. Tonight he'd had a huge tantrum when she'd stopped him playing with his toy speed boat in the bath.

He was sleeping now, and as she'd gazed down at her beautiful son she had felt both pride and panic, for he so resembled his father. A father he would never know.

She felt a rush of guilt and self-pity. This wasn't what she'd wanted for herself or for her son. In her dreams she'd wanted to give him everything she'd never had—two loving parents, financial security—but she'd tried marriage and it had been a disaster.

Even before Aristo's obsession with work had blotted out the rest of his life she had felt like a gatecrasher in her own marriage. But then what had they really known about one another? How could you really know someone after just seven weeks?

Maybe if their marriage had had stronger foundations it might have been possible for them to face their problems together. But they'd had no common ground aside from a raging sexual attraction which had been enough to blind both of them to their fundamental incompatibility. He had been born into wealth. She, on the other hand, had grown up in a children's home with a mother dosed up on prescription drugs and a father in prison.

And sex wasn't enough to sustain a relationship—not without trust and openness and tenderness.

Divorce had been the only option, and, although she might be able to face that fact she still wasn't up to facing Aristo. Thankfully, though, she would never have to see him again.

Her pulse twitched as she remembered telling him to talk to her through her lawyer. She could hardly believe that she'd spoken to him like that. But she'd been so desperate to leave before she said anything incriminating about George, and even more desperate to ensure that he would be out of her life for good.

Stifling a yawn, she picked up her phone and gazed gloomily down at the time on the screen. All she wanted to do was crawl into bed, pull the duvet over her head and forget about the mess she'd made of her life.

Unfortunately Elliot was dropping round to discuss the Claiborne meeting.

For a moment she considered calling him to cancel. But being on her own with a head full of regrets and recriminations was not a great idea.

Anticipating Elliot's partisan comments as she relayed an edited version of the day's events, she felt her mood lighten a fraction and, standing up, she walked into the tiny kitchen that led off from the living room.

She was just pulling a bottle of wine from the rack when she heard the entryphone.

Thank goodness! Elliot was early. Buzzing him up, she picked up a bottle of wine and two glasses.

'Don't be thinking we're going to finish this—' she began as she yanked open the door.

But her words trailed off into silence. It wasn't Elliot standing there, with that familiar affectionate grin on his face. Instead it was Aristo, and he wasn't smiling affectionately. In fact, he wasn't smiling at all.

CHAPTER TWO

'I WOULDN'T DREAM of it,' he said softly.

He held out his hand, his eyes locking with hers, and his sudden, swift smile made her heart lurch forward.

'You forgot these, and I was passing so...'

It was the pack of cards she'd left at his hotel.

She felt her breathing jerk. For a few seconds she couldn't answer—couldn't find the words to express her shock and confusion at finding him on her doorstep. Actually, not *on* her doorstep—he was already leaning against the frame, one foot resting negligently over the threshold so that shutting the door wouldn't just be a challenge, but a virtual impossibility, given the disparity in their respective weights.

'You were passing?'

She felt a shiver run over her skin as his dark gaze made a slow inspection of her, from the damp hair tumbling over her shoulders to her bare toes. Even if she'd been fully clothed she would have felt naked under his intense scrutiny, but she was wearing nothing but a T-shirt that was barely covered by her bathrobe.

There was a pulsing silence and then, tilting his head slightly, he glanced past her into the apartment. 'Aren't you going to invite me in? Or do you always entertain your guests in the corridor?'

'You're not a guest. Guests are invited, and I didn't invite you.' She stared at him suspiciously. 'And I didn't tell you where I lived either, so how did you find me?'

'I looked up "beautiful female magician" in the phone book.' His dark eyes glittered with amusement. 'You were there—right at the top.'

Her skin was suddenly prickling, her stomach flipping over in response to his words. She'd spent so long remembering his flaws that she had forgotten he could make her laugh and it was an untimely reminder of why she'd fallen in love with him.

Only, even as her mouth began to curl upwards she knew she was making a mistake. The last thing she needed right now was to give him any hint of her continuing vulnerability where he was concerned so, tuning out the erratic beat of her heart, she shook her head. 'Aristo—'

'Okay, that was a lie.' He shifted against the doorframe. 'I actually looked up "*angry*, beautiful female magician".'

Heart banging against her ribs, she took a deep breath, a rush of panic swamping her as she tried to gauge his mood. Surely if he'd found out about George he would be the angry one.

'Did you follow me?'

His smile widened. 'Of course. I have a second job as a private detective.'

Resisting the overriding urge to slam the door on his obviously expensive handmade shoes, she held his gaze. 'Very funny. So you had somebody find out where I lived?' She shook her head again. 'That's classy, Aristo.'

'You gave me no choice. You left before we'd finished talking.'

His complete inability to understand what had happened back at the hotel sucked her breath from her lungs.

'No, *I* had finished talking, Aristo,' she said irritably. 'That's why I gave you the number of my lawyer.'

'Ah, yes, your lawyer.' Pausing, he glanced over his

shoulder and frowned, pretending concern. 'Are you sure you want everyone hearing about your private business?'

Teddie stared at him helplessly. She could tell from the glint in his eyes that he was not going to leave without saying whatever it was he wanted to say, and she couldn't physically remove him herself.

Maybe she should call for back-up. But who would she call? Her maintenance charge for the apartment included a caretaker who was nominally responsible for security, but she had no idea how to get in touch with him, and Aristo might make a scene and wake George.

So that left her with the choice of having a conversation in the hallway or in her apartment. Her heart contracted with apprehension. Every instinct she had was screeching at her like a banshee not to let him into her apartment, but what if he met one of her neighbours and they mentioned her son?

Maybe there were other options, but right now she was too tired and strung out to work them out—and besides, she wanted him out of the hallway and her life.

Quickly she did an inventory of the apartment—thankfully she had tidied George's toys away, and the only photos of him were in her bedroom. Her skin felt suddenly hot and tight, but of course there was no way Aristo would be going within a mile of that particular room.

'Fine. You can come in,' she said briskly. 'But you can't stay long.'

Mentally crossing her fingers, she hoped that tonight wouldn't be the one occasion when Elliot was on time. She had, of course, given him an abridged version of her ill-starred marriage, only she had carefully edited out all mention of the tangle of unresolved feelings she still carried around with her.

But Elliot would only have to walk through her front door to know that she was upset, and right now she had enough going on with Aristo. She certainly didn't want to have to deal with Elliot as well.

'Ten minutes, Aristo, that's all. And you'll have to be quiet. I have elderly neighbours,' she lied, 'and I don't want to disturb them.'

His dark, unwavering gaze fixed on hers and she felt a sudden rush of panic, for it seemed as though he could not only sense her lies, but also the reason behind them—as if the T-shirt she was wearing was printed with the truth.

'I can do quiet, Theodora. Or have you forgotten?'

Her pulse fluttered, cheeks suddenly burning. No, she hadn't forgotten. They had often been caught out by the strength of their desire, and on one particularly memorable occasion in a park they had satisfied their passion beneath the shade of a tree, hidden from passers-by. Quickly she pushed the thought away, wishing her brain hadn't chosen to save that particular memory for posterity, but not even divorce proceedings had weakened the devastating pull of desire between them.

Ignoring the quivering tension of her body, she lifted her chin and smiled at him coolly. 'It must have slipped my memory.'

Turning, she let the door fall back on his foot, his grunt of pain giving her a momentary but sharp satisfaction.

Stopping what she considered a safe distance away from him, she watched as he strolled into her living room, his assessing gaze travelling over the modest interior and no doubt contrasting it with the luxury of the apartment they'd once shared. But who cared what he thought? He was only here under sufferance, and she needed to make that clear to him.

'I gave you my lawyer's number for a reason. So why are you here?' she asked stiffly.

She didn't much care, but now that he was standing in her living room she realised there was no such thing as *safe* for her where Aristo was concerned. He was still wearing his suit, but he'd unbuttoned his shirt and lost the tie. Only, instead of making him less intimidating, his more relaxed appearance only seemed to emphasise his natural authority.

Add to that the fact that they were completely alone, it was no surprise that her head was starting to swim.

But it wasn't just the tantalising temptation of his nearness that was making her hold her breath. Earlier she'd been so concerned about inadvertently revealing something about George that she'd been able to ignore her guilt at not doing so. In the unfamiliar surroundings of the Kildare Hotel it had felt almost like someone else's life.

Now, though, it felt real, *personal*, and she could feel herself wavering. Could she really go through with this? Could she really cheat him out of knowing his son? Shouldn't she at least give him the chance? And what about George? He'd already asked her why he didn't have a daddy.

So far he was too young to really focus on the issue, but that would change...

'I didn't speak to her.'

It took her a moment to realise that he was replying to her question about her lawyer.

He was standing with his back to her, studying the books on her shelves, and she stared tensely at him, remembering how he'd loved to lie with that same head on her lap and how she'd loved to run her fingers through the thick, black hair...

She jumped slightly as he turned, her cheeks flushing with colour as his all-seeing dark eyes fixed on hers.

'There was no point,' he said blithely. 'Why pay legal fees when we can talk for free?'

Her skin felt suddenly too tight. There was a long, steady silence as she stared at him incredulously. If she hadn't been so stunned, she might have laughed. 'Are you giving me advice?'

There was another long silence, and then he shrugged. 'Somebody has to. Clearly whoever has been doing so up until now can't have had your best interests at heart.'

He watched her green eyes widen, feeling childishly but intensely gratified that his words had clearly scored a direct hit. And then he caught sight of the two glasses and abruptly his mood changed, for clearly she hadn't been planning on spending the evening alone.

Ever since she'd more or less fled from him, he'd been questioning her motives for doing so. Although he knew their relationship was purely professional, Edward Claiborne and Teddie had looked good together, and it had got to him—for, just like his mother, Teddie was not the kind of women to be alone. Despite her denial, he had no doubt that somewhere in the city there was a nameless, faceless man who had stepped into his shoes.

In fact that was why he'd found himself standing on her doorstep. Even just imagining it made a knot of rage form in his stomach, and that enraged him further—the fact that she still had the power to affect him after all these years.

His shoulders tensed. 'Or perhaps they have their own agenda.'

Teddie felt a rush of anger spread over her skin like a heat rash. '*Nobody* has been giving me advice. I make my own decisions—although I wouldn't expect you to understand that.' Heart thumping, she lifted her gaze to his. 'It was always a difficult concept for you, wasn't it, Aristo? My being an independent woman?'

His eyes flickered, and she could almost see the fuse inside of him catch light.

'If by "independent" you mean self-absorbed and unsupportive, then, yes, I suppose it was.'

She caught her breath. The room felt suddenly cramped and airless, as though it had shrunk in the face of his anger—an anger which fed the outrage that had been simmering inside her since meeting him earlier.

'*You're* calling *me* self-absorbed and unsupportive?' She glared at him, the sheer injustice of his statement blowing her away. She could feel her grip on her temper starting to slip. How dare he turn up here, in her home, and start throwing accusations at her?

But even as she choked on her anger, she wasn't really surprised. Back when she'd loved him, she'd known that he had a single-minded vision of the world—a world in which he was always in the right and always had the last word. Her refusing to talk to him now simply didn't fit with that expectation.

Her motives, her needs, were irrelevant. As far as he was concerned she had merely issued him with a challenge that must instantly be confronted and crushed.

Queasily, she remembered his cold hostility when she'd refused to give up her job. Was that when their marriage had really ended? It was certainly the moment when she'd finally been forced to acknowledge the facts. That marrying Aristo had not been an act of impulse, driven by an undeniable love, but a mistake based on a misguided hope and longing to have a place in his life, and in his heart.

But Aristo didn't have a heart, and he hadn't come to her apartment to return a pack of cards. As usual, he just wanted to have the last word.

Crossing her arms to contain the ache in her chest, she lifted her chin. 'If you believe that, then perhaps I should have given you the number for my doctor, as you're clearly delusional,' she snapped. 'Wanting to carry on doing a job I loved didn't make me self-absorbed, Aristo. It was an act of self-preservation.'

Aristo stared at her, his shoulders rigid with frustration. 'Self-preservation!' he scoffed. 'You were living in a penthouse in Manhattan with a view of Central Park. You were hardly on Skid Row.' He shook his dark head in disbelief. 'That's the trouble with you, Teddie—you're so used to performing you turn every single part of your life into a stunt, even this conversation.'

They were both almost shouting now, their bodies braced against the incoming storm.

Her eyes narrowed. 'You think this is a conversation?' she snapped. 'You didn't come here to converse. I bruised your ego so you wanted—'

'Mommy—Mommy!'

The child's voice came from somewhere behind her, cutting through her angry tirade like a scythe through wheat. Turning instantly, instinctively, Teddie cleared her throat.

'Oh, sweetheart, it's all right.'

Her son, George, blinked up at her. He was wearing his pyjamas and holding his favourite toy boat and she felt a rush of pure, fierce love as she looked down into his huge, anxious dark eyes.

'Mommy shouted…'

He bit his lip and, hearing the wobble in his voice, she reached down and curved her arm unsteadily around his stocky little waist and pulled him closer, pressing his body against hers. 'I'm sorry, darling. Did Mommy wake you?'

Lifting him up, she held him tightly as he nodded his head against her shoulder.

Watching Teddie press her face against the little dark-haired boy's cheek, Aristo felt his stomach turn to ice.

He felt winded by the discovery that she had a child. No, it was more than that: he felt *wounded*, even though he could come up with no rational explanation for why that should be the case.

His pulse was racing like a bolting horse, his thoughts

firing off in every direction. He could hardly take it in, but there could be no mistake. This child was Teddie's son. But why hadn't she told him?

Thinking back to their earlier conversation, he replayed her words and felt an icy fury rise up inside of him. Not only had she said nothing, she'd lied to his face when he'd asked her about her family. Of course he'd been talking about siblings, cousins, aunts—but why hadn't she told him then? Why had she kept her son a secret?

At that moment the little boy lifted his face and suddenly he couldn't breathe. At the periphery of his vision he could see Teddie turning to face him, and then he knew why, for her green eyes were telling him what her mouth—that beautiful, soft, deceiving mouth—had failed to do earlier.

This was his son.

Like a drowning man, he saw his whole life speeding through his head—meeting Teddie at that dinner, her long dark hair swinging forward half-hiding a smile that had stolen his breath away, the echoing emptiness of his apartment, and that moment in the Kildare when she'd hesitated…

He breathed out unsteadily, and abruptly his pulse juddered to a halt.

Only, he wasn't drowning in water, but in lies. Teddie's lies.

The resentment and hostility he'd felt after she'd left him, the shock of bumping into her today—all of it was swept aside in a firestorm of fury so blindingly white and intense that he had to reach out and steady himself against a bookcase.

But the luxury of losing his temper with Teddie would have to wait. Right now it was time to meet his son.

'I'm sorry too,' he said gently, making sure that none

of the emotions roiling inside his head were audible in his voice as he smiled at his son for the first time.

'But you don't need to worry.' Skewering Teddie with his gaze, he took a step closer. 'Mommy and I are going to have a chat, aren't we?'

He turned to Teddie, making sure that the smooth blandness of his voice in no way detracted from the blistering rage in his eyes. Hearing her small, sharp intake of breath, he felt the glacier in his chest start to scrape forward. It had been barely audible, but it was all the confirmation he needed.

Forcing herself to meet his gaze, Teddie nodded mechanically, but inside her head a mantra of panic-stricken thoughts was beating in time to her heartbeat. *He knows. He knows George is his son. What am I going to do?*

Clearing her throat, she smiled. 'Yes, that's right. We're going to have a grown-ups talk. And you, young man, are going to be taken back to bed.'

Although, given that her legs felt as though they were made of blancmange, that might be easier to say than do.

Aristo stared at her coldly. 'But not before you've introduced me, of course.'

Her chin jerked up, but his glittering gaze silenced her words of objection.

'This is my son, George,' she said stiffly.

'Hello, George.' Aristo smiled. 'I'm very honoured to meet you. My name is Aristo Leonidas, and I'm an old friend of your mommy's.'

Gazing into his son's eyes—dark eyes that were almost identical in shape and colour to his own—he felt his stomach tighten painfully. George had his jawline and his high cheekbones; the likeness between them was remarkable, undeniable. At the same age they would have looked like twins.

As George smiled uncertainly back at him he felt almost

blinded with outrage at Teddie's deceit. His son must be three years old. How much had he missed during that time? First tooth. First word. First steps. Holidays and birthdays. And in the future, what other occasions would he have unknowingly not attended—graduation, wedding day...

He gritted his teeth.

Maybe he'd not actually thought about becoming a father, but Teddie had unilaterally taken away his right to be one. How was he ever going to make good the time he'd missed? No, not *missed*, he thought savagely. Teddie had cheated him of three years of his son's life. Worse, not only had she deliberately kept his son a secret from him for all that time, she had clearly been planning to keep him in ignorance of George's existence for ever.

Hell, she'd even lied to him tonight, telling him that he had to be quiet because of her elderly neighbours.

Glancing up, he refocused on his son's face and, seeing the confusion in George's eyes, pushed his anger away. 'I know you're not ready to shake hands yet and that's a good thing, because we need to get to know each other a bit better first. But maybe we could just bump knuckles for now.'

Raising his hand, he curled his fingers into a fist, his heart contracting as his son copied him, and they gently bumped fists.

'Hey, what's that? Is that a boat?' Aristo watched as George uncurled his fingers.

'It's my boat,' he said solemnly.

'I love your boat.' Aristo glanced at it admiringly. 'I have a real boat like that. Maybe you could come for a ride on it with Mommy. Would you like that?'

George nodded, and Teddie felt her chest hollow out with panic.

Watching the sudden intimacy between her ex-husband and their son, she felt something wrench apart inside her, for the two of them were so close—not just physically but in their very likeness. It was both touching and terrifying, almost overwhelmingly so.

Clearing her throat, she smiled stiffly. 'That would be lovely, wouldn't it, George? Right now though, it really is time to go back to bed.'

In his bedroom, she tucked him under his duvet, keeping up a steady stream of chatter until his eyelids fluttered shut.

If only she could just crawl in beside him and close her eyes too. Remembering the look on Aristo's face as he'd worked out that George was his son, she felt her pulse begin beating in her neck like a moth against glass. Despite his outer calm, she knew that he was angry—more angry than she had ever seen him, more angry than she could have imagined possible.

Not that she could blame him, she thought, guilt scraping over her skin like sandpaper. Had their roles been reversed she would have been just as furious. And the fact that part of her had always wanted to tell him the truth didn't feel like much of a defence.

She really should be relieved, though, for it had been getting harder and harder to keep lying.

But now she would have to pay the price for those lies and face his anger. That was bad enough, but more terrifying still was the sudden knife-twist of realisation that Aristo had both a moral *and* a legal right to be in his son's life. It didn't matter about their divorce. George was his son, and if he wanted to press that point home he had the power and the money to do so emphatically—not just here in her apartment but in court.

The thought of facing Aristo in court made her want to throw up.

So face him now, she ordered herself. And, taking a deep breath, she stood up and made her way back to the living room.

He swung round towards her, and her heart began beating so fast she thought it would burst through her ribs. She had thought he was angry before, but clearly each minute that had passed during her absence had increased his fury exponentially, so that now, as he walked towards her, it was the arctic blast of his contempt that held her frozen to the spot.

'I knew you were shallow and unscrupulous,' he said, his eyes gleaming like black ice, 'but at what point exactly did your morals become so skewed that you decided to keep my son a secret from me?'

'That's not fair—'

His black eyes slammed into hers. *'Fair?* You're really quite something, Teddie. I thought you just stole money from me. Turns out you stole my son.'

'I didn't steal him—' she began, but he cut her off.

'Oh, I'm sure you've post-rationalised it. What did you tell yourself? *What he doesn't know won't hurt him?*' he imitated her voice. *'It'll be for the best.'*

'I did do it for the best.' Her voice was shaking, but her eyes were level with his. 'I did what was best *for me*, Aristo, because there was only me.'

He felt his breathing jerk. 'Not true. You had a husband.'

'Ex-husband,' she snapped. 'We were divorced by then. Not that it would have made any difference. You were never there.'

His eyes didn't leave hers. 'You really can't help yourself, can you? It's just lie after lie after lie.'

Teddie swallowed. It was true—she had lied repeatedly. But not because she'd wanted to and not about the past. It wasn't fair of Aristo to judge her with hindsight. He might be in shock now, but she'd had just the same shock four years ago when, thanks to him, she'd been homeless and alone.

'I was going to tell you—' She broke off as he laughed, the bitterness reverberating around the small room.

'Of course you were.'

'I didn't mean now—today. I meant in the future.'

'The future?' He repeated the word slowly, as though not quite sure of its meaning. 'What's wrong with the present? What was wrong with this morning?'

'It all happened so quickly.' She looked at him defensively. 'I wasn't expecting to see you.'

Aristo stared at her in disbelief. 'And that's a reason, is it? Reason enough for my son to grow up without a father? Or have you got some surrogate daddy in mind? Is that why you ran out on me this morning?'

The thought stung. He might not have been celibate, but dating—certainly anything serious—had been the last thing on his mind for the past four years. Work—in particular the expansion of his empire, and more recently his upcoming flotation on the stock exchange—had taken up so much of his time and energy. On those occasions when he'd needed a 'plus-one', he been careful to keep her at a distance.

Clearly Teddie had found him far easier to replace.

His eyes narrowed. 'I mean, it's just what you *do*, isn't it, Teddie? That's your real act! Not all this nonsense.' He held up the box of cards. 'You set it all up.' *Set me up*, he thought savagely. 'Then take what you want and move on.'

'If you're talking about our marriage, I had plenty of reasons to leave. And I didn't take anything.'

She felt a sudden sharp pang of guilt as she thought of her son—*their* son—but then she repeated his sneering reference to her work as 'nonsense' inside her head, and pushed her guilt aside.

Glaring at him, she shook her head, whipping her dark hair like a horse swatting flies with its tail. 'And not that

it's any of your business but there is no man in my life, and
there's certainly no daddy in George's.'

The outrage in her voice sounded real, and he wanted to
believe her for his pride's sake, if nothing else. But, aside
from the faint flush of colour creeping over her cheeks,
she had already told so many different lies in such a short
space of time that it was hard to believe anything she said.
Clearly lying was second nature to her.

His heart was suddenly speeding and his skin felt cool
and clammy with shock—not just at finding out he was a
father, but at how ruthlessly Teddie had played him.

'So let me get this clear,' he said slowly. 'At some un-
specified point in the future you were planning on telling
me about my son?'

Teddie hesitated. If only she could plead the Fifth
Amendment but this was one question that required an
answer. Actually, it required the truth.

'I don't know. Honestly, most days I'm just trying to deal
with the day-to-day of work and being a mom to George.'
And grieving for the man I loved and lost.

Blocking off the memories of those terrible weeks and
months after they'd split, she cleared her throat. 'We were
already divorced by the time I found out I was pregnant.
We weren't talking, and you weren't even in the country.'

His eyes bored into eyes. 'And so you just unilaterally
decided to disappear into thin air with my child? He's my
son—not some prop in your magic show.'

Stung, and shocked by the level of emotion in his voice,
she said defensively, 'I know and I'm sorry.'

He swore under his breath. 'Sorry is not enough, Teddie. I have a child, and I fully intend to get to know him.'

It wasn't an outright threat, more a statement of intent,
but she could see that his shock at discovering he was a father was fading and in its place was that familiar need to
take control of the situation.

She felt a ripple of apprehension run down her backbone. Where did that leave her?

Last time she and Aristo had gone head to head she'd been cast out from his kingdom, her unimportance in his life no longer just a private fear but an actuality.

But four years ago she'd been young and in love, unsure of her place in the world. Now, though, she was a successful businesswoman and a hands-on single mother—and, most important of all, she understood what she'd been too naive and too dazzled to see four years ago.

Aristo had no capacity for or interest in emotional ties. She'd learned that first-hand over six agonising months spent watching his obsession with work consume their marriage and exclude her from his life.

She brought her eyes back to his. Yes, she should have told him the truth, but he'd given her no reason to do so— no reason other than biology for her to allow him into George's life.

And now? Maybe if Aristo had been a different kind of man she would have caved, but she knew that no matter how insistent he was now about wanting to get to know their son, it was only a matter of time before he lost interest—like her own father had. But George would not grow up as she had, feeling as though he was at the bottom of his father's agenda.

'*Our* son is not some chess piece you can move about on a board to suit you, Aristo. He's a person with feelings and needs—'

He cut her off. 'Yes, he is, and he needs to see me— his father.'

Folding her arms, Teddie glared at him, anger leaping over her skin in pulses. 'He needs consistency and security—not somebody offering him trips on a speedboat and then disappearing for days.'

He shook his head dismissively. 'I'm standing right here, Teddie.'

'For how long?' she countered. 'A day? A week? I mean, when exactly *is* your next business trip?'

His jaw tightened. 'That is irrelevant.'

'No, it's not. I'm being realistic about your limitations.'

Looking away, she clenched her fists. And her limitations. Her life might be bereft of romance and passion, but it was peaceful. The thought of having Aristo flitting in and out of her and George's life was just too unbearable to contemplate.

'I have rights, Teddie,' he said quietly, and something in his voice pulled her gaze back to his face. 'I'm guessing you can live with ignoring that fact—you've managed it for four years. But George has rights too, and I'm wondering what's going to happen when he realises that he has a father—a father you kept at arm's length. Can you live with that?'

Teddie stared at him, her heart pounding, hating him for finding the weakness in her argument.

'Fine,' she snapped, her hands balling into fists. 'You can see him.' But it was absolutely, definitely *not* going to be in her apartment. 'I suggest we find somewhere neutral.'

'Neutral—that's an interesting euphemism.'

He suddenly sounded amused, and she felt her pulse accelerate as she realised that his anger seemed to have faded and he was now watching her intently in a way that made her breathing come to a sudden, swift stop.

'If you're trying to find a place where you and I will feel "neutral" about one another, then I think you might need a bigger planet. Maybe a different solar system.'

She swallowed. His words were reverberating inside her head, bumping into memories so explicit and uncensored that she had to curl her fingers into her palms to stop her hands shaking.

'I don't know what you're talking about,' she said hoarsely, trying her hardest not to notice the way her stomach was clenching.

She felt heat break out over her skin as he took a step towards her.

'Yes, you do, Teddie. I'm talking about sex. And about how, despite all this, you still want me and I still want you.'

An ache like hunger, only more insistent, shot through her and she stared at him, her green eyes widening in shock at the bluntness of his statement.

He raised an eyebrow. 'What? Are you going to lie about that too?' He shook his head dismissively. 'Then you're a coward as well as a liar.'

'I'm not a coward,' she snapped. 'I just don't happen to agree with your unnecessary and rather crude remark.'

His dark eyes locked onto hers and she knew that this time her lie might as well be written in block capitals across her forehead.

'Yes, you do. You're just scared that you feel this way. Scared that you want me.'

Teddie breathed out shakily. He was close now—close enough for her to see the tiny flecks of grey and gold in the inky pools of his eyes. Close enough that she could smell his clean, masculine scent. So close that she could not just see the curves of muscle beneath his sweater but reach out and touch them—

'You're so arrogant.'

He took another step closer and lifted his hand. Her pulse fluttered as he traced the curve of her jaw with his thumb.

'And you're so beautiful, but neither of those statements changes the facts.'

She could feel his gaze seeking hers and, looking up, she saw that his eyes were shimmering with an emotion she recognised and understood—because she was feeling it too.

'Like it or not, we still burn for one another, and I know you feel it too. There's a connection between us.'

She stared at him, hypnotised not just by the truth of his words but by the slow, steady pulse of heat in her blood. And then, in a split second of clarity, she saw herself, saw his hand capturing her face, saw where it was heading, and was instantly maddened by his audacity and ashamed of her weakness.

Jerking her head away from his hand, she lifted her chin. 'You're wrong, Aristo. It's all in your head. It's not real,' she lied again.

He stared at her, his gaze taking in her flushed cheeks and the pulse beating at the base of her throat. 'Not real?' he softly. 'It looks pretty real from where I'm standing.'

Her whole body throbbing, she breathed out unsteadily. 'That's magic for you, Aristo. It plays tricks with the senses…makes you believe in the impossible. And you and I are impossible.' Fixing her green eyes on her ex-husband's breathtakingly handsome face, she gave him a small, tight smile. 'You being George's father changes nothing between us.'

His expression was unreadable, but as his dark, knowing gaze locked with hers she knew that she wasn't fooling either of them, and his next comment reinforced that fact.

'You're right, it doesn't,' he said into the tense silence. 'So perhaps from now on we can both stop playing games.'

He took a step backwards, his satisfied expression making her heart thump against her chest.

'I'll call you, but if in the meantime you want me desperately…'

Eyes gleaming, he reached into his jacket and held out a small white card. 'That's my number.'

'Well, I won't be calling it,' she snapped. 'As the chances of me wanting you "desperately" are less than zero.'

He smiled. 'Of course they are.'

She wanted to throw his remark back in his face, to claim that he was reading the signals all wrong, but before she had the chance to think of a suitably withering response he turned and strolled out of the room with the same swagger with which he'd entered it.

Heart pounding, she waited until she was sure that he'd left the building before darting across the room to close and bolt the door. Only, like the stable door, it was too late, she thought as she sank down onto her sofa with legs that were still unsteady. She'd not only let him back into her home, but into her life.

CHAPTER THREE

WALKING INTO HIS APARTMENT, Aristo stared blankly across the gleaming modern interior, a stream of disconnected, equally frustrating thoughts jamming his brain. He'd barely registered the hour-long drive home from Teddie's apartment. Instead he'd been preoccupied by that simmering undercurrent of attraction between them.

They'd both been so angry, and yet even beneath the fury he had felt it, strumming and intensifying like the vibrating rails beneath an express train.

Of course he'd known it was there since this morning—from that moment when he'd turned around in the Kildare and his stomach had gone into freefall. It had been like watching flashes of lightning on the horizon: you knew a storm was heading your way.

And he'd wanted the storm to come—and so had Teddie—right up until she'd told him that it was all in his head.

Not that he'd believed her. It had been just one more lie in a day of lies.

He breathed out slowly, trying to shift the memory of her final stinging remark to him.

'You and I are impossible. You being George's father changes nothing between us.'

Wrong, he thought irritably. It changed everything.

No matter how much she wanted to deny it, there *was* a connection between them—and it wasn't just based on sex, he thought, his heart tightening as he remembered his son bumping fists with him.

He still couldn't believe that he was a father. A *father*!

The word kept repeating inside his head like a scratched record.

Suddenly he needed a drink!

In the cavernous stainless steel and polished concrete kitchen, he poured himself a glass of red wine and made his way to the rooftop terrace that led off the living area.

Collapsing into a chair, he gazed moodily out at the New York skyline. Even from so high up he could feel the city's energy rising up like a wave, but for once he didn't respond to its power. He was too busy trying to piece together the life that Teddie had shattered when she'd walked into his hotel.

And if that hadn't been enough of a shock, she'd then lobbed a grenade into his perfectly ordered world in the shape of a three-year-old son.

Welcome to fatherhood, Teddie-Taylor style.

Thanks to her, he'd gone from nought to being the father of a miniature version of himself in a matter of seconds, with Teddie presenting George to him like the proverbial rabbit being pulled from a hat.

He ran his hand slowly over his face, as though it might smooth the disarray of his thoughts. It felt surreal to be contemplating even the concept of being a father, let alone the reality. He'd never really imagined having a child—not out of any deep-rooted opposition to being a father, but because work and the expansion of his business empire required all his energy and focus.

He frowned. But maybe there were other reasons too? Could his father's decision to opt out of his responsibilities have made him question his own programming for parenthood? Possibly, he decided after a moment's thought. Apostolos Leonidas had been an intermittent and largely reluctant presence in his life, and maybe he had just assumed that he'd be the same.

And up until now he'd more or less given his father a free pass—having been made to look a fool, his father had understandably wanted nothing to do with his adulterous wife, and that had meant having nothing to do with his son either.

But even when Aristo had been blinded with shock and anger earlier he'd felt no resentment towards George, no sense of panic or dismay. Gazing down into his son's dark eyes, he had felt his heart tighten in recognition—and love.

His shoulders stiffened. The same love that Teddie clearly felt for George?

Resentment still simmered inside him, but he couldn't stop himself from reluctantly admiring his ex-wife. Whatever else she might be, Teddie was a good mother. George clearly adored her, and she loved their son—not with his own mother's chilly, grudging variety of love, nor the nod of recognition that had passed for love in his father's head. Just love—pure, simple and unselfish.

Imagining how it must feel to be the focus of that kind of affection and tenderness, he felt something tauten inside him—not just a sense of responsibility, but of resolve. He was George's father, and it was his job to make sure his son had the love and security that he himself had been denied as a child.

His parents' divorce and subsequent remarriages had left him rootless and unsure of his place in the world, and he knew instinctively that George needed both his parents. But if that was to happen then this time Teddie wouldn't be running anywhere—ever. Only, judging by how quickly she had bolted from his life last time, he needed to make that clear sooner rather than later.

'Well, if you ask me, it could have been a lot worse.'

Elliot raised his elbows swiftly off the breakfast bar as

Teddie swept past him with a wet cloth, cleaning the evidence of George's cereal from the surface and wishing she could wipe Aristo from her life just as effortlessly.

Elliot hadn't appeared the night before but had arrived at breakfast, bringing doughnuts and his usual reassuring patter, and she'd been both grateful and relieved to see him.

It wasn't that he could do anything to change what had happened, but he made her feel calmer, more rational. Less like the woman she'd been last night.

Her fingers tightened around the cloth and she closed her eyes.

That, in short, was the problem. Maybe it was because he was so uncompromisingly masculine physically, but Aristo made her feel like a woman—fierce and wild and hungry to touch and be touched. They'd felt so right together; he'd felt so right against her. And, even though she despised herself for being so shallow, she couldn't pretend that anything had changed. When he was near her she was still so aware of his body, his breathing, the heat of his skin...

Her insides felt suddenly hot and tight and, breathing out a little, she opened her eyes. She'd done everything she could to excise the memory of what it felt like to be held in Aristo's arms, only for him to turn up on her doorstep and make a mockery of all her efforts. It wasn't fair—but that didn't mean she was going to roll over and let him turn her and George's lives upside down.

'It could?' Turning, she stared at Elliot disbelief. 'How, Elliot? How could it be worse?'

He shrugged, his expression innocent. 'He could have kissed you.'

Remembering how close she'd come to letting that happen, she scowled at him, a blush of colour heating her cheeks. 'He didn't.'

'Or you could have kissed him— Hey, it was a joke.'

Grinning, he caught the cloth that Teddie threw at him. 'Where's your sense of humour?'

Collapsing onto the stool beside him, she shook her head. 'It packed its bags and left shortly after Aristotle Leonidas arrived.'

She felt a sudden rush of panic, remembering that stand-off between them—the prickling of her skin and the intensity of his gaze, his dark eyes scanning her face, all-seeing, hungry, unwavering... Her stomach tightened, her hands curling into fists. She might not have given in last night, but this thing, this 'connection' between them wasn't going to just disappear.

But she could.

The thought popped into her head unbidden, fully formed, because of course that was still her gut instinct. Before Aristo, years of her life had been spent living out of suitcases, staying in hotels and motels, always ready to leave, to flee like a getaway driver after a heist. Running away had been her quick fix, her go-to solution for dealing with any problem in her life, any time things got hard.

It was a hangover from a childhood spent dodging unpaid bills and bailiffs and a legacy from her father—not that she'd ever thought of him as that. Wyatt Taylor had never stayed around long enough for the name 'Dad' to stick. Just long enough to teach her a couple of magic tricks and to make her miss him when he left.

Her heart began to pound.

Only, how could she run with a child? George's life was here, in New York. He went to nursery here, he had friends, a routine. He was the reason she'd stopped running.

As though sensing her panic, Elliot reached over and pushed a stray strand of hair away from her face.

'Come on, Teddie, I know he was a pig to you, and maybe it wasn't ideal, him turning up here out of the blue, but...' He hesitated, his expression becoming uncharacteristically serious. 'But whatever you're telling yourself, you're wrong. You can't run this time, babe.'

As she glanced up guiltily he gave her a lopsided smile.

'I've known you since I was twelve years old. I don't need supernatural powers to read your mind. This isn't something you can run away from, and deep down I don't think you really want to.'

She lifted her chin, narrowing her green eyes. 'And yet strangely, on a superficial level, I feel completely certain that I absolutely do.'

Elliot poked one of her clenched hands with his finger. 'No, you don't. I was there, remember? I know how often you tried to call him. I know how many messages you left, how upset you were.' His jaw tensed. 'I'm no fan of Aristotle Leonidas, but—' he frowned '—he's still George's father and he's got a right to see his son. Right now it's a shock, but once you get used to the idea it'll be okay, I promise. I mean, loads of couples share custody of their children.'

Teddie gave him a small, tight smile.

Thinking about a future in which she would have to see Aristo on a regular basis, speak to him and have him turning up on her doorstep, was not her definition of okay. But maybe over time her feelings for him would diminish, like radioactivity—only didn't that take, like, decades? Not that it mattered how she felt, or where she was. She could run but, as Elliot said, she couldn't hide from the truth any more. Aristo was George's father and she was just going to have to suck it up.

Pushing back his stool, Elliot stood up. 'I gotta go, but I'll call you later.' Sliding his arms into his jacket, he kissed her forehead. 'And don't worry. Leopards don't change their spots, baby, and from everything you've ever told me about your ex he's not the kind to stick around long enough for this to become a problem.'

Watching Elliot let himself out of the apartment, she

knew he was trying to reassure her. And she should feel reassured—it was, after all, what she wanted, wasn't it? For Aristo to disappear from her life for good? Only, for some strange reason, that thought didn't seem quite comforting as she'd imagined it would.

While George took his afternoon nap Teddie tidied the apartment, moving automatically to pick up the tiny toy cars and miniature dinosaurs that were scattered everywhere. Eventually she stopped beside her bed and, kneeling down, pulled out a cardboard box.

Feeling a lump start to build in her throat, she hesitated, and then sat on the floor. Lifting off the lid, she gazed down at the contents.

Was that it? Had her marriage really amounted to nothing more than a shoebox shoved under a bed?

Pushing aside the letters and documents, she reached to the bottom of the box and pulled out a small blue box.

Her hand twitched and then slowly, heart thumping erratically, she opened it and stared down at the plain gold band. For a moment she couldn't move, but as her breathing steadied she picked up her wedding ring and slid it onto her finger.

She still wasn't sure why she had kept it. But the answer to that was not as simple as the question implied.

At first, in the weeks after she'd moved out of Aristo's apartment—and it had always felt like *his* apartment—she'd kept wearing it because even though it had become clear to her by then that her husband was a different person from the impulsive lover she'd promised to love and honour and cherish, she hadn't been ready to give up on her marriage.

And then later it had been the one thing he'd given to her that he hadn't and could never take away—of course that had been before she found out about George.

Her throat tightened. She could still picture the exact moment that she'd finally decided to stop wearing it.

It had been on the taxi ride home from that night she'd spent in Aristo's arms, hoping and believing that they'd been given a second chance.

He'd followed her out of their meeting with the lawyers earlier and they'd argued, both of them simmering with fury, and then they'd looked into each other's eyes and desire had been stronger than their anger combined. Unreasonable, but undeniable.

But then what did desire ever have to do with reason?

They'd rented a hotel room like newlyweds, kissing and pulling at each other's clothes in the lift, hardly noticing the other guests' shocked or amused expressions as they'd run to their room.

But even before the sheets tangled around their warm, damp bodies had grown cold she'd realised her mistake.

That night hadn't been some eleventh-hour reprieve for their marriage. Aristo hadn't acknowledged his part in their marital problems, or been willing to listen to her point of view. Instead he'd just wanted to get his own way and, having failed to convince her with words he'd switched tactics. Like the hopeless, lovestruck fool she had been then, she'd let herself be persuaded by the softness of his mouth and the hard length of his body.

But, waking in the strange bed, she'd realised her mistake instantly.

She breathed out unsteadily, remembering how his face had grown hard and expressionless, the post-coital tenderness in his eyes fading as he'd told that he'd pay for the room, but that would be the last dollar she'd see of his money.

It hadn't been. Three weeks later she'd emptied one of the bank accounts they'd shared—the one with the least amount of money in it—partly to prove him wrong, but mostly so his unborn child would have something from its father.

Sliding the ring off her finger, she put it back in the box and got slowly to her feet. Elliot was right. She needed to face reality, and it would be easier to do so if she was in control of what was happening rather than sitting and stewing, waiting for Aristo to call.

Walking back into the living room, she picked up the card he'd given her the night before and punched out his number on her mobile before she had the chance to change her mind.

'Hello, Teddie.'

She hadn't expected him to pick up quite so quickly, or to know it was her, but that wasn't why she slid down onto the sofa. It was just that hearing his voice down the phone again felt strangely intimate, and for a split second she was reminded of how they'd used to talk when they'd first met. Conversations in the early hours of the morning after she'd finished performing and she was lying in bed in some hotel on the other side of the country.

It hadn't mattered what time she'd called—he'd always answered and they'd talked sometimes for hours. She felt her skin prickle. And not just talk... Sometimes he'd made up stories to help her fall asleep.

Curling her fingers around the phone, she gripped it more tightly. Remembering Aristo doing that for her was like waking to find a handcuff around her wrist, linking her to him in a way she hadn't imagined.

Steadying her breathing, she pushed the memory to the back of her mind. 'We need to talk,' she said bluntly. 'About George.'

'So talk.'

'No, not on the phone. We need to meet.'

There was a short pause, and her chest tightened as she

imagined him leaning back in his chair, a small triumphant smile curving his mouth.

'I can come to your apartment.'

'No.' Hearing the panic in her voice, she frowned. But there was no way he was coming to the apartment again, not after what nearly happened last time. 'I'll come to your office.'

She glanced at the time. She could drop George off at Elliot's and then go on into Manhattan.

'Shall we say about five?'

'I look forward to it,' he said softly.

At exactly five o'clock she was staring up at a tall, gleaming tower as all around her crowds of tourists chatted and laughed—no doubt on their way to see the Empire State Building or some other world-famous landmark.

If only she was a tourist too, enjoying a well-earned holiday, instead of having to face her clever, calculating ex-husband. But the sooner she faced Aristo the sooner she could return home, and so, heart pounding, she slipped through the revolving doors into the cool smoked glass interior of the Leonidas Holdings' headquarters.

Five minutes later she was riding up in an elevator, only just managing to force her mouth into a stiff smile as the doors opened.

'Ms Taylor.' Smiling politely, a young male assistant stepped forward. 'If you'd like to come with me, Mr Leonidas' office is this way.'

But not Mr Leonidas, Teddie discovered as the assistant showed her into the empty office. She wondered if Aristo had absented himself on purpose. Probably, she decided. No doubt he was trying to psyche her out by making her wait, by giving her a glimpse of his personal fiefdom.

She glanced slowly around the room, her narrowed gaze taking in the dazzling panoramic views of New York, the

Bauhaus furniture and the huge abstract painting that hung behind his desk.

'Sorry to keep you waiting.'

She turned, her body tensing automatically as Aristo strolled into the room, his dark eyes sweeping assessingly over her black cigarette trousers, burgundy silk shirt and towering stiletto heels.

He stopped in front of her and she felt her stomach flip over. He'd taken off his jacket, and the sleeves of his corn-flower-blue shirt were rolled up, the collar loosened. Her eyes darted involuntarily between the triangle of golden skin at the base of his neck and the fine dark hair on his forearms.

Her breath pedalled inside her chest. He looked both invincible and stupidly sexy, and any hope she'd had that she might have miraculously developed an immunity to him in the intervening hours since she'd seen him evaporated like early-morning mist. Even just being in the same space as him was sending her body haywire, her chest constricting and a prickling heat spreading like a forest fire over her skin.

If Aristo was feeling as uncomfortable as she was, he wasn't showing it. But then in the six months of their marriage she'd never really known what he was thinking—she might be a mistress of illusion on stage, but he was a master at disguising his feelings. Her lips tightened. Although that, of course, presupposed that he had any.

'It's fine,' she said stiffly. 'I know you're a busy man.'

His gaze hovered over her face and she cursed herself silently, for she knew what he was thinking.

Aristo's obsession with work had quickly become an issue for her. The long hours he'd spent at the office and his single-minded focus on building his business had slowly but inevitably excluded her from his life. Not that either of them had done much to stop it eroding their marriage.

For Aristo it had only ever been *her* problem, and she had found it impossible to tell him the truth. That she wanted the man who had craved her, who had been so hungry to share her life that he hadn't been willing to wait.

She swallowed, pushing back against the sudden swell of misery spreading through her. It was her own fault. She should have known what to expect when he'd cut their honeymoon short to fly halfway across the world to buy a resort. But of course when he'd pulled her into his arms and told her it was a one-off she'd believed him. She'd wanted to believe him, and to believe that she hadn't just made the biggest mistake of her life.

Only, her brief doomed marriage was not what she wanted to talk about now. They'd moved way past the point where there was even a 'them' to discuss. As far as she was concerned, the less she had to do with him the better, and after this meeting hopefully there would be no reason for her to see him except briefly and occasionally.

Watching the conflicting emotions flitting across his ex-wife's face, Aristo felt a ripple of frustration. She had always been so unsupportive of his career, when all he'd been trying to do was build a life for her, for them.

Glancing round his office, he steadied his breathing. Surely now she could understand what he'd been trying to do? But, either way, he wasn't going to let it get in the way of what really mattered.

He shrugged. 'Very busy,' he said softly. 'But let's not get distracted. I'm sure you didn't come here to talk about my work.'

She gave him a small, tight smile. 'We need to make arrangements. Something stable and uncomplicated. Because what's most important to me is that George feels happy and safe.'

He nodded. 'And I want that too.' Gesturing towards a cluster of easy chairs and a sofa grouped in front of the windows, he smiled slowly. 'So, why don't we sit down and talk about how we can make that happen?'

Teddie gazed at him warily. So far it was all going better than she'd expected. Her heartbeat scuttled forward. Only, it wasn't fair of him to smile like that. It would be so much easier for her to keep a clear head if he was cold and dismissive. When he smiled that extraordinary smile it was difficult to think straight. Difficult to think about anything other than that beautiful mouth.

Feeling his dark gaze, she ignored both his hand and the sudden rapid pounding of her heart and nodded, then walked as casually as she could manage across the room.

She purposely avoided the sofa and sat down in one of the chairs, but regretted her decision almost immediately as, dropping down into the chair closest to hers, he stretched out his long, muscular legs and began to speak.

'Look, Teddie, before we start I have something I need to say to you.'

'So say it.' She had been aiming to sound casual, offhand. Instead, though, her voice sounded stiff and unnatural.

His eyes fixed on hers. 'I know this can't be easy, having me back in your life and in George's life. But I'm going to try to make it as painless and unproblematic as possible for both of us. All I want is to be a good father.'

She held his gaze. It was on the tip of her tongue to tell him that he *wasn't* back in her life. But to be fair he was trying to meet her halfway, and it seemed churlish to nitpick over his choice of words.

Glancing away to the skyline, she shrugged. 'I hope so. That's why I'm here.'

It was true, and she wanted to believe Aristo, to take his words at face-value—only after everything he'd said and done in the past it was just so hard to trust him. But if this was going to work, for her son's sake, she was going to have to put the past behind her and concentrate on the present.

She took a quick, steadying breath and said quickly, 'I know it probably doesn't seem like it to you, but I really do want George to get to know you.'

The air seemed to still, like a held breath, and, looking up, she found Aristo watching her so steadily and intently that for a moment she forgot where she was. Suddenly the huge office seemed as though it had shrunk, and his body seemed way too close to hers.

Before she could stop herself she shifted in her seat, drawing her legs in tighter and then regretting it immediately as his eyes dropped to her throat, taking in the jerkiness of her pulse.

'So what do you suggest?'

It was a straightforward enough question, and his expression was blandly innocent, but something in his eyes made her body tense, her muscles popping and suddenly primed for flight as she quickly went through the options she'd rehearsed on her journey to his office.

'I thought perhaps we could meet in a park,' she said hopefully. 'George loves swings, and we have a nice park just down the street.'

She felt her pulse begin to hopscotch forward as slowly he shook his head.

'I was thinking of something more than just a trip to the swings. How about you bring George to the apartment for a weekend? That way we'll have more time, and plenty of space, and of course there's the pool.' He raised his dark gaze to hers. 'You *have* taught him to swim?'

She glared at him. 'Yes, of course I have. But—'

'Excellent, so we're agreed.' His smile widened but she started to shake her head.

'No, Aristo. We are not agreed.' She gritted her teeth. How had she ever thought this would be easy?

'Then I'll come to yours,' he said coolly.

Her back stiffened. He absolutely definitely wasn't coming to her apartment, and nor did she want to go to back to the apartment that had once been her home, with all its many reminders of their shared past.

So tell him what you do want then, she told herself.

'I don't think that's a good idea.' She spoke quickly, trying to inject a businesslike tone into her voice.

'No? But you do want to *arrange* something, right?'

He lounged back, his arm resting easily against the side of the chair, and suddenly she wanted to reach out and touch the golden skin, run her fingertips over the smooth curve of muscle pressing against the fabric of his shirt.

'Yes—yes, of course I do.' She dragged her eyes away, up to the compelling dark eyes and dangerous curves of his face.

He nodded. 'Something stable and uncomplicated, I think you said.'

'Yes, that's what I want, but...' She gazed at him uncertainly, wondering exactly where the conversation was going.

'Then the solution is staring us in the face.'

He went on as if she hadn't spoken, his voice curling over her skin, soothing and unsettling at the same time.

'What do you mean?' she said hoarsely.

He smiled. 'Isn't it obvious? We need to get married.'

The air was punched out of lungs. She stared at him in a daze, the beat of her heart suddenly deafeningly loud inside her head. She was mute with shock—not only at the audacity, the arrogance of his words, but at the heat building inside her.

How could she feel like that? Their marriage had been a disaster, and yet she could feel a part of herself responding with an eagerness that shocked her.

Ignoring the quivering sensation in her stomach, she forced herself to meet his gaze. 'That's not funny, Aristo.'

'It's not meant to be.' He looked at her, his gaze impassive. 'If I'm to be a permanent fixture in George's life then I need to be a permanent fixture in yours. Marriage is the simplest solution. We marry and George gets two parents and a stable, uncomplicated home life.'

She stared at him in disbelief. 'Is that what you think our marriage was like? Stable and uncomplicated?' She wanted to laugh, except that it wasn't even remotely amusing, just horribly familiar—for wasn't this exactly why they'd got divorced? Because Aristo had made assumptions without so much as considering her point of view or her feelings.

'I am not marrying you—*remarrying* you,' she corrected herself.

Tipping back his head, he stared down into her eyes. 'Why not? It's not something you haven't done before.'

She gaped at him. 'And it didn't work.' She enunciated each word with painstaking emphasis.

His dark gaze roamed so slowly over her face that she felt it like a caress.

'As I recall it worked very well.'

Her breath was trapped in her throat. 'I'm not talking about that,' she said quickly. 'I'm talking about everything else about our marriage. None of that worked.'

'Didn't work *last time*.' He dismissed her remark with a careless lift of his shoulders. 'But engaging with past mistakes is crucial to an improved performance, and this time we'll be operating from a position of experience, not ignorance.'

She felt her heart beat faster. He sounded as if he was presenting a business plan, not discussing getting married. But then, even before their marriage had ended work had already consumed his life to the exclusion of everything else—including her.

'This isn't some management strategy,' she said witheringly. 'This is my life, Aristo.'

His eyes didn't so much as flicker but she felt a sudden rise in tension.

'No, Teddie. This is our son's life. A son who doesn't know who I am. A son I've already let down. No child should feel like that.'

He stopped abruptly, his jaw tightening, and Teddie felt some of her anger deflate. There was something in his response that made her flinch inside, as though the words had been dragged out of him.

Aristo caught his breath. Remembering his own childhood, the constant nagging sense of not belonging, he felt suddenly sick. Whatever else happened, his son was going to feel wanted by *both* his parents.

'You haven't let him down.'

Teddie's voice jolted him back into real time and he gritted his teeth. She might have been his wife, but he'd never discussed his childhood with her. But the past was history. What mattered was George.

'I wasn't there—' He broke off and stared away, his face taut and set. 'All I want to do is make it up to him. And that is going to take more than a couple of trips to the swings.'

'You're right. I'm sorry.'

Teddie stared at his profile, her heartbeat rocking back and forth like a boat on a choppy sea. She could sense pain beneath his stilted words and she felt ashamed. Up until that moment she hadn't truly considered his feelings beyond shock and anger, and that had been unfair of her— for how would she be feeling right now if the situation was reversed?

'Maybe we should go away somewhere. That way you and George can spend time getting to know each other and we can start being open and honest with each other, because that's the only way we're going to make this work.'

Her words echoed inside her head, and for a moment she couldn't believe that they had actually come out of her mouth. But it was too late to take them back—and anyway, with a mixture of shock and relief she realised that she didn't actually want to. She needed to know now if Aristo was capable of being the father he claimed he wanted to be. Not in a few months, when it would destroy George if he left, just as she had been destroyed whenever her own father had disappeared from her life.

'Do you mean that?' His eyes were on hers, almost black, steady and unblinking.

'You want to get married again?' She phrased it as a question deliberately. 'Well, let's see if we can manage to spend a week together without wanting to kill each other.'

His eyes on her face were dark and intent. 'Or to tear each other's clothes off.'

Her pulse jolted forward, her body rippling into life as a wave of heat skimmed over her skin. For a moment she couldn't speak. Her brain seemed to have seized up and she stared at him in silence, stalling until finally she could lift her chin and meet his gaze.

'It would mean you taking time off work.' She tried and failed to keep the challenging note out of her voice.

There was a fraction of a pause. 'How does next week sound?' he said softly.

Her head snapped up. 'Next week?' The words made her feel giddy, but she could hardly back down now. 'That sounds fine. But won't it be a problem, going somewhere at such short notice?'

His eyes didn't leave hers. 'It won't be a problem at all. You see, I have an island—near Greece—and a plane to take us there.'

His mouth curled at the corners, his smile knocking the air out of her lungs.

'All you have to do is pack.'

CHAPTER FOUR

'Look, Mommy, look!'

Glancing up from the magazine lying open on her lap, Teddie smiled across the cabin to where George was waving a toy car at her.

'I can see, darling. Oh, wow!'

She made a suitably impressed face as he made the car fly up and then crash land on the headrest of his chair.

Over the top of her son's dark head her eyes met Aristo's, and quickly she looked away, not quite ready to share the moment with him.

She was still coming to terms with the fact that she was sitting on a private jet that was flying above the Atlantic Ocean. Obviously it had been her idea that they take a holiday. But, aside from her foreshortened honeymoon in St Bart's, she'd only ever been on day trips away. Now she was on her way to Greece! And not to the mainland but a private island—Aristo's island.

Out of the corner of her eye she could just see his smooth dark head, his black hair and light gold skin gleaming in the sunlit cabin. He was dressed casually, in jeans and some kind of fine-knit grey sweater, but he still exuded the same compelling air of authority and self-assurance.

She felt her heart beat faster. Everything was moving so fast. A part of her was glad about that, for if she'd had longer to think she would probably have been paralysed with indecision. And yet something about the speed with which everything had been set in motion made her feel uneasy.

Tucking a strand of dark hair behind her ear, she gazed meditatively out of the window at the horizon.

No doubt some of that feeling was down to being suddenly confronted by the true scale of Aristo's wealth. Four years ago his empire had been in its infancy—now, though, evidence of the Leonidas billions was visible everywhere, from his chauffeur-driven limousine to the powerfully built men in identical dark suits who had accompanied him onto the plane and were now seated at the other end of the cabin, studiously examining their phone screens.

She glanced over to where George and Aristo were playing with a sturdy wooden garage. It had been a gift from Aristo, supposedly to help occupy George during the long flight to Greece, but she had sensed that, more importantly for Aristo, it was an opportunity to connect with his son.

Her throat tightened. He could give George anything he wanted and, although she knew her son was happy and contented with his life, he was just as susceptible to the excitement of new toys or a promised trip on a speedboat as any other child. What would happen as he grew up? What if George chose to live with his glamorous, prosperous father?

One day he would have to choose because, whatever Aristo might think, she had no intention of marrying him again—ever.

Beneath the magazine, her hands balled into fists. *Don't go there*, she told herself, letting her long dark hair fall in front of her face. But it was too late. Like a dog proudly retrieving a stick for its owner, her brain had revealed the real reason why the haste and impulsiveness of this holiday had got under her skin.

She and Aristo had first got together after a particularly demanding week for her, and a charity dinner that she'd thought would never end. Aristo had been a guest at one of the tables.

Aged twenty-two, she'd had boyfriends, but never fallen in love, and she certainly hadn't been intending to fall in love that night. Even now she still wasn't quite sure how it had happened. Just that there had been something about the tilt of his head and the intensity of his gaze that had jolted her.

She'd picked him out to be her 'assistant', correctly identifying the card he'd chosen and then pickpocketing his watch.

Of course he'd had to come to the bar to retrieve it, and then he'd stayed, and when the bar staff had started to clear up around them she had leaned forward and kissed him.

He'd kissed her back, and she'd taken his hand and led him upstairs to her room. They'd only just made it.

That first time had been fast, abandoned and fully clothed. The second time too. When finally they'd managed to undress, and were lying naked and spent in one another's arms, she had already been half in love with him.

To her surprise, they'd carried on seeing one another—meeting in hotels across America whenever his frequent trips abroad and her show schedule had permitted them to do so. And then, less than two months after they'd met, he'd surprised her in Las Vegas and said the words that had changed the course of her life.

'You can't keep on living out of a suitcase and I can't wait any longer—for you to be my wife.'

Given the example set by her parents, marriage had been the last thing on her mind, and yet she hadn't hesitated.

Her chest tightened. And look how that had turned out.

Two hours later George had finally succumbed to the excitement of the day, and lay sleeping across two seats, his car clutched tightly in his hand. Gently, she reached over and smoothed his dark hair away from his forehead, her heart contracting painfully.

He was so beautiful, so perfect, even given a mother's bias, and she loved him completely and with an intensity that made her feel both superhuman and yet horribly defenceless.

More importantly, he would be out for the count for at least an hour, so now was her chance to send Elliot the text she had promised him and have a little freshen up at the same time. In the small but luxurious bathroom, she splashed some water onto her face, retied her thick, dark hair and then, walking back to the jet's bedroom, she tapped out a short but reassuring message to Elliot and sent it before she could change her mind.

Whatever she wrote, she knew he was still going to worry, but all he needed to know right now was that she had everything under control. But as she sat down on the chair beside the bed, she felt a sliver of panic slip down her spine, and the cheery bravado of her text seemed suddenly a little premature, for standing in the doorway, two cups of coffee in his hands, was Aristo.

Her body tensed, her heart thudding against her ribs like a wrecking ball as he held them up by way of explanation.

'I thought you might like a coffee as we had such an early start.' His dark eyes rested on her face. 'You always used to hate getting up early.' There was a short, suspended silence.

Teddie felt her insides tighten and a prickling heat began to spread over her suddenly over-sensitised skin as she remembered exactly what it had felt like to wake in Aristo's arms.

Tuning out the memory of his hard golden body on hers, she lifted her chin. 'Now I have a three-year-old son,' she said coolly. Her breath fluttered in her chest as he put one of the cups on the cabinet beside her bed.

'How long does he normally sleep?'

'An hour and a half—maybe two today. He was so excited last night he couldn't settle.'

His mouth curved upwards into a slow, sweet smile that made it impossible for her to look away.

'I would have been just the same at his age. Will it mess up his routine?'

She shrugged. 'A little. He didn't eat much breakfast, so he's probably going to be really hungry.'

'We can have lunch when he wakes up.'

She felt a cool shiver shoot down her spine as Aristo dropped down into the bed opposite her. Clearing her throat, she nodded. 'That's a good idea.'

He hesitated. 'I don't know what he likes—I thought pasta, maybe, or pizza.'

He sounded conciliatory, disarmingly unsure, and she felt some of her tension ebb. Maybe this was going to work—and she wanted it to, for George's sake at least.

Nodding, she gave him a stiff smile. 'Pasta or pizza will be fine. Although he's actually not fussy at all.'

She hesitated. Aristo had never been good at small talk or casual conversation—the silence between one of her questions and his answer had once stretched to twenty-three long drawn-out seconds—and the only times he'd ever unbent and seemed relaxed enough to chat had been during those long-distance phone calls late at night. But now, glancing up at his dark eyes, she saw that he was watching her without any hint of impatience.

'If he sees me eat something then he seems to think it's all right for him to eat too.'

'Smart boy,' Aristo said softly, and his eyes gleamed. 'Must take after his mother.'

It was the corniest of compliments, the sort of remark that didn't really warrant a response, but despite that she felt her cheeks grow warm beneath his dark, unblinking gaze.

'So,' he said softly into the taut silence, 'George seems to be getting used to me.'

'He likes you.' She raised an eyebrow. 'But I'm sure that will change when he gets to know you better.'

He stared at her steadily. 'We can make this work, Teddie.'

'I'm sure we can,' she said evenly. 'It would be pretty difficult not to. I mean, it's a holiday on a Greek island.'

She picked up her coffee, wishing that the cup was large enough for her to climb inside and hide from his dark, level gaze.

'I wasn't talking about the holiday.'

His expression was gently mocking, and she felt her heart start to beat faster. She'd known, of course, that he wasn't talking about the holiday, but she'd been hoping to keep away from that particular subject. But if he wanted to talk about it, then, fine.

She breathed out slowly. 'I know that you want this week to be some kind of first step towards me changing my mind about marrying you, but that's not why I'm here,' she said firmly. 'I'm happy for you to be in George's life but, honestly, something truly incredible—unimaginable, in fact—would have to happen for me to want to be your wife again. So could we drop this, please?'

He didn't respond, but she could sense a shift in his mood, sense something slipping away.

'What alternative is there?'

The bluntness of his question caught her off-guard. 'I don't know. The usual options, I suppose. Shared custody. Holidays and weekends— What?'

He was shaking his head and she felt a flare of anger.

'We don't work as a couple. You know that.' She stared at him, a beat of frustration pulsing in her chest. 'So stop pretending that marriage is an option.'

His eyes hardened. 'Only if you stop being so stubborn and try see it from my perspective for once.'

She glared at him. 'We should never have got married in the first place, so why would I ever want to do it again? In fact—' she took a breath, and straightened her shoulders '—why would *you* ever want to do it again? No, please, Aristo—just explain to me why you'd want to do something that made you so unhappy and angry.'

Aristo stared back at her in silence, his heart pressing against his ribs, caught off-guard by this unexpected and startling assessment of their relationship. 'I wasn't angry,' he said finally. 'I was confused because you were so dissatisfied.'

He watched her shake her head.

'Angry…dissatisfied…what does it matter anyway? We were both unhappy, so why would we do it again?'

His chest tightened and he felt a rush of anger and frustration with her for pushing—and with himself for thinking she would understand.

Before he could stop himself—before he even fully understood what he was about to do—he said, 'Because I know what it feels like when your father turns into a stranger.'

Listening to his words bounce around the quiet cabin, he felt his back tense and a hum of panic start to sing inside his head. What was he thinking? He'd never discussed his past with anyone. *Ever.* So why choose this of all moments to start spilling his guts about his childhood?

There was a tiny, sharp silence, like a splinter of ice, and through his dark lashes he could sense her confusion.

'I thought you inherited the business from your father?' she said slowly.

'I did.' His voice sounded sharp, too sharp, but he didn't care. He just stared past her, his back aching.

'So, when did he—?' She stopped, frowned, and then

tried again. 'How is he a stranger? Did something happen? Did you argue?'

Looking up, he found her watching him, and for a second he felt light-headed, almost as though he was floating. He was shocked to see not just confusion in her wide green eyes, but genuine concern too.

He hesitated. Now the words were out, he wasn't sure what to say next, or what Teddie was expecting to hear. The truth, probably. But the truth was way more complex and revealing than he could bring himself to admit, and to Teddie most of all.

'No, we didn't argue,' he said finally, with a firmness that he hoped would dissuade further discussion. 'Just forget about it.'

Teddie stared at him uncertainly, her mind doing cartwheels. She felt as if she had stepped through a wardrobe into a strange new country. This was not the Aristo she knew.

But then what did she really know about her aloof, uncompromising ex-husband? Their relationship hadn't been based on mutual interests or friends. The first few weeks of their affair had been carried out long-distance, and those long phone calls that she'd so come to enjoy had been about the present—his latest deal, her hotel room—and how much they missed one another, how much they missed making love.

They had never once been about their pasts or their families. She hadn't asked and he hadn't volunteered— and in a way hadn't she been grateful? In fact, she might even have encouraged it. She'd certainly discouraged speculation about her background and awkward conversations about her own parents. Maybe a part of her had even found it romantic that he'd wanted it to be just about the two of them.

Now, though, it seemed his reticence had been based not

on romance, or the speed of their relationship, but something more fundamental.

Watching Aristo rub the corners of his eyes, Teddie felt a sudden ache of misery, for it was exactly the same gesture that George made when he was tired or upset. And suddenly she knew why he was so insistent that they remarry.

'Did they get divorced?'

The question sounded ludicrously, simplistically trite, but she didn't know how else to begin—how else to get past that shuttered expression on his face. All she knew was that it had taken six months of a failed marriage and four years of separation to get to this moment, and she wasn't about to back off now. Even if that meant nudging at the boundaries of what he clearly considered off-limits.

Finally, he nodded. 'When I was six.'

His face was carefully blank, but she could hear the strain in his voice. Once again she had that sense of words being forcibly pulled out of him, and she knew that he'd never told this story before.

'That's young,' she said quietly.

He stayed silent for so long that she thought perhaps he hadn't heard her speak, and then, breathing out slowly, he nodded. 'My mother got remarried to this English lord, so they sold the house in Greece and I moved to England with my mother, to live with her and my stepfather, Peter.'

Her mind rewound through her rudimentary knowledge of Aristo's life. How had she not known about this? She'd been married to this man, loved him and had her heart shattered by him, and yet she knew so little. But she was starting to understand now why he was being so insistent about them remarrying. The adults in his life had made decisions based on their needs, not their son's, and in his eyes it must seem as if she had done the same with George.

'And what about your father?'

His shoulders stiffened, as though bracing against some hidden pain. 'He moved to America.'

She stared at him in silence, wanting to pull him close and hold him closer, to do anything that might ease the bruise in his voice and the taut set to his mouth. Except she was too afraid to move, afraid to do anything that might make him stop speaking.

'How did you get to see him?' she asked softly.

His shoulders shifted almost imperceptibly again. 'With difficulty. After we moved I was sent to boarding school, so there was only really the holidays, but by then my mother had a new baby—my half-brother, Oliver—and my father had remarried so everyone had got other stuff going on.'

Everyone but me.

She heard the unspoken end to his sentence, could picture the lonely, confused six-year-old Aristo, who would have looked a lot like their own son.

A muscle flickered in his jaw. 'After a couple of years it sort of petered out to one visit a year, and then it just stopped. He used to call occasionally—he still does.' He looked away, out of the window. 'But we don't really have anything to say to one another.'

He hesitated.

'I dream about him sometimes. And the crazy thing is that in my dreams he wants to talk to me.' His mouth twisted. 'Probably the longest conversation I actually had with him was when he signed the business over to me.'

He fell silent and, her heart thudding, she tried to think of something positive to say. 'But he did give you the business. Maybe that was his way of trying to show how much he cared.'

'I hope not.' Aristo turned to meet her eyes, his mouth twisting—part grimace, not quite a smile. 'Given that he was on the verge of filing for bankruptcy. The company was a wreck and he was up to his neck in debt—he hadn't even been paying the staff properly.'

'And *you* turned it around,' she said quickly. 'He could have just walked away, but I think he had faith in you. He knew you'd do the right thing.'

Her chin jerked upwards, and he watched her eyes narrow, the luminous green like twin lightning flashes.

'You've worked so hard and built something incredible. I know he must be proud of you.'

Teddie stared at him, her heart thudding so hard that it hurt. At the time of their marriage she'd hated his business, resented all the hours he'd spent working late into the night. But this wasn't about her or her feelings, it was about Aristo—about a little boy who had grown up needing to prove himself worthy of his inheritance.

She felt a little sick.

Was it any surprise that he was so intently focused on his career? Or that success mattered so much to him. He clearly wanted to prove himself, and felt responsible for saving his father's business—that would have had a huge impact on his character.

She felt his gaze, and looking up found her eyes locked with his.

'I don't expect you to understand how I'm feeling,' he said eventually. 'All I want to do is be the best father I can possibly be. Does that make sense?'

She bit her lip.

'The best father I can possibly be.'

His words replayed inside her head, alongside a memory of herself on the night that George had been born. Alone in her hospital room, holding her tiny new son, seeing his dark trusting eyes fixed on her face, she'd made a promise to him. A promise to be the best mother she could possibly be.

'I do understand.'

She was surprised by how calm and even her voice

sounded. More surprised still that she was admitting that fact to Aristo. But how could she not tell him the truth when he had just shared what was clearly such a painfully raw memory of his own?

'I felt exactly the same way when I was pregnant. And it's what I wake up feeling most mornings.'

Hearing the edge in her voice, Aristo felt something unspool inside his chest. She looked uncertain. Teddie—who could stand in front of an audience and pluck the right card out of a deck without so much as blinking. He hated knowing that she had felt like that, that she still did.

When he was sure his voice was under control he said carefully, 'Why do you feel like that?'

It seemed irrational: to him, Teddie seemed such a loving, devoted mother.

She shrugged. 'My mom struggled. And my dad was…'

She hesitated and he waited, watching her decide whether to continue, praying that she would.

Finally, she cleared her throat. 'My dad was always away on business.' The euphemism slipped off her tongue effortlessly, before she was even aware that she was using it. 'And my mom couldn't really cope on her own. She started drinking, and then she had an accident. She fell down a staircase and smashed two of her vertebrae. She was in a lot of pain and they put her on medication. She got addicted to it, and that's when she really went downhill.'

Even to her—someone who was familiar with the whole squalid mess that had been her childhood—it sounded appalling. Not just tragic, but pitiful.

Breathing out unsteadily, she gave him a tiny twist of a smile. 'After that she really couldn't cope at all—not with her job, or the apartment, or me…with anything, really.'

He frowned, trying to follow the thread of her logic, aching to go over and put his arms around her and hold her close. 'And you thought you would be like her?' he asked, careful to phrase it as a question, not a statement of fact.

She pulled a face. 'Not just her—it runs in the family. My mum was brought up by foster parents because *her* mother couldn't cope with her.' Her lips tightened.

'But you do cope,' he said gently and, reaching out, he took her hand and squeezed it. 'With everything. You run your own business. You have a lovely apartment and you're a wonderful mother.'

Abruptly she pulled her hand away. 'You don't have to say those things,' she said crossly, trying her hardest to ignore the way her pulse was darting crazily beneath her skin like a startled fish. 'You can't flatter me into marrying you, Aristo.'

Dark eyes gleaming, he leaned forward and pulled her reluctantly onto the bed beside him.

'Apparently not. And I know I don't have to say those things,' he added, his thumbs moving in slow, gentle strokes over her skin. 'I said them because I should have said them before and I didn't. I'm saying them because they're true.'

Releasing her, he reached up, his palms sliding through her hair, his fingers caressing then tightening, capturing her, his touch both firm and tender.

'So could I please just be allowed to say them? To you? Here? Now?'

Teddie blinked and, lifting her hand, touched his face, unable to resist stroking the smooth curving contour of his chin and cheekbone. She felt her fingertips tingling as they trailed over the graze of stubble already darkening his jawline.

Somewhere in the deepest part of her mind a drum had started to throb. She wanted to pull away from him—only not nearly as much as she wanted to feel his skin against hers, to lean into his solid shoulder.

'I suppose so.'

His thumb was stroking her cheek now. It was tracing the line of her lips and she could feel her brain slowing in time to her pulse.

'Aristo…' she said softly. The nearness of his drowsy, dark gaze nearly overwhelmed her.

'Yes, Teddie?'

'I don't think we should be doing this.'

The corners of his mouth—his beautiful mouth that was so temptingly close to hers—curved up into a tiny smile. 'We're not doing this because we should,' he said softly. 'We're doing this because we want to do it.'

Her stomach flipped over and she stilled, too scared to move, for she knew what would happen if she did. She knew exactly how her body would melt into his and just how intensely, blissfully good it would be.

But if she gave in and followed that beating drum of desire where would it lead? She might consider herself to be sexually carefree and independent, and maybe with any other man she could be that woman. But not with Aristo. Sharing her body with him would be fierce and intimate and all-consuming. She knew she would *feel* something—and that would make her vulnerable, and she couldn't be vulnerable around this man. Or at least not any more vulnerable than she already was.

And, whatever Aristo might argue to the contrary, when he talked about wanting to marry her again she knew deep down that what he was really thinking about was sex. Only, no matter how sublime it was, there was more to a relationship than sex—as their previous marriage had already painfully proved. She wouldn't—she couldn't—go there again.

Yes, she wanted to touch him, and she wanted him to hold her, and she was fighting herself, torn between wanting to believe that they could try again and knowing it was an impossibility. Maybe in another life, if the timing had been different…

But Aristo was already her first love, her ex-husband and the father of her child. Did she really need to add another layer of complication to what was already a complex and conflicted relationship? And besides, she should be looking forward, not back, and that meant keeping the past where it belonged.

'I know,' she said quietly. 'But this isn't about what you and I *want* any more. It's about being honest and open.'

His eyes moved over her face. 'So tell me, honestly, that you don't want me.'

He was so close she could see herself reflected in the dark pools of his eyes, and it took every atom of will in her body to resist the tractor beam of his gaze and her own longing.

'I can't. But I also know that I can't have everything I want. Maybe I thought I could once, but not any more.'

As the words left her mouth she knew that they were just that—words—and that if he chose to challenge her or, worse, if he leaned forward and kissed her, she would be lost.

She stared at him, mute, transfixed, mind and body wavering between desire and panic.

But he didn't lean forward.

Instead, his dark eyes calm, his expression unfathomable, he gently ran a finger down the side of her face and then, standing up, walked slowly across the cabin. As the door closed she breathed out unsteadily, searching inwardly for the relief she'd expected to feel.

But it wasn't there. Instead she had never felt lonelier, or more confused.

CHAPTER FIVE

STEPPING OUT OF the shower, Aristo reached for a towel and rubbed it briefly over his lean, muscular body. He smoothed his damp hair against his skull and, still naked, stepped into his dressing room. Stopping in front of the shelves, he let his dark eyes scan their colour-coded contents momentarily, before picking out a pair of dark blue swim shorts and a lighter blue T-shirt.

He sighed. If only the rest of his life could be as organised and straightforward.

Sliding his watch over his knuckles, he glanced down at the time and frowned. It was early—far too early for anyone else on the island to be awake. But although it was the first day of his holiday his body still insisted on acting as though it was just another day at the office.

Actually, not *all* of his body, he thought grimly.

Twelve hours on a plane with Teddie had left him aching with a sexual frustration that made not just sleep but relaxing almost impossible.

He grimaced. Only, in comparison to what was going on inside his head, the discomfort in his groin seemed completely inconsequential.

His heart began to beat unsteadily.

Had he really told Teddie all that stuff about his father? He could hardly believe it.

He'd spent most of his adolescence and adult life suppressing that hurt and disappointment, building barriers between himself and the world, and especially between himself and his wife. Ordinarily he found it easy to deter personal questions. But yesterday Teddie had refused to take no for an answer. Instead she had waited, and listened, and coaxed the truth out of him.

Not the whole truth, of course—he would never be ready to share that with anyone—just the reason why he was so determined to remarry her.

It had been hard enough to reveal even that much, for it had been the first time he'd ever really tried to untangle the mess of emotions he felt for his father. The first time he'd spoken out loud about Apostolos's indifference and almost total absence from his life.

It had been a rare loss of self-control—one that he still couldn't fully explain. But Teddie had been, and was still, the only person who could get under his skin and make him see fifty shades of red. She alone had overridden all his carefully placed defences, and it wasn't the first time it had happened. Despite her being the wrong woman in the wrong place at the wrong time, he'd not only led her to his bedroom but up the aisle.

His mind took him back to the moment when he'd first become aware of the existence of Teddie Taylor at the opening of his first major project—the Rocky Creek Ranch. It had been a vision nearly two years in the making: a luxury resort offering all-American activities on a three-thousand-acre mountain playground.

He'd wanted his mother, Helena, to be there, but inevitably—and despite his reminding her frequently about the date—there had been a clash. His half-brother, Oliver, had been playing in some polo match, so his mother had missed what had been up until then the most important moment in his career.

He'd almost not gone to the opening. But as usual business had overridden emotion and he'd bitten down on his disappointment and joined the specially selected guests to watch the evening's cabaret.

He wasn't entirely sure when Teddie had stopped being just the entertainment. He'd barely registered the other acts and, although he'd thought her beautiful, she was not his usual type. Only, at some point, as she had effortlessly shuffled and cut the cards in front of her captive audience, he'd been unable to look away—and, despite believing himself indifferent to magic, he'd found himself falling under her spell.

Catching a glimpse of green eyes the colour of unripe olives, he'd willed her to look at him, and just as though he'd waved a magic wand she picked him out from the crowd. Even now he could still remember the jolt of electricity as their hands had touched, but at the end of the performance she'd turned away to mingle with the other guests.

Only, of course that hadn't really been the end of her performance.

She'd been waiting for him in the bar.

With the watch she'd removed from his wrist.

Seven weeks later they had been married, and six months after that they'd been divorced.

Angry and hurt, he'd cast her as the villain, believing that she'd seen him as a warm-up act—a means to gain access to the kind of society where there would be rich pickings for a beautiful, smart and sexy woman like Teddie Taylor.

Now, with hindsight, he could see that it had been easy to persuade himself that those were the cold, hard facts, for there had been a deeper anger there. An anger with himself. Anger because he'd allowed himself to be drawn to a woman like her after all he'd been through and seen.

He frowned. Four years ago it had all seemed so simple. He'd thought he understood Teddie completely.

Now, though, it was clear that he'd never really understood her at all. Worse, his previous assessment of her seemed to bear no relation to the woman who had been so worried about him on the plane. Or to the woman who had financially supported herself and their child on her own.

A light breeze ruffled the white muslin curtains and he turned towards the window, his eyes lingering on the calm blue sea that stretched out to the horizon in every direction. Had the single-mindedness that had always been his greatest strength actually been a weakness? Had he put two and two together and made minus four?

Frowning again, he stepped towards the window, pondering how that could be the case.

Although he'd condemned her as shallow and grasping when they'd split up, he couldn't ignore the facts, and the truth was that Teddie had neither challenged the modest settlement she'd received at the time of their divorce—a settlement which had obviously not included raising George—or pursued him for more money.

In fact she had successfully supported both herself and their son *without him*, and reluctantly, he found himself contemplating the astonishing possibility that he might actually have misjudged Teddie. That maybe he'd cut and pasted his parents' mismatched and unhappy relationship onto his own marriage, making the facts fit the theory.

But what *were* the facts about his ex-wife? What did he really know about Teddie?

He breathed out slowly and started walking towards the door. Judging by that conversation on the plane, not as much as he'd thought he did. Or as much as he should.

Teddie had been his wife. He might not remember his vows word for word—there had been too much adrenaline in his blood, and a sense of standing on the edge of a cliff—but surely her husband should have been the person who knew her best.

Thinking about her baffling remarks on the plane, he felt his shoulders tense.

Yesterday she'd as good as admitted that she wanted him—why, then, had she held back? And what had she meant by telling him that she couldn't have everything she wanted?

He felt his heartbeat slow.

In principle, this holiday was supposed to be all about getting to know his son, but clearly he needed to get to know his ex-wife as well. In fact it wasn't just a need—he *wanted* to get to know Teddie, to get close to her.

His legs stopped moving, and something exploded inside his chest like a firecracker as he realised that he wasn't just talking about her body. No, what really fascinated him about his beautiful, infuriating, mysterious ex-wife was her mind.

His heartbeat doubled, a flare of excitement catching him off-guard.

Last time they hadn't got to know each other as people. It hadn't been that kind of relationship, or even any relationship really—just desire, raw and intoxicating as moonshine.

Marriage had been the furthest thought from his mind. Even now he didn't understand why he'd done it. Watching his father be taken for a fool should have been warning enough to steer clear of matrimony, but Teddie had slipped past his defences.

And now she was the mother of his child, and the logical and necessary consequence of that fact was that they should remarry, for it was his job to take care of his child and the mother of his child.

Only, this time it would be different—more like a business deal. There would be no messy emotions or expectations. He would set the boundaries, and there would be no overstepping them, and then he would have it all—a global business empire, a beautiful wife and a son.

All he needed to do now was convince Teddie to give him a second chance.

He blew out a breath. Judging by her continued resistance to even the possibility of renewing their relationship, that was going to be something of a challenge—particularly as he didn't know where or how to start.

But so what if he didn't have all the answers? What he did know for certain was that as of now he was going to do whatever it took to find out what made Teddie Taylor tick.

And, feeling calmer than he had in days, he started walking towards the door again.

'Wait a minute, George.' Turning her son gently to face her, Teddie rubbed sunscreen into the soft skin of his arms, marvelling as she did every morning that she'd had anything to do with producing this beautiful little human.

His small face was turned up towards hers, the dark eyes watching her trustingly, and she felt her heart contract not only with love but at the knowledge that she had never felt as her son did. He had been raised to feel secure in a world where he was loved and protected. Whereas she had known nothing but a life spent in flux, with parents who had been absent either in body or mind.

She thought about herself at the same age. Of her mother, drifting through the house in a haze of painkillers, barely registering her small daughter. And then she thought of herself a few years later, at school, when her constant fear had been that her mother's fixed smile and narcotised stare would be obvious to others.

It had felt like a dead weight inside her chest, a burden without respite—for of course her father had been away, his wife and daughter no match for whatever get-rich-quick scheme he had been chasing.

'Mommy, are we going in the pool now?'

'We are.' She smiled down at her son's excited face. He

had been talking about nothing else since he'd woken up. 'Just let me find your hat.'

He frowned. 'I don't want to wear it.'

'I know,' she said calmly. 'But it's hot outside and you need to protect your head. I'm going to be wearing *my* hat.' She pointed to the oversized straw hat she'd seen and then impulse-bought in a shop on her way home from work.

George stared up at her. 'Does Aristo have a hat too?'

Her smile stiffened. 'I don't know. He might do.'

Looking down into her son's dark eyes—eyes that so resembled his father's—Teddie felt her stomach flip over, as it did every single time George mentioned Aristo's name.

But it was a small price to pay for being permitted into paradise, she thought, closing the tube of sunscreen as she glanced at the view from her window. The island was beautiful. Although just an hour by motorboat from the mainland, it felt otherworldly, mythical.

It was a wisp of land with bleached sandy beaches and coves, and luminous turquoise water so clear you could see every ripple on the seabed. The villa itself looked like something you might read about in one of those glossy lifestyle magazines, dazzling white beneath the fierce sunlight. There were views everywhere of the sky and sea, and occasional glimpses of the elliptically-shaped pool—blue on blue on blue. And if all that wasn't enough, there was a garden filled with fruit trees and the drowsy hum of bees.

It was untouched and timeless, and in another life she could have imagined switching off and losing herself in its raw, unpolished beauty and sage-scented air.

But, despite the sun-drenched peace of her surroundings, and her own composed appearance, she felt anything but calm.

She'd woken early from a dream—something familiar but imprecise—and it had taken her a wild moment to remember where she was. Lying back against the pressed white linen pillowcase, she had steadied her breathing. Her restless mind, though, had proved harder to soothe.

Ever since she'd walked out of Aristo's office she'd been trying to come to terms with everything that had happened and how she was feeling about it.

Or, more specifically, how she was feeling about the man who had just barged back into her life—for, as much as she'd have liked to pretend otherwise, it wasn't this heavenly island that was dominating her thoughts but her ex-husband.

Perhaps, though, that was progress of a sort. For at least now she could admit, even if only to herself, that Aristo had always been in the background of her life.

Of course she'd wanted to forget him. She'd tried hard to make it appear as though he'd never existed. And outwardly she'd succeeded. She had a job and friends and an apartment, and they were all separate from her life with Aristo. But she could see now that her unresolved feelings for him had continued to influence the way she lived. Why else had she kept every other man except Elliot at a distance? Even the sweet single dads she met at nursery.

Her fingers tightened around the sunscreen.

Not that it would have made any difference if she'd welcomed them with open arms. What man was ever going to be able to match Aristotle Leonidas? He had shaped her life and he was an impossible act to follow on so many levels—not just in terms of his wealth or even his astonishing beauty. There was an elusive quality to him that fascinated her. He was like a mirage that shimmered in the distance, hazy and tantalising, always just out of reach, slipping between her fingers like smoke.

Her heart began to beat faster.

Except yesterday, when out of nowhere he'd suddenly unbent, opening up to her about his childhood in a way that she would never have imagined possible. It had been a brief glimpse into what had made him the man he was, but also a fairly damning reflection on their marriage— for how could she have known so little about the man who had been her lover and her husband?

It wasn't all her fault, though, she thought defensively. Aristo had been as reluctant to discuss his past as she had, and a part of her couldn't help but wonder if it wouldn't have been a lot easier if they'd had that conversation four years ago,

Instead, though, he had stonewalled her, and she'd run away.

And if she hadn't been marooned on an island on the other side of the world that was what she should be doing now—beating a dignified but hasty retreat from his unsettling, dangerously tempting presence.

Picking up George's hat, she shivered at the memory of how close she'd come to giving in to that temptation. She was just so vulnerable where Aristo was concerned… Only, it went deeper than that. Her need to exonerate and turn a blind eye was rooted in a childhood spent craving and competing for her father's attention.

It had been the pattern of her early life: Wyatt's intermittent absences followed by his inevitable reappearance. No matter how unhappy and angry she'd been, every time he'd come back she'd let herself believe his promises, allowed herself to care. And every time he had left she had felt more worthless than the time before.

And that was why she wasn't going to fall into the same pattern with Aristo.

No matter how sexy or charming he was, one shared confidence couldn't change the facts. It was too little, too late. They didn't trust each other, and that was why their marriage had failed—why she couldn't give in to the sexual pull between them now.

Making love with Aristo again would undoubtedly be unforgettable, but she knew from experience that the people she cared about found it exceptionally easy to forget *her*.

That episode in the plane had hinted at what would happen if she gave in, how quickly everything would start to unravel...

She breathed out slowly. Was that true, or was she overreacting? After all, what was really so wrong about two people who had once shared a unique and powerful chemistry getting together again? Plenty of people did it: Elliot for one.

Only, this was different. There was George to consider, so there would be no way out...nowhere to run.

Her mouth was suddenly dry and she felt a rushing panic, like a stone dropping into the darkness. And besides, this wasn't some game of spin the bottle—and Aristo wasn't some old flame she could casually reignite.

He was a forest fire.

One touch was all it had taken to awaken her body from hibernation. One more touch and she would be lost. And next time she felt like giving in to the heat of his body and the strength of his shoulders she needed to remember that.

Outside on the terrace, George instantly tugged his hand free and scampered towards Aristo. She followed him reluctantly, suddenly conscious of the fact that both she and Aristo were semi-naked, and wishing that she'd packed a one-piece as well as her bikinis.

George was gazing up at his father. 'I want you to take me swimming.'

Aristo laughed. 'So let's go swimming.' He hesitated. 'Is that all right?' Glancing over, he stared at her questioningly, and she almost burst out laughing, for his expression so closely mirrored their small son's.

Nodding, she turned towards George. 'Yes, but you have to do what Aristo tells you.'

She felt it on her skin before she saw it: the slow upturn of his mouth, the teasing glitter in his dark eyes.

'Does that go for you too?' he asked softly.

Her heartbeat faltered. Somewhere beyond her suddenly blurred vision she heard the faint splash of waves as a pulse of excitement began beating beneath her skin. For a sharp, dizzying second they stared at each other, and then, glancing pointedly back at George, she smiled.

'I'm going to read my book, darling. I'll be just over here, okay?'

Ignoring the amusement in Aristo's eyes, she quickly sat down on one of the loungers that had been arranged temptingly around the pool. Unwrapping her sarong, she stretched out her legs and glanced over to where Aristo had been sitting. Instantly her mood shifted. A mass of documents were spread out over the table and beside them, open in the sunshine, was his laptop.

Seriously? Had he really brought work with him?

Her eyes narrowed. But when had Aristo ever put work anywhere but first on his agenda? She thought back to the long, empty evenings she'd spent alone in their beautiful cavernous apartment, feeling that same sense of failure and fear that she was not enough to deserve anyone's unswerving attention.

Fleetingly she considered saying something—but it was only the first day of their holiday, so maybe she should give him the benefit of the doubt. After all, he had walked away from his office at a moment's notice, and that would have meant unpicking a full diary of meetings and appointments.

Out of the corner of her eye she caught a glimpse of hard, primed muscle, and instantly a heat that had nothing to do with the Mediterranean sun spread slowly over her skin.

Picking up her book, she opened it at random, irritated

that, even when faced with evidence of his continuing obsession with work, her body still seemed stubbornly and irrationally determined to ignore the bad in favour of the good.

There was a loud splash, and automatically her eyes darted over to where the 'good' was unapologetically on display. In the shallow end of the pool Aristo was raising George out of the water on his shoulders, droplets of water trickling down the muscles of his arms and chest, and in the dazzling golden light he looked shockingly beautiful.

She gritted her teeth. Why couldn't he own a ski lodge? Some snowbound chalet where quilted jackets and chunky jumpers were practically mandatory? she thought, her heart thumping as Aristo stood up and began to walk out of the water, the wet fabric of his shorts clinging to the blatantly masculine outline of his body.

Fully clothed and in a crowded hotel he had been hard to ignore, but half naked on a private island he was almost impossible to resist.

As though reading her mind, Aristo chose that particular moment to look over at her, and she felt a cool tingle run down her spine as his dark eyes drifted over her face, homing in on her mouth in a way that emptied the breath from her lungs.

She wanted to look away, but forced herself to meet his eyes—and then immediately wished she hadn't as his piercing gaze dropped to the pulse beating agitatedly at the base of her throat, then lower still to the curve of her breasts beneath the peach-coloured bikini.

'Look at me, Mommy! Look!' George waved his hands excitedly.

'Don't worry, George,' Aristo said softly, his dark eyes gleaming. 'Mommy's looking.'

Her skin was prickling as, still carrying their giggling son, he walked slowly towards her. Depositing George onto his feet, he dropped down lightly onto the lounger beside her, his cool, damp body sending a jolt over her skin like sheet lightning.

'Here.' Grabbing a towel, she unceremoniously pushed it into his hands. 'Why don't you dry off?'

'I thought you might like to take a dip with me.'

His voice was cool and controlled, but the taunting expression in his eyes made her breath catch in her throat.

'Or are you scared of getting out of your depth?'

Their gazes locked and she wondered how it was possible that one little sentence could make her feel her so naked and exposed.

She tried to think of something smart to say, but she was struggling to control her voice. 'No, of course I'm not scared.' She glared at him.

His eyes hadn't left her face. 'Did you hear that, George?' He glanced slyly over at his son. 'Mommy's going to come swimming with us.'

'I didn't say that—' But as George began jumping up and down, she gave up. She held up her hands. 'Okay, okay— I'll go swimming. But later.'

Her face grew warm as she felt his dark eyes slowly inspect her, his narrowed gaze rolling over each of her ribs like a car over speed bumps.

'That colour really suits you,' he said softly.

Leaning forward, he tipped her book upwards to glance at the cover and she felt his thigh press against hers. Her mouth suddenly dry, she stared across at him.

'Thank you.' She felt her lips move, heard her voice, but none of it felt real. Nothing felt real, in fact, except the hard length of his leg.

'Mommy? Please may I have a juice?'

Turning towards her son, she nodded. 'Of course, darling.'

'I'll take him.' Aristo stood up, and she clenched her

muscles against the sudden, almost brutal feeling of loss as she watched her son trotting happily beside her ex-husband towards the villa.

Later, she joined them in the pool, and then she dozed in the sunshine while Aristo taught George to do a kneeling dive.

It felt strange, watching the two of them. In fact she felt the tiniest bit jealous of her son's fascination with Aristo, for up until now it had always been just the two of them. Mainly, though, she was stunned but happy at how quickly and effortlessly they had bonded, and at the fact that Aristo seemed as enchanted by George as she was.

A knot began to form in her stomach. It had caught her off-guard, Aristo being so gentle and patient with his son. Growing up, that had been all she'd ever wanted from her own father—to be more than the fleeting focus of his wandering attention. And the blossoming relationship between Aristo and George was not merely a reminder of what she'd missed out on growing up, it also confirmed what she'd already subconsciously accepted—that there was no going back. They were going to have to tell George the truth.

Gazing down at the open but unread page of her book, Teddie felt a flicker of panic. Not about her son's likely reaction to the news, but about what would happen when they left the island and returned to normal life.

Aristo might appear to be fully focused on George right now, but this was the honeymoon period, and she knew how swiftly and devastatingly things could change. Back in New York, her son would no longer be the only item on Aristo's agenda. He was going to have to compete for his father's time against the allure and challenge of work.

The tension in her chest wound tighter and tighter and she gripped the edges of the book, remembering how glorious it had been to feel the warmth of his gaze. And how cold it had felt when she'd been pushed into the shadows.

But it was too late to worry about that now. George wasn't going to stay as a three-year-old for ever, and sooner or later he was going to want to know who his father was. And—as she'd already discovered—there was never a right time to tell the truth.

'I thought we might eat together later tonight. Just the two of us.'

Aristo's voice cut into her thoughts and her chin jerked up. They were lazing by the pool beneath a gleaming white canvas canopy. His gaze was steady, his voice measured.

'We need to talk,' he said quietly. 'And, much as I love having our son around, it'll be easier to do that when he's not there.'

She knew her face had stilled. Her heart had stilled too, at the thought of spending an evening alone with him. But, ignoring the panicky drumming of her heart, she nodded. 'I agree.'

And then, before her face could betray her, she lowered the brim of her hat and leaned back against the sun lounger.

Three hours later, the heat of the day was starting to drop and a faint breeze was riffling the glassy surface of the pool.

Glancing down at her cup of coffee, Teddie felt her spine tense. The meal would soon be over, but she still hadn't managed to say even one word of what was whirling inside her head.

Looking up, she felt her heart drop forward like a rollercoaster. Aristo was watching her, his gaze so calm and knowing that she felt as if she'd been caught with her hand in his jacket. Except he wasn't wearing a jacket.

Just a washed-out black Henley and a pair of cream linen trousers.

'You're quiet,' he said softly.

'Am I?' She felt her cheeks flush, hearing the nervousness in her voice.

'Yes, unnervingly so.' His eyes looked directly into hers and she suddenly wished that it was whisky, not coffee that she was drinking.

She frowned. 'I'm just thinking…'

'Whoa! I wasn't getting at you. I don't want to fight.'

He held up his napkin and waved it in a gesture of surrender, but she barely noticed; she was too busy following the lazy curve of his smile.

Her own smile was instant, instinctive, unstoppable. 'I'm not looking for a fight either…' She hesitated. 'I was just thinking about us, and George, and…'

He sat watching her, waiting, and she looked away, fearful of what she would see in his eyes.

'And… Well, I think we should tell him tomorrow that you're his father.'

There was a stretch of silence.

Aristo studied her face.

Caught between the flickering nightlights and the darkness she looked tense, wary, apprehensive and he could sense the effort her words had taken.

Of course, logically, now he and George had met, it was inevitable that they should tell him the truth, and it was what he wanted—or at least a part of what he wanted. But, as much as he wanted to acknowledge his son as his own, these last few days had taught him that the decision needed to come from Teddie.

And now it had.

He exhaled slowly, relief vying with satisfaction. It wasn't quite the hand of friendship, but it was a start.

His eyes wandered idly over the simple yellow dress she was wearing, lingering on the upward curve of her breasts. And anyway, he wanted Teddie to be a whole lot more than just a friend.

'Are you sure?' He spoke carefully. 'We can wait. *I* can wait.'

He was rapidly becoming an expert in waiting. Shifting against the ache in his groin, he gritted his teeth and glanced away to the white line of slow-moving surf down on the beach.

Teddie felt her heart jump against her ribs. Incredibly, Aristo was giving her a choice, but to her surprise she realised that now was the right time.

'I'm sure.'

And once they did then there really would be no going back.

She felt a spasm of panic, needle-sharp, like a blade beneath her ribs. Was she doing the right thing? Or had she just doomed her son to the same fate that she'd endured? A childhood marked with uncertainty and self-doubt, with a father who would cloak his absences beneath the virtuous task of supporting his family.

'He needs to know.' Hearing the words out loud, she felt tears coming. Quickly she bolstered her panic. 'But I need to know that you understand what this means.'

He frowned. 'If I didn't I wouldn't be here.'

Pushing back her chair, she stood up unsteadily. 'So this is all about you, is it?'

'That's not what I'm saying.'

He was standing now too.

'That's what it sounded like.'

She heard him inhale and her anger shifted to guilt. It wasn't fair to twist his words when she wasn't being honest about her own feelings.

'I just mean that being a father is a lifetime commitment.'

His face hardened. 'I'd like to say that's not something I'm going to forget but, given my own childhood, I can't.

All I can say is that I am going to be there for George—for you.'

Teddie fought the beating of her heart. He was saying all the right things and she wanted to believe him—only believing him set off in her a whole new spiral of half-thought-out fears and uncertainties.

'Good.' She was trying hard to let nothing show in her eyes but he was staring at her impatiently.

'Is it? Because it doesn't sound like it to me.'

He moved swiftly round the table, stopping in front of her. The paleness of her face made her eyes seem incredibly green, and he ran his hand over his face, needing action to counteract the ache in his chest, unsure of his footing in this uncharted territory.

'Teddie…' He softened his voice.

She lifted one hand to her throat and raised the other in front of her, as though warding him off. It was a gesture of such conflicting vulnerability and defiance that he was suddenly struggling to breathe.

'I'm not just saying what I think you want to hear.'

'I know.' She gave him a small, sad smile. 'And I want you to be there for George. It's just it's only ever been me and him. I know you're his father, but I've never had to share him before and it feels like a big deal.'

Aristo stared down at her. The fact that Teddie loved her son so fiercely made something wrench apart inside his chest and, taking a step forward, he pulled her gently towards him.

'I'm not going to take him away from you, Teddie,' he said softly. 'I couldn't even if I wanted to. You're his mother. But I want to be the best father I can be. The best *man* I can be.'

He felt some of the tension ease out of her spine and shoulders, and then, leaning forward unsteadily, she rested her head against his chest.

Listening to the solid beat of his heart, Teddie felt her body start to soften, adrenalin dissolving in her blood, his clean masculine scent filling her chest.

The air around them was suddenly heavy and charged. She felt weightless, lost in the moment and in him, so that without thinking she curled her arms around his body, her fingers following the contours of the muscles of his back. And then she was pushing up his T-shirt and touching smooth, warm skin.

His hand was sliding rhythmically through her hair, tipping her head back, and his mouth was brushing over her cheeks and lips like the softest feathers, teasing her so that she could hear her own breathing inside her head, like the waves rushing inside a seashell.

She took a breath, her hands splaying out, wanting more of his skin, his heat, his smooth, hard muscle. Her heart was pounding, the longing inside of her combusting as she felt the fingers of his other hand travel lightly over her bare back. And then her stomach clenched as he parted her lips and kissed her open-mouthed, his tongue so warm and soft and teasing that she felt the lick of heat slide through her like a flame.

Her head was swimming.

She wanted more—more of his mouth, his touch, his skin—so much more of him. Reaching up, she clasped his face, kissing him back, pulling him closer, lifting her hips and oscillating against him, trying, needing to relieve the ache radiating from her pelvis.

Heat was spilling over her skin and, arching upwards, she felt his breath stumble, and then he was sliding a hand through her hair, holding her captive as he kissed her more deeply, his warm breath filling her mouth so that she was melting from the inside out.

Her fingers were scrabbling against his skin... She moaned...

There was a second of agonising pulsing stillness, and then slowly she felt him pull away.

His eyes were dark with passion. For a moment he didn't speak, and she knew as he breathed out roughly that he was looking for the right words, looking for *any* words because he was as stunned as she.

'Sorry. I didn't mean to do that.'

She stared up at him, an ache like thirst spreading outwards. 'Me neither.'

'So I suppose we should just forget it ever happened.'

He made it sound like a statement, but she knew it was a question from the dark and unblinking intensity of his gaze. Suddenly she could barely breathe.

Should they? Would it really be so very bad to press her foot down on the accelerator pedal and run the red light just once?

She could feel something inside her shifting and softening, and the urge to reach out was so intense and pure that she almost cried out. But her need for him couldn't be trusted on so many levels—not least the fact that no man had come close to filling the emptiness that she'd been ignoring for four years.

'I think that would be for the best,' she said quickly, lifting her gaze, her green eyes meeting his. 'Just be a father to him.'

His steady, knowing gaze made her heartbeat falter and she glanced away, up to a near perfect moon, glowing pearlescent in the darkening sky.

'Thank you for a lovely evening, but I should probably go and check on George.'

And, taking a fast, hard breath, she sidestepped past him and walked on shaking legs towards the villa.

In the darkness of her son's room she leaned against the wall, seeking solace in its cool surface.

She shouldn't have agreed with him.

She should have told him that he was wrong.

Then remembering his open laptop, she tensed. They might have called a ceasefire, but she still didn't trust him.

And it wasn't just Aristo she didn't trust. She didn't trust herself either.

Four years ago she'd let her libido overrule not just her common sense but every instinct she'd had, and it had been a disaster. Nothing had changed except this time she knew the score.

Aristo might be the only man who had made her body sing, but she knew now that if she allowed herself to be intimate with him then she ran the risk of getting hurt—and she'd worked so hard to un-love him.

So that left friendship. Not the sort of easy affection and solidarity that she shared with Elliot, but the polite formality of former lovers now sidestepping around each other's lives and new partners.

Her heart lurched as visions of Aristo with a new wife flooded her head and she felt suddenly sick. It had been hard enough getting over him last time. Far worse though was the thought of having to witness him sharing his life with someone else.

CHAPTER SIX

IT WAS THE most perfect peach Teddie had ever seen. Perfectly plump, sunset-coloured, it was half concealed by a cluster of pale green leaves, like a shy swimmer hiding behind a towel on the beach.

She'd spotted it yesterday evening, when she and George had joined the housekeeper, Melina, as she'd wandered around the garden, choosing ingredients for the evening meal. In the end they had collected fat, dark-skinned figs to go with the salty feta and thyme-scented honey that had followed a dessert of delicious homemade strawberry ice-cream—George's favourite.

She let out a quiver of breath, remembering her son's reaction as she'd told him that Aristo was his father. Watching his face shift from confusion to shy understanding, she'd felt her heart twist—as it was twisting now at the memory, although not with regret. And she knew George had no regrets either, for he was happily 'helping' Melina crack eggs for the *strapatsada* they were having for breakfast.

Standing on tiptoe, she stretched out her arm, her fingers almost touching the peach's skin. If only she was just a little bit taller...

She breathed in sharply as a hand stole past her and gently pulled the peach free.

'Hey!' Turning, she stared up at Aristo in outrage. 'That's mine.'

He looked her straight in the eye and kept on looking. 'Not according to the evidence.'

Her fingers twitched. She was tempted to make a grab for it, but already his proximity was sending her senses haywire and she didn't want to risk reaching out to touch the *wrong* soft, golden flesh...

She swallowed. Her desire for him chewed at her constantly, and already her insides felt so soft and warm it was as if she was melting.

Watching the play of emotions cross her face, Aristo felt his body tense. He could sense the conflict in her and it was driving him crazy. For once they'd had only to be alone and they would be reaching for one another—his hand circling her waist, her fingers sliding over his shoulders...

His blood seemed to slow and thicken and his limbs felt suddenly light as he stared at her profile, at the dark arch of her eyebrow above the straight line of her nose and the full curving mouth. There was a sprinkle of freckles across her cheeks and he wanted to reach out and touch each and every one.

Instead, though, he glanced down at the peach, turning it over in his hand, his thumb tracing the cleft in the downy flesh. 'What will you give me for it?' he asked softly, his mouth curving upwards.

Teddie swallowed. This was Aristo at his most dangerous. That combination of tantalising smile and teasing dark, dark eyes. And, even though she knew she shouldn't, she held his gaze and said lightly, 'How about I *don't* push you into that lavender bush if you hand it over?'

Laughing, he held out the peach. 'And I was going to offer to share it with you.'

His fingers brushed against hers as she took the peach and she felt a tremor down her spine like a charge of electricity. 'So let's share it,' she said casually. 'There's a knife in that basket.'

'Are you sure it won't spoil your appetite?'

A suspended silence seemed to saturate the air around them and, staring past him, she said quickly, 'The basket's on the bench.'

She watched as carefully he halved the peach, then pitted and sliced it, his profile a pure gold line against the intense blue sky. The creamy golden flesh was still warm from the sun and heavy with juice, and as she bit into it the intense sweetness ricocheted around her mouth.

'Wow! They don't taste like that in New York.'

Folding the knife, he dropped it back into the basket. 'No, they don't. But then everything tastes better here.'

She frowned at the edge that had entered his voice. 'You make that sound like a *bad* thing.'

A light breeze stirred between them and the air felt suddenly over-warm, the sunlight suddenly over-bright.

He shrugged. 'It's not a bad thing—just a consequence of living in a fantasy. When you go back to civilisation, reality doesn't quite match up.'

Her heart was pounding against her chest. He was referring to the peach, but he might easily have been talking about their marriage—for wasn't that what had happened? They had married on impulse, without really knowing anything about one another—certainly not enough to make till-death-do-us-part vows. And even before the honeymoon had been over it had become clear to both of them that what they'd shared in all those hotel rooms across America was too fragile to survive real life.

And yet here they both were in this idyllic sun-drenched garden sharing a peach.

She felt a flutter of hope. Okay, this wasn't real life, but they weren't newly weds either and Aristo wanted to make this work. They both did. And that was the difference between now and then. Four years ago they hadn't wanted the same things, but that had been before George.

Remembering how at breakfast Aristo had answered their son's questions about his motorboat patiently, giving him his full attention, she released a pent-up breath.

'I think you're looking at it the wrong way,' she said slowly. 'I mean, peaches in New York might not taste like the peaches here—but what about the cheesecake? You can't tell me that they have cheesecake here like they do at Eileen's.'

He frowned. 'I wouldn't know. I've never eaten there. Actually, I've never had cheesecake.'

'Really?' Teddie stared at him in disbelief. 'Well, that's not right. As soon as we get back to New York we're going out to have to fix that.'

Aristo laughed. 'We are?'

He seemed pleased.

'They do all kinds of flavours. When I was pregnant I had these terrible cravings for baked cheesecake and it just kind of carried on. Now it's a regular thing. Last Saturday in the month. You could come too.'

'It's a date,' he said softly.

Her heart was suddenly beating too fast. 'I didn't mean just the two of us,' she said quickly.

Was that how it had sounded? Or was he just accepting her invitation?

Aristo held her gaze, but the anticipation that had been flickering through his veins had abruptly dissolved. His shoulders tensed. After the moment of intimacy the swift rejection was unsettling, but it was the confirmation he needed that he couldn't be casual with her in the way he'd been with other women in his life.

She had been his wife, and he was determined that she would be again. Only, he wasn't going to get emotionally played.

He turned and looked at her, his expression unreadable.

'Of course not. Are you supposed to be picking something for Melina?'

Reaching down, he picked up the basket and she nodded, grateful for a shift in conversation.

'Yes, I was—lemons and thyme.'

For a moment she thought he was going to offer to help her. Instead, though, he held the basket out to her. 'Then I'll leave you to it.'

And before she had a chance to respond he had turned and was walking back towards the villa.

'Hurry up, Mommy.'

For the second time in so many minutes Teddie felt George's hand tug at the edge of her shorts.

'I'm trying, sweetie. Just let me check this one last pocket.'

Fumbling in the side of her suitcase, she smiled distractedly down at her son, who was sitting on the floor of her dressing room.

Her hat was great when she was sitting on the sun lounger, but it was difficult to wear in the pool and she was trying to find the hairbands that she'd packed—or at least thought she'd packed—so that she could put her hair up to protect her head.

'Mommy, come *on*!'

'Darling, the pool will still be there—' she said soothingly,

But, shaking his head, George interrupted her. 'I don't want to go to the pool. I want to see the pirate boat.'

Pirate boat! What pirate boat?

Giving up on her search, she pushed the case back into the wardrobe and turned to where George was sitting on the floor beside a selection of toy vehicles, his upturned eyes watching her anxiously.

'What are you talking about, darling?' Gently, she pushed a curl away from his forehead.

'The pirate boat.' He bit his lip, clearly baffled by his mother's confusion. 'Aristo—I mean, *Daddy...*'

He paused, and her heart turned over as he looked up at her. The word was not yet automatic to him.

'They left it behind and Daddy said he'd take us to see it.'

Teddie frowned. She had some vague memory of Aristo talking about pirates when they were eating breakfast that morning, but she'd been only half paying attention, she thought guiltily. Most of her head had still been spinning from that almost-kiss they'd shared last night.

'Okay—well, we can do that. I was just going to tie my hair back.' Leaning forward, she gave him an impish grin. 'But I've had a much better idea!'

Ten minutes later she was walking through the villa with George scampering by her side. Both of them were wearing blue and white striped T-shirts and Teddie had drawn a moustache and stubble on their faces.

'Shall we scare him?' George whispered, accelerating into a little run.

He seemed giddy with excitement at the prospect, and Teddie nodded. But as they crept out onto the terrace the giggle she'd been holding back subsided as she saw that the pool was empty.

'Where is he?' George's hand tightened around hers and instinctively she gave it a squeeze.

'He's probably getting changed.' She gave him a reassuring smile.

Ten minutes later, though, they were still waiting by the pool.

'Do you think he's forgotten?' George whispered.

He was starting to look anxious, and she couldn't stop a flicker of uncertainty rippling down her spine.

She shook her head. 'No, of course not,' she said firmly. 'Why don't we give it another five minutes and then we'll go and look for him? I'm sure he'll be here any moment.'

But Aristo didn't arrive. Finally, Teddie took George's hand, and they walked back into the villa just as Melina came rushing towards them.

'I was coming to find you! I completely forgot Mr Aristo said that he was going to be in his office. He has a very important work call.'

Nodding, Teddie pinned a smile on her face, but inside she could feel a rising swell of angry disappointment as she asked Melina to take George to the kitchen. Disappointment and relief—for hadn't she been expecting this to happen?

She bit down on her misery. An important work call! No, scratch that, a *very* important work call, she thought bitterly. Her throat tightened. Had she really thought that things could be different? Or that Aristo could change? She should have realised how this holiday was going to pan out that first morning, when she'd spotted his laptop crouching like some alien in the blazing Mediterranean sunshine. But, idiot that she was, she'd assumed it was a one-off.

Aristo's office wasn't hard to find, and his voice was clearly audible as she walked stiffly up to the open door.

'No, we need total transparency. I *want* total transparency—exactly.'

He was standing by his desk, his phone tucked against his ear, the tension in his body at odds with the casual informality of his clothing. She stepped into the room, her heartbeat ringing in her ears as he looked up from his laptop, his frown of concentration fading.

'I'm going to have to call you back, Nick,' he said quietly. Hanging up, he stared at Teddie impassively. 'So you got my message?'

'Loud and clear,' she snapped. Stalking into the room, she stopped in front of the desk. 'I was a bit stunned at first, but I suppose it wasn't that much of a surprise. You put work first during the whole of our marriage, so why should a holiday to get to know your son be any different?'

His face creased into a frown. 'I don't know what you're talking about. It's *one* call—'

Her response to his words was instant, visceral, making her heartbeat accelerate, emotion clog her throat. It was everything she'd dreaded—only it had happened so much more quickly than even she had thought possible. Literally within hours of him claiming that he wanted to be there for her and George.

But how many times had her father made just such a claim?

'I'm talking about *this*,' she interrupted him. 'About you, sneaking off to close some deal—'

She broke off abruptly. The misery inside her chest was like a block of ice and she was starting to feel sick.

Aristo felt the pulse of anger start to beat beneath his skin. Ever since they'd told George that he was his father Teddie had been acting strangely, oscillating between a suspended tangible hunger and a maddening aloofness, but this—her anger, her baseless accusation—was so unexpected, so unfair.

And she was dressed as a pirate—although clearly she had forgotten that fact.

Just at that moment his phone started to ring and, glancing up at the ceiling, she rolled her eyes in a way that made him want to find a plank and make her walk it.

'I'm not going to answer that,' he said coolly. 'And I wasn't *sneaking* anywhere. Something important came up and I needed to deal with it. I told Melina to give you a message, and she did.'

Why was this so hard for her to understand? He'd taken a week off work, but that didn't mean his business was on hold. And who did she think he was doing all this for— and why? Women might talk about needing love and being loved, but what that translated into was a relentless desire for money and status—as his mother had proved.

His phone was still ringing and her green eyes narrowed like a cat's. 'We're not some junior members of your staff you can just fob off.'

'I wasn't fobbing you off.'

She stared at him incredulously. 'George is *three years old*, Aristo. He was so excited.' Her voice quivered and she paused, then straightened her shoulders determinedly. 'You didn't even give him a second thought, did you? But the thing about three-year-olds is that if you say you're going to do something then you have to do it. You can't lie to him.'

His phone had finally stopped ringing, but his chest felt suddenly so tight that he couldn't breathe.

'That's rich—coming from you.'

He watched the colour drain from her face, but he told himself that she deserved it.

'You lied to him from the day he was born. And you lied to me too.' He shook his head dismissively. 'All those years, and not once did you consider telling me the truth.'

'That's not true.' Her face blazing with anger, Teddie took a step forward. 'I did try and tell you.'

'Don't give me that.' The coldness in his eyes made her stomach churn. 'You could have contacted me in any number of ways.'

'I did,' she said flatly, the flame of her anger dying as quickly as it had ignited, smothered by the memory of the phone calls she'd made to his various offices around the globe, and the polite but cool indifference of the Leonidas staff.

'I tried them all. By the time I realised I was pregnant, you'd left America, so I tried calling you, but you blocked me on your phone, so then I called your offices and left messages with your staff asking you to call me back but you never did. And I wrote to you, every year on George's birthday but I never got a reply.'

There was a long silence.

Aristo could feel his heart pounding, the shock of her words pricking his skin like bee stings. She was telling the truth. He could hear it in the matter-of-fact tone of her voice. And yes, he *had* blocked her number, told his staff not to bother him with any kind of communications from Teddie... And they had done what they'd been told. But he'd been angry and hurt—and also scared that if he even so much as heard her voice he would do something stupid, like listen to his heart...

He'd just wanted to put it all behind him—to forget her and his marriage—

'So you gave up?' His pride might have contributed to him not finding out about his son, but the bulk of the responsibility was still hers.

Watching her eyes widen with anger and astonishment, seeing the sudden shine of tears, he felt harsh, cruel—only before he could say anything she took a step towards him.

'Yes, I gave up! Because I was on my own and I was sick and I was scared.' She breathed out unsteadily. 'But even if I hadn't given up, and you had got my messages, you wouldn't have called me anyway. No doubt something *very important* at work would have come up and you'd have had to deal with that instead.'

He stared at her in silence, his face set and tense, his dark eyes narrowing like arrowheads. 'Not this again.' He shook his head. 'Unlike you, Teddie, I'm not a magician. I can't just pull a hotel out of a hat and take a bow. I work on global projects that employ tens of thousands of people. I have responsibilities, commitments.'

His face looked cold and businesslike. It was the face he'd used on her when he'd been late home from work, or cancelled dinner, or spent all weekend on the phone. Behind him, through the window, the flat, shifting blues of the Mediterranean seemed an oddly serene backdrop to their heated argument.

'*Responsibilities...commitments...*' Her voice echoed his words incredulously. 'Yes, you do, Aristo. Four years ago you had a wife—me—and now you have a son—George.'

'I was working to build up the business for you, so you didn't have to worry about money!'

Surely she could understand his motives for working so hard? Had they stayed together she would have been the first to complain, for women were never satisfied with just enough—they always wanted more.

'Well, I didn't marry you for your money.'

He heard the catch in her voice and his chest tightened as he watched her lip tremble.

'And you're already fantastically wealthy. So why are you still working as though your life depends on it?'

There was a short, strained silence, and then, as his phone started to ring again, she took a deep breath.

'You should probably answer that,' she said quietly. 'We clearly have nothing left to say.'

And, turning, she walked swiftly out of the room.

Twenty minutes later, having got directions from Melina, she and George reached the right cove. The pirate boat was at the back of the beach on the dunes, its wooden hull bleached like the bones of some marine animal. It was more of a rowing boat than an actual pirate ship with masts, but it was still recognisably a boat and, on seeing it, George began towing her down the dunes.

'Look, Mommy, *look*!'

'I can see it, darling,' she said quickly.

He'd been unusually quiet during the walk, and she was grateful to hear a hint of his former excitement back in his voice.

After walking out of Aristo's office she had collected him from the kitchen, explaining in an over-bright voice that, 'Daddy is very sorry that he can't come right now, but he wants us to go without him.'

Watching her son's face fall, she had wanted to storm back into Aristo's office, snatch his phone and hurl it out of the window along with his laptop. She knew exactly how George was feeling, and the fact that *she* had somehow let it happen, by letting her selfish, workaholic ex-husband into his life, felt like a dagger between her ribs.

'Do you want to have a look inside?' she whispered.

He nodded and, leaning down, she picked him up. They inspected the ship carefully, but aside from a few small startled crabs they found nothing.

George sighed and, glancing down at him, she saw that his eyes were shining with tears. With an intensity that hurt, she wished she had planned ahead and hidden something for him to find.

'Daddy would know where the treasure is,' he said sadly.

She breathed out silently. *But Daddy isn't here. He's holed up his office, expanding his empire.*

'He might—but we haven't really looked properly. And most treasure is buried, isn't it?' she said reasonably.

'Yes, it is,' said a familiar male voice as a shadow fell across her. 'And no self-respecting pirate would ever leave his treasure lying about on his ship.'

'Daddy!'

George launched himself at his father.

Looking up at Aristo, Teddie felt her heartbeat accelerate. He was wearing a white shirt unbuttoned at the neck, and a pair of rolled-up dark trousers. He'd borrowed what looked like a scarf and tied it bandana-style around his head. The stubble, however, was his own.

He looked incredibly sexy—but she wasn't about to let his looks or her libido wipe the slate clean, and nor was she about to expose George to any further disappointment.

'I think we should be getting back now,' she said stiffly. 'We can look for treasure another time.'

Their eyes met, and she glared at him above George's head.

'Trust me,' he said softly. 'I've got this.'

He headed off along the beach with George scampering beside him. Gritting her teeth, she watched them crouch down near a rocky outcrop, then stand up again. And now they were heading back towards her.

'Mommy, *look*!'

George was jumping up and down, and even at a distance she could see that his eyes were wide with excitement.

'I'm coming,' she called.

She half-walked, half-ran across the sand, to where he was pointing excitedly at a large white stone clearly marked with an *X*. Her heart seemed to slide sideways and she glanced up at Aristo in confusion.

The sun was behind his head, casting a shadow across his face, but she could feel his eyes, sense their intensity, and suddenly she understood what he'd done.

'We must have walked right past it,' she said, when she was completely sure her voice was composed.

Aristo lifted the stone, and then he and George scooped out sand with their hands until finally their fingers found the edges of a wooden box. To Teddie's eyes it was obviously far too well-preserved to be a pirate's relic, but she could see that her son had no doubt that it was genuine.

She watched him pull it free, and open it.

'Oh, George,' she whispered. The box was filled with gleaming golden coins. 'You are so lucky.'

He looked up at her, his face trembling with astonishment. 'Can I take it home?'

'Of course.' Reaching out, Aristo cupped his son's chin in his hand. 'This is my island, and you're my son, and everything I have is yours.'

* * *

Back at the villa, they ate early. George was exhausted, and could barely keep his eyes open, so Aristo put him to bed and then joined Teddie on the terrace.

There was a short, delicate pause.

'I wanted to say thank you for earlier,' she said quietly. 'It was magical, and so thoughtful of you.'

'All I can say is that real pirates had it easy.' He groaned. 'Honestly, cleaning those coins nearly killed me. It took so *long*.'

She laughed. 'Aristo Leonidas wearing his fingers to the bone! I really wish I'd seen that.'

His eyes on hers were suddenly serious. 'Well, I'm glad you didn't. It was my turn to make magic happen for you.' His mouth twisted. 'I'm sorry about the phone call.'

'I'm sorry too.' She squeezed his hand. 'I shouldn't have jumped to conclusions.'

'You didn't. I took the call and I shouldn't have done,' he said simply.

Turning his gaze towards the blue sheet of water below, Aristo frowned. Crossing the dunes earlier, his breath had seemed to choke him, and with every step he'd grown more convinced that he'd blown it.

Now, though, beneath a pink sunset, with Teddie sitting opposite him wearing that same simple sundress, his reaction seemed ludicrously out of proportion.

Or it would have done but for the unasked question that was reverberating inside his head and had been since she'd stormed out of his office.

'Did you mean it?' he said abruptly. 'Did you mean what you said earlier—about not marrying me for my money?'

He could see the confusion in her eyes. 'Yes, of course. I would have married you if you'd been penniless.'

'So why did you keep working, then?' Another question—this one older, but just as pressing. 'In New York?'

She frowned. 'I needed to—I need to have that control.'

The words left her mouth unprompted, unedited, and she stared at him, embarrassed and angry, because up until that moment that fact had been private, not something she could even really admit to herself.

Sensing his curiosity, she hesitated, but his dark gaze was calm and unfazed and she felt her heartbeat steady itself.

'My mum was terrible with money. She was so out of it sometimes she'd forget to pay the rent. And she was always upping her medication, so it would run out, and then we'd have to buy other people's prescriptions. Otherwise she'd steal them.' She swallowed. 'I know my life isn't like that any more, but…'

Gazing down, she saw that her hands were clenched in her lap, and with an effort she forced her fingers apart.

'I can't seem to stop that feeling of dread.'

'I didn't know that was how you felt,' he said slowly.

She shrugged. 'Having a regular income, however small, just makes me feel calmer.' Finishing her sentence, she glanced towards the door. 'We should probably go back in.'

For a moment Aristo didn't respond, and then he nodded slowly and they stood up and walked back through the silent house.

'You asked me why I work. And you're right—it's not the money, or even how work makes me feel…'

He had stopped at the top of the stairs and was staring back down, as though considering his next step, his next sentence. Finally he turned to face her.

'I do like being in control…having a focus—but it's more than that. It's about creating something that matters beyond just making me rich.' His gaze fixed on her face. 'I want my brand, my name—George's name now—to be indelible.'

And he was prepared to work relentlessly to reach his

goal, Teddie thought miserably. Even when he was just talking about it, she could see the fire in his eyes, the relentlessness and determination to succeed, and her stomach clenched. How could she or George compete with that?

As though reading her thoughts, he shook his head. 'I know what you're thinking. And you're right. Work was too important to me—more than it should have been. But only because I let it be. I can change. I'm already changing.'

He took a step forward and his fingers brushed against hers lightly, then he caught her hand in his.

'We both are. Look at us talking.'

His hand tightened around hers and he sounded so vehement that she found herself smiling.

It was true. Last time he had stonewalled her, and she had run away rather than face their problems, but here they were discussing things. Only...

'Aristo, I'm glad we're talking, but...' She hesitated. 'I'm not sure that's enough for us to find a way back to how we used to be.'

'Good.' He pulled her against him so that suddenly their eyes were level. 'Because I don't want what we had before. What we had before needed improving. This time you and George are going to be my top priority.'

Her heart was beating too fast; she couldn't keep up with him. Or with the rush of longing that was racing through her blood. 'Did *everything* about us need improving?'

His dark gaze rested on her face. 'No, I can think of one thing at least that was utterly incomparable,' he said softly. 'But if you don't believe me then maybe I could remind you.'

His words rippled over her skin like the softest caress. He looked so handsome, so certain. She could feel the smooth tension of his hard body next to hers, and his eyes were darker than the night sky. She knew she should disentangle herself, but instead she reached up and touched his face.

She heard him breathe out softly, and the sound made something inside her chest crack apart like ice breaking. She wanted him so badly that she felt she might catch fire. So why was she fighting it? Fighting herself? What point was she really proving to Aristo, or herself, by denying the attraction between them?

They already had a bond through George. Nothing could be more permanent and binding than a child, and she had managed to come to terms with that by setting boundaries.

So stop making everything way more complicated than it needs to be, she told herself. *Than you want it to be.*

His hand was firm against her waist, his eyes steady on her face, and she could feel his longing, sense the power beneath his skin. But she knew that he was holding himself back, waiting for permission.

She ran her finger along the line of his jaw and tilted his head down so that their mouths were almost touching. 'I don't need reminding,' she whispered.

His mouth brushed against hers, barely touching, teasing her, and his hand slid up to cup her breast, his fingertips grazing her nipple. Feeling the swell of blood beneath her skin, she breathed in sharply, leaning into him, and then, taking his other hand, she led him slowly towards his bedroom.

They were just over the threshold when he pulled back, then stopped, his eyes narrowed, his face taut with concentration.

'Is this what you want, Teddie?' he said hoarsely. 'Me... this?'

She stared at him in silence, her body throbbing. Maybe it was just the island working its magic on her, subtly, irresistibly, but it—*he*—was what she wanted.

'Yes.'

In one swift movement he pushed the door shut and, leaning forward, kissed her fiercely, his hand sliding up beneath her hair to cup her head, his kisses spilling like warm liquid over her mouth and throat and breast.

The touch of his warm mouth was making everything tingle and tighten, so that she could hardly bear it. She moaned softly and then her body started to shake and she began pulling at his clothes, her hands clumsy with desire.

Sucking in a breath, he lifted his mouth and, stepping back, peeled off his shirt, reached for his shorts.

'No, wait, let me,' she said hoarsely.

His eyes narrowed in protest, but as she reached out and ran her fingertips over the muscles of his stomach he stayed still. Gently, she caressed his smooth skin, following the path of dark hair down to his waistband, then lower still. As she traced the thickness of his erection, feeling it twitch and swell and harden beneath his shorts, she heard him groan and felt his hand lock in her hair.

Slowly, carefully, she undid the cord around his waist and pulled him free. Heart thudding, she stared at him in silence, her mouth dry, her breath quickening.

'My turn now,' he said softly.

His fingers were light but firm. Unbuttoning her dress, he let it slip to the floor and breathed in sharply. She was wearing no bra, just a pair of the palest peach panties, and her body was flecked with sand. He stared at her, spellbound, and then, taking her hand, he led her into the bathroom and pulled her into the shower.

As his hands spread over her ribs, Teddie closed her eyes. Warm water was trickling over her skin and her belly was tight and hot and aching. She curled her hands into his wet hair, reaching out for his hard, muscular body, trying to shake some of the dizziness in her head. She wanted him so much, wanted the ache inside her to be satisfied, and helplessly she arched up against him, pressing, pulling, pleading with her fingers...

But as he lowered his mouth and sucked fiercely on her nipples she gasped, stepping unsteadily back against the wall of the shower.

Aristo stilled, the soft sound bringing him to his senses. Closing his mind against the heavy, insistent beat of hunger in his groin, he lifted his head. 'Are you protected?'

She stared at him dazedly, then shook her head.

Groaning, he backed out of the shower, his heart pounding. When he returned she had stripped off her panties and his body stiffened in instant response. Gritting his teeth, he rolled the condom on and then kissed her again, parting her lips, plundering her mouth with his tongue. His hands were roaming over her belly and between her thighs and, feeling her move against his fingers, he was suddenly struggling to breathe.

Teddie moaned softly. Her body was aching now and, reaching out, her hand found his erection. Hardly breathing, she slid her fingers over the rigid, pulsing length, pulling him closer, opening her legs. She heard him breathe in raggedly and then he was lifting her up, bracing himself against the wall. Shifting against him, panting, she guided him inch by inch into her trembling body to where a ball of heat was starting to implode.

Flattening himself against her, Aristo began to thrust, out of sync at first, then in time to the pulse beating in his head. His mouth found hers and he felt her respond, deepening the kiss. His heartbeat was accelerating and, closing his eyes, he felt his body start to cut loose from its moorings. Teddie arched upwards, her hands gripping his shoulders, nails cutting into the muscle. He felt her tense, heard her cry out, and then his body shuddered and he erupted into her.

CHAPTER SEVEN

IT WAS EARLY when Teddie woke up. She wasn't sure what time it was, but as she opened her eyes she could tell from the pale wash of light spreading through the room that dawn was not far away.

She blinked. They must have forgotten to close the shutters—but then they'd had no thought for anything except each other. Her face grew hot as she remembered how Aristo had stripped her naked, his hands smooth against her skin, smooth and hard and urgent.

How she had needed his touch, craved the frenzy of release that he alone had given her. And she had wanted to touch him too, splaying her fingers over his body, pressing her thumbs into the muscles of his shoulders and down his back, her hands shaking with eagerness.

Glancing over at Aristo, she felt her breath still in her throat. He was deeply asleep, his long dark lashes grazing his cheekbones, one arm loosely curling over the pillow. She loved how smooth his skin was—and his smell: salt and sunlight and some kind of citrus. She lay for a moment, trying to hear his heartbeat in the silence, feeling the gravitational pull of his body.

And she would have carried on lying there, except that her mouth felt dry, and there was a sharp ache beneath her ribs, like thirst only more intense. Pushing back the sheet carefully, so as not to wake him, she slid out of bed.

Tiptoeing into the bathroom, she turned on the tap and,

grabbing her hair to one side, held her mouth open beneath the running water. It tasted good and she swallowed greedily, and then, standing up, she caught a glimpse of her reflection in the mirror.

She stilled. She had been fighting herself for days now, and giving in to her desire had felt like such a big step, with such serious, far-reaching consequences, that she had expected to see a sign. But then when it had finally happened she had never felt more certain of anything—except when she'd found out she was pregnant and had decided to keep the baby.

Some things were just meant to be, and leading him into his bedroom had given her a peace that came from being part of something greater and beyond her control.

And now? How did she feel *now*?

She searched anxiously inside herself for feelings of regret—but how could she regret what had happened last night? He'd felt so right against her, their bodies seamless against one another, and even now the memory of his touch made her head swim. It had been wonderful, incredible… The corners of her mouth turned up and she realised she was grinning stupidly at herself in the mirror. *Magical!*

And it wasn't just the sex. She'd been there before, tumbling into bed with Aristo after that meeting with their lawyers, but then it had felt so different—off-key, every word a misstep, their bodies desperately seeking a way to resolve what they hadn't even tried to address.

Only, now they'd talked—really talked—and there had been no desperation, just a sense of irrefutable rightness.

So, no, she didn't regret any of it—but nor, she realised, had the ache in her chest subsided. It wasn't water she wanted.

Back in the bedroom, she slipped under the sheets and felt him shift beside her. Gazing down, she saw that his eyes were open, and then his hand was sliding over her stomach and her body rippled into life and she reached for him urgently.

An ivory-coloured light greeted Aristo when he blinked his eyes open several hours later. For a few moments he lay on his back, watching the white muslin curtain flutter weakly in the barely there breeze, and then slowly he stretched out his arms above his head.

For days now, ever since he'd walked into the Kildare lounge and spotted Teddie, his body had been on edge, vibrating with the muscle memory of what it had been like to hold his ex-wife in his arms, to feel her body arching beneath his and hear her soft gasp of climax.

Last night had transformed memory into reality, and now, lying among the warm mussed-up bedding, breathing in the scent of her skin, his body was already craving her again.

Unsurprisingly.

Right from the moment she'd reached for him he'd been enslaved. And not just by her beauty or the way her body had melted into his. She'd taken the heaviness from his heart, made the blood run more lightly in his veins, and he'd never met anyone like her before or since.

Despite the undeniable attraction between them, Teddie had been keeping him at arm's length. Until last night, when she had led him to his bedroom and he had felt like an exile returning to the promised land.

He breathed out once, then got up swiftly and walked into the bathroom. Stepping under the shower, he closed his eyes, tipping his head back under the warm water, and instantly he felt his body harden, his brain dazzled by the memory of Teddie naked, sliding down his body, cupping him in her mouth—

His eyes snapped open and he punched off the water. It

still didn't feel real: to be able to touch her again, to have her consent to kiss and caress her freely, to stretch out her body beneath his.

But it had happened.

And the relief was unimaginable—as intoxicating and potent as wine. And even more potent was the knowledge that she had felt the same way too. Even if she hadn't stated her desire out loud, he'd have felt the urgency in her, felt a need as explicit and unequivocal as his own, and the tautness of her nipples and the slick heat between her thighs had been answer enough.

And holding her whilst she slept… He had liked it that she had curled against him, had enjoyed almost against his will the possessive feeling it had provoked, even though it was the kind of primitive he-man response he would normally despise.

But it was daunting, knowing how easy it would be to lose himself in Teddie. Look at how he was feeling now. Already he could feel the previously insurmountable barriers around his heart starting to crack apart, like pack ice feeling a spring sun.

Only, that wasn't going to happen.

Not this time.

Yes, he wanted Teddie back in his bed full-time. But now, knowing now what he did about her childhood, he knew what was required to make her stay there—she needed stability and certainty, something vast and unshakable, and with his business about to go public he was in a position to give her and George what they deserved.

Because last night hadn't been just about sex.

A muscle flickered in his jaw. It had been about momentum and, just like in business, once you had momentum that was the time to push on to the next step.

In Teddie's case that meant convincing her to marry him.

Outside, he heard George's voice and Teddie's reply. Instantly his skin was prickling, his heart bumping against his ribs as he walked out of his bedroom, down the stairs and into the brilliant sunshine.

Teddie was leaning forward, laying the table, her dark hair swinging loosely across her shoulders, and in her pale pink sleeveless blouse and sawn-off denim shorts she looked like a very sexy castaway. Beside her, George was eating a bowl of yoghurt.

'Daddy—Daddy, we're having…we're having…' Looking up from his breakfast, George hesitated, a small frown of concentration creasing his forehead. 'What are we having, Mommy?'

Glancing over to where Aristo was standing behind her son, Teddie felt her heart start to beat unevenly.

Waking for the second time, she had found it agonisingly hard to leave the lambent warmth of Aristo's body. But she'd had no choice. Like most young children, George woke early and, although he'd been sleeping in longer since they'd arrived on the island, she hadn't wanted to risk him waking up and discovering her bed empty.

Her pulse fluttered forward like a startled deer.

Or, worse, waking up and finding her in Aristo's room.

Daylight hadn't changed her mind. But although she was willing—eager, in fact—to share his bed, she had no illusions. Sublime sex hadn't been enough to save their marriage four years ago, and it was not enough to rebuild their relationship now.

That didn't mean that she regretted what had happened. On the contrary, she knew it would happen again and she wanted it to—because she wanted him: the one, the only man whose touch left her begging for release.

Especially here, on this beautiful island paradise. Here they were far away from the demands of real life, and it was easy to live in the moment and not think further. And when it ended, as it undoubtedly would, when they returned to New York, she would move on with her life.

So why expose George to this sudden temporary change to her sleeping arrangements? He was three years old. Plus, he'd only just found out that Aristo was his father and, although he'd taken it very well, she understood enough about children—and her son in particular—to know that it was a huge, *permanent* tectonic change to his life.

Besides, he had no understanding of sex, let alone the complex dynamics of his parents' relationship, so how could she hope to explain that she and his father hadn't loved each other enough to make their marriage work, but the sexual charge between them was too powerful to resist?

The thought of trying to do so made her brain feel as though it was being pressed in a vice.

She cleared her throat. '*Pites*—I think that's what Melina said they're called.' She forced herself to look at Aristo.

He nodded. 'You mean the little pies?' Reaching down, he ruffled George's hair. 'They used to be my favourite when I was your age. They're delicious.'

George twisted round to look at Teddie. 'I want to have them *now*, Mommy.'

He tugged at her hand and she let him pull her from her chair. 'Well, I don't know if they're ready…'

'Can I go and ask Melina? Can I?'

Her arm tightened around her son but, resisting the urge to draw him against her leg like a shield, she nodded. 'Don't run—and don't forget to say please,' she called after him.

There was a small sea breeze shimmying across the terrace and she tucked a stray strand of hair behind her ear. She knew she should say something, only she couldn't think of a single word.

As Aristo took a step closer she felt a rush of panic. What if he tried to kiss her and George saw?

Edging behind the table, she gave him what she hoped was a casual smile. 'Did your mother make them?'

'Make what?'

He stared at her in a way that made her muscles tense. Not quite hostile, but wary. Her smile stiffened, her heartbeat suddenly swift-moving, erratic.

'The pies?' she prompted. 'You said they were your favourite when you were George's age. I thought your mother...' Her voice faded. His expression hadn't altered outwardly, but there was a slight tension in his manner that hadn't been there before.

Aristo shrugged. 'My mother's more of a hostess than a cook.'

He studied her face calmly. Last night she had not only acknowledged and accepted the irresistible sexual pull between them, but she had also shared her past with him, and he'd been hoping that if he could get her to drop her defences again then maybe, finally, she might consider sharing the future with him.

Only, judging by Teddie's cool demeanour this morning, she was still not ready to trust him completely. For a moment he considered giving her some space, but he had a responsibility to make this work, to make her see why it had to work.

'What are your plans for later?' he asked abruptly.

She glanced up at him, her eyes wide and clear. 'Nothing. The pool, probably—why?'

'Because I thought you and I might spend the afternoon together.' His dark gaze roamed her face. 'Just the two of us. There's something I want you to see...'

'You're sure that Melina is okay about this?'

Turning towards Teddie, Aristo picked up the hand that

was clenched between her knees and squeezed it. It had taken some persuasion to convince her to leave their son back at the villa. Now that she was here, though, he was determined to let nothing interfere with his plans.

'I'm one hundred per cent sure,' he said firmly. 'You *are* allowed to have child-free time. Besides, Melina adores George, and he loves spending time with her—and if there's any problem we can be back in ten minutes. That's why we're taking the boat.'

Grinning, he gestured towards the front of the speedboat, where Dinos sat with one hand resting lightly on the wheel.

'And Dinos gets to go fishing without Melina getting on his case, so everyone's happy.'

Teddie shook her head, smiling back. 'I've never really understood fishing—it seems so boring.'

'It's not boring—it's shopping, but with a rod.'

His eyes gleamed and she punched him lightly on the arm. 'Clearly you've never been shopping.'

'Clearly you've never been fishing,' he countered.

Her eyes widened. 'And *you* have, I suppose?'

She felt a rush of heat as his gaze swept over her.

'Only once.'

He lowered his head, brushing his mouth against her cheek, his warm breath sending a flutter of sensation across her skin so that she felt a bite of hunger low down.

'But I was careless and I let her get away,' he whispered.

His head dipped and he kissed her mouth softly, his hands tangling in her hair, pulling her closer as the boat's engine slowed and then stopped.

Lifting his mouth, he glanced past her. 'We're here.' Turning towards her, he held out his hand. 'Come on—let's go see the rest of my island!'

It was more rugged at this end, Teddie decided as Aristo led her away from the beach and an extremely happy Dinos.

Instead of being sandy, the beach was pebbled and the sea was a deep nautical blue.

The light was soft through the olive trees, but as the path climbed upwards she soon started to feel breathless.

'Sorry!' Slowing his pace, he glanced down at her, his expression contrite.

Frowning, she stared at the olive grove. 'It didn't seem like a hill from down there.'

He grinned. 'It's not far now.'

She could hardly believe it was the first time she had left the villa since arriving. But it was hard to keep track of time on the island, and the days had blurred in a haze of eating, swimming and sleeping.

Although neither of them had slept much last night.

The thought popped into her head and this time the heat on her face had nothing to do with the sun.

'This is it.'

Aristo had stopped beside her and, turning with relief to where he was looking, she felt her heartbeat skip backwards as she stared down at the ruins of some kind of monument.

She breathed out softly.

'It's actually why I bought the island.'

He spoke quietly but she could hear the emotion in his voice.

'It's incredible.'

She shook her head, hardly able to take in what she was seeing. Juxtaposed against an impossibly turquoise sky, the pale stone columns looked fantastical, so that she half expected a centaur to step out from behind one.

'Can we get any closer?'

Nodding, he drew her against him, his hand sliding up her back as his mouth covered hers.

Heat flooded her and she could feel herself melting, her body softening against the hard breadth of his chest.

Breathing out unsteadily, he lifted his mouth, and stared down at her, his dark eyes gleaming. 'Is that close enough?'

Heart thudding, she gave him what she hoped was a casual smile and lightened her voice. 'I was talking about the ruins.'

'Come on, then.'

He caught her hand in his and they followed the sage-scented track down the hillside, past clumps of almost violently pink cistus.

Up close, the ruins were breathtaking. Standing in the shadow of the columns, it was impossible for her not to be impressed by their size—and the fact that they were still standing. But it wasn't just about size or age, she thought, gazing at them in silence. It was about the human cost of building it. How had they got the stone there? And how long had it taken for them to carve it with such precision?

His hand closed around hers and, turning to him, she smiled. 'Is it a temple?'

He nodded. 'To Ananke,' he said softly. 'Goddess of destiny and necessity. She's very important because she directed the fate of gods and mortals.'

He was kissing her as he spoke, feather-light but feverish kisses against her mouth and throat. She was losing concentration, losing herself in the feel of his lips on her skin.

Drawing back slightly, she frowned. 'I've never heard of her.'

'Shh!' He held up his finger to his lips, but he was smiling. 'I need to keep in her good books until after I've floated the business.'

Teddie glanced at him uncertainly. Why was he bringing up work now—here? It seemed almost sacrilegious, not to say out of place, but the hazy sunshine was touching his dark eyes with gold and she felt dizzy with a longing that was almost like vertigo.

'I thought it was hard work and a go-getting attitude that built your empire,' she said teasingly.

His mouth curled upwards and he took a step closer, so that suddenly she was breathless with his nearness.

To hide the tangle of desire and excitement twisting inside her, she slipped free of his grip, stepping sideways and behind a pillar, darting out of reach as he followed her.

'You're not telling me you really believe in all that stuff about destiny?' she said, as he caught her wrist and spun her against him. Her pulse butterflied forward as she felt his muscles tighten.

'I used to not,' he said slowly.

She swallowed. There was a tension in the air, a stillness and a silence, as if a storm was about to break, and she had to count the beats of her heart to steady herself.

'So what changed your mind?'

He lifted his head, and their gazes locked. 'You did. When you decided to meet Edward Claiborne in my hotel.'

She looked startled—and confused, Aristo thought as her green eyes widened.

'I don't understand.'

'That's okay. I didn't either. Not until we got here.'

He stared past her at the ruined temple, his pulse oscillating inside his head, wanting, needing to find the words that would make her change her mind—

'That first evening, when you and George went to bed, I was so tense I couldn't sleep. So I went out for a walk and I ended up here.' He frowned, remembering how he'd felt suddenly calm and resolute as he'd wandered between the columns. 'I couldn't stop thinking about everything that's happened. You being at the Kildare. Me going to your apartment. All of it so nearly didn't happen—and yet it did.'

Her hand tightened in his. 'I wasn't even supposed to be there. Elliot was. But he'd double-booked himself so I had to go instead,' she said quietly.

'That's exactly what I'm talking about. Don't you see, Teddie? You and me meeting again—it's fate. Every single thing that's happened could have gone a thousand different ways, but each time fate's pushed us closer. We're meant to be together...we belong to each other.'

Teddie blinked. She wanted to believe him, and he made it sound so compelling, so plausible, so certain. It was why she'd fallen in love with him.

Remembering those long late-night phone calls, she felt her pulse jump in her throat. But then Aristo had always been able been a good storyteller. Only, she already knew how their story would end.

Something of her thoughts must have shown on her face. Dropping her hand, he took a step closer and captured both her arms, tightening his hands around her shoulders.

'Are you happy?'

She looked up at him in confusion. 'What do you mean?'

'Are you happy? Here? With me?'

His words sent her stomach plunging, but even as she considered lying, she was nodding slowly. 'Yes, but—'

'But what?'

She frowned. 'But it's not that simple.'

'It could be,' he said fiercely. 'And I want it to be. I just need you to give our relationship a second chance. To give *me* a second chance so I can be the husband you deserve and the father George needs. I want you to marry me.'

She couldn't speak. She was too scared that she would agree to what he was asking—just as she'd done four years ago.

Her heart gave a thump.

She was scared too, of what would happen if she said yes. Their marriage might have lasted six months on paper, but even before their honeymoon had ended she had taken second place to his work. And now his empire was even bigger, his workload more demanding. How was he going to find the time for a wife *and* a child?

Wyatt had certainly never managed it, and she and her mother had just learned how to live with his absences. But she didn't want that for George. To know what he was missing but be powerless to change it.

Only, what would happen if they split up? How would George react? Having only just bonded with his father, he might choose to stay with Aristo. Would she lose her son as well this time?

The thought made her legs start to shake.

'George needs me.'

'Of course he does.' He sounded genuinely shocked. 'I would never take him away from you. You've done an incredible job, caring for him on your own for three years, but I don't want you do have to do it on your own any more. I want to be there for you—for both of you.'

'I can't marry you.' She pressed her hands against his chest until she felt him release his grip, and then he took a step backwards, giving her space. 'I'm sorry, Aristo, but I can't—I know it feels like things can work out between us, because I feel it too. But this isn't real life, and once we leave the island it won't be the same—you know that.'

Her throat felt as if it was lined with sandpaper.

'You and I—' she looked up at him, her eyes blurry with tears '—we are impossible.'

'Any more impossible than Elliot choosing to meet Claiborne at *my* hotel? Or you stepping in for him at the last moment?' His dark gaze was burning into her face. 'The impossible happens all the time, Teddie.'

She shook her head. 'You hurt me.'

The tremble in her voice seemed to belong to a completely different person. She hadn't meant to say it so bluntly, let alone out loud and to Aristo, and the shock of her admission silenced her.

'We hurt each other,' Aristo said after a pause. 'But we're not those people any more, so let's forget them and what happened then. Marry me and we can start again.'

Teddie stared at him in silence. It would be so easy to say yes. So much between them was good, and she knew how happy it would make George, and how miserable he was going to be if they returned home without Aristo. But how much worse would it be if his father was a full-time presence in his life?

She gave a small shake of her head. 'That's not going to happen, Aristo.'

Her voice was calm. Everything was so beautiful—the sunlight, the temple, the shimmering blue sea stretching away to the horizon, their new mood of intimacy and of course Aristo himself—and she didn't want to make it ugly with a stupid, pointless argument.

Nothing moved in his face. He held her gaze. 'We could make it happen.'

'But we don't need to.' She tried again to lighten the atmosphere between them. 'You asked me if I'm happy, and I am. We both are. So why add unnecessary complications?'

She could almost see him examining her words, deliberating and weighing up his response. Her heartbeat accelerated. His expression was one she recognised, for she'd seen it often, when he had been on the phone or at his laptop at their home, and it hurt that he was treating his ex-wife and child like some glitch at work.

Aristo frowned. He could sense her retreating from him—could feel their mood of easy intimacy starting to shift into something more strained—and even though he'd been the one to introduce the topic of marriage he felt irrationally angry with her.

'For someone claiming to want honesty and openness you're being a little disingenuous. Surely marriage would simplify matters between us. It will certainly simplify matters for George.'

Teddie stared at him in silence for a moment. 'How? By moving him away from the only home he's ever had to live in some uptown mausoleum? I told you before—he has friends, a routine, a life.'

'And now he has a father. Or am I less important than some random three-year-old he sits next to at lunch?' He shook his head dismissively. 'Kids change friends all the time at that age, Teddie.'

'I know that,' she said sharply. 'And, no, I don't think you're less important—just deluded. Listen to yourself! We bumped into one another in a hotel less than a week ago and now you want us to remarry. I mean, who does that, Aristo?'

He kept his gaze hard and expressionless. 'We did. Four years ago. Okay, it was seven weeks, not one.'

'And look how that turned out!' She stared at him in disbelief. 'It was hardly a marriage made in heaven.'

Aristo steadied himself against the pillar. The script he'd prepared inside his head was unravelling—and faster than he could have imagined. *Focus*, he told himself. *Remember why you brought her here.*

'This time will be different. In six weeks I'm floating my business on the stock exchange. Leonidas Holdings will soon be a household name. I can give you and George everything you need, everything you've ever wanted.' Some of the tension left his muscles and he exhaled slowly. 'You could both come to the ceremony. They might even let George ring the bell.'

Teddie felt as though her legs were going to give way. She felt dizzy, misery and fury tangling with her breath. She'd thought they were talking about getting married, and yet somehow they'd ended up talking about his business.

Even now, when he was proposing, she was somehow relegated to second place.

'So that's what this is about? Some photo op for the Leonidas empire.'

'No, of course not.'

'Why "of course not"?' she said shakily. 'Everything you do is ultimately about business.'

Uncoupling her eyes from his, she took a step backwards, her shoulders tensing, her slim arms held up in front of her chest like a boxer. Only, somehow the gesture made her look more vulnerable.

'We should never have married. Whatever happened in your bed last night doesn't change that, and it certainly doesn't mean we should marry again.'

'Teddie, please...'

'Can't you see? I don't have a choice.' She could feel the tears, and knew she couldn't stop them. 'There's no point in talking about this any more. I'm going to go back to the boat now.'

As she darted past him she heard him swear softly in Greek, but it was too late—she was already halfway up the path, and running.

CHAPTER EIGHT

SLAMMING HER BOOK SHUT, Teddie tossed it to the end of her bed.

It was a romantic novel, with a heroine she really liked and a hero she currently hated. She'd been trying to read for the last half-hour, but she couldn't seem to concentrate on the words. Other more vivid, more significant words kept ping-ponging from one side of her head to the other.

She could practically hear Aristo's voice, feel the intense, frustrated focus of his dark gaze, smell the scent he wore on her own skin—even though she'd showered, his phantom presence was still flooding her senses. Her heart was suddenly beating too fast.

The walk back to the boat had seemed never-ending. She had half expected him to follow her, if only to have the last word. Then she'd been scared that he'd wait and make his own way back, leaving her to somehow explain his absence to Dinos.

But she needn't have worried on either count. He had turned up perhaps five minutes after her and seamlessly picked up where he'd left off earlier in the day, engaging Dinos in conversation about his day's catch.

Back at the villa, their son's innocent chatter had been a welcome distraction, but the whole time she'd been dreading the moment when they would be alone again.

Only, again she needn't have worried, for Aristo had politely excused himself after kissing George goodnight.

And she should have been pleased—grateful, even— that he had finally got the message. Instead, though, she had felt oddly disappointed and, lying here now, she still couldn't shift the sense of loss that had been threatening to overwhelm her since she'd turned and walked away from him at the temple.

Rolling on to her side, Teddie leaned over and switched off the light, reaching inside herself for a switch that might just as easily switch off her troubled thoughts.

But her brain stayed stubbornly alert.

Perhaps she should close the shutters.

Normally she only shut the muslin curtains, liking the way the pale pink early-morning light filtered softly through them at daybreak. But tonight the room felt both too large and yet claustrophobic, and she knew closing the shutters would only add to the darkness already inside her head.

Besides the temperature had risen vertiginously during the afternoon, and she wasn't prepared to shut out the occasional whisper of cool sea air.

It hardly seemed possible that only this morning she had made peace with herself, accepting that the sexual longing she felt for Aristo was not shameful in any way, nor something she would come to regret. That it just *was* and there was no point in questioning it or fighting it.

But, although she was willing to give in to the temptation of a sexual relationship with Aristo, marriage was something she was going to continue resisting. She'd spent too long dealing with the chaos and devastation caused by the men in her life to let it happen again to her or her son.

Gazing at the moonlight through the curtains, she felt her heart contract. Maybe a fling wasn't what she would chosen if she could have had exactly what she wanted. But, as she'd already told him, she couldn't have that, and right now it was enough. All she wanted to do was live each minute as fully as possible until the inevitable moment of their separation when they returned to New York.

And it could have worked—only, typically of Aristo, he'd had to push for more—

Her stomach muscles tensed, frustration slicing through her. Nothing was ever good enough for him. He had a beautiful home in one of the most vibrant, exciting cities in the world, another in Athens, this mythically beautiful island and who knew how many other properties scattered across the globe? He owned a string of hotels and resorts and could probably retire now. But she knew he would never stop, that there would always be something driving him onwards, chasing him to the next goal.

Right now it was getting Teddie to marry him. And if she agreed to that then it would be something else.

Why couldn't he have left things as they were? Why couldn't he have just enjoyed the absence of complication in this new version of their old relationship? What was so wrong with allowing things to remain simple for just a few more days?

She didn't understand why he couldn't be satisfied, and she was tired of not understanding. Suddenly and intensely she wanted to talk to him.

Swinging out of bed, she snatched up a thin robe, pushing her arms into the sleeves as she walked determinedly across her bedroom. But when she reached the door she stopped, the rush of frustration and fury that had propelled her out of bed fading as quickly as it had arisen.

Did she really want to have this conversation now?

No. *Only, how could she not?*

Maybe he wasn't her husband any more, but she was going to have to deal with Aristo on a regular basis—and how would that ever work if she allowed the issue of re-marrying to sit unquestioned, unanswered between them?

Knowing Aristo as she did, he wasn't going to give up without a fight. So why not take the fight to him?

Heart thumping, she opened the door and walked purposefully out into the softly lit hallway. But before she had gone even a couple of paces her feet faltered and she came to an abrupt standstill, her pulse beating violently against her throat as though it was trying to leap to freedom.

Aristo was sitting on the floor, his long legs stretched out in front of him and blocking her way. As she stared down at him in stunned silence his dark gaze lifted to her face, and instantly she felt her shoulders stiffen and her heart begin to beat even faster.

'What are you doing?' she said hoarsely.

Holding her breath, she watched as he got to his feet in one smooth movement.

He shrugged. 'I couldn't sleep. So I got up to do some work, only I just couldn't seem to concentrate.' He looked up at her, his mouth curving crookedly. 'This may come as a surprise to you, but apparently everything isn't ultimately about business after all.'

She recognised her own words, but they sounded different when spoken by him. Less like an accusation, more self-deprecating. But even if that was true, she knew he was probably just trying a new tactic.

'So...what? You thought you'd stretch your legs instead?' she said, glancing pointedly at his long limbs, her green eyes wide and challenging. 'What do you want, Aristo?'

His gaze didn't shift. 'I want to talk to you. I was going to knock on your door.'

'But you didn't.'

'Your light was off. I thought you must be asleep.'

She hesitated, then shook her head. 'I couldn't sleep either. Actually, I wanted to talk too. I was coming to find you.'

Aristo felt his chest tighten.

Watching Teddie practically sprint away from the temple, he'd had to summon up every atom of willpower to stop himself from chasing after her and *demanding* that she agree to what was clearly the only possible course of action open to them. Despite his frustration at the relentless circular dynamics of their relationship, and her stubborn, illogical opposition, he'd held back.

He'd felt too angry. Not the cold, disbelieving anger he'd felt four years ago, when he'd returned to their apartment to find her gone, or even the gnawing, twisting fury at learning he was father to a three-year-old he'd never met.

No, his anger had been hot and tangled with fear—an explicable fear, not new but still nameless—and that had angered him further because he couldn't control what he didn't understand. He'd known that he needed time to cool off, so he'd forced himself to stand and watch her disappear, to wait until his heart beat more steadily. And then back at the villa, he'd made himself turn in before her.

Of course he hadn't been able to sleep. His room still resonated with her presence from the night before. But even if it hadn't, he would have been incapable of thinking about anything but her.

And it wasn't just about the sex.

In a lot of ways that would have been easier, more straightforward. He gritted his teeth. But then nothing about Teddie was straightforward. She was an impossible to solve magic trick—thrilling and compelling and mystifying.

Look at her now. She might say she wanted to talk, but the expression on her face was an almost perfect hybrid of defiance and doubt, and he could sense that she was holding her body ready. Maybe ready to fight but, knowing Teddie, more likely ready to flee.

He felt the muscles of his face contract. He didn't want to fight with her any more, and he certainly didn't want to make her run.

Only, they couldn't just stand here in the darkness for ever.

'I don't want to force this…' He spoke carefully, willing her to hear his words as an invitation, not a trap. 'So I'm going to go downstairs and sit by the pool. If you want to join me that's great, and if not then I'll see you in the morning.'

Outside, the air was slightly cooler and he breathed in deeply, trying to calm the thundering of his heart. Had he said enough to reassure her that they could survive this conversation?

He wasn't sure, and as the silence stretched out into the night he was on the verge of turning and walking back into the villa. Then he saw her walking stiffly out onto the deck.

She stopped in front of him, close enough that he could see her eyes were the same colour as the wild pines that grew in the centre of the island, but not so close that she couldn't bolt back into the darkness.

'I don't want to argue,' he said after a moment.

She held his gaze. 'And you're saying I do?'

He held up his hands. 'No—that's not what I meant. Look, Teddie, I'm not looking for a fight. I'm just trying to fix this.'

'Fix what?' She glanced up at him, and then away into the darkness. 'Me? Us? Because I don't need fixing, thank you very much, and there is no us.'

'So what was last night about?'

'Last night was about sex, Aristo.'

'Not sex—passion,' he said softly.

'Whatever! It's just chemistry, pheromones.' She made her voice sound casual, even though her fingernails were digging into the palms of her hand. 'That's all.'

'That's all?' he repeated incredulously. 'You think last night was run of the mill?'

'No, of course not.' Her cheeks flushed. 'I'm not saying what we have isn't special. I know it is—that's why we've got this arrangement. So can't we just enjoy it? Do we have to keep talking about marriage?'

A muscle flickered in his jawline. 'Yes, we do. This "arrangement" works here, but it's not practical long-term.'

'Practical?' She took a deep breath. 'I thought we were talking about passion, not putting up some bookshelves.'

He gazed at her steadily, but she saw something flare in his dark eyes.

'So how do you see it working, then, Teddie? Is it going to be sex in the afternoons, when George is at school? Are we going to have to get up early and move beds every time one of us sleeps over?' His lip curled. 'But I'm guessing you don't even have a spare bed, so what will happen? Are you expecting me to sleep on the sofa?'

Her hands clenched into fists. 'That's the point. I'm not expecting anything. And you shouldn't expect anything from me—particularly marriage.'

She might as well not have spoken. Even as she watched him searching through that handsome head of his for some new line of attack he was already speaking.

'You told me you wanted us to be honest with one another.'

Heart pounding, she stared at him in mute frustration. 'So be honest! What you really want from me is sex, but you *need* me to be your wife because you want a wife.'

'Not just *a* wife. I want *you*.'

She shook her head. 'You don't want me—not really.'

'I know you don't believe that.'

'You don't know anything about me,' she snapped. She was starting to feel cornered, hemmed in by his refusal to see anything except from his own point of view. 'And what's more you don't want to know.'

Watching his jaw tighten, she knew that he was biting down on his temper.

'That's not true.'

'Yes, it is. You have this idea of what a wife should be, and I'm not it, Aristo.' She took a breath, trying to stay calm. 'Please don't bother trying to pretend I'm wrong. There's no point. I know I'm not enough. I've known that since I was five years old—'

She broke off, startled not just by the stunned look on Aristo's face but by the words she'd spoken out loud, for up until now her the subject of her father had always been a conversational no-go area.

'What are you talking about?' he said slowly.

She shook her head, not trusting herself to speak, frightened by what she might say next. 'It's nothing,' she said finally. 'Just a sad little story you don't want to hear.'

His heart in his mouth, fearful of losing her but more fearful of chasing her away, he watched her walk into the darkness, counting slowly to ten inside his head before following her.

She was sitting by the pool, head lowered, feet dangling into the water.

'I do want to hear it. I want to hear everything.'

The beams from the underwater lights lit up her fine features as though she was standing on a stage, about to perform a monologue—which she was, in a way, he thought, watching her slim shoulders rise and fall in time with her breathing.

There was a tight little pause, and then she said quietly, 'The first time my dad left I didn't miss him. I was too young—just a baby. He came back when I was about George's age, maybe a bit older.'

She lifted her face and his breathing stilled at the expression on her face. She looked just as he imagined she would have done as a little girl, just like George had looked when he'd told him that he was his father—solemn and shy, eyes wide with wonder.

'What happened?' He made himself ask the question but he already knew the answer. He could see it in the pulse beating savagely in her throat.

'He stayed long enough that I minded when he left, which was when I was about five. And then again when I was eight, then nine.'

She looked up at him briefly and he nodded, for he had no idea what to say.

'He was always chasing some get-rich-quick scheme, making promises he couldn't keep, borrowing money he couldn't pay back, gambling the money he did have on the horses. And sometimes he'd get out a pack of cards and teach me a trick. He was good—he probably could have made a career out of magic—but he liked taking risks and that's what he did when I was fourteen. He pretended to be a lawyer and got caught trying to con some widow out of her life savings.'

She looked away, and Aristo could tell that she was fighting to stay calm.

'I think he'd been lucky up until then. He was so handsome and charming he could usually get away with most things. But maybe his luck had run out or his charm couldn't hide all his lies any more. Anyway, he got sent to prison for eight years.'

Her eyes met his and she gave him a small, bleak smile that felt like a blade slicing into his skin.

This time he couldn't stay silent. 'I'm so sorry... I can't imagine what that must have been like for you.'

Nor had he ever tried. Of course he hadn't known the full story, but he had been too wrapped up in his own fears and doubts to consider it.

He'd sensed a wariness in her but, looking back, he knew that each time she'd hesitated he had simply ignored the signs and used his charm to convince her—just like he'd done in Vegas.

'Do you know what's the really sad part? Him being in prison was okay. It was actually better than how it was when he normally disappeared. You see, it was the first time I actually knew where he was. And he was pleased to see me, and that had hardly ever happened before. Usually he was distracted by some stupid scam.'

And then she'd met *him*, Aristo thought, swallowing, feeling shame burning his throat. A man who had brought her to a tall tower in a strange city, showered her with gifts and promises he hadn't known how to keep, then neglected her—not for some stupid scam, but for the infinitely more important and pressing business of building an empire.

No wonder she found it so difficult to trust. Her father had laid the foundations and he had unthinkingly reinforced her reasons to feel that way.

'I don't know how you survive something like that,' he said quietly. Except Teddie hadn't just survived. She'd faced insurmountable obstacles and triumphed.

She shrugged. 'It got worse before it got better. My mum lost it—big-time. I kept having to stay home to take care of her so my school got involved, and then I had to go and live with foster parents. Only, we weren't a good fit and I kept running away, so basically I ended up in care.'

Teddie swallowed. She couldn't look at him, not wanting to see the diffidence or, worse, the pity in his eyes.

'It wasn't all bad, though. That's where I met Elliot,' she said defiantly.

'Teddie…'

She tried to block the softness in his voice, but then she felt his hand on hers.

'Don't be nice to me.'

She pushed him away. If he touched her she would be lost, but he was taking her hand again, wrapping his fingers around hers, and she was leaning into him, closing her eyes against the tears.

'I don't want your pity.'

'Pity? I don't pity you.'

He lifted her chin and, looking into his fierce, narrowed gaze, she knew that he was telling the truth.

'I'm in awe of you.'

She bit her lip, stunned by his words. Four years ago she'd thought that hearing the truth would give him a bulletproof reason to walk away, and yet he was here, holding her close, his heartbeat beating in time to hers.

'I should have told you the truth before. But I thought you'd get bored with me before then.'

He shook his head, clearly baffled. 'Bored! Yeah, you're right—I can understand why you thought that might happen.' When she didn't respond, he frowned. 'Seriously?' he said softly. 'Don't you *know* how smitten I was?'

Her heart gave a thump; her eyes slid away from his. 'It was all so quick…and I guess you weren't really my type.'

His eyes looked directly into hers. 'You had a type?'

'Yes—no. I just meant the other men I dated weren't like you.'

Her cheeks felt hot. How could she explain his beauty, his aloofness, the compelling polished charm of a man born to achieve?

'They were scruffy guys I met in bars. You didn't even look at the bill before you paid it.'

The faint flush of colour on her cheeks as much as her words did something to soothe her remark about him not being her type, but he was still trying to understand why she thought he would have got bored with her.

There was a drawn-out silence. Teddie could feel the curiosity behind his gaze, but it was hard to shape her thoughts, much less articulate them out loud.

'It wasn't about you really—it was me. Even before we

got married I felt like an imposter. And then when I moved into the apartment I panicked. It felt like when I was child, with my dad. I just couldn't seem to hold you—you were so focused on work.'

'*Too* focused.'

He breathed out unsteadily, knowing now how difficult it would have been for her to admit how vulnerable she was—how difficult it must still be.

'You're an incredible person, Teddie, and your father was a fool not to see that. You deserved better than him.'

He brushed his lips against her forehead, the gentleness of his touch making her melt inside.

'You deserved better than me.'

Reaching up, she rested the back of her hand against the rough stubble of his cheek and his arm tightened around her.

'I never meant to hurt you,' he said. 'I just wanted it to be different with you.'

'Different from what?' she asked.

He frowned. It was the first time he'd ever spoken those words out loud. The first time he'd really acknowledged his half-realised thoughts to himself.

'From what I imagined, I suppose.'

She glanced down into the pool and then back up to his face, her expression suddenly intent. 'What *did* you imagine?'

He hesitated, his pulse accelerating, but then he remembered her quiet courage in revealing her own painful memories and suddenly it was easier to speak. 'My parents' marriage.'

Her green eyes were clear and gentle. 'I thought you said it was civilised?'

His mouth twisted. 'The divorce was civilised—mainly because they had nothing to do with it. But the marriage was positively toxic. Even as a child I knew my mother was deeply unsatisfied with my father, their friends, her home...'

He paused, and she felt the muscles in his arm tremble.

'And me,' he said.

Teddie swallowed. She felt as though she was sitting on quicksand. Aristo sounded so certain, but that couldn't be true. No mother would feel that way. But she knew that if she was upset George always worried that he'd done something wrong...

'She might have been unhappy, but I'm sure that didn't have anything to do with you. You're her son.'

He flexed his shoulders, as though trying to shift some weight, and then, turning, he gave her a small, tight smile. 'She has two sons, but she prefers the other one. The one who doesn't remind her of her mediocre first husband.'

Her hand fluttered against his face and she started to protest again, but he grabbed her fingers, stilling them.

'When I was five she moved out and took an apartment in the city. She left me behind. She said she needed space, but she'd already met Peter by then.'

Catching sight of Teddie's stunned expression, Aristo felt his throat tighten. But he had told her he was going to be honest, and that meant telling even the most painful truths.

'It's fine. I'm fine with it.' He stared down at the water and frowned. 'Well, maybe I'm not. I don't know any more.'

Teddie stared at him uncertainly. Her own mother had been hopeless, but she had never doubted her love—just her competence.

'But she must be so proud of you—of everything you've achieved. You've worked so hard.'

His profile was taut. He was still like a statue. 'Yes, I work. Unlike my half-brother, Oliver, who has a title and an estate. Not that it's *his* fault,' he added. 'It's just that her feelings were more obvious after he was born.'

His voice was matter-of-fact, but she could hear the hurt and her chest squeezed against the ache of misery lodged beneath her heart.

'But you like him?' she said quickly, trying to find something positive.

He shrugged. 'I don't really know him. He's seven years younger than me, and I was sent to boarding school when he was born. I guess I was jealous of him, of how much love my mother gave him. I've spent most of my life trying to earn that love.'

Her fingers gripped his so hard that it hurt, and he smiled stiffly.

'She left my father because she thought he wasn't good enough, and I guess I thought all women were like her— always wanting more, wanting the best possible version of life.'

'I never wanted that,' she said quietly.

The crickets were growing quieter now as the evening air cooled.

'I know. I know that *now*,' he corrected himself. 'But back then I suppose I was always waiting for you to leave me. When I came back from that trip after we argued about you giving up work, and you'd gone to see Elliot, I overreacted. I convinced myself that you were lying. That you didn't just want space.'

He could still remember how it had felt—that feeling of the connection between them starting to fade, like a radio station or mobile phone signal going out of range so that there would be periods when they seemed to skip whole segments of time and conversation. He'd been terrified, but it hadn't been only the sudden shifting insubstantiality of their relationship that had scared him, but the feeling that he was powerless to stop it.

'I did just want space.' She looked at him anxiously. 'I wasn't leaving you.'

'I *know*.' He pressed her hands between his. 'I'm to blame here. I was so convinced that you'd do what my mother did, and so desperate not to become my father, only I ended up creating the perfect conditions to make both those things happen.'

'Not on your own, you didn't!'

He almost smiled. 'Now who's being nice?'

She struggled free of his grip, clasping his arms tightly, stricken not just by the quiet, controlled pain in his voice but by what they had both pushed away four years ago.

'I was lonely and unhappy but I didn't address those problems—I didn't confront you. I ran away just like when I was a teenager.'

'I'd have run away from me too.' His face creased. 'I know I wasn't a good husband, and that I worked too hard, but it was difficult for me to give it up because work's been so important to me for so long. I didn't understand what it was doing to you—to us—but I've changed. I understand now, and you're what's important to me, Teddie—you and George.'

She wanted to believe him, and it would be so much easier to do so now, for she could see how her panicky behaviour must have appeared to him.

Last time the spectre of her parents' marriage—and his parents'—had always been there in the background. They'd both been too quick to judge the other. When the cracks had appeared he had overreacted and she had run away.

Her eyes were blurred with tears as she felt barriers she had built long before they'd even met starting to crumble.

Maybe they could make it work. Maybe the past was reversible. And if they both chose to behave differently then maybe the outcome would be different too.

Aristo reached out and drew her closer and she splayed her fingers across his chest, feeling his heartbeat slamming against the palm of her hand.

'Please give me a second chance, Teddie. That's all I'm asking. I just want to put the past behind us and start again.'

His gaze was unwavering, and the intensity and certainty in his eyes made her heart race.

'I want that too,' she said hoarsely. 'But there's so much at stake if we get it wrong again.'

She thought about her son, and the simple life they'd shared for three years.

'I know,' he said softly. 'But that's why we won't get it wrong.'

If he could just get her to say yes...

She hesitated, her green eyes flickering over his face. He felt a first faint glimmer of hope, and had to hold himself back from pulling her into his arms and kissing her until she agreed.

'This time it will be good between us,' he said softly. 'I promise.'

Her head was spinning. It was what she wanted—what she'd always wanted. *He* was all she'd ever wanted, and she'd never stopped wanting him because she had never stopped loving him.

From the moment she'd chosen him to walk up onto that stage, his intense dark eyes and even darker suit teasing her with a promise of both passion and purpose, the world had been *his* world and her heart had belonged to him.

Her pulse fluttered. Around her there was a stillness, as though the momentousness of her realisation had stopped the crickets, and even the motion of the sea.

She searched his face. Could it be possible that Aristo felt the same way?

Looking up into his rigid, beautiful face, she knew that right now she wasn't ready to know the answer to that question, or even to ask it. She still hadn't replied to his marriage proposal—and, really, why was she waiting? She knew what she wanted, for deep down it was what she'd never stopped wanting.

'Yes, I'll marry you,' she said slowly, and then he was sliding his fingers through her hair, pulling her closer, kissing her deeply.

And there was only Aristo, his lips, his hands, and a completeness like no other.

CHAPTER NINE

SHIFTING AGAINST THE MATTRESS, Teddie blinked, opening
her eyes straight into Aristo's steady gaze. It was the last
morning of their holiday. Tomorrow they would be back
in New York, and they would spend their first night as a
family in what she thought of as the real world.

It was three days since she had agreed to become his
wife—again—but even now just thinking about it made
her breath swell in her throat.

She loved him so much—more, even, than she had before. Four years ago she had been captivated by his perfection. Now, though, it was his flaws that had enslaved
her heart, the fact that he could feel insecure and trust her
enough to admit it.

'What time is it?'

She stretched her arms slightly, her eyes fluttering down
the line of fine dark hair on the smooth golden skin of his
chest to where it disappeared beneath the crumpled white
sheet. His hand slid over her stomach and she felt something shift and spiral down in her pelvis.

'What time do you want it to be?'

His finger was tracing the shape of her belly button, and
suddenly she was struggling to speak.

'Early,' she whispered.

'Then you're in luck.' He gave her waist a gentle tug,
pulling her closer so that she could feel the warmth radiating from his body.

Leaning forward, he kissed her softly, brushing his lips against her mouth, then down her throat and back to her mouth, and she pulled him closer, her fingers splaying over his shoulder as he stretched out over her.

He pushed inside her, gently at first, easing himself in inch by inch, then with more urgency. He breathed in sharply, his face taut with concentration, and she knew that he was having to hold himself back. She shivered, enjoying the power she had over him.

As though sensing her thoughts, he swore softly under his breath and then rolled over, taking her with him so that she was lying on top of him. Reaching up, he covered her breasts with his hands, playing with the nipples, feeling them harden, his dark eyes silently asking for and receiving her unspoken consent as he grasped her arms and pinned them against her body.

And then his mouth closed around her nipple, nipping and sucking at it fiercely, moving to the other breast until he felt her arching against him. He heard her gasp and, lifting his mouth, gazed up at her flushed cheeks, his dark eyes narrowed and glittering.

'You're so beautiful,' he murmured. 'I want to watch you.'

Teddie rocked against him. She could feel the impossibly hard press of his erection, could feel him growing thick, then thicker still, and she rocked faster, guiding his movement, wanting the merciless ache inside her to be satisfied.

Groaning, he let go of her arms, pulling her closer for more depth, driving into her until she began lunging forward, her whole body shaking as he tensed against her, his muscles clenching in one last breathless shudder.

Afterwards, they lay sprawled against one another, bodies damp and warm, fitting together with a symmetry that seemed to her as miraculous as any magic trick. The morning light was growing sharper, and soon they would have to get up, but for now it felt as though the beating of their hearts and the soft shadows at the edge of the room were holding back time.

Lifting her fingers, he flattened her hand against his. '"And palm to palm is holy palmers' kiss",' he said softly.

Tilting her head back, she looked up at him, her green eyes widening. 'Are you quoting Shakespeare?'

She felt her face grow hot and tight. Despite privately acknowledging her feelings for Aristo, something still restrained her from telling him that she loved him. Of course, she'd rationalised her behaviour, arguing to herself and to her conscience—in other words, Elliot—that the baseline of her love needed no public announcement or reciprocation.

Only occasionally did she wonder if it had more to do with a fear of how he would react.

Either way, it was getting harder to stay quiet—particularly if he added an ability to quote romantic lines to his armoury of charms.

He raised an eyebrow. 'Don't look so surprised. I don't just sit hunched over my laptop drooling over my bank balance. I have seen the occasional play.'

His fingers were lazily caressing her hip, and her breath caught as his lips brushed her collarbone. She leaned closer. He was so wonderfully sleek and warm, and the ceaseless rhythm of his fingertips was making it difficult for her to concentrate.

'So you like *Romeo and Juliet*?'

'Of course.'

His eyes gleamed, and she could hear the smile in his voice even before his mouth tugged upwards.

'Although I always thought there was scope for a sequel, where the paramedics arrive with an antidote.'

She held his gaze. 'You think they deserved a second chance at happiness?'

'Doesn't everyone?' He stared down at her intently, and she felt her pulse accelerate.

'That's not fair,' she said lightly. 'You can't quote Shakespeare and then look at me like that.'

Glancing down at her naked body, he groaned, and she felt him harden against the soft curve of her buttocks, felt her skin tighten in instant uncontrollable response.

'You're in no position to talk about fairness.'

Shifting forward, she slid her hand over his stomach. 'Who said anything about talking?'

Later, body aching, muscles warm and relaxed, she lay curled on her side, listening to the splash of water as Aristo showered. Outside, nothing was moving, and the faded crescent of last night's moon hung in the washed-out sky, a pale, fragmented twin for the blush-coloured sun that was starting its morning ascent.

She felt incredibly calm—and happy. There was hope now, where before there had been only doubt and fear and two damaged people circling one another. She knew Aristo now—not just as a lover but as a man. She knew where he came from, the journey he'd made to reach her, and he knew her journey too.

And from now on it would be *their* journey.

Her stomach flipped over as he walked back into the bedroom, a towel wrapped around his sleek, honed torso. His body looked as though it had been spray-painted bronze, and she lay breathless with heat and longing as he stood in front of the open doors, sunlight falling on his bare shoulders.

'Don't look at me like that,' he said without turning.

She blinked, her fingers clenching guiltily against the sheets. 'Like what?'

He walked towards her, and the single-minded focus in his dark eyes made a sharp, tugging current shoot through her.

He didn't answer, just dropped onto the bed beside her and leaned over, sliding his hands over her waist, pulling her body closer, kissing her, opening her mouth and, just like that, she was melting on the inside all over again.

Groaning, he lifted his mouth and rested his forehead against hers. 'You're not making this very easy for me...' he said softly. He shook his head. 'I can't believe we have to leave for New York this evening.'

Curling her fingers underneath the edge of his towel, she pulled him gently onto the bed beside her. 'Is that a problem?'

He sighed. 'I just want to stay here with you for ever.'

She rubbed her face against his cheek, then shifted against the pillows to meet his gaze. 'I want that too, but...'

'But what?' Reaching out, he ran his fingers through her hair, wrapping it around his hand, drawing her head back, letting his eyes roam hungrily over the length of her throat. 'We could easily stay a couple more days—a week, even.'

She stared at him, her head spinning. Did he even realise the full magnitude of his words? It wasn't just that he was offering to stay on the island but that he was prepared to neglect his business to do so.

Her heart was thumping. She'd been trying to ignore it, but their imminent return to reality had been ticking away in the back of her mind like a timed explosion, waiting to go off.

For the last few days she had been sublimely happy. They'd hardly spent a moment apart, and Aristo had never been more attentive, but part of her hadn't been able to help but wonder if that would change when the plane touched down in New York. If his promise of change would disappear along with the sand in their shoes.

Now, though, she realised that—incredibly—he had meant what he'd said, for he had just given her the proof she'd been subconsciously seeking that she didn't need to measure her happiness in days or weeks any more.

'We could...'

Sitting back, he studied her face assessingly. 'You're turning me down?'

Green eyes flaring, she nudged him with her foot. 'I don't want to wear you out. I mean, you're not as young as you used to be—'

She broke off, yelping as he grabbed her foot and jerked her towards him, his dark eyes gleaming with amusement.

'Is that right?'

His fingers began sliding up her legs, over her ankles, moving lazily over her skin, and she breathed out unsteadily, feeling her body tighten in response.

'Of course I want to stay...'

She hesitated. Her job had always been such a contentious issue between them, but she couldn't run away this time. More importantly, she didn't want to.

'But I've got opening night at the Castine on Saturday. I have to be there.'

She wondered how he would respond to her putting *her* job first, but his eyes were impossible to read.

There was a short silence, and then, leaning forward, he kissed her gently. 'Then we'll be there.'

For a moment she didn't register his choice of words, and then suddenly she realised what he'd said.

Taking a breath, she said tentatively, 'I didn't know you were planning on coming.'

His gaze was steady and unblinking. 'I wouldn't miss it for anything.'

And, tugging her body towards him, he lowered his mouth and deepened the kiss.

* * *

The next two days fell into a pattern. They woke early, then made love until the morning light grew bright enough to wake their son. They had their meals on the terrace, swapping between the pool and the beach as the sun rose. Then, after George had gone to sleep, they retreated to Aristo's bedroom where they stripped one another naked, making love until they fell asleep.

It was the hottest day today, and they had gone to the beach in search of a breeze.

Stretching out her legs, Teddie gazed up at the cloudless sky. 'I forgot to tell you—Elliot texted me.'

Aristo frowned. 'Is there a problem?'

He watched as she glanced across to where George was jumping over the tiny waves that were undulating across the pale sand. Her uncomplicated connection with their son was still a source of wonder and joy to him. As was the new easiness between them.

She shook her head. 'No, it's good news. Apparently Edward's invited a whole bunch of his celebrity friends to come to the opening night. There's a tennis player, some actors, and that singer who sang at the Super Bowl—I can't remember her name.'

Picking up her hand, Aristo kissed it. 'It doesn't matter. They're going to love you.'

Teddie smiled automatically. *But not as much as I love you.*

Her heart beat faster as he leaned forward and brushed a few grains of sand from her arm, apparently unmoved by her words.

Unsurprisingly, as they'd been inside her head.

She glanced up at him, and then quickly away. Why was she being so spineless about this? It was the perfect opportunity to tell him the truth, but the words stayed stubbornly in her throat as he laced his fingers with hers.

'Of course they probably won't all turn up.' She smiled.

'They will. And I'll be there too,' he whispered, nuzzling her neck, his warm breath making her pulse jump.

'Thank you for doing this.' She gave his hand a quick squeeze. 'You'll probably find it insanely dull as you already know all my tricks.'

His eyes gleamed. 'Not *all* of them,' he softly. 'If last night was anything to go by.'

He had never felt so relaxed. No—not just relaxed, he thought reflectively. He felt liberated. Not only had he won Teddie back, he hadn't thought about work for days. Of course he was checking his email, once in the morning and once again in the evening, but the project he'd been working towards for years no longer seemed quite as important as the woman sitting beside him and their son.

How could anything compete with getting to know George and sharing his bed with Teddie?

He glanced down at their hands, at the way her fingers were entwined with his. And it wasn't just about sex. He wanted to hear her laugh, to *make* her laugh. He wanted to watch her fix her hair into that complicated bun thing that seemed to defy gravity. To hear her mischievous voice as she pretended to be the lonely giraffe in George's favourite bedtime story.

Four years ago he'd always had a sense that she was holding herself back, and he'd mistakenly assumed it was because she wasn't committed to him. Now, though, she had admitted the truth about her past. He had gained her trust. And that knowledge was an aphrodisiac more potent than any sexual act.

He looked up as, pulling her hand free, she nipped his arm with her fingers.

'You're about to be taken off the guest list,' she said threateningly, but she was laughing.

He grinned. 'Wouldn't matter. It's your big night. Whatever happens, I'm going to be there in the front row—that's a promise.'

She leaned against him. 'I can't believe it's happening.'

She couldn't. Nor that Aristo was going to be there. It was a touching sign of his commitment both to her *and* her career. And yet another reason to reveal the depth of her feelings.

But right now she needed to concentrate on her upcoming show. She never got stage fright on the night, but in the days running up to a performance her nerves always got the better of her. And she hadn't so much as picked up a deck of cards for nearly two weeks.

Thankfully she'd brought a couple of packs with her, and now, leaving George and Aristo building an elaborate fortress out of sand on the beach, she returned to the villa and worked her way through her repertoire of tricks, some of which had taken five years to perfect.

As usual, she lost track of time, and it was only when she heard the sound of Dinos's motorboat, returning from its morning trip to the market, that she realised how long she'd been practising.

Packing away her cards, she ran quickly through the villa, down to the beach.

'Sorry,' she said breathlessly. 'I didn't realise how late it was.'

'Look what we built, Mommy!'

Grabbing Teddie by the hand, George hauled her over to where Aristo stood grinning beside a huge sandcastle.

'Wow! That's amazing! I think that is the best sandcastle I've ever seen.'

Eyes dancing, she stood on tiptoe and kissed Aristo softly on the mouth.

'And the biggest!'

Drawing her closer, he laughed.

'Daddy, can you take a picture?'

'Yes, of course he can, darling.' Teddie glanced down at her son. 'Do you want to be in it?'

Pulling out his phone, Aristo took a step backwards.

'Okay—hold your spade up, George.'

Aristo held his arm above his eyes to shield them from the sun, and was just starting to crouch down when his phone vibrated.

'Hang on a minute...' Glancing down at the screen, he frowned. 'I'm going to have to take this.'

Teddie watched in confusion as he held the phone up to his ear.

'What?' he said tersely. 'Well, can you explain to me why that's even happening?'

Without even looking back, he began walking away.

'Mommy?' George was standing beside her, staring uncertainly after his father. 'Where's Daddy going?'

'He's just got to talk to somebody. He'll be back in a couple of minutes,' she said quickly.

But five minutes later Aristo was still talking.

As Teddie tried to distract their son she could see Aristo out of the corner of her eye, pacing in circles, still talking, his shoulders braced.

It was obvious the call was work-related and, judging by the palpable frustration in his voice, there was some kind of problem—but was it really that urgent?

After another five minutes she took a reluctant George back up to the villa, having promised that Daddy would definitely not forget to take a photo of his sandcastle.

Standing in the living room, she gazed down at the beach, feeling her frustration starting to rise. But Aristo was the CEO of a huge global company, and she couldn't really begrudge him one phone call, no matter how long-winded. She was just lucky to have Elliot at home, fielding any potential work problems for her.

She glanced down to where Aristo was still pacing across the sand. It was obviously not a happy conversation, but a cup of his favourite *sketos* coffee would help restore his mood.

She was just about to head off to the kitchen when she saw him heading up the steps from the beach, moving fast, the phone still pressed his ears.

'I agree. I can't see a way round it. Okay. Thanks, Mike. We'll speak on the flight.'

Striding past her into the room, he tossed his phone onto one of the sofas. His jaw was tense, the skin of his face stretched taut across his cheekbones and, her heart hammering against her ribs, she stood in silence, feeling invisible, extraneous, frozen out.

'Is everything okay?'

He turned and stared at her blankly, almost as if he didn't know who she was, and then, frowning, he shook his head. 'No, it's not.' His eyes narrowed and he ran his hand over his jawline. 'But it's my own fault. This is what happens when I go off-grid.'

'What's happened?'

The air around him seemed to vibrate with tension.

'There's a problem in Dubai. For some incomprehensible reason they've been using single-use bottles out there and I need them replaced.'

Was that all? She felt a rush of relief. 'It's obviously just a mistake. Surely all you have to do is get someone to replace them?'

He stared at her impatiently.

'This isn't just about replacing bottles, Teddie. Leonidas hotels and resorts are supposed to be eco-friendly. If this gets out it's going to look like I'm greenwashing my business, and I can't have publicity like that—particularly when I'm about to float the company.'

Glancing down at his swim-shorts, he grimaced.

'I need to change,' he muttered and, turning, he began walking purposefully towards the stairs.

Change? She followed him, feeling slightly off balance. 'Are we going somewhere?'

He stopped, one foot on the first step, and to her agitated mind, he looked ominously like a sprinter waiting for the starter gun to be fired.

'Not we.' Turning, he locked his eyes with hers.

'I don't—'

'You don't need to go anywhere.'

Finishing her sentence, he smiled politely and she had a rush of *déjà-vu*—a familiar unsettling sensation of being demoted to 'any other business'.

'Look, this shouldn't take more than a couple of days,' he said calmly. 'Melina and Dinos will take care of you while I'm away.'

She felt a head-rush, his words pulling the blood away from her heart.

'What? You're going to Dubai?' Her legs felt flimsy suddenly, and she reached out to grip the bannister. '*Now?* Can't you send someone else?'

He stared past her, his features hard and closed. He could see the confusion in her eyes, and the disappointment in her clenched fists, and it hurt knowing that he was the cause, but he couldn't risk handing this over to someone else.

'Of course not. I need to be on the ground. I'll need to talk to the staff, and if anything's leaked out then I'll need to talk to the media. Otherwise it'll look as though I don't care about the promises I make.'

'*Promises?*'

Her grip against the bannister tightened. There was an ache inside her chest, cold and dark and heavy, spreading like an ink stain. 'What about the promises you made to *me*?' she heard herself saying.

His eyes didn't so much as flicker. 'Teddie, this is important. Otherwise—'

She cut him off. 'You said I was important to you,' she said flatly. 'You promised me that this time it was going to be good between us. You promised that you'd be at the opening of the Castine. In the front row.'

He frowned. 'And I will be—'

'How?' She interrupted him again. 'The opening show is on Saturday. Did you forget? Or maybe you just don't care.'

He said nothing and the chill seemed to spread to her limbs.

Aristo stared at her in silence. Her accusations stung— primarily because he couldn't deny them. He hadn't forgotten about her show, but he'd downgraded its importance—obviously, how could he not have done? There were always going to be other shows, but if he didn't go to Dubai then he would be jeopardising everything.

'Of course I care. That's why I'm going to Dubai.' His face felt so rigid with tension that it hurt to speak. 'Look, I don't want to leave you—'

'So don't!' Her eyes were fierce, the green blazing like the Aurora Borealis. 'Stay here with us—that's what you said you wanted.'

He stared at her, their conversation washing over him like the waves outside, pulling him in and drawing him away all at the same time.

He didn't want to leave her, but they couldn't stay here for ever, and this happening now was a reminder of what was at stake back in the real world—what he risked losing. Teddie might have told him that she didn't care about money and status, and he believed her, but now that she'd agreed to marry him he was determined that this time it would be perfect.

And if things got out of hand in Dubai then that wouldn't happen.

Glancing over, he saw that her eyes were too bright, but he let his anger block the misery twisting in his throat. He hadn't planned any of this, and he had no choice but to fix it in person. So why was she making it so hard? Just for once couldn't she just give him her unconditional support?

Reaching out, he took both her hands and, gripping them tightly, pulled her closer. 'Of course I care. Look, it's just one show. And I wouldn't be going to Dubai if there was any other option. But I can't risk the damage it will do to my reputation.'

Nor the knock-on consequences that damage would have when he came to issue a share price—because that was his goal. Then he would be able to join the business elite and leave his rivals in the dust.

That was his priority, in his role as husband and father.

Teddie swallowed past the lump in her throat.

She didn't recognise the man standing in front of her. Had he really just spent hours building a sandcastle with their son? Looking down at his hands, she felt her heart contract. She could feel his pulse beating frantically, urgently through his fingertips, and suddenly she understood.

This wasn't about some mess in Dubai, or his business reputation, this was about a childhood spent trying to win the love of his mother. And now he was trying to do the same with her and George. To earn their love.

That was why work mattered so much to him and why he wanted his name to be indelible.

But what would happen if he found out he was already loved? Unconditionally. Now and for ever. Maybe she could quiet the urgency inside him.

'I don't want you to go,' she said softly. Looking up into his eyes, she smiled unsteadily. 'And you don't need to go.

If you don't ever float your business, whatever that means, it won't change how I feel about you, or how George feels about you.'

She cleared her throat.

'I love you, Aristo.'

Silence.

His dark eyes rested on her face and then, lifting her hands to his mouth, he kissed first one and then the other gently.

'I can't do this now.'

His voice was quiet, careful, almost as though he was scared of breaking something.

She stared at him, her heartbeat slowing. She'd never told anyone she loved them before—not even Aristo. Other phrases of love, maybe, but not those three specific words. But she knew that the correct response wasn't, *'I can't do this now.'*

'Is that all you're going to say?' she said shakily. 'I just told you I love you...'

'I can't, Teddie.' He let go of her hands.

Her chest was too tight, and then she felt her veins flood with shock and misery as she realised that what he'd been scared of breaking was *her*.

She opened her mouth to speak, but no words came out. She'd thought she knew what heartbreak felt like but she'd been wrong.

'I'm sorry,' he said stiffly. 'I really need to change. We can talk properly when—'

Her body felt numb, and it took an effort to shake her head. 'There's nothing to talk about.'

What was there to say? That she had stupidly fallen in love with a man who saw marriage as a means of tying up loose ends? She wasn't even going to try and deny the sexual chemistry between them, but everyone knew that passion burnt itself out. And if she hadn't been the mother of the heir to the Leonidas empire their relationship would no doubt have ended when they'd finally satisfied their hunger for one another.

He frowned. 'We'll talk when I get back. If you don't want to stay here, then go to the apartment. I'll make arrangements.'

'There's no need.' She was striving for calm. This wasn't going to turn into some slanging match. At least then this trip would be a happy memory for George. 'We won't be moving into the apartment. I'm not going to marry you, Aristo.'

His eyes narrowed. She could feel his disbelief, his frustration.

'Because I'm flying to Dubai? Don't you think you're overreacting a little?'

Time seemed to wind back four years, and suddenly it was as though they were back in the bedroom of that tall tower in New York, when he'd told he was going on yet another business trip.

She shook her head. 'No, I don't. This isn't about you flying to Dubai, it's about us being honest—or did you forget that too?'

He didn't respond, but his jaw tightened. 'I have been honest. I didn't plan this mess, and I can't just delegate it to someone else.'

He looked so serious, and so very beautiful, and she loved him so much, but it wasn't enough to make her turn a blind eye like her mother had done. She knew Aristo was telling the truth—only they were small, inconsequential truths. She needed security in her and George's life, the emotional not the financial kind, and there was nothing to be gained by avoiding the bigger, uglier truths.

She took a deep breath. 'Just tell me the truth. Would you honestly have asked me to marry you if I hadn't had George?'

He glanced away, and in that small gesture she knew that it was over.

Her face didn't change. 'You should change, and then we need to tell George you're leaving.'

Silently, she willed him to look at her, but after a moment he turned and began walking upstairs.

CHAPTER TEN

TAKING A DEEP BREATH, Teddie closed the door to her wardrobe and gazed at her reflection in the mirror.

It was the first time she had been able to look at herself since getting back from Greece. Up until now she'd been too hollowed out with misery and despair to face the red-eyed proof of her failure, but tonight she had no choice.

Tonight was the opening night of the Castine, and she was going to be up on stage in front of the fifty personally invited guests of Edward Claiborne. Getting to this moment had been brutal, and the pain had been like nothing she'd ever experienced. But tonight was her night—hers and Elliot's—and she wasn't going to let herself or him down.

Turning slowly, she glanced over her shoulder. The jumpsuit was black…fitted. The top was guipure lace, long-sleeved, buttoning up the front to a high collar. The trousers were plain except for the long fringe that was really only visible when she moved.

Spinning round on her towering heels, she stared at herself critically, pressing her hand flat against her stomach in an effort to calm the jumping jacks twitching inside her.

She looked serious but that was okay. Perhaps a little intimidating. But that was okay too. An audience should have a healthy respect for magic, not see it as some kind of sideshow at a kids' party.

And it was a beautiful jumpsuit. Too expensive, of

course, but she would be earning real money now, and for the past few days she had been uncharacteristically reckless in her spending. She'd given Elliot a new evening suit, as a thank-you for looking after the business, and she'd been lavishing George with presents too.

Her throat tightened. Not to say thank-you to him, but sorry. Sorry for giving his stupid, selfish father a second chance.

As soon as she'd seen Aristo in the lounge at the Kildare she should have walked straight past him and into a lawyer's office. Instead she'd not only let him back into her bed, but into her heart, had even agreed to marry him.

Her mouth trembled. She could forgive herself for falling into his arms. Given the sexual pull between them, it had been inevitable. But she had no excuse for falling in love with him again.

Breathing out unsteadily, she closed the wardrobe door.

She'd always been so concerned about not turning into her mother, but maybe she was actually more like her father, for she had let herself be seduced by daydreams instead of seeing the reality. And, just like Wyatt, she'd stupidly believed she could beat the house.

Gazing at her reflection, she let her hand drop.

One small mercy was that, thanks to some last vestige of self-preservation or common sense, she hadn't told George that she and Aristo were getting married. But she'd still had to explain to their overtired and confused son why they weren't going to Daddy's apartment.

She blinked back tears as she remembered their journey back from Greece.

When Aristo had left the island George had been moderately upset. But he'd assumed that they would be staying there until his father returned. It had only been when Teddie had told him that they were going back to New York without Aristo that he'd got hysterical.

She hadn't wanted to lie, and the truth was that she didn't know when—*if*—George would see his father again, but she had told him how much Aristo loved him, how much *she* loved him, and just saying the words had made her feel more confident. Whatever happened, she would be there for her son.

Her stomach clenched and she felt suddenly sick. She wished that she hadn't actually thought of Aristo by name. Ever since she'd got back home she'd been trying not to do so, even in her head. It just seemed to make her feel so much worse, and right now she didn't want to feel anything.

George had been inconsolable, refusing to leave Melina and then crying himself to sleep on the plane. Then and only then had she allowed her own tears to fall.

Thankfully, Elliot had been waiting outside her apartment. Opening the door of the taxi, he'd pulled her into a bear hug with one arm, scooped George into the other. He'd taken charge of everything—paying the driver, carrying in the suitcases and then ordering pizza.

He hadn't cross-examined her, but then he hadn't had to ask anything. He knew her well enough to see the pain behind her careful smile as she'd cut the pizza into triangles.

George had calmed down, but she was still worried about him. He hadn't slept in his own bed since they'd got back, and he seemed quieter than usual. Thankfully he loved his babysitter, Judith—a retired pre-school teacher and grandmother of twelve—so at least she wouldn't have to worry about leaving him tonight.

She heard the doorbell ring and instantly froze, her heart hammering against her ribs. But of course it was only Elliot's voice drifting through the apartment.

'Teddie?'

She took a breath. 'I'll be right there,' she called, knowing that she was wasting her time. He would see right through the over-bright note in her voice.

She felt suddenly guilty and stupid for wishing that it was Aristo waiting patiently in the living room for her to emerge instead of her friend—her good, loyal friend.

Guilty because Elliot deserved better, and stupid because right now she had no reason to believe that she would ever see Aristo again, given that he hadn't so much as texted her once.

Her mouth trembled and, feeling the threat of tears, she picked up her bag and walked quickly across her bedroom. She'd promised herself that tonight she was not going to cry any more tears for Aristotle Leonidas until the show was over.

And that was what was going to happen, for—unlike her ex—she actually kept her promises.

'You okay, babe?'

Edward Claiborne had sent a limo to collect them and, glancing across its luxurious interior, Teddie saw that Elliot's face was soft with worry.

She nodded. 'I will be.' She gave him a small crooked smile. 'And this evening will help, you know—being up there. I'll forget everything but the cards.'

Maybe she might even forget her shattered heart.

'I know.' He grinned. 'And I know I'm your buddy, and that makes me not really a guy, but I gotta say you look smoking hot tonight, Teds!'

She managed a real smile then. 'You look good too, Els.'

The limo was slowing, and she could see the doorman stepping forward to greet the car. Her pulse started to accelerate. They had arrived.

Elliot held her gaze. 'You ready?' he said quietly, holding out his hand.

Nodding, she reached out to take it as the door swung open.

The Castine was the perfect setting for a magic show.

There was no sign outside the door, and it was situated in a side street far away from the hustle of the city. On the first floor there was a bar and dining room, and on the second a jewel-coloured lounge that, despite its size, offered both intimacy and drama.

She could hear the buzz of people talking and the clink of glasses beneath the beating of her heart, and as she stepped under the spotlight she knew that all eyes were on her.

They just weren't his eyes.

And, despite knowing it was pointless, she still couldn't stop herself from quickly scanning the front row, unable to quell one last tiny hope that he would be there.

Of course he wasn't.

But they were an easy crowd to please—and not just because of the waiters discreetly circulating the room with bottles of *prestige cuvée* champagne. Clearly, like their host, they appreciated magic, and as their applause filled her head she was finally able to admit what she had been fighting so hard to deny. She missed Aristo. Missed him so much that words were simply not adequate to describe the sense of loss, the loneliness, the aching bruise of his absence.

She already knew that she would never again share that dizzying chemistry with a man. But, together with their son, it was something nobody could ever take away from her—it would always be there inside her. And now, looking out into the blur of faces, she felt a tingling heat run down her spine, for she could almost feel him there in the audience, a shadow memory of that first time they'd met.

Two hours later it was over.

'Teddie, that was marvellous.' Edward Claiborne was the first to offer his congratulations. 'I honestly think she's a genius, don't you, Elliot?' He massaged his forehead. 'I've watched a lot of very talented magicians in my time, but with you I find it impossible to separate technique from performance. When you're doing a trick, I know something's happening but I just don't see it.'

'Well, he's happy,' Elliot said softly as they watched him shaking hands with an Oscar-winning actress. 'And he has some great connections.' He grinned. 'Hollywood, here we come!'

She punched him lightly on the arm. 'Hollywood is in California. You hate California, remember? That's why you moved to New York. Besides, it's hardly convenient for George's nursery.'

She made her way slowly back to the dressing room. In some ways the evening had been a triumph, but it had been a bittersweet triumph, for she knew now that no amount of applause and admiration would ever make her feel as complete as lying in Aristo's arms.

But there was no point in thinking about that now. *This is supposed to be your night, remember*, she told herself. And, taking a deep, cleansing breath, she walked into her dressing room.

And stopped.

Aristo was sitting on a chair, his head bowed, what looked like a phone clamped between his hands. As she took a faltering step backwards, her fingers gripping the door frame for support, he looked up, his dark eyes fixing on her face.

'Aristo.'

He was wearing a dark suit, and it was a shock seeing him dressed so formally, but of course this was real life now, and that meant work. Her stomach clenched as he stood up, but she forced herself to hold his gaze.

'Hello, Teddie.'

She stared at him in disbelief, trying to ignore the pain ripping through her chest. 'What are you doing here?'

Her arms had lifted to cross automatically in front of her body, and she willed her legs to stay upright.

'I came back for the show,' he said quietly. 'I told you I wouldn't miss it for anything.'

Her heart thumped inside her chest. 'Except you did. It just finished. But it doesn't matter.'

Her voice sounded wrong, too high and breathless, and she knew it didn't match her careless words, but she was past caring what he thought of her.

'You had something more important to do. You had to fix a crisis in Dubai.'

He shook his head. 'There was no crisis in Dubai.' His mouth twisted. 'Only, I'm such an idiot I had to go all the way there to work that out.'

'I thought you had to be there to talk to your staff and the media.'

Staring down into her eyes, he let out a long breath. 'I was wrong. I realised the only person I needed to talk to, the only person I *wanted* to talk to, was you. That's why I flew back to New York.'

He ran his hand across the face, and with a jolt she realised that although he was dressed in a suit, he looked nothing like the suave businessman who had left her on the island. His shirt was creased, and his unshaven face looked paler than usual, and he was actually holding his passport, not his phone.

He must have come straight from the airport and he must be exhausted. The two thoughts collided inside her head.

But, remembering how he'd let go of her hands when she'd told him she loved him, she pushed the thought away.

'Well, I'm sorry you had a wasted trip,' she said stiffly. 'Two wasted trips.'

'Teddie, please—'

'No, Aristo. I don't want to do this.' She shook her

head. Her whole body was shaking now. 'If you want to see George, then talk to my lawyer.'

'I don't want to talk to your lawyer. I want to talk to you.'

He took a step forward, and even if she hadn't heard the strain in his voice she would have seen it around his eyes.

'I made you a promise. I said I'd be here, and I was. I know I wasn't in the front row. I got here too late for that. But I was at the back the whole time.'

She stared at him, blinking, remembering that moment when she'd felt his presence, how she'd thought it was just a phantom memory of the first time they'd met.

'I should never have left you. I knew I was making a mistake, but...' He paused, then frowned. 'But when you told me you loved me I panicked.'

His choice of words felt like a slap to the face. Could he make it any plainer that her feelings were not reciprocated? Her heart was a lead weight in her chest and she felt suddenly brutally tired.

'I don't need to hear this, Aristo,' she said flatly. 'I just want to go home.'

He shook his head. 'Not until you understand.'

Reaching out, he took hold of her arms, but she shook him off.

'I do understand. You don't love me and you only wanted to marry me because of George. I get it, okay? And now I want to go home.'

'Your home is with *me*, Teddie. And not just because of George.'

She started to shake her head, but he took her face between his hands and this time she didn't pull away.

'Look at me,' he said softly.

At first she resisted, but finally she lifted her chin.

'Maybe it was true at first, but not any more. George is our son, but he's not the reason I want to marry you. I want you to be my wife because I love you.'

'If you love someone you don't panic when she tells you she feels the same,' she said stubbornly.

He shook his head, his dark eyes narrowing. 'Not true. I love you, Teddie. And I did panic. As soon as you said those words I couldn't think straight. I just knew that I couldn't let anything mess up my business, the sale of the shares.'

'But I told you I don't care about any of that.'

He nodded. 'I know you don't—but I did. Look, I know it sounds crazy, but I've been chasing perfection all my life—first at school, then with work. And each time I reached my goal I'd set myself a new one.'

He frowned, as though baffled by what he was saying.

'When you told me you loved me I couldn't just say the words back to you. I wanted to *show* you how much I love you, and I thought that meant fixing things in Dubai, that if I couldn't do that then I didn't deserve to win you back. I was so desperate to make that happen, and so scared that it wouldn't. But as soon I got there I realised that I wasn't fixing anything, only breaking *us*, and that's why I came back to New York—'

His voice cracked, and he breathed out unsteadily.

'Because I can't lose you again, Teddie. The business, my career—none of that matters if we're not together. That's all I want…to be with you.' He stopped, his dark eyes on hers. 'If you'll have me. Do you think that's possible?'

Her heart was fluttering against her ribs, but her love for him felt solid and unbreakable. 'I do,' she said softly. Holding her breath, she searched his face, saw hope and love shining in his eyes.

He pulled her closer, wrapping his arms around her, burying his face against her hair. 'I thought I'd broken us.'

She felt his grip tighten.

'I was so scared that I'd ruined it, that I'd lost you.'

'You can't lose me. You're my husband, my heart.' Lifting her face, she smiled weakly. 'But if you'd told me you were coming I'd have saved you a seat.'

He loosened his grip. 'I think I left my phone on the plane.'

She looked up at him. 'What about Dubai?'

'I don't know.' He frowned, then slowly began to smile. 'And what's more I don't care. I really don't.'

'I need to sit down,' she said shakily.

He led her into the dressing room and pulled her onto his lap, his arms curving around her body so tightly that she could feel his heart beating in time to hers.

'You're an incredible magician, Teddie.'

Leaning back into his chest, she felt her face grow warm. 'Thank you. It went really well. But Elliot and I are definitely going to have to find some other acts to keep it fresh. Maybe a hypnotist—people always love watching that.'

'Maybe I could have a go. I've been practising a trick.'

His eyes were warm and steady on her face.

'You have?'

'You can never have too much magic in your life.'

His gaze drifted slowly over her face and she felt her pulse start to accelerate.

'Well, you can certainly audition.'

'Right now?'

'Okay.' She laughed. 'Do you have a stage name?'

He shook his head. 'I don't think I'm going to need one. It's going to be a one-off performance.'

She smiled. 'So what trick are you going to do?'

'It's one I made up myself.'

His face was soft and unguarded and she stared at him, transfixed by the glitter in his dark gaze.

'It's called the reverse disappearing ring.'

'Do you want me to tell you when to start?'

His eyes locked onto hers and she felt her blood lighten as he shook his head.

'No need. I'm done.'

She frowned, and then as he lifted her hand she felt her heart open up as she gazed down at the beautiful emerald ring on her finger.

'It was a bit last-minute in Vegas,' he said hoarsely. 'But I wanted to do it right this time.'

'I love it,' she whispered, her eyes filling with tears. 'And I love you.'

'I love you too.' Dipping his head, he kissed her gently. 'More than I ever believed I could love anyone. So much more. And it's going to be so good between us.'

Reaching up, she stroked his cheek. 'Do you promise?'

'Oh, yeah,' he said slowly.

And she believed him because she could see the certainty and love he was feeling reflected in his eyes as he lowered his mouth to kiss her again.

EPILOGUE

DESPITE THE WEATHER forecast predicting rain, the clouds emptied from the sky just as the limousine turned slowly into Broad Street. Glancing up at the sun, and then back down to the diamond ring on her third finger, Teddie smiled. She knew from personal experience that predicting the future was an extremely unreliable business.

'Do you like it?'

Looking up into Aristo's face, she nodded slowly. The ring was a surprise gift to mark six months of married life—*happily* married life—and it was stunning, but the soft grip of his hand around hers was what was making her heart swell with love.

Any fears she might have had of history repeating itself were long forgotten. Aristo had been true to his word and as eager as she to make sure that the mistakes of the past stayed in the past.

'Of course I do.' Reaching up, she stroked his cheek, her green eyes suddenly teasing.

'Do I get one every six months?'

He laughed, and then his face grew serious. 'I know it's not an official anniversary—it's just that I wanted to give you something…you know, because last time—'

'I know.' Leaning forward, she kissed him, cutting off his words.

Their engagement had lasted a year, and both of them had enjoyed the wait. They'd argued a little, and laughed a lot, and then finally they'd had a small private wedding with friends and colleagues that they'd planned together. Elliot had given Teddie away, and George had been a very solemn page boy, and now six months had passed and they had never felt closer.

'I love you,' she said softly.

Sliding his hand around her waist he pulled her closer. 'I love you too.' His eyes were steady and unblinking. 'And I know it's been a difficult lately, but that's going to end today.'

'It's fine. I understand.'

Today, after months and months of intense preparation, Aristo was finally floating his business on the New York Stock Exchange. He'd been working long hours, and she knew he was trying to reassure her now, but it was something she no longer needed.

The unhappy memories of their first marriage were just memories.

Now, instead of staying late at the office, he'd invite his team back to the apartment so that she and George could be a part of the process, and she wasn't left feeling isolated and lonely. And on the odd occasion when he had been forced to travel he had kept his trips as short as possible, often returning earlier than expected or taking her and George with him.

She squeezed his hand. 'And today's going to be better than fine.' Feeling the limo start to slow, she kissed him fiercely, her eyes burning with love. 'I'm so proud of you, Aristo.'

He shrugged. 'I work with some good people. They're really what's made this possible.'

'You do, and you've worked incredibly hard too.' Her gaze fixed on his face. 'But I wasn't talking about the business,' she said softly. 'I was talking about you.'

Aristo stared down into her clear green eyes, his heart pounding.

The limo had stopped. If he looked out of the window he would be able to see the six Corinthian columns of the New York Stock Exchange. For so long he had dreamed of this moment—the short walk to the legendary neoclassical building that would turn his business into a global brand.

But over the last eighteen months he'd made a far more important journey with the woman sitting beside him. Teddie had transformed his life. She had taught him how to hope, to believe and to love.

Of course he was pleased that the IPO was happening, but the appeal of the big deal had dimmed. His life with Teddie and George was far more satisfying and exciting than any boardroom negotiation, and he savoured every moment spent with his wife and son for he had come so close to losing them.

As soon as they stepped out onto the pavement time seemed to speed up exponentially, so that one moment the second bell of the day was ringing to start trading on the Leonidas stock and the next they were mingling with underwriters and executives from the business.

And now they were back in the limousine, on the way to a party for the staff at Leonidas headquarters.

Teddie breathed out slowly. After the frenzy of the trading floor the car seemed incredibly calm and quiet.

She felt Aristo's gaze on her face and, turning, she smiled up at him. 'Happy?' she said softly.

He nodded. 'It went well.' Leaning forward, he tapped on the glass behind the driver's head. 'Bob, can you take us to the apartment now, please?'

Teddie frowned. 'But what about the party? Don't you want to celebrate?'

He shook his head. 'I spoke to the staff this morning. They know how pleased I am, and this party will be a lot more fun for them without the boss breathing down their necks.'

Biting her lip, she touched her fingertips to his cheek. 'Does that mean I get to have you all to myself?'

Pulling her into his arms, he laughed.

'Yes.' He paused. 'And no. I thought we needed some time as a family, so I've arranged for us to spend a week at the island. We're just going to pick up George on the way.' His eyes dropped to her mouth. 'But once we're there we should have time to celebrate...*privately.*'

The dark heat in his gaze took her breath away. 'I like the sound of that,' she said slowly. 'And we have got a lot to celebrate.'

More than she would ever have imagined, and more than Aristo knew.

Watching her expression shift, Aristo frowned. 'I'm happy it's all over, Teddie, but going public with the business isn't what I want to celebrate.'

His face was so serious, so open, that she could keep the secret to herself no longer.

'I wasn't just talking about the business.'

Leaning closer, she fixed her eyes on his handsome face, wanting to see his reaction. He looked at her uncertainly and, picking up his hand, she pressed it gently against her stomach.

'We're having a baby.'

For a moment he didn't speak—neither of them could: their emotions were too intense, too raw. But it didn't matter. She could see everything he was feeling in his heart, everything she needed to see burning in his eyes as he pulled her closer and kissed her passionately.

* * * * *

RETURNING TO CLAIM HIS HEIR

AMANDA CINELLI

For those who have grieved.

May the sun always shine after the storm.

CHAPTER ONE

IT WASN'T OFTEN that a man could say he'd looked upon his own grave. Duarte Avelar stood frozen in the sleepy English village graveyard, staring at the elegant family crypt where he and his twin sister had laid their beloved parents to rest seven years before.

But now a third name had been added to the marble plaque.

His own.

Dried wreaths and bouquets lined the resting place, with small notecards and offerings of condolences from friends and business colleagues alike. He'd been told his memorial service had been a grand affair, filled with Europe's wealthy elite, come to pay their respects to one of their favourite billionaire playboys.

His mind conjured up an image of his twin sister, Dani, accepting their sympathies, standing in this very spot to watch as they lowered an empty coffin into the ground...

His stomach lurched, nausea burning as he turned away and moved swiftly through the empty cemetery grounds. A sleek black car awaited him outside the gates, the young male chauffeur studiously staring at the wet ground as he held the door open. A pair of hulking bodyguards in plain clothes stood nearby, quietly focused on monitoring the surrounding countryside.

He had once enjoyed a certain level of familiarity with his staff. Had prided himself on being considered a likeable employer, easy-going and approachable. And yet for the past two weeks, since his shock return, he had been a pariah. It seemed everyone had been forewarned of his unpredictable temperament and had decided that ignoring him was the safest option.

Still, he caught them trying not to stare at the thick crosshatched scarring that spanned his face from the centre of his left eyebrow to the tip of his ear. He saw their stricken gazes upon seeing the scars along the rest of his torso when he went for his twice-daily swim.

He had gone from being the kind of man who could command a boardroom and charm any woman in his path to being one who avoided his own staff so as not to make them nervous.

His sister had managed the media, laying down an embargo for a couple of weeks until Duarte was ready for the attention. He had walked out of their first press conference less than an hour ago, knowing he hadn't been ready, but there was nothing to be done now.

The press had called him a walking ghost, a man returned from the dead. They had jumped at the chance to paint him as some kind of hero to fit their own sensational narratives.

No one seemed to understand that his survival was not something he wished to be celebrated for. Not when he was sure that his disappearance and the suffering he had endured had been entirely his own fault.

By rights, he *should* be dead.

He sat heavily against the back seat of the car, running his hand along the length of the long scar that traced the side of his head above his ear. It turned out that the nightmarish recovery process he'd endured after a gunshot wound to the head had been child's play compared with trying to fit back into a world where Duarte Avelar had ceased to exist.

As they drove away he watched the sun shine over the picturesque countryside hamlet that his family had adopted as their home after moving from Brazil. As a young boy he had been angry and homesick, barely even ten years old, but this quiet place had soon become home. Even when he had made his fortune, owning homes in every corner of the world, nothing had compared to the feeling of this small slice of peace and paradise.

Now...nowhere felt like home.

Everything was wrong. *He* was wrong.

He saw it in the glances his sister shared with Valerio, his business partner and best friend. They had witnessed his shifting moods, his restless lack of focus and his irritation with the debilitating headaches that could hit at any moment.

Two weeks previously, when they had been informed that he had miraculously survived, they'd both rushed to where he'd been kept, at an elite private medical facility on a tiny island off the coast of Brazil. Up until that point he'd had no memory of who he was, and had been singularly focused on rebuilding the physical strength he had lost during the months he'd spent confined to a hospital bed.

Talking to them had been painful, but he had started to recover some memories with their help. Coming back to England had been Dani's idea, and he had seen her eyes fill with hope that he would somehow come back to their childhood home and magically be restored to his former self.

It had worked to a certain extent. With their help, the gaps in his memory had begun to fill, but he still felt a strange disconnection from it all. Dani was determined to think positively, but Duarte felt nothing but apathy for the strange world he had re-entered. At times he even longed for the peaceful solitude of his anonymous life on the island, then felt guilt for his own selfishness.

In his absence, so much had changed. With every passing day he continued to be reminded of how people had moved on and adapted, growing over the hole he had left behind. Growing together mostly. He scowled, thinking of the look on his best friend's face when he'd revealed that in Duarte's absence he and Dani had fallen in love and were now engaged to be married.

His best friend and his twin sister were going to be man and wife. The fact that their relationship had begun as a measure to protect Dani from the corrupt forces who had been behind his kidnapping had only angered him further.

It wasn't that he didn't want them to be happy. But they'd buried him. Mourned him. And then they had moved on— all while he had been trapped alone in a living hell.

His anger was a constant presence and it shamed him. They had done nothing wrong. No one could have known he was still alive. In fact, his father's oldest friend in Brazil had ensured that no one knew until the time was right.

But Duarte hadn't told them that part of the story yet… He hadn't told anybody. Telling the truth behind the events that had led to him and Valerio being captured and tortured at the hands of Brazilian gangsters would mean admitting his own part in what had happened. Revealing the secrets he'd kept from them both. Secrets that now had gaping holes in them, thanks to his memory loss.

Dani had been subtle, but pointed in her questions about when he might feel ready to get back to work. Velamar, their luxury yacht charter company, was just about to open new headquarters in the US and in the Caribbean. It was something that he and Valerio had been building towards for more than a decade. His answers to her repeated questioning had been hostile and he had refused to commit to attending.

After the press conference that morning he'd told them both that he was going back to Rio for a while, to assist with securing one of the Avelar Foundation's charity developments—a sizeable portfolio of prime urban development sites in Rio De Janeiro, which had been the catalyst for all the trouble he had brought into their lives.

Of course the charity was only one of the reasons he was returning to Rio, but he hadn't told them that.

Dani had been stone-faced and had walked away from him without a single word. Valerio had been torn between them both, his mouth a grim line as he'd urged Duarte to take a large security detail and be careful.

He knew his sister was hurt by his distant moods, but he felt stifled by her company, by her obvious happiness with Valerio and by her questions about his time in recovery. But he didn't want to talk—didn't want to remember the pain of learning to walk again and pushing his broken body to its limits. Not when he was so consumed with bringing down the wealthy criminals behind his ordeal and making sure they paid for their crimes.

The insistent chime of his phone grabbed his attention. The screen showed a text message from an undisclosed number.

We found her.

Duarte felt his body freeze for a moment before he tapped a few buttons on the phone to open an encrypted server. His team of private investigators and ex-law-enforcement operatives had been hard at work in the past week, since he'd set the course for his revenge. They'd already recovered and collated every photograph and video of him from the past year, trying to create a map of his movements. Judging by the most recent files added, they'd uncovered a wealth of photographs taken at a political event he had attended directly before his kidnapping.

He scanned through the countless images, one after the other, seeing that a trio of pictures at the end had been flagged for his attention. The photographs showed him standing away from the main podium area, towards the back of the large event hall. Something thrummed to life in his gut as he clicked through the files until finally a glimpse of long red hair made him freeze.

It *was* her. *Cristo*, he'd finally found her.

Of all his tortured dreams as he'd recovered on the island, those of the beautiful redhead had plagued him the most. When he'd first come out of a medically induced coma, the only clear memory he'd had was of her holding him as he bled out. He hadn't been sure if it was his imagination that had conjured such a vivid picture or if it was truly a memory he'd managed to retain.

She'd kept him warm with her body around his, her hand holding his own as she'd spoken his name so softly. Her bright silver eyes had been filled with tears, and the scent of lavender had cocooned him as she'd tried to stem the blood-flow.

'*Duarte...please don't die,*' she'd sobbed, before cursing in colourful Portuguese.

Her words had been like a mantra in his mind.

'*You need to stay alive for both of us.*'

That voice in his mind had kept him going throughout his intense recovery process. And now he couldn't shake off the feeling that she was...*important*, somehow. That she was real. But, despite all the people that Angelus Fiero had tracked down and arrested in the last two months, there had been no mention of a woman anywhere near that shipping yard.

But now, looking at the photo on his phone screen...

One look at her face and he knew it was her. He knew she was real, not a dream. She had been his very own angel that night. She had saved his life with her bare hands, but she had left before anyone saw her.

Why?

He ignored the countless theories his mind produced, knowing none of them painted her as having nothing to hide. He would think about that later. For now, this woman was possibly the only link to what had happened that night and he needed to find her.

He looked up, noticing that they had arrived at a small private airfield outside London. His pilot, Martha, stood on the Tarmac to greet him, along with the small crew of one of the Velamar fleet of private jets.

Duarte smoothed a hand over his jaw as he tried not to think of his sister's words, begging him to forget his ordeal, to let the police continue to handle it while he focused on getting back to his normal life. Now, after seeing the woman's face, knowing she was real, he felt as if he was finally doing something that mattered. The cogs in his brain were turning, giving him purpose.

But was he just tracking her down to find out what she knew, or was it something more?

He brushed off the thought and dialled a number on his phone, hearing the rasping voice of his chief investigator as he answered the call and began griping about the various data protection laws standing in the way of facial recognition and searching for the mystery woman. Duarte growled back that he didn't care what he had to pay or what had to be done. He added that if his team had eyes on her by the time he landed in Rio their fees would be doubled.

The other man swiftly changed his tune.

'You will wait for my arrival before you make a move. Nobody is to approach her or bring her in—understand?' Duarte felt anticipation build within him as he growled the warning. 'She's mine.'

Nora Beckett took one last look at the empty space of her tiny apartment and felt the weight of uncertainty descend, choking the air from her throat.

She wouldn't cry. She'd done enough of that in the last six and a half months to last her a lifetime. Crying was for people who could afford that weakness, she thought miserably as she opened her phone one last time and looked at the list of missed calls and unopened voicemails. The name on the screen read 'Papai'. Such an innocent word to cause such a violent reaction in her gut.

She placed the phone in one of the boxes, knowing she couldn't take it with her. As far as she was concerned she had no father. Not any more.

She'd thought she was almost free of his reach...

She'd thought she still had time...

Her powerful father had been in hiding somewhere outside of Brazil for months, and Nora had taken the time to finish her studies at university, cramming in as many repeat classes as she could to try to undo some of the damage of the last year.

She'd barely managed to scrape through her final exams when the first messages had begun to arrive. She had no idea if she would even be allowed to graduate with her patchy attendance record, but sadly, that was the least of her worries right now. She had to get out of Rio.

The open boxes on the floor overflowed with books on engineering and environmental studies. They were the only possessions she owned other than her small case of clothing, but they were too heavy to take with her. She'd already done far too much today, bending down and scrubbing the place all morning so she could get her meagre deposit back.

As though agreeing with the thought, her lower back throbbed painfully.

As she descended the five flights of stairs to the street below she cradled the enormous swell of her stomach, taking care not to go too fast for fear she might jostle the precious cargo nestled within.

She had agonised over booking the four-hour flight to Manaus at this late stage of her pregnancy, but the nurse at the clinic had assured her that spending three days crammed in a bus to travel across the country would pose far more of a risk.

Her legs and feet had already been swelling painfully in recent days. And arranging her swift escape had put her under so much stress that her head throbbed constantly and insomnia plagued her. When she did manage to sleep she had fevered dreams of walking into her mother's arms in the quiet, peaceful safety of the remote animal sanctuary where she'd grown up on the banks of the Amazon.

She just hoped that Maureen Beckett would welcome her runaway daughter's sudden, unannounced return…and forgive her for the past five years of silence…

Whenever she thought of the last words they'd spoken to one another shame burned in her gut and stopped her from calling, but she had at least sent a letter. She'd written that she was sorry. That she'd been a naïve, sheltered eighteen-year-old with a desperate hunger to see the world and her father's promises ringing in her ears.

She'd received no response.

The sanctuary was the only place she could imagine raising her baby without fear or threat. She wouldn't be alone there, amidst the bustling community of ecologists and volunteers, with her fierce Irish mother at the helm. There was a small birthing clinic in the nearby village, and she'd arranged to rent a room with the last of her savings in the event that her mother turned her away.

But deep down she hoped her mam would forgive her.

It was the beginning of May, technically the start of the dry season, and yet the torrential downpour that now descended on Rio De Janeiro was like something from a catastrophe movie.

Nora tried her best to stay dry under the narrow porch, craning her neck to do a quick scan of the street. The bells from the cathedral nearby began to chime midday and, as she'd hoped, there was no sign of the dark blue car that had been parked in the alley all week. Even criminal henchmen took predictable breaks, it seemed.

Even though Lionel Cabo hadn't set foot in Rio in months, he still made it his mission to make his only daughter's life hell. Having her watched was only one of the ways he'd been tightening the noose, showing her the power he wielded. When she'd continued to ignore his calls he'd somehow managed to get to her landlord and have her evicted.

He knew she wouldn't dare go to the police, who were mostly in his pocket. He knew she was utterly alone here.

She bit her lower lip as she rubbed small circles on her aching lower back.

A small group of teenagers in hoods moved out from their spot in a nearby doorway as a sleek black sports car prowled slowly up the narrow street and came to a stop a short distance away. The young boys crowded around it, peering into the windows through the rain which was now beginning to ease.

Nora felt her senses shift into high alert. Usually the

wealthy residents of Rio stayed far away from the more dangerous streets in this part of the city.

The teenagers moved aside as a tall figure emerged from the expensive vehicle. Rain instantly soaked his dark coat and he looked up, amber eyes glowing bright against the dark skin of a sinfully handsome face.

She was hallucinating.

Either her brain was playing tricks on her or she had fallen asleep, and was still upstairs, dreaming the same dream she'd had for more than six months.

The man closed the distance between them with a few long strides, stepping under the canopy with a strange stiffness to his movements. Nora fought to breathe as her headache intensified, her heartbeat thundering in her ears as she waited for him to speak.

'Nora Beckett?' he asked softly.

His voice contained the slightly clipped undertone of an English accent that she knew came from more than two decades living away from his homeland.

He extended a hand towards her in polite greeting. 'I hope you don't mind me coming to find you like this?'

Nora remained frozen, feeling as if she was watching herself from above, standing with this man who had Duarte's face and Duarte's voice. He dropped his hand after a moment, frowning, and looking back to where the boys were still investigating the exterior of his fancy car.

'I don't know if you remember me.' He spoke quickly. 'My name is Duarte Avelar. I was in an…an incident about six months ago—'

'Duarte Avelar is dead.'

Nora heard the hysteria in her own voice and willed herself to calm down, willed herself to find a logical solution for this madness.

'I'm quite alive, as you can see.'

His smile was forced, his movements strangely stilted as he reached for a split second to rub his hand across the slightly uneven hair growth on the left side of his head.

Nora followed the movement, noticing the thick dark brown line of puckered skin that began at his temple. What had once been soft, springy jet-black curls was now a tight crop that was barely more than skin at one side. She could clearly see the tiny marks where stitches had once sealed a wound that ended above his left ear.

The exact same place where she had tried to stem the blood flow with her own hands, had felt it spill over her dress and onto the cold ground around her feet.

She swallowed hard against the awful memories and focused on the man before her. His lips were still curved in a polite smile that was nothing like the man she had known. He seemed so real she almost felt as if she could reach out and touch him…

Frowning, she stepped forward and impulsively placed her hand on his chest. His sharp intake of breath took her by surprise, and she felt her insides quake with a strange mixture of fear and relief. She hardly dared to hope. She was unable to move, completely entranced by the blazing heat of his skin under her fingertips through the expensive material of his dove-grey shirt.

Almost of its own volition, her hand skimmed up a hard wall of muscle to where a glorious pulse thrummed at the base of his neck. *Alive.* She closed her eyes and felt a painful lump form in her throat at the cruelty of such a vision if this wasn't real. If it was just another one of her vivid dreams, after which she would awake in the middle of the night and expect to see him lying beside her.

Tears filled her eyes and she blinked them away, tipping her head up to find him staring down at her. His skin was still that rich caramel-brown, vibrant and healthy, so unlike the deathly pallor of that awful night.

She heard the tremor in her voice as she whispered, 'Duarte...this is impossible...'

'I've thought the same thing over the past months, believe me.' One side of his mouth twisted in the same sardonic way she remembered. 'But here I am.'

'You're actually here. You're alive...' Her voice was a breathless whisper as she felt a long-buried well of hopeless longing burst open within her.

Before she could stop herself, she closed the space between them and buried her face against his chest. He froze for a split second, and she feared he might push her away. She wouldn't blame him, considering she was essentially the reason he had received that scar in the first place.

She stiffened, bracing herself for rejection, only to feel his strong arms close around her. She was instantly cocooned in his warm spicy scent and the glorious thumping rhythm of his heart. His beating, perfect heart.

Emotion clogged her throat as she was consumed by the urgent need to feel him, to hold on to him as though he were an oasis of hope in the unbearable desert of her grief. Her breathing became shallow and she was overcome with the need to kiss him, to feel his lips on hers once again.

From the moment she had first laid eyes on him in that crowded Samba club almost a year ago he had affected her this way. She had never reacted to another man with such primal desire, and he had told her that she affected him just the same way.

'You bring out the animal in me, querida.'

He'd whispered that in her ear right before their very first kiss. They'd almost made love on the beach, in full view of the pier. It had been madness, and she felt that same desire humming through her veins just from being in his arms now.

She leaned back, looking up and expecting to see a reflection of the intense emotion she felt. Instead his face was utterly blank, and so confused it was like being doused with ice water.

This was wrong. Something was very, very wrong.

Suddenly she felt a tiny kick within her, wrenching her back to the present moment. She forced herself to take a step back, putting space between them as she composed herself and took in a lungful of air. The rain had died down and around them the sound of the boisterous youths filled the street.

Suddenly the weight of reality came crashing down upon her. If this wasn't a dream then it was a living nightmare. There was no question that this man was Duarte. And that meant her life had just become even more complicated.

She wrapped her bulky raincoat even tighter around herself and held her handbag in front of her stomach. If he was here, they were both in danger. This changed *everything*.

She looked around the streets once more, praying the blue car hadn't returned.

'How…?' she breathed. 'How are you alive?'

'It's a very long story.' He rubbed at his freshly shaven jawline. 'One that involves a medically induced coma and many months of painful rehabilitation. Let's just say I'm a hard man to kill.'

She heard the gasp that escaped her throat and closed her eyes against the image it created in her mind. He'd been alive all this time…in pain, broken…

She fought the urge to cling to him once again, never to let him go. But a tiny voice in her mind was screaming at her to run away as fast as she could and pretend she'd never seen him. Even if walking away from him now might be more painful than losing him the first time.

It was too much… She could hardly breathe…

'I hope you don't mind me tracking you down,' he said, and he spoke with a strange politeness to his tone that made her uneasy. 'You were there with me, the night I was shot.'

'Yes, I was there.' She frowned, watching the relief that crossed his face at her response. He smiled, and her heart seemed to pulse at the sight of it.

'Your care and kindness were the first things I remembered when I woke up.' His gaze softened for a moment before he seemed to shake himself mentally, then cleared his throat. 'I have a few things I'd like to ask you, if you wouldn't mind?'

'You don't remember me.' She spoke half to herself, processing the polite detachment in his gaze, the way he'd introduced himself to her—as though they were strangers.

It all came painfully into focus, like a movie replaying in her mind. He had no idea who she was…no idea what they'd been to one another.

'My injury has caused some slight memory loss. It's been a process—one I'm hoping you might help me with, actually.' He put his hands in his pockets and looked at her through his thick lashes. 'Is there somewhere private that we can talk?'

To any other woman his overtly calm posture would appear benign and almost welcoming. But Nora wasn't any other woman, and she knew when she was being baited. He might not have any memories of her, or their history, but that didn't mean he didn't still possess the killer instinct he was famous for.

He'd noticed her lengthy pause and the skin around his mouth had tightened with barely restrained irritation. She felt a shiver run down her spine. He wanted answers and he had managed to track her down. She suddenly felt as if he was a predator on the hunt and she a small rabbit heading straight for his trap.

She looked up the street and saw her bus, just beginning to turn the corner.

Duarte followed her gaze and narrowed his eyes.

'I'm sorry. I have to go. I have a flight to catch.' She forced the words from her lips, trying not to let him see the tears that threatened to spill from her eyes at any moment.

'Let me drive you to the airport. I just want to talk.'

Nora stared at the face of the man she had once loved. The man she'd *thought* she loved, she corrected herself.

If he said he had no memory of her, did that mean he had no recollection of what had passed between them all those months ago?

Guilt and anger joined the swirl of emotions warring within her. She had made her own mistakes, but he had ensured she was punished in return. He had shattered her trust and broken her foolish heart.

She had grieved for him and mourned the father her child would never have. But a small, terrible part of her had whispered that at least with his death she would be safe from his wrath. Her child would be safe.

She needed to get away. Fast.

If there was one thing she had inherited from her crime boss father, it was the sheer will to survive. She closed down her emotional reaction to his miraculous return and focused instead on the worst moments they'd spent together. The pain he'd put her through.

She lowered her hand to her stomach, reflexively protecting her unborn child from the threat of danger. That was what Duarte Avelar was to her, she reminded herself. Dangerous. That was what he had always been.

Nora opened her mouth to tell him she had no interest

in answering his questions, but instead let out a silent gasp as her entire lower body spasmed with pain. Her handbag fell to the ground and she gripped her stomach, feeling the dull throbbing that had been torturing her back all morning shifting around to her front and burrowing deep inside.

The twisting heat took her breath away. She could do nothing but breathe for a long moment.

'Are you okay?'

His voice came from close beside her, and his hand was warm on her elbow. She pushed him away, not able to look up into his face. She needed to get on that bus before her father's men returned. She needed to get out of Rio today. But she couldn't think straight.

'*Cristo*, you're pregnant…' Duarte breathed reflexively, slipping into heavily accented English. 'You're really, really pregnant.'

'Excellent observation.' She spoke through clenched teeth.

'Do you need to get to a hospital?'

'No… I was just lifting some heavy boxes. I'm moving out of town today.'

She breathed in through her nose and out through her mouth, praying this was just the shock of him showing up on her doorstep and her body was simply reminding her to take it easy.

In the back of her mind she heard the noise of the bus drawing closer along the street. She needed to *move*. 'I'll be fine. I need to get to the airport or I'll miss my flight.'

She moved to walk around him, throwing her arm out to hail the *ônibus*, but then she felt another wave of pain tighten inside her abdomen so swiftly she cried out.

Clutching onto the nearest object for balance—a very firm male bicep—she squeezed hard and prayed that this wasn't the moment her child would choose to be born.

As that thought entered her mind she felt a strange pop and the trickle of what felt like water between her legs.

This could not be happening.

She kept her eyes closed tight, a low growl escaping her lips through the waves of pain that seemed to crash into her body.

'I think my waters have just broken.'

CHAPTER TWO

NORA WAS VAGUELY aware of the sound of a loud engine slowing to a stop beside them and the bus driver calling out to see if she needed help.

'Não obrigado.' Duarte's voice boomed with authority.

She wasn't sure how many minutes passed before she opened her eyes and saw the bus had gone. She looked down to find herself clutching him like a limpet and groaned inwardly. She knew she should feel embarrassed, but she was rapidly becoming unable to think straight—or stand up, for that matter.

'Is there someone I can call for you?' he asked. 'The baby's father?'

Fighting the urge to sob, she shook her head and closed her eyes as she began to realise the gravity of her situation.

He frowned, pressing his lips together in a firm line as he looked down at her small suitcase. 'Can you walk? I'm taking you to a hospital right now.'

She allowed him to hold her arm as they moved carefully towards his car. She'd just made it to the door when another pain hit. He seemed to understand that she was unable to move, and he took off his coat and draped it over her while she breathed and tried not to curse.

'It's too early...' she breathed. 'I'm not due for four and a half more weeks. I'm not meant to be here in this city.'

He helped her into the car, bending down to carefully buckle her seatbelt around her before he looked deeply into her eyes. Warm amber filled her up with the same magnetic strength she remembered so well.

'Just try to relax.'

'Are you saying that for my benefit or for yours?' she groaned, closing her eyes against the beautiful sight of him.

She heard him chuckle low in his throat and opened her eyes once more.

'I'm going to drive now, okay?'

She nodded, staring up at this man she had once thought herself in love with, this man who now had no idea who she was.

This couldn't be happening. He couldn't be with her when she was about to give birth to her child.

Their child.

'I can't do this…' She closed her eyes once again, a sea of thoughts overwhelming her, and sent up a prayer to everyone and anyone who might be listening. To keep her safe. To keep her baby safe.

She felt a warm hand cover hers. When she opened her eyes he was looking at her, and there was nothing but kindness and concern in his warm whisky-coloured eyes.

Maybe it was the pain, or maybe she was just in shock, but she heard herself whisper, 'I've been so afraid of doing this alone…'

'You are not alone.' He squeezed her hand once more before turning and starting the engine of the powerful sports car with the push of a button. 'If my memory is correct, I'm pretty sure I owe you my life. I won't leave you.'

Duarte burst through the hospital doors carrying a wild-eyed pregnant woman in his arms. The drive to the hospital had been blessedly swift, and free of the usual Rio traffic, but he had still feared they might not make it in time. He was famous for pushing himself beyond his limits, but delivering an infant in the passenger seat of a rented Bugatti was not exactly the way he'd imagined this meeting going.

This hospital wasn't the nearest medical facility, but when she told him she'd been attending a community birth centre in one of the poorest areas of the city he'd been hit by a strange protective urge so strong it had taken his breath away.

She was important to his investigation, he told himself. He needed her safe and well if he was to find out the information she might have.

Nora seemed to be delirious with pain as the nurses performed some preliminary checks. In between each contraction she became more frantic, her eyes glazed as she repeated that she had to get to the airport.

Duarte saw the questioning looks that passed between the nurses as they looked at the reading on the blood pressure monitor. The atmosphere in the room changed immediately. A bright red call button was pressed and soon the room seemed to fill with people—doctors and specialists, anaesthetists and paediatricians.

Nora clutched his hand tightly as the team moved around her, performing more checks. Her nails bit into his skin as she cursed through another intense wave of pain, her neck and back arching and her hair tumbling around her face in a wild cloud of red curls.

He felt utterly dumbstruck by her ferocious beauty. This woman was a stranger to him, and yet he was witnessing one of the most intimate moments of her life. He felt the strangest urge to reach out and comfort her, but was keenly aware of her boundaries. In the end he settled for the simple touch of his hand on top of hers.

Her back relaxed as the pain eased off again and she looked up at him, pinning him with eyes the colour of the sky after a heavy rainstorm at sea—deep silver with a ring of midnight-blue. He was so captivated by her gaze that he hardly noticed as she looked down at his hand and frowned at the quartet of scarlet crescent moons left by her fingernails.

'Did I do that…?' she breathed, horrified.

Duarte leaned close to speak softly near her ear. 'Don't worry about me. This hand is yours for the duration. If you need to crush my fingers in the process, so be it.'

She shook her head, the ghost of a smile crossing her lips.

Duarte couldn't help it; he laughed at the crazy turn his day had taken.

She looked up at him through thick lashes, her eyes filled with surprise, and for a moment, Duarte felt the strong pull of *déjà vu*. His mind grasped at the feeling, but it was like trying to hold on to water and feeling its weight slip through his fingers.

Why did he feel as if seeing her was the key to unlocking some hidden compartment in his memory?

A young nurse chose that moment to interrupt, looking at Duarte as she explained that she needed to talk to the baby's father for a moment.

Nora's entire body froze, and a sudden lucidity that was almost akin to blind panic entered her eyes.

'No! He needs to leave.' Her voice lowered to a growl as another contraction hit her and her body began to arch forward. 'Get him *out* of this hospital.'

Duarte took a stunned step back just as another doctor entered the room and announced that they would be preparing her for immediate emergency surgery.

He was swiftly whisked away from her and taken down

the hall to fill out some paperwork. The surgeon was a kind-faced young woman who assured him that his partner and the baby would be well taken care of.

Duarte opened his mouth to correct her, only to find she was already rushing away.

Keeping his mind occupied, he strode down to the nurses' station and set about filling in more paperwork. He had no idea what her date of birth was, or even her nationality so, against all his instincts, he opened her handbag and her suitcase and began to search.

For a woman who said she was leaving town, she had packed suspiciously light. Her bags contained no identification nor any clues as to where she might have been headed. She didn't even have a mobile phone. Baffled, he listed his own details as next of kin and made sure it was known that no expense should be spared in her care.

The nurse's eyes widened, her gaze flickering between the name scrawled on the form and the long scar on the side of his face. For a moment Duarte was confused, but then he winced and cursed under his breath. In all the drama he'd forgotten that technically he was supposed to be dead. His family name was well known in this part of Brazil, thanks to their wealth of charity work.

He walked away from the stunned recognition in the woman's eyes, knowing that at some point he was going to have to contact Dani and explain how he'd come to be spotted in Rio, in hospital with a pregnant woman.

His shoulder twinged again, the pain hot and uncomfortable under his designer shirt. He had missed out on his evening swimming regime due to the long flight, and already he could feel his muscles seizing in protest. He seemed to be in a constant state of management, swimming against the tide and trying to live a normal life with his new damaged body.

After what felt like hours, he walked back down the corridor towards the operating theatre, feeling like a caged animal pacing its enclosure. Running a hand along the stubble growing on his jaw, he ignored the tension in his gut and instead puzzled over the way Nora Beckett had embraced him in the rain.

She'd thought him dead and had seemed overwhelmed at the sight of his return. She'd *known* him. He could have sworn he'd felt the echo of some fierce connection between them every time she'd looked at him. And yet she'd looked at him with fear in her eyes, and had bellowed for him to be taken from the room.

Something didn't make sense…

Unable to stay put a moment longer, he moved purposefully down the corridor to demand an update. At the same moment a nurse emerged from the double doors that led down to the operating theatres with a bundle of white linen in her arms.

'*Senhor*, I was just coming to get you.' She beamed. 'Baby boy is completely healthy. We'd like you to get settled in the suite while the team finish with Senhora Beckett.'

'Is she okay?' he asked, swallowing hard as he peered down at the small face, barely visible in the folds of material.

'The procedure required heavy anaesthesia and she is still sedated.'

The nurse ushered him down the hall to a large private suite. The small bundle was placed in a cot beside the bed and then the nurse apologised as she was suddenly called from the room by a beeping device at her hip.

Alone, and utterly out of his depth, Duarte felt his chest tighten with anxiety as the infant began to wriggle. Did they usually abandon babies to the care of clueless billionaires around here? Give him a priceless antique catamaran and he would know how to take it apart and put it back together blindfold. But children had never exactly been a part of his wild playboy lifestyle.

Duarte walked to the side of the cot and peered down at the infant, its tiny features scrunched up, its hands flailing. Without thinking, he reached into the cot towards one tiny hand. His heart seemed to thump in his ears as his index finger was instantly grasped in a tight fist and the wriggling stopped.

'There you go, *pequeno*,' he murmured, rubbing his other hand against his sternum, trying to control the frantic beating of his heart as he marvelled at the force of the boy's grip. 'You can hold on tight if that helps. Your *mamãe* will be here soon.'

Nora opened her eyes to find she was still dreaming.

Often in the past six months she had fallen asleep to dream of Duarte, his amber eyes alive and full of happiness as he cradled their newborn baby. In that perfect life there was no anger or lies between them, no danger or threat of punishment from her villainous father.

She blinked at the vision before her in the luxurious hospital room—the painfully handsome man in his perfect designer shirt, shirtsleeves rolled up as he cradled the tiny infant in his powerful arms. She closed her eyes briefly at the memory of how she'd embraced him so passionately in her shock, then clung to him as he'd rushed her to the hospital.

But he didn't remember her at all.

A small tear slid from her eyelids and down her cheek as she realised that perhaps that was a blessing to them both.

To all three of them.

'You're awake,' that gravelly voice murmured from

across the room. 'The nurse told me to tell you not to try to sit up by yourself.'

'My baby…' Nora croaked, her throat painfully dry. 'Give him to me.' She raised her voice, hearing the edge of panic creeping in but feeling too weak to hold it back.

Duarte frowned, but immediately did as she asked. The soft bundle was placed gently on her chest and Nora looked down at her son's perfect face for the first time.

'The nurse just fed him and she asked me to hold him for a moment.'

'Thank you…' Nora whispered, inwardly mourning the fact that her baby's first feed had not come from her.

She mentally shook herself, sending up a prayer of thanks that they were both safe. All those plans she had made for a natural birth had been thrown out of the window when the doctors had told her she was in an advanced stage of pre-eclampsia and they would need to sedate her immediately in order to operate.

Her headaches, the swelling… She was lucky they were both alive. She was lucky they had got to the hospital so quickly.

If she'd been alone…

Tears welled in her eyes at the thought.

'My sweet, sweet Liam,' she whispered, closing her eyes and brushing her lips against jet-black downy soft hair. He was beautiful, and so impossibly small she felt something shift within her. Something fierce and primal.

'Liam? An interesting name.' Duarte's voice seemed to float towards her from far away.

'It's short for the Irish for William,' she whispered, her eyes still fixed on examining the tiny bundle.

She almost couldn't believe that in the space of one day her life had changed so dramatically. She moved her fingertips over ten tiny fingers and toes, puffy cheeks and a tiny button nose. He was perfect.

She closed her eyes and placed her cheek against her son's small head as a wave of emotion tightened her throat once more.

'It's easier to pronounce than our version. My father always shortened his name to Gill.'

Nora refused to look up, unsure if he was baiting her somehow. But there was no way he could know she had chosen her son's name to honour the great Guilhermo Avelar.

She heard him take a step closer.

'You have Irish ancestry? You speak Portuguese like a native, but the red hair...'

Nora looked up and wondered if she imagined the shrewdness in his gaze, fearing that he was remembering... The reality of her situation came crashing down on her, dampening the euphoric pleasure of holding her child for the first time. She felt her chest tighten, but schooled her features not to show a thing, not wanting to give him any more information than needed.

'My mother is Irish, but I've lived here my whole life.'

'Here in Rio?' he asked.

'No. Not here.' She let her words sit and watched as he realised she wasn't going to play along.

He nodded once and took a few steps away, towards the window. Nora was briefly entranced by the sight of his handsome features in the glow of the afternoon sun. The blue sky formed a heavenly backdrop behind him, making him look like a fallen angel.

How could someone so beautiful cause her so much heartbreak? How could he remember nothing of the time they'd spent together? She'd told him of her Irish mother's lifelong work as an ecologist and about the remote Amazon village where she'd been born. He'd told her stories of his own idyllic childhood, and how happy they had been as a family until their move to England.

They'd bonded over a shared sense of having felt stifled and restless when growing up. She had never felt such a connection to another person, such an urge to speak the first thing that came into her mind. He had seemed like a good man then—before everything had become so twisted between them. But his anger had made him cold.

The last time they had spoken he had vowed to find her, to hunt her down and put her in prison alongside her criminal father. Even now she could clearly remember the simmering rage in his gaze as her father's men had dragged him away.

He might not remember that night, or all the events that had led to it, but he still felt that hunger for vengeance— she'd bet her life on it. Why else was he back here in Rio, digging around?

What would he do if he knew she had hard evidence that could put Lionel Cabo in prison for the rest of his life? The slim thumb drive sewn into the lining of her suitcase was the insurance she had used to secure her own freedom, but that same evidence would also serve as evidence of a damning connection. A connection that someone could use against her.

Trusting Duarte in the past had led to betrayal. Did she dare ask him for help, knowing that he might choose to use her past against her?

She closed her eyes and thought of the innocent life she had just brought into this battlefield. This should have been a moment of celebration for both of them.

For a split second she contemplated throwing caution to the wind and telling Duarte that Liam was his son. Maybe if she told him everything and explained herself he would see that she was not the same as her father after all. She had made her share of mistakes, but she was not the black-hearted criminal he had accused her of being.

But then she remembered his promise and imagined being thrown in jail for her crimes. She felt torn between silence and blind faith, but she was a mother now and she had a responsibility to raise her son. She couldn't risk it.

'I hope you don't mind me bringing you to a different hospital.' He gestured around them at the clean sleek lines of the private mother-and-baby suite. 'I know the staff here from my charity work. It's one of the best facilities in the city.'

'I will try my best to repay you.' Her voice shook slightly and he instantly waved away her offer.

The gesture held so much lazy arrogance that her hands automatically tightened at the reminder that Duarte Avelar wasn't just rich, he was powerful. More powerful than any of the people she'd met while working for her father among Rio's high society.

Even without the fact that he was descended from one of Brazil's oldest dynasties, he was rich as Croesus in his own right. He was the kind of man who didn't have to worry about anything. He probably had world-class lawyers on retainer just in case he needed matters dealt with. If his memory came back, if he remembered what she had been a part of…

'Nora…' Duarte didn't move, but his eyes held her captive with their sincerity. 'Was there a reason you were leaving the city today, alone and in such a vulnerable condition?'

'That's hardly your concern.'

She kept her tone firm, the anxiety roaring within her a reminder of her own vulnerability. She *was* alone and he knew it. That meant it was even more important for her to keep the upper hand. Keep what little power she had left.

She looked up at his dark features, feeling the weight of fear crush any of the remaining traces of hope she might have had upon seeing him alive. She had far too much knowledge of what happened to a woman when she put herself in the orbit of a powerful man's control. Her son deserved to be safe, and she would die before she allowed him to be used the same way she had been as a child.

Her eyes darted to the window. She was trying to pinpoint where they were in the city. Trying to plan a way out, just in case.

Powerful men did not often give up their children—even illegitimate ones. Her own mother had found that out the hard way. Sometimes a child served as the ultimate form of control.

'I had to search your bag for identification in order to fill out your chart.' His eyes met hers, searching. 'I noticed you were packing very light. You don't even have a mobile phone or your passport.'

'I must have forgotten them at home.'

The lie fell easily from her lips and she felt a pang of relief that he hadn't found the hidden pocket in the lining of her luggage that she'd used to hold her savings, the thumb drive and her emergency documents.

'I thought that…so I had my assistant go back to your apartment to retrieve them.'

Nora fought the urge to growl, feeling his eyes on her, watching her reaction. Apparently his injury hadn't addled the entirety of his wonderful mind; he was still sharp. He must have been told that her apartment was empty, that she'd been evicted suddenly and without notice.

'What exactly are you asking me?' She assumed her best poker face, feeling as though she was walking a tightrope and might fall into the web of her own lies at any moment.

'Your landlord seemed terrified that he might be harmed and refused to give the reason for your eviction. In fact, he seemed quite concerned for your wellbeing, despite having no knowledge of your pregnancy. According to him, before today you had barely left your apartment in months.'

Nora felt her pulse hammer against her chest. How could she tell him that hiding behind the walls of her shabby apartment and living in anonymous squalor for months on end had been preferable to anyone in her father's criminal network seeing her growing stomach and using it against her? Her father would have known instantly whose child she carried, and he would not have hesitated to use the knowledge for his own gains. He'd always got her under his control so easily—it was one of his talents.

She had been eighteen when she'd first moved to Rio, home-schooled and painfully naïve, with her father's wonderful promises ringing in her ears. She hadn't reacted when he'd told her she stood out in all the wrong ways, with her simple outdoorsy style and her wild red curls. When he'd hired stylists to dress her and soften her looks she had foolishly seen it as him taking care of her. To a girl who had grown up fatherless and isolated, any attention from him had seemed wonderful.

Then he'd started asking her to gather small pieces of information for him. Her successes had been met with affection and gifts, and she'd never felt so happy and loved. She hadn't known then, but he'd been grooming her for his organisation, teaching her the tricks she would need to become one of his network of spies.

She'd obeyed his every command and completed every mission perfectly...until Duarte.

She looked up at the object of her thoughts and wondered which of the men in her life had hurt her more...

'I get the feeling that we knew one another, Nora. Maybe we were friends?' Duarte's whisky-coloured eyes bored into hers, assessing her with a razor-sharpness. 'If you're in trouble, I might be able to help.'

'I'm not in trouble.' Shaken, she tried to keep control of the conversation, hoping he wouldn't notice the tremor in her hands. 'And you are *not* my friend.'

'Well, that makes your earlier reaction to my reappearance even more interesting.'

Something within her bristled at the superior tone in his voice and the evident suspicion in his gaze. The Duarte Avelar she had so briefly known had not had this hardness in him. But, then again, that version of him hadn't been almost murdered as part of a blackmail plot involving the woman he claimed to have loved.

Still, she was a vulnerable woman with a newborn baby in a hospital bed and, as far as he knew they were perfect strangers.

Duarte stood up straight, his eyes sweeping over her and the small infant, something strange in his gaze. 'You've been through a lot today. I still need to speak with you, but my questions will keep until you have recovered.'

'Did you come back to Rio looking for answers...or for revenge?' She asked the question, holding her breath as she waited for the answer that would determine their fate.

His brows knitted together, and when he spoke his voice held a mixture of surprise and keen interest, as though he were dissecting a puzzle. 'You fear revenge from me, Nora?'

'You haven't answered my question.'

She spoke with steel, despite the frantic thrumming of her heartbeat. She was exhausted, and likely still in shock from the events of the past few hours, but she knew she needed to have this conversation for her son's sake. For her own sake too.

She forced herself to hold his gaze, trying not to be entranced by the features that seemed like a mirror image of the tiny face on her chest.

He seemed to hesitate for a moment, his eyes shifting to take a sweeping look out over the city. When his eyes at last met hers, there was a haunted darkness to them.

'I came here to find out what truly happened in that shipping yard. For now, that is enough to satisfy me.'

For now.

Nora felt the threat of those words as clear as day. He might not know it yet, but he was on a direct path to retribution. His memories might be missing but his heart was still the same. He would never let this go. He would never forgive her for the part she'd played, unwittingly or not.

The silence stretched between them like an icy lake and she felt whatever slim hope she'd clung to begin to fade to nothing.

She looked up to see him watching her, his brow furrowed with concentration. Time seemed to stop as he opened his mouth to speak, then closed it, taking a few steps towards the window. He braced his hands on the sill, one deep inhalation emphasising the impressive width of his shoulders.

He was leaner than he had been before, his muscular frame less bulky but somehow more defined. The long, angry scar stood out like a kind of tribal marking along the side of his skull. She breathed in the sight of him, knowing that it might be the last time she could. That it *needed* to be the last time.

'I will leave you to rest for a few days.' He spoke with quiet authority. 'I am not so cruel as to interrogate you in your condition. But I *will* have my answers, Nora.'

She opened her mouth to order him to leave, fury rising within her at the barely concealed threat in his words, but she froze as she saw the unmistakable look of curiosity he sent towards the tiny baby she held in her arms.

'Seeing as you don't have a phone, would you like me to notify anyone about the birth?' Duarte asked, taking a step closer and peering into Liam's small sleeping face. 'Who is his father?'

CHAPTER THREE

NAUSEA TIGHTENED NORA'S already tender body, emotion clogging her throat as she inhaled and prepared herself for another performance. Another cruel twist, cementing her own web of lies beyond repair.

Just as she'd opened her mouth to respond, like an angel of mercy the nurse returned. Nora smiled politely as her son was lifted from her chest and put gently into his cot before the young woman began efficiently taking vitals, asking about her pain and making notes on a detailed chart.

Nora's vague realisation that she'd still been pregnant only hours ago was laughable, considering that her current sense of fear had completely overshadowed any of the strange sensations in her body from the Caesarean section.

She was painfully aware of his dark eyes watching her from the corner of the room. Her heartbeat skittered in her throat as the nurse widened her eyes at her blood pressure reading and then left the room, mumbling about getting a second opinion.

Nora fought the urge to call after the nurse and beg her to stay. *Please, stay.*

She wanted to delay the inevitable answer she had to give. The lies she needed to tell to keep her son safe. To keep them all safe.

In an ideal world she would celebrate finding out that the

father of her child was alive and had returned to find her. In an ideal world this would be a reunion… But she had long ago learned that no happy endings lay in her future—only an endless fight for survival. The world she lived in was filled with nothing but danger and dire consequences if she took a single step wrong.

She had a tiny life relying on her now; it wasn't just her own future at stake. She could not let her heart lead her—not again.

'Who is the baby's father?' Duarte repeated.

She avoided his eyes as she folded and refolded the linen blanket on her lap. She bit her lip, trying to come up with a convincing lie, but found she simply couldn't. So she just went with omission instead, forcing words from her throat. 'I'm a single mother. I have no family here in Rio.'

Silence fell between them. She wondered if he was judging her for her situation, then brushed off the thought with disgust. She had far bigger problems in her life than worrying about the opinion of a powerful man who had never known the true cruelty of life at the bottom of the pecking order. He might think her in the habit of random flings, but that seemed preferable to the embarrassing truth.

The only man she'd ever let her guard down with was standing five feet away from her.

And he didn't remember a single thing.

She reached out and laid one hand on the small cot beside the bed, reminding herself of the tiny life that now relied on her strength. She needed to convince Duarte to leave, to forget all about her and Liam. Once that part was done, she would get back to her original plan.

Her heart seemed to twinge with the pain of knowing she would never see him again, but she forced the pain away, knowing she must survive losing him all over again for the sake of her son.

She had to.

'You said you wanted details about what happened that night? I'll write down everything I can remember and send it to you.' She spoke quickly. 'I'll tell you everything you need to know.'

Strong arms folded over an even more powerful chest as he stared down at her. Nora ignored the flare of regret screaming within her. The urge to confess everything and beg him to take her and Liam away from Rio, away from the reach of her father and the memories of all the mistakes she'd made, bubbled up inside her.

But she couldn't trust him—not after everything that had happened. She couldn't put her child's future in his hands, or gamble on the hope that he might be merciful. She needed to be strong, even if it meant doing something that felt fundamentally wrong to her on every level.

'Why do you act as though you are afraid of me?' Duarte asked darkly, his jaw tight enough to cut through steel. 'I pose no danger to you. You can trust me.'

'I trust no one—especially not men like you.' The words slipped from her mouth and she saw them land, anchoring him to the spot. '*Please*...just leave.'

She closed her eyes and lay back against the pillows, willing him away along with the one million worries that had come with his reappearance in her life. She lost track of how long she lay there, eyes closed tight against the sight of him. She fought against the need to reach out and beg him to stay, to breathe in the scent of him one last time.

When she opened her eyes again he was gone.

She didn't cry, but the walls of the hospital room blurred into one wide canvas of beige and white as she stared upwards into nothingness.

If this was what shock felt like, she welcomed it—welcomed the cold that set into her fingers and the heavy exhaustion deep in her bones.

She had no idea how long she stared up at the ceiling before she drifted off to sleep, one hand still tightly clutching the railing of her son's cot at her bedside.

Duarte left the hospital in a foul mood, instructing one of his guards to remain for surveillance. Whether that was to protect Nora Beckett or to ensure she didn't try to disappear he didn't quite know yet. But one thing was for sure: his mystery woman was deeply afraid of something. And, even though it made no sense, he had the strangest feeling that that *something* might be him.

The drive out of the city and high up into the hills to his modern villa passed in a blur. He had purchased the house a few years ago, but had very few memories of staying there. It was a visual masterpiece of clean lines and open living spaces, designed by an award-winning architect. Every feature took the natural surroundings into account, so that the building seemed to slot effortlessly into the rocky mountain face that surrounded it.

As a man who had taught himself to conceptualise and build ships just by observing the masters and trusting his feeling for what was right, he had a deep appreciation of design in all its forms. Usually the sight of this home filled him with awe and appreciation for such a feat of skilled, thoughtful engineering. But today he just saw a load of concrete and glass.

Duarte parked in the underground garage and found himself staring at the wall, processing the turn his day had taken in just a few short hours. He felt the sudden urge to grab a full bottle of strong *cachaça* and switch his mind off. To another man, the lure of getting rip-roaring drunk might have been attractive after a day like he'd had. But he was not another man, he reminded himself.

Perhaps he should have gone into the city, to one of the trendy upscale night spots along the coast. The bars would be teeming with beautiful women only too happy to help a man like him forget his troubles... But he doubted he'd even remember how to chat up a woman it had been so long.

Since he'd woken in the hospital all those months ago his days had been consumed only by recovery and, more recently, revenge. But maybe it was exactly what he needed. To indulge himself, to shake off the edge that had refused to pass since his dreams of the redhead began. Dreams of the woman who had saved him.

Nora.

He shook off the thought of her and made his way into the spacious entrance hall just as his phone began to ring. He looked at the name on the screen and answered the call from his father's oldest friend with a weary smile.

'Angelus—*tudo bem*?'

The old man was eager to hear about his meeting with the mystery redhead and apologised for believing Duarte had simply imagined the woman.

'She must have been the one to alert me that night,' Fiero mused, not needing to elaborate any further. They both knew what night he referred to. 'I got a text from your personal phone number simply stating the address of that shipping yard and the fact that you were in danger. You and Valerio had been missing for seven days at that point.'

Duarte swallowed his frustration at his lack of memories of his captivity. He had no clue as to what had occurred other than the scars that covered his body and the haunted look in Valerio's eyes. His best friend had refused to go into detail about whatever had befallen them during their long days and nights of captivity, stating that he was better off not knowing.

Nora had saved him—but why had she disappeared?

The thought suddenly occurred to him that perhaps they had been together. Perhaps she had been taken captive too? But surely Valerio would have mentioned a woman.

Angelus interrupted his musings, launching into a detailed briefing on the latest developments in their joint sting operation.

The corrupt politician who had paid for the kidnap had already been brought to justice, shot by Angelus himself in self-defence. But they had evidence to prove the man hadn't been working alone. That there was a criminal kingpin behind the operation and he was hell-bent on taking control of the large area of land that the Avelar family owned and used for their charitable operations in Rio and Sao Paolo. Tens of thousands of tenants stood to be displaced and abandoned.

Thankfully, Angelus had arranged for the land to become untouchable, locked it into use by the Avelar Foundation, securing the homes and livelihoods of the families they assisted.

Duarte hadn't yet told Angelus that he remembered having lunch with that same politician just over a year before his kidnapping. Considering that Angelus was currently still recovering from near death because of his efforts to help Duarte, he didn't think his revelation would be well received.

It plagued him—why would he choose to meet with a man who so vehemently opposed the Avelar family's work in Rio? Their refusal to sell or redevelop prime land in what was considered an upper class area of the city had been the cause of a decades-long argument, dating back to his father's inception of the foundation. His parents had taken on the cause of the most vulnerable in society by building quality, sustainable housing projects. They had directly opposed and ignored the handful of corrupt developers that wanted to earmark the area for a luxury tourism development.

Duarte vaguely remembered the months before his kidnapping. He had been tired from spreading himself too thinly between Velamar and his own fledgling nautical design firm, Nettuno. When the Avelar Foundation had needed his immediate presence in Rio due to a large and embarrassing fire safety scandal, he'd been furious and resentful.

He'd had a few drinks with the politician and somehow they'd got into talks about what might happen if he sold the land with their family name kept solely as a front. He'd had plenty of his own charitable projects going on. He simply hadn't had the time required to pursue such a demanding cause.

Shame burned in his gut at the memory of that conversation.

But he would never have acted on it…he was almost sure. He vaguely remembered flying out of Rio determined to find another way to carry on his parents' legacy and uphold his duty to the people relying on the foundation.

His memories were non-existent from that point, but his passport showed that he'd returned to Rio three times after that trip. Whatever he'd come back for, he'd kept secret and eventually he was going to be forced to admit his suspicions to Angelus… That the person who had started this hell was possibly himself.

The infinity pool on the boundary of the villa had been serviced and readied for his arrival, as per his instructions. He had never been more grateful as he tore off his clothes and dived under the water in his boxer shorts. The fresh salt water engulfed him, cutting off the frantic hum of his mind and replacing it with a calming nothingness that soothed the anxious roar within him. Even if the relief was only temporary.

Anger and frustration had him doing more laps than usual, pushing his body to its physical limits as though reminding himself of his strength.

Teaching his damaged body how to walk and move again had been a nightmare, but he had done it. He had shocked his team of physiotherapists and smashed all their expectations. So much so that soon the staff and other patients would gather to watch him slice through the water at incredible speeds.

He'd thought that was the reason he'd become a minor celebrity in the small community, never realising that many of the staff had already been aware of his identity and had been paid heavily by Angelus for their silence.

Even without his memories he had felt the same connection to water, the same need that he'd had his whole life to swim or be out on the open sea.

· It had been on that same beach that a strange man and woman had arrived and introduced themselves as his sister and his best friend. He'd remained silent as they tried to gauge how little he remembered. He soon found out that not only had he been a competitive swimmer and sailor throughout his teenage years and into his twenties, but he had apparently turned that passion into a career and was the co-founder of one of the biggest luxury yacht charter firms in the world.

Going from being an abandoned John Doe with no knowledge of his past to having his dream life presented to him should have been enough, he thought darkly. And yet he had been plagued by the thought that there was something vital he was missing—something he needed to do before his spirit would rest and accept his survival for what it was.

A second chance.

He lifted himself from the water with only minimal pain and stepped under the blistering hot spray of the outdoor waterfall shower. The heat loosened his muscles the rest of the way, ensuring that he would sleep without medication.

The heavy painkillers he'd been given on the island had become a dangerous crutch in the weeks after he'd awoken. His pain had been a relentless presence, along with the anxiety that stopped him sleeping or eating. Soon he'd begun to crave the oblivion those pills offered, and he had progressed to hoarding his dosages to achieve the maximum effect. Luckily, the nurses had recognised the signs and had made it impossible for him to continue down that path.

When a man was in constant pain, anything could become a vice, so he had adopted a strict, clean lifestyle and focused on healing his body naturally. But even now that he had his physical regimen under control, he still felt that restless hunger within him at times. It was as if he had come back to life with a great big chunk of himself missing, and no matter what he did…nothing filled the space.

His thoughts wandered back to the first moment he'd laid eyes on the woman from his dreams. Nora. How she had looked at him in that rain-soaked street, the shock and relief on her delicate features right before she'd embraced him. He'd felt something shift within him, as if something in his broken mind had awoken and growled *mine*.

Perhaps they had been lovers before his accident? She was certainly eye-catching, with her vibrant red waves of hair and large silver eyes. The thought of the two of them together filled him with a rush of sensual heat—until he remembered that she had been heavily pregnant with another man's child when he'd found her.

If they had been lovers, she had clearly moved on quickly.

Shrugging off the dark turn his thoughts had taken, he reminded himself of the more pressing matter that she was clearly in need of help and fearful of some unknown force. Afraid enough to pack up her life and move cities in an advanced stage of pregnancy.

He winced, remembering how he had told her he *would* get his answers. Suddenly the idea of getting answers seemed overshadowed by the idea that she might fear *him*. She was made of steel, that much was clear, and yet he'd seen flashes of vulnerability on her face that had made him tense with the primal need to protect.

His fists clenched tight and he shut off the water with an impatient growl. From the villa's hilltop vantage point he could see the last rays of the late evening sun glittering on the waves of the Atlantic below. He took a deep breath and wrapped a towel low on his hips, inhaling and exhaling the salty spray until he felt a sense of calm logic return.

If he had any chance of getting information from Nora he would first need to gain her trust. She was a new mother, in dire need of help, but he got the feeling that she would not accept help from him easily. Luckily for him, patience had always been something he had in abundance.

He let out a deep exhalation, a plan already taking shape in his mind.

He would get what he needed from Nora Beckett—one way or another.

'This can't be legal.' Nora stood by the edge of her hospital bed, her suitcase packed at her feet and the small bundle of her son in his baby carrier. 'It's been a full week and you've said yourself I am well enough to leave.'

'You're well enough to go home—not to fly across the country.' The doctor spoke in a firm tone. 'Miss Beckett.

You will not be cleared to fly in your condition. I won't allow it. Recovery from pre-eclampsia needs to be closely monitored, and you will both need regular check-ups here in Rio for at least another five weeks.'

'I can't stay here,' she said weakly. 'I have nowhere to go.'

'You have a home address listed, right here in Rio.'

Nora looked down at the form on the doctor's clipboard, seeing Duarte's name at the top and noting that the address listed was for his palatial villa up in the hills. A place where she had stayed before, numerous times.

'That's *not* my home.'

'We have been advised to stop you leaving.'

'Advised by who?' She raised her voice, looking around at the burly security man who had suddenly appeared outside her door and the slightly uncomfortable look in the doctor's eyes. 'Has someone asked you to keep me here?'

'I asked them.'

Duarte Avelar appeared in the doorway, impeccably dressed in a sleek navy suit and light blue shirt. How unlucky could she get? He had become even more gorgeous, while she had been in a haze of sleepless nights with a newborn and had barely mustered the energy to brush her hair in the week since she'd last seen him.

'I told you I didn't need your help.' Nora squared her shoulders.

He gestured to the doctors and the guard to leave, closing the door behind them. His eyes drifted down, narrowing as he took in the small suitcase at her feet and the baby bundled up in the infant carrier she'd asked one of the nurses to order for her. Thankfully she'd set aside a small provision of cash for clothing and supplies for her son, but she hadn't expected to need everything so soon.

'You have no right to intrude on my privacy this way.' She shook her head in disbelief. 'I told you I didn't need your help.'

'I'm listed as your next of kin. The doctors called and filled me in on your plans to leave because they have concerns. I'll admit that I do too.'

His eyes met hers with an intensity that took her breath away.

'Packing a bag and then asking for internet access to book a flight?'

Nora swallowed hard, looking away from him and crossing her arms, ignoring the tender pain that still lingered in her chest from repeated failed attempts to nurse her son. She felt raw inside and out, and having Duarte reappear was just another thing sending her closer to the edge of her control.

'I am not doing anything wrong.' She forced a tight smile and deliberately slowed and calmed her voice. 'The doctor has said herself that both Liam and I are ready to be discharged. Not being allowed to fly has put a snag in my plans, but I will find a way.'

His frown deepened even more. 'Planning to leave the city?'

She looked down at her hands, feeling the heavy weight of her situation take hold. Without a flight, Manaus was almost three days away—at the other end of the country by the mouth of the Amazon. It was utterly ridiculous even to try to plan that kind of journey with a newborn and in her condition, putting them both at the mercy of public transport and cheap motels. She'd spent almost every last *real* she had paying to rebook her flight.

'I need to get out of Rio.'

She heard the desperation in her voice but didn't care. For all she knew, her father's men were waiting outside at this very moment. She had never felt so helpless and she hated it.

'Tell me why,' he said softly. 'Are you in danger?'

She bit her lower lip, looking away from him as she felt her eyes fill with panicked tears. She was losing every ounce of control she'd gained for herself, for her son. It infuriated her, feeling so utterly powerless.

Beside her, Duarte cursed softly under his breath and looked away for a moment. 'Nora, you must know you can't travel right now. If you need protection…' He seemed to measure his words for a moment. 'We've got about three minutes before the doctor returns, most likely in the company of someone from social services, who is going to ask some pertinent questions about the welfare of your child.'

Nora clutched at her throat, feeling it clamp tight with fear and realisation. She couldn't afford for anyone to go digging into her background right now. She needed to keep herself and her son out of her father's reach.

Closing her eyes, she inhaled deeply, completely aghast at the severity of her situation. Was this how she was starting her journey as a mother? Every single plan she'd made had gone wrong and now she was going to be investigated for child endangerment barely a week into her son's life!

'My home is nearby.' His eyes were steady on hers. 'You can stay there as my guest until they say you can fly. You'd have almost an entire wing of the house to yourself, along with anything you might need.'

'I can't fly for five weeks…' She half whispered the words.

'There is no time limit on my assistance,' he said softly. 'I believe that you played a vital role in saving my life and I would like to help.'

'Does this assistance come with a catch?'

She forced herself to look at him, to analyse his face so

she could see if he was sincere. He seemed genuine as he spread his hands wide and shrugged one powerful shoulder.

'I believe you have valuable information that will help me to bring a very dangerous man to justice. I understand why that must seem overwhelming in your current position, so I won't press you for answers yet. Right now, it's my job to prove to you that I am trustworthy, and I am willing to wait and work for your trust.'

Nora bit her lower lip, focusing on calming her thoughts and laying out all her options in her mind. The way things stood, she was trapped between two utterly terrible outcomes. If she tried to leave alone she risked the attention of the authorities, and thus her father, who had webs in every area of the city. But the alternative was accepting an offer from a man who at any moment might remember who she was and what had happened and bring her whole world crashing down. A man she had spent six months mourning and dreaming of.

Could she hold herself together for five weeks?

'I want my flight changed to a later date, when I'm cleared to travel,' she said quietly, standing up straight in an effort to project an air of confidence. As though any of this was actually *her* choice...

'I will have it taken care of immediately.'

The door of the room opened suddenly and the doctor appeared, introducing a stern-faced woman in a pale grey suit as a representative from social services.

As Nora felt her body go slack, Duarte's hand reached out to her elbow and held her upright. She looked up at him, seeing the question in his eyes. Like a woman about to sign her own death sentence, she nodded once. She watched his pupils dilate, the briefest flash of triumph glowing in his amber eyes before he turned away, using his body as a shield between her and the others.

Nora felt as though she had entered a twilight zone version of her life as Duarte easily commanded the situation in a way that somehow managed to be both dazzlingly charming and authoritative.

As she watched his bodyguard gather her things, she tried to shake off the feeling that, after spending months ensuring she escaped her father's control, she had just volunteered to step into another shiny cage.

CHAPTER FOUR

DUARTE TRIED TO ignore his strange feeling of relief at having Nora agree to come under his protection.

Once they were safely within the gates of his home he allowed her some privacy to settle in, instructing his housekeeper to give her a tour of the rooms he'd had set up for her and to serve her lunch in private while she rested. He was painfully aware of the fact that he had no idea what a newborn needed, so he'd enlisted the help of his assistant at the Avelar Foundation, a young mother herself, and had instructed her to spare no expense.

Not wanting to crowd his guest, he spent the afternoon in various meetings at his city offices. With Angelus Fiero still recovering from his injury, it fell on Duarte to step in and oversee the final stages of locking down their lands for future renovation projects.

He returned to the house much later than he'd expected, his back and shoulder aching from exertion. The house was strangely silent as he slipped into the kitchen and grabbed a premade salad from the refrigerator. Usually he took pleasure in cooking his own meals, but tonight he just wanted to eat quickly and get some sleep. He was not used to being back in the world of boardrooms and business deals, surrounded by the hum of conversation. It made him restless and edgy, as if he wanted to crawl out of his own skin.

He knew he needed to get back into practice if he had any hope of returning to his full workload as CEO of Velamar. His sister had sent him an email with details of the launch of their new headquarters in Florida the following month—a week of grand events in Fort Lauderdale to celebrate their new US and Caribbean charter routes.

A noise jolted him upright and he looked up to see Nora, standing frozen in the doorway of the kitchen. She held an empty baby's bottle in one hand and her small son in the other.

'Can I help?' he asked, standing up.

'No, thank you.'

She moved with impressive agility, balancing the infant in one arm as she prepared his milk with the other. Duarte frowned, making a mental note to call in a nurse tomorrow. If she wouldn't accept help from him, he'd ensure she got it elsewhere.

'I hope you have everything you need?' he said.

'You ordered a lot of things…' She met his eyes for a brief moment. 'I can't repay you for any of this.'

'I'm happy to help you any way I can.'

'In return for information?'

She spoke with a practised lightness to her tone, but he could see shrewd assessment in her gaze.

He placed both of his hands on the marble counter between them. 'I meant what I said at the hospital. Five weeks. I am a patient man, Nora. Right now my priority is keeping you safe while you rest and recover. Nothing more.'

She hovered in the doorway for a long moment, her red hair seeming to glow under the lamps of the corridor behind her. 'What if in five weeks… I still can't tell you anything?'

He heard the fear in her words, noting her use of the word *can't* rather than *won't*. He measured his words carefully. 'I think you should think about the kind of power

I might hold over whatever it is that you fear. I might be able to help.'

She shook her head once, a sad smile on her lips. 'I wish it were that simple.'

She turned and disappeared back up the corridor, leaving Duarte alone with his thoughts.

Nora practically tiptoed around the palatial villa, in an effort not to run into Duarte. For the most part she was successful. She spent her days adjusting to Liam's needs, and was grateful for the help of the kind young nurse Duarte had provided to keep on top of her own aftercare.

Breastfeeding had turned out to be impossible with her terrible supply of milk, and she'd sobbed with guilt when her nurse recommended she stop before Liam had even reached his two-week milestone. Without the pressure of her own failure hanging over her, she found she became slightly more relaxed. In a matter of days, her blood pressure readings returned to normal range and she began to smile again.

She was slowly beginning to feel a little more human, but still she found herself scanning the exterior grounds and refused to walk outside the house.

In the early hours of the morning that marked the start of her third week as Duarte's guest Nora awoke in a blind panic, her skin prickling with awareness as she jolted upwards in the gigantic four-poster bed. Blinking in the darkness, she placed a hand over her heart as though trying to calm her erratic breath. Her skin felt flushed, and the sheets were twisted around her legs as though she'd been thrashing in her sleep.

It wasn't the first time her dreams had been invaded in such a fashion, but this one had been by far the most X-rated. In it, Duarte had touched her with such gentle reverence, his eyes drinking her in as though she were the most beautiful thing he had ever seen. She had heard herself moan that she never wanted him to stop, her voice husky in a way she'd never heard before. She had felt every touch of his mouth as he kissed a path of sensual heat down her neck…

Shaking off the shiver of awareness that still coursed down her spine, she took a deep breath and peered over into the small cot beside her bed to ensure that Liam still slept peacefully. She adjusted his blanket and tried not to think of her handsome host or his frequent appearances in her subconscious.

If she'd expected Duarte to break his vow and demand answers, she'd been completely wrong. If anything, he'd gone out of his way to give her space. He spent much of the day out of the house, likely working somewhere in the city. Some nights he didn't return at all, like tonight.

She hated it that she was so hyper-aware of his movements, his presence. She'd tried her best to train herself to think of him as a benign stranger, but it was hopeless—especially while she was staying in this villa where memories of their time together assailed her.

Every time she walked into the living room she remembered the first night he'd taken her there…his mouth on hers as they failed even to make it to a bed. He'd been shocked to discover she was a virgin, and he'd insisted on bathing her afterwards. He'd sat behind her in a large claw-foot tub, overlooking the mountain view, and his hands had stroked over her body so reverently…

After that, she'd come to the villa countless times, always after the staff had been excused for the night. She'd been living in her own fantasy, imagining that she would build up to telling Duarte the truth of her identity and never incur his wrath or suspicion.

And all the while her father had been completely aware of her movements, plotting his revenge for her lies and deception. She'd been nothing but a pawn. A disposable entity to both powerful men in her life.

Now, lying back on the pillows in the silent house, she felt on edge. Earlier that day she'd tried to take a walk outside, for the first time since arriving. But while wandering around the courtyard, with Liam tucked tight against her chest, she'd thought she'd seen a familiar dark blue car parked at the end of the driveway. Her heart had stopped and she'd moved quickly back into the house, peering out of the window to see the car remain in place for another half-hour before slowly moving further down the road.

She'd had such a broken sleep tonight that it was possible she was being overly sensitive. It was only natural that she would be feeling the effects of her captivity. She wasn't technically a prisoner here, but she knew she couldn't leave. Not yet.

Frustrated, she gave up on trying to go back to sleep, wrapped herself in a thin cotton robe and clipped the portable baby monitor to the pocket. The clever gadget had been delivered the day after her arrival, along with a whole host of other items, including boxes and boxes of clothing for both her and Liam. In the haze of her sleep deprivation at the time she hadn't had the energy to insist she would pay for the items. But she knew she must repay Duarte somehow. She refused to fall under the spell of a rich man and then begin to feel like she owed him something.

Lost in thought, she almost missed the faint sound outside the house, but her heightened senses alerted her to the fact that something wasn't right. Frozen in place, she hardly breathed as the sound came closer to the large plate-glass windows that lined the back of the house. In the absence of the moon, she could see nothing but shadows and the crash of the waves in the distance below the cliffs made it hard to distinguish what exactly was out of place.

But then she heard it again. Footsteps on gravel, slow and deliberate. Heavy steps—much too heavy for the delicate, swanlike nurse or the housekeeper, neither of whom would be outside in the dark in the middle of the night.

Her brain made quick calculations as she moved instinctively to the side of the doors, out of sight. A tall shadow moved along the glass in her peripheral vision and Nora felt panic climb in her throat. All too quickly the quiet sound of the catch sliding sideways in the doorframe became apparent. To her horror, it seemed to have been left unlocked.

She watched as the door slid slowly open and the intruder pushed their tall, hulking frame inside.

Duarte felt his breath rushing in his lungs, hardly believing the events of this night. He'd been less than ten minutes from the villa when one of his security guards had informed him there was a break-in in progress. Two large men in a dark blue car had arrived shortly after midnight and managed to scale the gates.

Duarte and the guard had arrived just as the intruders had overpowered the second guard he'd left in charge of the surveillance of his home and its occupants.

Fury such as he had never known had possessed him as he had attacked the men and subdued them, using perhaps a little more force than necessary. His knuckles had become bloody, marking his white shirt and dark trousers, and he'd growled into his phone for his investigation team to send a van to pick the intruders up and take them for questioning. He'd left his security team to handle the rest, needing to get inside and ensure that Nora and the baby were unharmed.

Something about the two burly intruders snagged on his memory. He stepped into the darkened kitchen, feeling a memory surface like a television screen coming into focus. He froze with one hand still on the door handle, his mind conjuring an image of himself being thrown into a dark room, the smell of damp earth mingling with the scent of the sea in his nose. And then there had been Valerio's furious voice, asking him if the woman had been behind everything.

The woman?

He pulled at the details, hoping for more, cursing as he felt them slip away.

He heard the movement behind him too late. Something hit him with sharp force behind his knees, jolting his equilibrium and sending him down onto the porcelain tiles. He landed on his left shoulder. The pain lanced through him like fire, a primal roar ripping from his throat.

A blur of white moved in his peripheral vision—someone trying to step over him in the narrow space. On autopilot, after months of running on his survival instinct he reached out, grasping bare flesh. The skin was butter-soft, his brain registered, and his thoughts were confused between defence and attack. He tightened his grip but did not pull, straining his eyes upwards in the darkness.

His hesitation was all his opponent needed to turn the tables.

Within seconds he found himself pinned to the floor, with something cold and metal pressed tight against his sternum. A familiar lavender scent drifted to his nostrils and his eyes finally adjusted enough for him to make out a cloud of familiar red curls.

'Nora…' he breathed, shocked to feel his body instantly react to the sight of the wide-open split of the white nightgown she wore. 'It's okay. I'm—'

'I've got a high-voltage electronic Taser here, so I wouldn't try to move.' She cut him off, pressing her knee down harder onto his shoulder to prove her point. 'I've already pressed the panic button, so don't try anything.'

'Listen, I'm not—'

'How did he find out I was here?' she gritted out, and there was a slight tremor in her voice even as she kept her aim firmly at the base of his throat.

Duarte froze, taking in the confidence in her pose, the steel in her voice. He had to admit he was both impressed by such obvious skill and worried about where she'd honed it. Why it might have been a necessity.

Suddenly, her hurry to leave the hospital took on a much darker tone...

'I don't know who *he* is.' He spoke slowly, trying not to wince at the pressure of her knee on his injured shoulder. 'I'm here because I own this house.'

She froze, easing up on her pressure with a single jerky movement. Her voice was a shocked whisper. 'Duarte...?'

'In the flesh.'

She scrambled to her feet and Duarte tried but failed to avert his gaze from another tantalising glimpse of those long bare legs. The lights were turned on suddenly, momentarily blinding him as he pulled himself up to a seated position. His left arm hung limply at his side, and a familiar burning pain was travelling from his neck to the top of his shoulder blade before disappearing into numbness.

Partially dislocated, he'd bet. After months of gruelling physiotherapy sessions, he recognised the symptoms of his recurring injury.

'I'm so sorry... I thought you were someone else.' She stood on the opposite side of the kitchen, arms folded across her chest. 'A burglar.'

'Do you routinely confront dangerous intruders and pin them down for questioning?' he drawled, moving to stand up.

The pain in his shoulder intensified, taking his breath for a moment and putting stars in his vision. He sat back against the glass door with a growl.

'You're covered in blood!' She moved towards him, her face a mask of shock and concern. 'What on earth…?'

'Not from you.' He breathed deeply against the lancing pain. 'I was in a fight.'

His first instinct was to brush off her concerns—male pride winning out over his need for assistance. His shoulder was the last stubborn remnant of his injuries, along with the memory loss. There was an angry, bitter part of him that would rather languish in agony than admit any further weakness. But then Nora leaned down, gently placing one hand on his arm, and his mind seemed to go blank.

'But this is from me.' She spoke softly, the flash of her silver eyes briefly meeting his own. 'Is it your shoulder or your arm?'

'Shoulder. It wasn't entirely your fault.'

He felt the warmth of her skin through the material of his shirt as she lifted the sleeve. The scent of lavender grew stronger.

Duarte closed his eyes, clearing his throat. 'It's fine. It's an old injury.'

She snatched her hand back as though burned and he tried not to mourn the loss of contact.

With a deep inward breath, he pinned his arm to his chest as he slowly moved to stand up. 'Besides, I was lucky you were far too busy threatening me and asking questions to do any real damage.'

The slim black device in her hand caught his eye; he could now see it was not a Taser at all but a digital monitor. The small screen showed an image of a sleeping infant. A hollow laugh escaped his lips.

Nora frowned, realising he'd noticed her deception. 'I... I had to think on my feet.'

'You're quite practised in that, it would seem.'

Her posture changed at his comment, her shoulders straightening and her lips pressing into a thin line. But still she offered no explanation for her belief that she had been found by someone. Nor did she explain who that someone was.

Duarte had always been good at reading people, and right now he could see distrust settle into her eyes. She was the very definition of a flight risk, and if he had any hope of keeping her safe and finding out what her connection to his kidnapping was he needed to keep her here.

Almost as though she could hear his mind working, she took a step away, towards the living room. 'I should be getting back to bed...'

'Not so fast.'

She turned back and placed both hands defensively on her hips.

'I need your help with this,' he said. 'I don't think your nurse would be happy to be awoken at this hour.'

'I... I'm not a medical professional. Could you take something for the pain?'

'I know what I'm doing. I just need your hands.'

'My hands?' she repeated, eyeing the space between them with a strange expression.

Duarte tried not to feel affronted by her obvious reluctance to touch him. 'It's the least you can do, really, after you knocked me to the ground without effort.' He raised a brow in challenge.

When the barest smile touched her lips Duarte felt something inside him ease. She had clearly known fear in her life, and to think she had been afraid of him had made something dark and heavy settle right in the centre of his chest.

When she moved to stop beside him he deliberately avoided her gaze, needing a moment to clear his thoughts and ready himself for the manoeuvre.

'Will it hurt?' she asked quietly, her teeth worrying her lower lip.

'It's not without pain, but it's quick and then I'll be able to sleep. If you let me guide your hands, I'll show you.'

She placed both her hands into his much larger ones and Duarte felt again that strange echo of memory in the back of his mind as he took in the contrast of her porcelain skin against his dark brown tones. Brushing off the sensation, he placed her palms on the front of his shoulder, right where the pain burned most. As expected, her touch intensified the discomfort, but he instructed her to hold her grip. Her eyes were wide with fear and yet she did as she was told, keeping her hands steadfastly in position.

He told her how and when to apply counter-pressure and then did a quick countdown, biting down on his lower lip as he quickly guided his joint to where it needed to go with a swift jerk. The muffled roar that escaped his lips was quite mild in comparison to other times, when he'd been forced to do this alone.

He took a few deep breaths as the pain ebbed, and when he opened his eyes she was in front of him with a glass of water and two aspirin, which he accepted.

'That's not the first time you've done that...' Nora frowned at him, her expression troubled as she watched him drink the water, leaving the medication untouched.

'My memory is not the only part of my body that has been injured. I have a whole collection of scars owed to my time in captivity and the men behind it all. They were an energetic bunch of guys.'

Duarte thought of the memory he'd recovered earlier and felt a shiver run down his spine.

She stood close enough for him to see her eyes move to the long thin scar that moved from his temple down behind his ear. 'Duarte, I'm so sorry.'

He hadn't heard her speak his name since that first day in the rain. The sound of it on her lips, the way it rolled smoothly off her tongue…something about it called to him.

'Why should you be sorry? It's not your fault.'

At that she looked away, clearing the glass into the sink. With her back turned, Duarte took a moment to sweep his gaze along the length of her body, noticing her narrow waist and lush curves. It had only been a month since she'd given birth and the woman looked like she could step onto a catwalk.

His initial attraction to her had deeply perplexed him, considering her delicate condition, as had the depth to which she had become engrained in his thoughts in the weeks since. He'd deliberately been staying late at work in the city so he could get past whatever madness had taken over his mind since finding Miss Nora Beckett and becoming her unwitting protector.

He was not usually the kind of man who got off on rescuing damsels in distress; he didn't feel the need to bolster his own masculinity. She was a beautiful woman and his libido responded to her as such—nothing more. The fact that he had not felt a similar attraction to any other equally attractive woman was just circumstantial.

Although truthfully, he hadn't been looking at women very hard, preferring to dive deeply into his work and avoid distraction as he fought to make up for the time he'd lost.

He had promised her five weeks before he would question her again, but tonight had changed everything. The suspicions he'd had that she was in danger had just been confirmed with that break-in—as well as her words as she'd pinned him down—and he needed answers.

* * *

Nora took deep breaths to push down the wave of sorrow that threatened to overtake her at seeing the extent of the pain Duarte had suffered up close. She had felt the strange effects of her hormones shifting since Liam's birth, but this was so much more. This was an echo of grief. The tears fell fast and heavy down her cheeks as she tried in earnest to turn her face away from Duarte's perceptive gaze.

'Are you crying?'

She heard him move from his seat and his hand was suddenly on her shoulder, turning her to face him before she could wipe her face or move away. His feather-light touch gently guided her chin so she was forced to look up at him.

'You didn't hurt me, honestly.' He spoke quickly, one hand covering hers and gently stroking across her knuckles with the pad of his thumb.

She shivered, remembering him doing that before, what felt like a lifetime ago. She felt an insane urge to ask him if he remembered that night. If he remembered that he had told her how breathtaking she looked right before he'd kissed her senseless.

It had been their first kiss—the first of many over the long month of their whirlwind romance.

With his golden eyes on hers, Nora experienced a mad desire to lean in and feel his lips under hers again. Just one more time. She felt her tongue trace the edge of her own bottom lip, saw him follow the movement. His fingers flexed on her wrist and she could see a muscle in his jaw tick ever so subtly.

'Why can't I stop thinking about doing this?' he murmured, his eyes dark as he leaned forward slightly and brushed his lips across hers.

Nora inhaled sharply at the contact, hardly believing it.

Judging by the sudden widening of his eyes, he was just as shocked at himself. But the shock was short lived and Nora reached up on tiptoe and wound her arms around his neck, touching her lips to his again, seeking the heat of him.

Without warning, he took a step forward and spanned her waist with his big hands, holding her in place as she was pressed back against the kitchen units. The sleek wood was cool against her back and the hard, blazing heat of him engulfed her front. There was no softness in his kiss now…only fire and need. He somehow managed to be delicate even as his lips took hers in an almost brutal sensuous rhythm.

She heard herself moan against his mouth and felt him move even closer, one hand cupping her jaw as he deepened the kiss.

In the months after she'd lost him she'd lain in bed and tried to conjure up the memory of his kisses. They'd only spent a month together—a month of scattered secret moments in between his travelling and her own duties to her father's organisation. They'd spent most of their time in bed…and yet it had felt like so much more.

She'd thought her memory vivid, but right now she knew nothing had done justice to what it actually felt like to be in his arms, his sinful mouth demanding and coaxing… And she also knew exactly what it would feel like to guide him up to the master bedroom and re-enact every detail of her dreams…

She froze, pressing her hands against Duarte's chest and putting a few inches of space between their lips. He frowned, his amber eyes black with desire. And then that frown deepened and she felt the atmosphere suddenly shift.

Duarte took a few steps away, bracing his hands on the marble counter of the kitchen island as he continued to breathe heavily.

'You have been lying to me, Nora.'

Duarte's voice was a sharp boom in the stillness. He turned back to face her, amber eyes narrowed with suspicion.

'That was not the first time we've kissed, was it?'

CHAPTER FIVE

NORA CLOSED HER EYES, knowing she had made a fatal error.

'Answer me,' he demanded.

All trace of passion from their kiss had gone from his face.

'No. It wasn't the first time.' Nora whispered, closing her eyes tightly as if to block out the weight of her words as she spoke them.

'We were together.' He said quietly.

It took her a moment to process the fact that his words were a statement rather than a question.

A strange look transformed his dark features. 'We were...lovers.'

His words were like a whip against her frayed nerves and for a moment she feared that he had got his memories back—that he would figure out that he was Liam's father and she would be completely at the mercy of his anger. But then she looked up into his eyes and saw a brief flash of uncertainty as he waited for her to speak.

She had always been a terrible con-artist. Her father had tried and tried to toughen her up and mould her to fit in with the other female operatives in his criminal empire, Novos Lideres. She was too innocent, he'd said. But that innocence had long ago been taken from her in so many ways.

She straightened her shoulders and met Duarte's eyes.

'We went on a couple of dates, Duarte. I saw no reason to further complicate things for you over a minor detail.'

'You are still lying.'

His words were a menacing growl. He took a step forward, closing the gap between them.

'My mind may not remember you but my body does. I know that if I kiss a certain spot on your neck you will lose control and your legs will begin to shake.'

Nora gasped, shaking her head in an effort to stop him. 'You're mistaken.'

'Stop! No more lies between us.' His voice was a seductive whisper. 'I remember touching you, Nora. I remember your beautiful face as you climaxed with the most delicious whisper of a scream.'

He looked into her eyes and Nora was utterly helpless, unable to move under the sensual weight of his amber gaze.

'I suddenly know all of these things and yet everything else is still in shadow. How can that be?'

Nora wasn't sure whether he was asking her or himself, but she inhaled a deep shuddering breath and found that the few distraction tactics and acting skills she was able to draw upon had thoroughly escaped her. She felt a mixture of arousal and fear creep up her spine, holding her paralysed and powerless to do anything more than stare at him in damning silence.

'Am I still mistaken?'

Nora closed her eyes and felt the echo of their passionate whirlwind affair rush through her like a hurricane, destroying all the hopes she'd had of talking herself out of this.

'It was a casual thing. Barely more than a few weeks until it was over.' She forced the words out and watched as Duarte's eyes blazed with triumph, then narrowed on her once again.

'When?' The word was a harsh demand.

'A year ago. Five months before your kidnapping,' she said, wondering if he was mentally doing calculations.

The idea that he was suspicious enough to ask for that confirmation was more fuel heaped onto the fire of anxiety within her. She had told him the truth. Their short-lived fling had ended the day he'd walked out of her father's home. But of course there had been that crazy day when he had appeared in the rain outside her university a couple of months later...

An involuntary shiver went down her spine as she remembered the anger and frustration of their conversation erupting into a single desperate explosion of passionate kissing in his low-slung sports car. They'd been parked near the beach in broad daylight, and she had shocked herself when she had moved to spread herself over him and felt Duarte enter her unsheathed.

The madness had only taken them briefly, before they had realised what they were doing and stopped, but apparently that was all it had taken for her to fall pregnant.

She wouldn't regret it—not when it had given her the greatest gift of her life. Her son.

Duarte took a deep breath, opening his mouth to speak, but just then they were interrupted by the arrival of one of his bodyguards in the doorway. Nora was shocked to see that the man was covered in blood and had a split lip. It suddenly dawned on her that Duarte had told her he'd been in a fight. What had happened?

'The intruders have been removed, sir.' The guard spoke quietly but his rasping voice carried on the wind. 'Senhor Fiero has confirmed that they are members of Novos Lideres.'

Nora felt the ground shift beneath her.

'There's been a break-in and you didn't tell me?' She gasped, feeling her body begin to shake as she desperately grasped for the baby monitor, half expecting to see her father's face there instead of her peaceful, sleeping child.

'Thank you—you can take the rest of the night off.' Duarte's mouth was a grim line.

'That's not all, boss.' The guard flashed a glance towards where Nora stood. 'I don't think they were here for you. There were months' worth of surveillance pictures and notes all over their car…photos of her.'

Duarte's face turned to pure thunder as he instructed the guard to gather the evidence and bring it to his office.

Once the man was gone, he advanced on Nora. He was dangerously still, his arms crossed as he looked down at her like an angry god. 'Have they approached you since that night in the shipping yard?'

'I knew I was being watched,' she answered truthfully.

He closed his eyes, torment in every inch of his face. 'This is why you fear me. Why you have been so mistrustful of my help. I'll bet even now you are making plans to run. To disappear from here.'

'Running is the only defence I have to keep my son safe. Away from the crossfire. From all of you.'

'All of us?' His brow darkened with sudden ferocity. 'You consider me the same as *them*?'

Nora turned to walk away, but her progress was hampered by a strong, muscular arm against the doorframe. She looked up to find him dangerously close, his eyes twin fires of fury.

'Don't *ever* compare me to that lowlife gangster and his cronies again.'

'You say you're trying to help me, but we both know why you've really taken me under your protection.' She steeled herself, determined not to back down in the face of his anger. 'You're keeping me here to get information against your enemies. What makes you any different?'

'I don't take people against their will.'

'Well, that's good news for me.' She felt her breath expand painfully in her chest. 'Because I won't be staying here a moment longer to be used as a pawn in your game.'

'I have been up-front with you from the start. I do not use women.' He moved forward, pressing his hand to her cheek and forcing her to look into his eyes. 'Whatever this connection is between us, it is not some kind of ploy. I didn't plan that kiss.'

Nora blushed, remembering the heat of his mouth on hers, but she pushed the feeling away. 'That is another reason I can't stay here.'

'You can,' he said softly. 'You can choose to be a witness in my case and help bring a criminal to justice. You can choose to trust me to protect you.'

She shook her head, hardly believing the words coming out of his mouth. He spoke of trust. What would he do if he knew the truth of her terrible past. Right now, he was assuming that she was an innocent victim, caught in the crossfire of his war. That she could simply go on the witness stand and give evidence without repercussions.

She closed her eyes, thinking of her father and his clever net of spies and his unending power. He would likely pay the judge to throw her in jail while he walked away with a smile on his face. She was simply circling under his net and he was waiting to make his move and catch her. She knew how he operated. She knew that even if he didn't know about Liam yet, the very thought of his daughter reunited with Duarte Avelar would be enough to tip him over the edge into one of his rages. He would want Duarte dead for sure this time. And he would make sure she watched it happen.

And her son? She shuddered to think of Lionel Cabo using Liam in his games.

Panic edged her voice and she didn't try to hide it. 'I can't be a witness for your case, Duarte. I can't willingly put myself in danger like that just so you can have your revenge. I have to protect my son. I just want to get away from all of this and raise my child in peace.'

'Nora, this isn't about me getting revenge for myself.' He walked to the window, turning his back to her. 'Those people almost burnt down a tower block full of apartments with living occupants inside. *My* tower, that *I'd* refused to sell to them. They have no morals, no limits when it comes to getting what they want. Those apartments were filled with hundreds of the most vulnerable people in society: elderly couples, people with disabilities and single mothers with their children.'

'The fire safety scandal…' She froze, remembering him telling her the reason he'd been in Rio, trying to save his parents' housing foundation. 'That was Novos Lideres?'

Duarte nodded. 'There is proof of a politician's involvement. A politician who was in Lionel Cabo's pocket. A friend of mine pursued the evidence and was almost killed as a result. But that politician was our only hope of pinning the crime on Novos Lideres and now he's dead. Cabo thinks he's untouchable. One of the things my business partner Valerio told me about the beatings we endured was that they threatened to kill my sister. They have no respect for human life, Nora.'

His fists pulled tight as he spoke the words and Nora was quiet for a long moment. Up until now her decisions had been solely focused on how to keep herself and her son as far away from this mess as possible. To keep them safe and out of her father's nefarious clutches. But in walking away would she actually give her father more power? She had evidence that could put him away; she was an eye witness to many of his crimes.

Wrapping her arms around herself, she shuddered out a long breath and stared at the ground. Perhaps if she helped Duarte he might forgive her. More importantly, she might undo some of her own poor choices and finally be able to forgive herself.

Until Duarte, she'd told herself that the effects of her father's business dealings had only been on the money and power of wealthy men. She had fooled herself into thinking that she wasn't a true criminal if she wasn't hurting people. The truth was, every time she'd stolen information before feeding it back to her father it had hurt someone in one way or another. There had been political coups, corporate espionage... But she had never considered that perhaps her father had only ever let her see areas of his business that wouldn't scare or upset her. She had been unbearably naïve not to realise that her actions had hurt vulnerable people through cause and effect.

Her silence was part of the problem.

When she looked back up Duarte was assessing her with his shrewd gaze. She shivered to think what might be going on in his mind. She was fast realising that keeping her son away from all this was impossible. Perhaps she'd be better off choosing the lesser of two evils and putting her faith in the man in front of her.

'I don't want to let them get away with it,' she said quietly. 'I don't want to be afraid any more.'

'Such a fierce little angel you are.' His eyes blazed with triumph.

'I'm far from an angel...'

She heard the hitch in her own voice and felt an urge to tell him everything. Every terrible detail of her sins. She craved his forgiveness. She craved the bond they had once shared—before the reality of her awful family connections had torn it all apart.

'I have a house a short helicopter ride down the coast. I'll help you pack now and we can have your nurse flown in for check-ups each day.'

'Now…?' she breathed, looking out at the inky blackness of the sky.

'It's best if we leave before dawn.' Duarte's voice was quiet and filled with sincerity. 'Let me keep you and your son safe.'

Our son. Something inside her shouted.

She felt a heaviness in her chest in the region of her heart. *Tell him*, it said. *Tell him everything.*

But she couldn't. Not until she was sure of him and of the man he now claimed to be.

An uncomfortable thought flickered in her mind. If he was truly a good man and she had kept his son from him… did that make her a villain all over again?

'I'm not ready to make any statements yet, Duarte…' She steeled her voice, trying to muster some strength. 'But I'll come with you because I can't stay here. I want to help you, but I need some time to think about all of this, to make sure my son and I will be safe.'

'I'm a patient man, *meu anjo.*'

They both froze at his use of the endearment. Nora's heartbeat seemed to thump in the region of her ears.

After a prolonged silence she mumbled that she would go and get packed before quickly turning away from the haunting amber gaze that saw far too much.

Duarte walked out onto the terrace and made a quick call to order a helicopter from one of his trusted private firms. Paranoia had his head snapping up at every small sound.

He sat down heavily in the nearest deckchair and rubbed a hand down his face, feeling the dull pain still throbbing in his shoulder. His skin seemed to be on fire after that surprising embrace and the revelations that had followed.

He closed his eyes, remembering the softness of Nora's hands on his skin.

They had been lovers.

The faint memory of their connection had come to him the moment her lips had first touched his. He'd seen her underneath him...over him... Everything else was still in the shadows, as though the way his body had responded to her wouldn't let him remember anything else.

The moment she'd admitted the truth he'd immediately thought of the child. But unless she'd had a year-long pregnancy, the dates didn't match. The boy had even been born early, he reminded himself. He should have been relieved, but something within him had been quietly furious at the thought of her finding pleasure with another faceless man and conceiving a child.

The image of her fiery passion being given to someone other than him made his fists clench painfully. He briefly considered asking his team to find out who the man was, simply so he could land a punch on the bastard's face for abandoning his pregnant lover...

Duarte might have spent most of his twenties enjoying women in all their forms and wonders, but he had always used protection. And if by chance one of his lovers had ever become pregnant he would have done his duty and cared for his own flesh and blood.

Nora was a mystery to him in so many ways still, but this new knowledge of their intimate history together had changed something within him. He no longer felt adrift and lost in his own body. That single kiss seemed to have created a tether between them, from his solar plexus to hers, reaching out across the house and pulling her towards him.

He could feel her presence like a moth being drawn repeatedly to the warmth of a burning flame.

He knew it was a bad idea to want her. He knew there was a chance she would refuse to tell him the truth of how she'd ended up in the shipping yard with him. And yet still he imagined having those soft curves underneath him once more. He imagined hearing her cry out her pleasure in real time and seeing if the vague memory he had did it any justice.

He didn't know how long he sat, staring out at the blackness of the night sky, but by the time the distant sound of rotor blades sounded around him he had made his decision.

He would have her in his bed again.

As the helicopter began to descend over the small coastal town of Paraty, Nora tried to quell the roiling anxiety in her stomach. In her arms, her son slept peacefully, completely unaware of the upheaval taking place around him.

When they touched down on a sprawling property on the beachfront outside of town, she watched as Duarte set about ordering his guards to secure the perimeter while he escorted her inside. This reminder of the danger she had been in back at his villa made her begin to tremble all over again.

She knew that Duarte's protection was the safest thing for her and Liam right now, but it was only a matter of time before he figured out that she was hiding far more than just her brief relationship with him.

Nora barely registered her surroundings as he showed her to the large master suite of the house, explaining that his cousin and her husband lived on this historically preserved property year-round, in a separate groundskeeper's cottage, and sometimes gave guided tours to tourists. He quickly added that the house would be secured and closed for their use for the duration of their stay.

Nora eyed the sumptuously inviting pillows on the large four-poster bed and felt all the tiredness and exhaustion of a sleepless night hit her.

'Get some sleep.' Duarte followed her gaze to the bed, his eyes darkening for a moment before he exited the double doors of the suite and left her alone.

Nora felt raw inside, as though all her emotions had been swept up into a swirling storm within her. Liam still slept soundlessly, his cherubic face so serene and innocent she felt her throat tighten with emotion.

She was fast beginning to entertain the idea that Duarte wasn't as cruel and ruthless as he'd shown himself to be all those months ago. She thought back to that night in her father's home, when she had arrived to overhear them together, using her as a pawn in the game they'd played.

Her father had told her that Duarte had been playing her all along. That his interest in her had been an attempt at getting inside information on the organisation.

Nora had refused to believe it. She'd fallen in love with a kind-hearted, creative soul. They'd talked about her dreams of travelling as a freelance architect, once she graduated. They shared a passion for design and he'd promised to take her to Europe, to show her some of the beautiful buildings she'd only ever seen in books. It had been real…or at least she'd thought it had been real.

She'd felt sick as she stood there outside the dining room, listening to her father threatening to have her punished for the affair unless Duarte agreed to marry her. And telling him that a stipulation of the marriage contract would be that the Avelar Foundation signed a certain piece of land over to Novos Lideres.

When Duarte had flatly refused the contract, her father had been furious. He'd revealed his ace in the hole, threatening to have Duarte's jet-setting playboy image ruined by bringing him up on charges of sexual assault. Her own father had told him that he had friends who would enjoy giving Nora some nice big bruises to create photographic evidence, saying that hopefully they wouldn't get too carried away with their task now that they knew their princess had been deflowered.

Nora had almost fainted with terror and disgust.

She had waited for Duarte's outrage, waited for him to swear to defend her from such violence, but the silence had been deafening. Then Duarte had dialled a number on his phone and three police officers had entered. The men had been listening to the entire conversation. He'd smiled and spat that *nothing* would make him marry a mobster's daughter or hand over his land to such a crook.

His parting words had cut through her like a knife.

'If you think your daughter is worth anything to me, you're a bigger fool than she is.'

She lay down in the bed, turning her face into the covers to try to stop the tears that threatened to fall from her eyes. She had always known that her father was a dangerous man, but she'd naively believed herself out of the bounds of his cruelty. Hearing him threaten to use violence against her had been the catalyst she'd needed to begin her plan to escape.

Realising how she had been duped—how she had let herself be duped because she had craved love and attention from her father—had meant she no longer trusted her own judgement when it came to anyone. Especially not men who had a motive to use her for their own gains.

But she was no longer sure about her decision to leave Brazil and hide her son's existence. She wasn't sure about anything. She needed to be sure Duarte was telling the truth before she made herself—and her son—vulnerable.

She fell asleep with the memory of Duarte's lips devouring hers and dreamed of him watching her from the shadows of the bedroom, his amber eyes filled with longing and unrest.

CHAPTER SIX

NORA AWOKE AFTER a few hours of restless sleep with her body still taut with anxiety from the night before. She contemplated a shower, but no sooner had she stood up from the bed and stretched than Liam began to wake and fuss for his morning feed.

She dressed in the first thing she pulled out of her case that wasn't wrinkled—a simple coral sundress that was loose and flowing around her legs. She still hadn't quite figured out how to dress for her new body shape, but there was a more pressing matter at hand: feeding the fussing infant who had begun to let out intermittent squeaks, demanding her attention.

Scraping her hair up into a messy bun, she set out for the kitchen. It had been too dark to see much the night before, so she didn't know what to expect.

A long narrow corridor led from her bedroom to a sweeping mahogany staircase. She paused halfway down and looked up, transfixed by the breathtaking original stonework on the walls and ceilings. She could see where the historic features had been lovingly preserved, creating a perfect balance with modern touches.

The large living area had been extended at some point, with a clever stone pillar holding a modern glass fireplace acting as a transitional centrepiece that reached from floor to ceiling. She shook her head, hardly able to take in every wonderful detail at once.

From her vantage point at one of the full-length windows she could see that the rear of the house was surrounded by a stone terrace. Marble steps led down to an ornamental garden that looked perfectly maintained.

The property was cocooned by tall trees on either side, with just enough space at the front to see the South Atlantic Ocean spread out before them.

It was a home fit for a king—or at least some form of nobility—and sure enough, when the housekeeper, who introduced herself as Inés, spied her and showed her to the long galley kitchen, she was only too happy to give her a brief history lesson, outlining the passage of Casa Jardim from being the home of eighteenth-century Portuguese colonials to its present incarnation, housing three generations of the wealthy Avelar family.

Nora bit her lip, looking down at her infant son in her arms. This was what she was denying him. Not just wealth, but history and heritage.

But that life would mean nothing without safety. She couldn't remember ever being carefree as a child. The shadow of her father and his power had always hung over her and her mother, even when they'd tried to live peacefully in Manaus.

On that long weekend when they'd first met, Duarte had told her of the dangers that came with being an Avelar. He was regularly subjected to threats and scrutiny, requiring security wherever he went. She didn't want that for her son. He deserved to grow up free from fear, free from threat.

Steeling herself, she fed Liam and then settled him to kick his legs in his pram before tucking into the delicious spread of fresh fruit and pastries Inés had laid out on the open terrace.

The gentle clearing of a throat caught her attention, and she turned to find the subject of her dreams standing at the end of the stone steps, his body only partially covered by the white towel slung low on his hips.

Nora felt her mouth go dry and a groan of pure disbelief threatening to escape her throat. Of course he would be in a towel…

'I hope you both slept well?' he asked as he took a seat opposite her and sent a single fleeting look down to where the baby now slept in the shade.

'He doesn't sleep longer than a few hours yet,' Nora answered truthfully. 'The bed was very comfortable though.'

'That must be difficult…losing so much sleep.' Duarte frowned, thanking Inés as she brought him out a fresh cup of steaming hot coffee.

'I have many tricks to make *o menino* sleep.' Inés leaned down to coo at Liam, who had woken and begun to fuss and pull up his legs as if with discomfort. 'May I hold him?'

Nora nodded and bit her lip as the dark-haired woman gathered the baby into her arms and expertly placed him over her arm. 'I call this *macaco em uma árvore*. Monkey in a tree.' She smiled and began to sway from side to side, as though dancing. Liam immediately let out a loud burp and relaxed onto her arm with a dreamy little gurgle.

Once Inés and the baby had moved slightly out of earshot, Nora looked up to see Duarte watching her intensely.

'You are exhausted,' he said.

'I'm a new mother.' She frowned, touching a hand to the hair she'd so carelessly thrown up earlier. 'I don't have time to hide my exhaustion under make-up and smiles just to look presentable for your comfort.'

'*Deus*, I'm not criticising your appearance, Nora.' He shook his head with a mixture of anger and surprise.

'Things must have ended badly between us if you think me such a shallow, callous bastard.'

'I don't want to talk about that right now.' She stiffened.

'I know. You asked for some time and I will give you that.' His eyes were sincere, his mouth a firm unyielding line. 'But, for the record, I don't think you need to *try* to look presentable. You have the kind of natural beauty that most women would kill for.'

He leaned back in his chair, showcasing the impressive deep brown expanse of his bare torso. Nora felt her gaze linger for longer than necessary, her eyes drinking in the smooth muscles that were so tautly defined in the morning sunlight. It had been so long since she'd felt the heat of his body on hers...

She bit her lip, turning to look out at the ocean in the distance.

'I do have one small stipulation,' he said gently, drawing her attention back to his amber gaze.

Nora felt trepidation shiver deep inside her at the predatory gleam she saw for a brief second before he disguised it.

'For the duration of our stay here I wish for us to have dinner together.' He steepled his hands over that magnificent stomach, his eyes never leaving hers. 'Just good food and conversation—no tricks or forcing the issue of the past or the future.'

Nora narrowed her eyes at him, processing his words slowly and trying to figure out his angle. 'What's in it for you?'

Duarte fought the urge to smile at the obvious suspicion in her gaze. 'Perhaps I just don't like to eat alone,' he said simply.

'You are a terrible liar.' She pressed her lips together, the faintest glimmer of a smile appearing on her lips before she stopped herself. 'Let me guess—you plan to play the gracious host and wear me down until I agree to give you what you want?'

'I don't need to wear you down.' He took another sip of his coffee. 'I have faith that you are going to do the right thing, and I am determined to make sure you are kept safe.'

'You don't need to be nice to me,' she said uncomfortably. 'You are a busy man and I'm sure you have things to do back in Rio.'

'Of course I do. But those things can be managed from afar. You cannot.'

'You wish to *manage* me?' She narrowed her eyes.

'I wish to get to know you, Nora.'

He heard in his own words a bare honesty that shocked him. He saw her eyes shift away from him uncomfortably, her hands twisting the napkin in her lap as she watched Inés pace with the baby, singing softly.

'Trust me—you don't.'

Her words were barely audible but he caught them. He heard the weight of sadness and hopelessness woven through each syllable and was consumed by the urge to stand up and gather her into his arms. To figure out what on earth had happened between them that could put such a miserable look on her face.

'Will you agree to my terms?' he repeated, knowing she had every right to say no and knowing that he wouldn't push the issue.

Inés walked back towards them and revealed the peacefully sleeping baby in her arms. Nora's face lit up with surprise and gratitude as the older woman settled Liam into his pram.

Duarte peered down at the small bundle wrapped in blankets. The child had grown significantly in the month since leaving the hospital, and yet he was still tiny. He took in the boy's dark colouring and once again thought of the man who had walked away from fatherhood. Anger coiled within him.

Inés's voice penetrated his thoughts, asking Nora if she would like to take a moment to rest or freshen up and offering to sit with the baby in the fresh air of the upstairs balcony.

Nora hesitated, looking towards Duarte for a moment. 'I don't mean to leave you alone in the middle of your breakfast...'

Duarte assured her that he would be working all day and instructed Inés not to take no for an answer. No one should be expected to do everything for an infant without a little help.

She smiled, and the two women began to make their way back into the house. A few footsteps from the door Nora stopped and turned around to face him.

'I'll see you at dinner, then.' Her voice was a little uncertain as she waited for him to nod before she disappeared through the doors.

Duarte tried not to roar at the small victory. He watched her walk away, his gaze lingering for far longer than was proper. He mentally shook himself and tucked into the spread of freshly cut papaya slices and warm bread rolls that had been filled with cheese and pan-fried.

This traditional dish of *pão de queijo* that Inés had prepared was one of his favourites, reminding him of long weekends and summers spent here as a child, when he and his sister would fight over the last piece while their father laughed and their mother scolded.

Every time he thought of his parents he wondered why his memory loss had not wiped away the grief he still felt from their death seven years ago. From the moment he'd set foot inside this, their special family vacation spot, he'd been instantly overcome with memories of when he was a child. Yet for some reason he had no memory of the past year of his life beyond blurred snatches here and there. It made no sense.

Shaking off the frustration, he opened his phone and dialled Angelus Fiero's number for an update. Upon hearing that the two criminal henchmen had escaped and gone straight back to Novos Lideres and Cabo, he clenched his fists on the table.

'Filho da mãe!' he cursed, banging his fists hard against the wood.

He quickly recovered and forced himself to think logically. Those men would never have testified against him anyway; it was a part of the sick code of the Novos Lideres. Men quite literally pledged their life to their *patrao*—their boss. And Lionel Cabo got to sit at the top of the pecking order, watching them all fall like good soldiers.

He wasn't prepared to tell Angelus any details about the woman staying under his protection. He simply said that he was working with a witness who was possibly willing to assist in their case. The older man's voice brightened substantially, and he assured Duarte that witness testimony would be enough to get an arrest warrant at least, but they still needed solid evidence to make the charges stick.

The idea of finally putting Lionel Cabo behind bars for his crimes was immensely satisfying. But what would he do if Nora decided not to do the right thing? What if fear won out over that tiny spark of fury he'd seen in her eyes when he'd told her the depth of the mobster's crimes?

Once she could leave, he wouldn't be able to stop her.

In an ideal world, he'd simply offer her a large sum of money in return for information—but he had a feeling that bribery would only send her running faster. She had seemed uncomfortable with his purchases for her and the baby, continuously offering to repay him.

His father had taught him to follow his instincts in business and he'd honed that skill to a fine art, using it to his advantage in all areas of his life. He needed to stay, to get under her skin and find out what she was holding back and why.

Nora Beckett was proving to be quite a perplexing distraction, but if there was one thing Duarte Avelar relished above all else, it was a challenge.

Nora waited patiently for her distractingly handsome host to disappear back to his busy life, as he had done while they'd been in Rio, but he surprised her by staying put at the villa. Shockingly, he didn't attempt to question her further about her revelations. Nor did he mention their kiss.

He spent most mornings doing laps of the pool at a punishing pace, while she tried to focus on tending to Liam, trying not to catch glimpses of his powerful body slicing through the water, or heading off bare-chested for a jog along the beach. The middle hours of the day were spent working, but she soon found that he was not the kind of man who holed himself up in an office all day in front of a screen. Instead, he took conference calls out on the terrace, as he paced back and forth like a lion in his den, issuing orders and asking questions in more languages than she could count.

He'd taken over the large dining table that overlooked the sea, filling it with complicated blueprints and large heavy books filled with technical information. Sometimes when she woke at night, to pad to the kitchen for milk for Liam, he would still be there, frowning as he fitted together odd-shaped plastic pieces and transferred calculations to technical-looking documents.

His yacht designs, she presumed, remembering how passionately he'd once spoken of his creative projects.

They had eaten dinner together for four nights in a row, and the conversation had been far from boring. He was a deeply intelligent, well-travelled man, and yet he didn't try to make her feel inferior because she didn't know about worldly things due to her sheltered life.

At their first dinner she had briefly mentioned she loved to swim, and the next day she'd found a brand-new powder-blue swimsuit in a package outside her bedroom door.

The next night Duarte had surprised her by showcasing his cooking skills, and had prepared a delicious platter of barbecued *picanha*, the meat so tender it had made her moan with delight. Afterwards, Inés had offered to rock Liam to sleep, and Nora had accepted Duarte's offer of a short walk down to the beach.

As she'd stared out at the wide expanse of the ocean, spread out ahead of them, she had found herself confessing to him her dream of travelling, of seeing in real life all the amazing places in her architecture textbooks.

He'd seemed genuinely interested, and impressed that she'd completed a degree during such a turbulent time in her life, and he had frowned when she'd revealed that she'd had to abandon all her books back in Rio.

The next day there had been an entire shelf of thick hardbacks installed in the formal study at the back of the house, along with a note from him instructing her not to give up on her dream.

He somehow managed to make her feel on edge and completely at ease all at the same time.

On the sixth day after their arrival, she found herself sitting outside in the sunshine with Liam peacefully asleep in his pram by her side. When she felt a strange prickle on her neck she turned to see a familiar pair of golden eyes watching her. Quickly he turned away, going back to his work, as though chagrined at being caught looking her way.

Nora bit her bottom lip, wondering if he felt the unbearable chemistry simmering between them just as much as she did.

That evening, Duarte passed a message through Inés that he had to leave for the city. Nora tried not to be hurt by his lack of a goodbye, reminding herself that she was a guest in his home and nothing more. But she had got used to their evenings together and felt silly for being disappointed.

The next morning she awoke, ready for the nurse's daily check-up, and was shocked when the woman reminded her that it was the day of Liam's six-week check-up.

She waited with bated breath until the nurse announced that her son had grown and developed at a typical rate over the past six weeks and congratulated her on a job well done.

Her own check-up was just as detailed, and ended with another smiling declaration that she had healed perfectly and the pre-eclampsia would have no lasting effects. She watched in silence as they were both officially declared fit for travel, and then gave the nurse a long hug as she bade the woman goodbye for the last time.

Duarte had kept his word and booked her flight, the details for which were printed out and safely stashed in the hidden compartment of her case.

There was nothing to stop her from leaving, she thought sombrely as she stood on the balcony and watched the helicopter recede into the clouds above. And yet she had already decided she would stay.

Her complicated feelings for her son's father had clouded her mind, making it impossible for her to come to a decision about trusting him. But really she knew she had to tell

him. Even if he had treated her terribly all those months
ago and broken her heart, was that enough of a reason for
her to deny him the right to see his own son?

Her body was on edge with tension as she tried over and
over to think of the best way to tell him that he was a father.
She hadn't outright lied to him about Liam, she told herself
as she worried at her lower lip. He had made assumptions
which she hadn't corrected, but she hadn't directly fabri-
cated the lie, had she?

As if sensing her turmoil, Inés insisted she take an hour
for herself to unwind in the pool. The older woman refused
to take no for an answer, so Nora changed into the powder-
blue swimsuit, covered her pale skin with sun lotion and
spent a delightful half-hour wading from one side of the
huge pool to the other, floating on her back and staring up
at the cloudless sky.

Taking a moment to lie back on a sun lounger and dry
off, she found herself able to take in the details of her surroundings. She was awed by the solitude of this cliffside
villa. The nearest neighbour was a five-minute drive away,
leaving no man-made sound to disturb her peace, only the
wind in the trees and distant rush of the waves on the rocks
below.

Inés had been right; she'd needed some time to reconnect
with herself. She had almost forgotten she could function
outside of the tiny bubble of motherhood.

When she got back to her room she found Inés had already fed Liam and put him down to sleep. Her son was
starting to slumber for longer stretches at night now, and
it was all down to Inés's magic touch. In the absence of
her own mother, Nora felt enormously grateful to have
such a caring maternal influence. And Inés had developed
quite a bond with her son too—although she often threw
strange glances Nora's way and commented that the boy

could almost pass for an Avelar, with his defined dimple and dark skin.

Nora only blushed and looked away.

The older woman told her that dinner would be at seven and gave her a stern look, instructing her not to be late. It was already getting dark outside, so she forced her tired body to shower and dress in a simple emerald-green shift dress and flat sandals, not wanting to be rude if Inés had prepared a meal.

Putting the baby monitor into the pocket of her dress, she padded downstairs.

In the short time she'd been gone the net of lights above the terrace had been switched on, and underneath was a small dining table, neatly set up for two. In the distance she could see two bodyguards, doing their nightly sweep of the property. She frowned. If there were two bodyguards, that meant Duarte had returned.

'Welcome, *senhorita*.' A slim waiter appeared, motioning for her to take a seat.

'I don't think this is for me…'

She looked around, half expecting a parade of wealthy socialites to come marching through the house. Instead, she saw Duarte emerge from the dining room, striding towards her as if he'd just stepped off the cover of a fashion magazine. He wore a crisp white shirt, unbuttoned at the neck. His short crop of hair was still damp and glistened in the twinkling lights, as did his eyes as he pinned her with an intense gaze.

'I decided I needed to make up for missing last night.' He smirked.

'You've done all this for me?' She frowned, a knot of anxiety twisting in her stomach as she looked around, seeing a man in full chef's uniform hard at work in the kitchen.

'Not exactly.' Duarte let out a low hum of laughter. 'Chef

Nico and his team have applied for the catering contract on the new superyacht I'm designing. I'm seeing if he lives up to the hype.'

'Oh.' She felt her arms relax slightly with relief. The name sounded vaguely familiar—she thought he was a minor Brazilian celebrity. 'They're cooking for you as an audition, then?'

'They are cooking for *us*.' He raised a brow. 'You need to eat, no?'

'Well, yes, but...'

'Inés made me promise to feed you. Besides, I found I rather missed your company last night,' he said softly, guiding her over to a chair. 'Do with that what you will.'

Her eyes widened at his admission and Duarte had to fight himself to look away, to ignore how his heartbeat sped up in his chest and pay attention to the dishes that began arriving in front of him for his judgement.

It turned out that Chef Nico's hype was more than justified. By the time the last of the dishes had been cleared away he had already decided to hire the man.

Nora glanced down at the slim monitor in her pocket every so often, but otherwise seemed to be genuinely enjoying herself, and kept up with his deliberately light tales of the day of manual work he'd completed at one of the Avelar Foundation's newest housing projects. He'd spackled walls and lifted furniture up and down steps all day, thanking his good luck that his body was strong despite his injuries.

It dawned on him that he hadn't had a headache in weeks, and that his mood had become more balanced and predictable—almost like his old self.

They took a small break before dessert, and Nora slipped up to her room to check on her son. When she returned,

Duarte suggested they take their drinks to the viewing deck and allow the serving staff to clear away the dishes.

She walked ahead of him, the gentle sway of her hips a naturally sensual sight. He shook off his errant thoughts, realising that while he should be planning his approach to secure her agreement to be a witness against Lionel Cabo, all he could think about was kissing her again.

'I love the view from up here. I can't remember the last time I left the city.' She sighed, taking a long sip of her drink.

'You said you didn't always live in Rio…?' Duarte said, keeping his gaze straight ahead. Still, he couldn't miss the way she visibly stiffened by his side, then forced herself to relax.

'Not always, no. My mother and I moved around a bit.'

'You said she's Irish?'

Nora nodded her head, her fingers twirling around the stem of her glass for a moment.

'Ireland's a beautiful place to live,' Duarte said. 'She moved all the way across the world for her work?'

'Something like that.' Nora cleared her throat. 'You know what that's like, though, I suppose?'

He nodded. 'We moved to England when I was just a boy and I started boarding school not long after. My parents wished for me to be a great scholar.' He laughed, seeing the ice in her gaze shift a little, and congratulated himself on his efforts.

'I wouldn't say their efforts were wasted, considering your success.'

He shrugged, tugging at his collar, which suddenly felt too constricting. He disliked it when others commented on his success—an old habit after the years of torment that had come with being the smartest kid in class. He always tried to be modest, to downplay the ease with which he seemed to accomplish certain tasks.

She seemed to sense his shift in mood and changed the topic to the yacht she'd seen him working on, asking if he was enjoying his work. To his own surprise he answered honestly—perhaps too honestly. He told her of the large-scale launch for their US operation, and the pressures his sister and his business partner had been under with Duarte's sudden reappearance and subsequent return to the company.

He didn't go into the guilt he felt about the pain his twin had endured when she'd thought him dead, or how his best friend had blamed himself for the events leading to their kidnapping.

'It sounds like you're feeling the need to prove yourself and your health by going above and beyond all your previous achievements,' she said quietly, turning to look up at him.

Duarte paused and smiled, shaking his head and sitting back in his chair to survey her.

'Did I say something wrong?' She frowned.

'It's more what you didn't say.' He raised one brow. 'I could have sworn I set out to learn more about *you*, and somehow I end up talking non-stop about myself for ten minutes.'

She moved to take a step away from him, and to his own surprise he found himself circling his hand gently around her wrist. Her eyes widened with surprise, but she made no move to pull away.

'You said you've missed my company…but you don't know me. Not really,' she said softly, barely audible above the rush of the breeze and the waves around them. 'If you knew all the things that had passed between us…'

He watched as she swallowed hard and moved further away from him. If she was hiding things from him, it was likely she had her reasons. But still, looking down at the small handful of steps that separated them, he found he didn't care about the circumstances. He looked at her and he wanted her as he had never wanted another woman. And if she were to give him the barest hint that she wanted him too he knew all bets would be off. He'd have them both naked and in his bed before they could take another breath, gourmet chef and their dessert be damned.

As if she sensed the intensity of his thoughts, she took a deep breath that seemed to shudder a little on the exhale. 'When you look at me like that I can't think straight.' She shook her head softly. 'Liam turned six weeks old today. The nurse declared us both fit for travel.'

Duarte froze, the news hitting him like a bucket of ice water. He leaned against the handrail, looking out at the ocean. 'Have you made your decision?' he asked.

She closed her eyes, as if some unknown emotion was threatening her composure. It dawned on him that he'd never seen her so undone, so close to tears. She was always so strong.

'Hey…hey…' He wrapped an arm around her. 'Look, I understand that you're afraid.'

'I'm not afraid of being your witness, Duarte.' She pulled away from him. 'But I can't tell you about what happened that night without revealing my part in all of it. Without revealing that *I'm* part of the reason you were there in the first place.'

She reached one hand into her pocket and pulled out a slim black thumb drive, placing it into his hand. 'This contains everything. It's encrypted with some kind of code, but I know it's more than enough to blow Novos Lideres apart for good.'

Duarte felt shock pulse through him as he absorbed her words. 'Explain.'

Her words were dull and emotionless. 'The reason Cabo's men were looking for me is because I was a part of his organisation. I… I worked for him for a while.'

She looked away from him, her lips pressing together in that tell-tale way he could now recognise.

'I was initially tasked with getting information from you that they could use to force you to sign over your land.'

She went quiet again for a moment, her eyes flickering between him and the horizon in the distance.

'But it all went wrong.'

'Clearly.'

He frowned, shocked and horrified at her words, and stared down at the black rectangle that supposedly held all the things he'd been working to find. Could it be true?

'I was already trying to get away by the time you were kidnapped. They held me captive in a different location, to ensure that I didn't go to the police. I got free and I got word to your friend, Angelus Fiero, but by the time I got to where they had you…you had already been shot.'

'Why save me?' he asked, watching her reaction closely. 'Why risk being arrested yourself or punished for your actions?'

'I may have done things I'm not proud of, Duarte, but I'm still human.' She shook her head. 'There was so much blood… But I couldn't risk being seen. I had to leave you there. The next thing I heard was your death announced on the news. And then your poor friend was found alive. I didn't even know he was still in there…'

'He suffered greatly but he is okay now. Physically at least.'

Duarte was silent for a long time, his mind working double-time to process the new information. He'd known she was hiding something, but this was unbelievable.

'Look, I'll get my things packed first thing in the morning and I'll be gone, okay?' She moved towards the door. 'I just want you to know that I am sorry for the part I played. I never meant for any of that to happen.'

'You saved my life. You risked your own life to save me,' he said softly. 'Did you love me, Nora?'

She shook her head, anger in her eyes. 'Don't make me out to be something I'm not. I'm not the worst of them, but I was still one of them. I still conspired to hurt you. To hurt other people through you.'

'Did you love me?'

He asked the question again, more harshly this time, and watched as her eyes drifted closed. She was consumed with guilt—that much was clear. And he should be furious at her deceit. So why did he have the urge to offer her comfort instead?

He closed the space between them, forcing her chin up so she met his eyes. Twin stormy grey pools of torment reached out to him and pierced him somewhere in the region of his heart.

'Yes…' she whispered, a choked sob escaping her lips. 'Despite everything, I loved you…so much.'

Duarte claimed her lips, swallowing her sadness and her guilt and wishing he could take the burden from her. She had been in a purgatory of her own making for months, believing him dead and believing she had been responsible.

Her hands clutched at his shoulders, pushing slightly, and Duarte froze, fully prepared to stop. He was not the kind of man who needed to force a woman to get his way, no matter how strongly his body had reacted to her touch. But before he could pull back she seemed to make a decision of her own, moving up on her toes and pressing her soft, full lips against his.

CHAPTER SEVEN

SHE HAD KNOWN it would come to this from the moment she'd taken a seat across from him at dinner and looked into his warm, whisky-coloured eyes. It was too much—having him this way but not having him at all. If there had ever been a more perfect torture, she'd like to see it. This man who had stolen her heart and then broken it into a million pieces…he was everything she remembered and more.

His strong muscular arms locked her in place as their mouths moulded together like twin suns re-joined. He was a skilled kisser, and the heat of his mouth on hers was sending delicious shivers down her spine. Nora felt her body sing out the 'Hallelujah Chorus' even as her mind screamed at her to stop. To think of the consequences of her actions.

She was sick of thinking.

She felt brazen and rebellious as she moved her body even closer into the cocoon of his arms, letting her tongue move against his in the sensuous rhythm he had once taught her on a darkened beach.

If she kept her eyes closed she could almost imagine that this moment was entwined with that one. That their lives had never been torn apart by the awful events in between. No. She couldn't think of that. It was just him and her and this glorious fire they created between them when they touched.

'I'd be lying if I said I wasn't hoping for this, but I'm not apologising,' he whispered, his head dipping to kiss a path along her neck.

She gasped as his teeth grazed along the sensitive skin below her ear. His hands slid down her back to cup her behind, holding her against him. She could feel the evidence of his arousal pressing against the fabric of her dress. It would be so easy to lift the fabric and feel him properly...

A long-ago memory of him lifting her legs around his hips and taking her in a public elevator rose to her mind unbidden, heightening her arousal. She had always been like this with him—like a moth to a flame. She'd never reacted at all to any of the men her father had allowed her to date...

The single errant thought of her father was enough for her to get a hold on her rapidly deteriorating rational mind and detangle herself from Duarte, moving a single step away.

'Why do you want me, Duarte?' she asked. 'Even after the things I've revealed, you still kiss me like that and it ties me up in knots.'

He shoved a hand through the short crop of his hair, golden eyes seeming luminous against his dark skin. 'I've tried to ignore my attraction to you, because you have made it more than clear that whatever we had before is over. But every time we're together I'm more drawn to you. You're intelligent, and beautiful, and I find myself thinking of you far more often than I should probably admit. I think you still want me too.'

Nora felt heat and desire prickle across her skin at his words. She didn't know what to say to that.

One half of her was crying out to kiss him again and throw caution to the wind—to take one selfish night of pleasure and deal with the consequences of her lies of omission tomorrow. The other half told her she needed to tell him everything, not just a half-truth. She was stalling and drip-feeding him all the terrible things in the hope that she might somehow manage to keep him. That they might make it through all her painful revelations with this fragile new beginning still intact.

The idea of tipping him over the edge into the kind of hatred she'd seen on his face once before was more than she could bear.

She closed her eyes, hardly believing the selfishness of her own thoughts. This wasn't just about her. Liam deserved to have his father in his life; he deserved the chance to know him. She had to tell him. She had to rip the sticking plaster off.

She opened her mouth to speak, but a small cry came from the monitor in her pocket. She looked at the screen, then up to Duarte.

'Go,' he said simply.

The cry sounded out again—faint, but enough to tell her she needed to go. It was a divine intervention, of sorts, saving her from her own uncontrollable libido. *Stupid, stupid girl.*

'Nora.'

She turned around and saw he was still standing where she'd left him. The night sky formed an impressive backdrop, making him look even more otherworldly than he already did.

'I have to leave again shortly for the city.' He cleared his throat and adjusted the collar of his shirt, looking up at her. 'Have dinner with me again tomorrow?'

She swallowed hard at the knowledge that she had a twenty-four-hour reprieve. She would figure out how to tell him about Liam. She had to. Nodding and throwing him a tight smile, she practically ran the rest of the way up to her room, her heart hammering in her chest.

* * *

Duarte stepped inside the entrance hall of the house and was struck by the utter silence. He'd spent the morning with Angelus, and they'd agreed to send the thumb drive for immediate decoding, finding a source they trusted so the information wouldn't be lost. The rest of his day in Rio had been spent in meetings with the future tenants of his new developments, figuring out what they needed and ensuring he was offering the best fresh start possible for them.

He'd eventually cut his day short and decided to return to the coast early, knowing he wanted to ask Nora more questions but also just wanting to be with her.

Upstairs, he passed the door to Nora's room. It was open. He saw the bed freshly made and the small cot. He entered the room, his gut tightening at how empty it looked. He felt his body poised to run downstairs, to investigate further, when a splashing noise outside caught his attention.

He reached the balcony in a few quick steps, peering down to see a blur of action in the pool. Nora sat at the edge, dipping her tiny infant's toes into the water. As though she felt his presence, she looked up and spotted him. A shy smile crossed her lips and she waved.

Duarte pressed his lips together, hardly able to manage the riot of emotions coursing through him. For that split second he'd believed she'd gone, he'd been ready to rip through the country in search of her. It was madness. He felt as if he was losing what little control he'd gained over himself in the past months. How was it possible to feel calmed by this woman's presence and yet so completely undone?

She had essentially admitted to being part of the syndicate that had tried to kill him. She was a criminal by her own admission. And yet something in him refused to believe that was all she was. He had witnessed her care for her son, her intelligence and heard of her determination to finish her studies.

She was a contradiction. He usually despised things that didn't make sense, and yet he kept moving back to her, time and time again, as if he was a magnet and she was his true north.

Even as he told himself he needed to keep his distance, and regain the upper hand in order to move forward with his investigation, he found himself moving down the stairs and through the house towards the sound of her gentle laughter.

Nora had felt as though she were breaking apart all day as she'd wrestled with her decision and her fear of staying too long here in this wonderful place. She didn't quite know how to accept the calm happiness of being so secure and cared for... Deep down, she knew this kind of life was never meant for someone like her. She knew she couldn't stay for ever. Especially once Duarte knew everything. She wished that everything could just stay the same in their little bubble, but it couldn't.

And then Duarte had come back early from the city, and he had looked down at her in his intense way and she'd felt her heart sing in response.

He'd stayed outside with them for much longer than he ever had before, even offering to hold Liam while she took a short swim. She'd felt her hands shake as she'd passed her precious child into Duarte's arms, trying not to stare at their identical colouring and the same little frown between their brows.

The urge to tell him in that moment that he held his son in his arms had been overwhelming, but Inés had been watching them, and Nora hadn't been prepared to do it in the middle of the day.

Coward, she'd told herself as she'd dived under the water to disguise the tears that had flooded her eyes.

And even now, as she showered and dressed for dinner, her stomach flipped as her mind replayed the image of the two of them together in her mind. Father and son…

She knew she couldn't stay there another moment, knowing she was keeping such a huge thing from him. Duarte was not the man she'd thought he was. He was not like her father. Yes, he would be angry at her deceit, but she didn't believe he would be cruel.

She no longer feared that he would want to take her son from her and she now knew she couldn't keep his son from him. Liam was an Avelar by birth, and no matter how much she wished it to be different she had no hope of competing with the kind of life such a birthright would offer him.

She needed to tell Duarte and hope that they could find a way through this together.

Duarte had taken his time showering and dressing for dinner, his senses heightened. Now he waited in the dining room, listening to the sounds above of Inés and Nora talking as they readied the infant for bed.

He had surprised himself with his interest in the boy, offering to hold him that afternoon out of pure curiosity. And something had tightened in his chest as he'd looked into the small silvery blue eyes so like Nora's. He'd felt something protective and primal that he'd feared examining too closely.

He didn't want to come on too strong, he reminded himself. This was just dinner between two people with a mutual attraction.

When Nora appeared, the sight of her curves encased in jade-green silk stole his breath. She always looked beautiful, but tonight she looked radiant. Her eyes looked wider, outlined with the barest sweep of shadow, and the apples of her cheeks glowed with vitality. Her soft full lips were painted a rose-pink that made his own mouth water at the memory of how she tasted.

'You're really dressed up.' She smiled nervously. 'Have you ordered another chef audition?'

'Not exactly.' His voice sounded a little rough even to his own ears, and he could see the way she looked at him a little uncertainly. He cleared his throat, running a hand along his freshly shaved jaw. 'I thought we could go out tonight—if that's okay? The old town is really not to be missed, and I know a place that makes the best *moqueca de peixe* in the whole of Brazil.'

She smiled, and Duarte felt his chest ease.

Nora felt slightly nervous at leaving the house for the first time, but Inés had practically pushed her out through the door, assuring her that Liam would be fine for a couple of hours.

He had begun sleeping for longer stretches of the night now, she reassured herself, trying to ignore the almost painful tug of anxiety as Duarte's car moved away from the house and along the dirt road.

As though he sensed her anxiety, Duarte began filling the silence with commentary, telling her about the small town of Paraty and its rich history dating back to the time of the gold rush.

The historic centre of town was a bustling labyrinth of pedestrianised cobbled streets, with pretty whitewashed buildings and a surprisingly cosmopolitan array of restaurants. Duarte had booked a table in a small modern-looking eatery near the pier, where the ambience was like stepping into a warm golden cavern.

True to his word, the *moqueca* was the best she'd ever

tasted. The traditional fish stew melted in her mouth and was washed down by a local wine. For a dinner with a billionaire, it was surprisingly low-key and cosy. She found herself slowly relaxing as she tried not to think of the words she had rehearsed all day.

All day she had been tortured with anxiety. She didn't want to lose him all over again. She'd made bad choices in her life and allowed herself to be controlled by her father, but she did not believe she was truly bad.

After the last of their food had been cleared, Duarte suggested they take a walk down the stone-walled pier to where he had something he wanted to show her. Nora walked alongside him, keeping her eyes ahead and trying to control the swirl of butterflies flapping around her stomach.

The way he looked at her and listened to her, his curiosity unmarred by the hatred she'd once seen... It was as if she'd been given a true second chance with him—with the Duarte she'd known before his betrayal and all the ugliness with her father.

'It's just down here.' Duarte smiled as he took her hand and led her down one of the narrow wooden walkways of the marina. Small fishing boats bobbed gently on either side, gradually getting bigger and more expensive-looking as they walked further on.

Duarte came to a stop at the end, gesturing to a gigantic dark-painted ship that looked completely out of place amongst the more modern white and grey giants that surrounded it. It had several tall sails and an elegant golden trim. A large painted sign along the side read *O Dançarina. The Dancer.*

'This was the first ship I ever set foot on. My father's pride and joy.' Duarte spoke quietly beside her. 'It's been in storage for seven years...ever since their accident.'

Seven years. Nora closed her eyes briefly. She knew

exactly when his parents had died, and felt sadness on his behalf.

Duarte pulled down the gangplank and gestured for her to follow him on board. She'd bet the deck alone was longer than her entire apartment back in Rio. It was polished teak and spotlessly clean, as though it had just come back from a week at sea with its wealthy owners. She half expected staff to be teeming below-deck, ready to offer refreshments and hors d'oeuvres.

'I had it cleaned. It still looks exactly the same.'

Duarte smiled, taking his time as he ran his hands along the wooden handrail that lined the sides. He reached down to a small panel and with one flick of a switch the entire ship was lit up with golden light.

'It's…beautiful…' Nora breathed. 'I always knew that you own a yacht empire, and that you design your own ships, but this is the first time I've seen you on one.'

He laughed, a glorious smile touching his full lips. 'I was thinking I might take her out on the water tomorrow, but for tonight we'll have to make do with a champagne picnic right here in port.'

He poured her a glass from the bottle waiting for them.

'This is…magical…' Nora mused, feeling the bubbles warm her throat as she swallowed. 'Thank you for tonight. For being such a kind host.'

He raised a brow in her direction, leaning forward to sweep a lock of hair from her face. 'I'm not here as your host tonight, Nora. I thought that was pretty clear.'

She blushed, turning her face away from him and feeling warmth spread down her body. When she looked up, she saw the twinkling lights of the marina reflected in his golden eyes. His arms circled her waist, pulling her closer so they stood barely an inch apart.

'I've thought about nothing but kissing you all day,' he

purred, his fingers softly sweeping along her cheek and down to cup either side of her neck. 'You almost made me sign half my paperwork with your name.'

'I'm sorry.' She smiled, shivering at the sensation of his touch branding her skin. She felt caged in by his large body and his leonine eyes. Trapped in the most sensual meaning of the word. She'd never felt happier.

'You don't sound sorry,' he growled. 'You sound quite delighted at the thought of me in my office, half mad with lust, hardly able to wait to get back to you.'

'I thought of you too,' she whispered. 'I... I missed you.'

Her voice broke on the words, on their heartbreaking truth. She had missed him so much. She needed to tell him everything—needed to take a leap of faith and believe that he wouldn't punish her—or their son—for her hesitation.

But then his lips were on hers, his hands sweeping down to caress her hips and the small of her back. As she sighed into the kiss, sliding her tongue against his, she felt her control begin to unravel. He pressed himself and his hard length against her and she had to fight not to groan against his mouth. Her body remembered his hands and seemed to heat up on command, until the fire within her threatened to consume her entirely.

As though he suddenly realised he was grinding himself against her, he broke the kiss and pressed his forehead against hers. 'I'm sorry... It's been a while for me. I swear I've never felt so out of control.'

'I know the feeling...' she breathed, her mind a tangle of desire.

He framed her face with his hands and kissed her again, slower and deeper this time. His tongue was her undoing, its slow seductive teasing sending her completely over the edge of reason. She groaned softly, sliding her hand under the edge of his shirt to touch his skin. Having him like this, feeling him under her palms...she was half afraid he would disappear if she blinked.

The truth was like an invisible barrier between them, and here in the golden light, with his eyes on hers, she felt as if she'd been given the cruellest gift. She thought back to all the times she'd wished for just one more night with him. She wanted to take this moment and live in it. To have him, even if it was selfish.

The thought jarred her. Of course it was selfish.

She bit her lower lip, feeling the weight of the moment press down on her like a ten-ton truck. She took a step back from him and the words she knew she needed to say seemed to stick in her throat, choking her.

'We need to stop.' She closed her eyes. 'There are things I promised myself I would tell you tonight, even though I know it could ruin everything between us. But now I'm standing here I have no idea how to begin.'

'Then don't,' he whispered. 'I promised you a night out and that means no serious business. Right now, all I want to do is keep kissing you.'

'You don't mean that,' she breathed. 'You're not thinking with your head.'

'I'm trusting my gut, and my gut is never wrong.' He met her eyes. 'Will these things still be exactly the same tomorrow? Are they time-sensitive?'

Nora breathed in a shaky breath, looking up into his gold-flecked eyes. 'It will still be the same.'

He leaned down, gently pressing his lips to her temple and pulling her close. 'Being here...being with you...it's the closest I've felt to happiness in a long time. Even long before what happened to me. I was always seeking new thrills, always on the move. I was never actually calm enough to just...*be*. But when I'm with you, I'm actually here. I feel present in a way I've never been able to tolerate or enjoy before. I think we owe it to each other to allow ourselves a moment of happiness, don't you?'

'Just a moment?' Nora breathed, half hoping he would draw the line at tonight.

If he ended it—if he showed her he was the careless billionaire she'd once believed him to be—maybe this would be easier. Because this version of Duarte—the one who spoke of happiness and called her beautiful... It broke her heart to imagine a life without him.

She had never stood a chance of resisting him from the moment he'd swept her off that dance floor all those months ago, she realised. She was hopelessly in love with this man and helplessly careening towards full-on heartbreak once she revealed everything to him. Her heart seemed to ache at the thought, as she imagined him looking at her and seeing the lying, deceitful criminal that she was.

Closing her eyes, she sank against him and kissed him with every ounce of love she possessed in her foolish, foolish heart.

When they were both finally out of breath, and in danger of committing a public indecency offence, Nora took a step back, meeting his eyes steadily, without a single doubt. 'Does this ship have a bed?'

Duarte fought the urge to throw her over his shoulder like a caveman and kick open the doors to the cabins below. He'd never been more grateful for the top-to-toe valet service he'd ordered before he'd arranged for *O Dançarina* to be skippered to Paraty. The ship was freshly cleaned and gleaming, ready to sail and with the cabins made up.

Taking Nora's hand in his, he led her down towards the master cabin, briefly giving her a lightning-fast tour as they passed through the ship. Her eyes sparkled with mirth as he pulled her into the large cabin and laid her down on the giant bed before she even had a moment to take in the sumptuous décor.

He adored *O Dançarina*. The ship was beautiful—one of the most exquisitely restored sailing yachts he'd ever known in his two decades of sailing. But right now nothing compared to the view of Nora spread out on the bed below him, her lips slightly parted and swollen from his kisses.

She reached up, looping her arms around his neck and pulling him down for another deep, languorous kiss. Her hands tangled in his hair, pulling roughly against his scalp and sending shivers down his spine.

'I don't think I can wait another minute,' she breathed, her hands exploring his ribcage, and lower, pulling at his belt.

He allowed her free rein for a moment, before taking hold of both her wrists and clasping them above her head. She gasped, her hips flexing against him with surprise and definite appreciation. His little lioness liked being commanded—he could see it in the darkness of her eyes and feel it in the way her heartbeat pounded.

'I didn't come prepared,' he said, groaning with sudden realisation of his lack of contraception. 'I wasn't expecting us to…'

Nora bit her lower lip, desire warming her cheeks. 'The nurse has already got me covered in that regard.'

Duarte fought the urge to sink into her then and there with relief. 'Remind me to send that woman a gift basket,' he said, and smiled against her skin. 'I know I'm clean.'

'Thank God,' she breathed.

Her nervous chuckle fast turned into a groan of pleasure as he licked the sensitive skin below her ear and gently bit down.

'I don't know where I want to kiss most,' he murmured, trailing a torturously slow path of kisses along her collarbone. 'The glimpses of you in that bathing suit have played in my memory for so long I could hardly imagine having you in the flesh.'

'You have me,' she breathed. 'I'm not going anywhere.'

Something blazed in her eyes and made his chest feel so tight he had to look away, his mouth seeking out her hardened nipples through the silk material of her dress. He focused on teasing the peak, feeling her gasp and thrust against him, following the delicious friction.

Heat, passion, desire. This he could deal with. Two people using one another for pleasure and release. His sex-starved body seemed to have gone into overdrive, wanting all of her at once. That was the only explanation for the overwhelming feelings coursing through him with each touch.

If he wasn't careful this would all be over before he'd even begun, and he wanted to make this good for her. For both of them. She wanted him just as badly as he wanted her—he could feel it in the gentle flex of her thigh muscles around his shoulders as he moved lower.

Letting go of her wrists, he looked up at her from the valley of her thighs. 'Take off your dress.'

She slid the material over one shoulder, then the other, drawing it down to her waist. Duarte pulled it the rest of the way, biting down on his lower lip as her perfect porcelain skin was revealed to him inch by inch. Her small firm breasts were tipped with rose, the skin leading down to the lush curves of her waist and hips flawless, with only the lightest silver streaks on her hips to give any hint that she'd been swollen with a child six weeks before.

His eyes fell to the thin pink scar at the bottom of her stomach, his fingers reaching out to caress it. She froze, her hands covering her stomach with a grimace. Duarte frowned, lowering his lips to kiss her navel through her fingers, distracting her and easing the tension away until she was molten beneath him once more.

The idea that she might want her to hide her body from him was ridiculous. Did she not see what he saw? She was beautiful. More than beautiful—she was intoxicating.

He remembered that once, a long time ago, he had believed himself to be an accomplished lover, but right now he felt as if he was drunk on her beauty, his senses overwhelmed and uncoordinated.

Using her responses as his map, he slowly found his rhythm again, leaning down to kiss the inside of one knee and moving slowly upwards. His hands held her hips in place and she gyrated against his grip, begging him to move faster. To take her where she wanted to go.

'Please, Duarte,' she breathed, her hands moving down to tangle in his hair once more.

Her words seemed to echo in his mind, and there was something so familiar in them, something so right. He felt as if he had been waiting a lifetime to claim her this way, as if something deep within him craved having her body under his command.

He focused on the slow torture of removing the delicate white silk that was the only barrier left between them. His lips moved slowly along her soft flesh to where a silken thatch of red curls was the last barrier to the heart of her. He knew exactly what she wanted, what she needed, as he set about stroking and kissing her exactly where she needed him most.

Her low, drawn-out moan of pleasure was almost enough to send him over the edge himself. He focused on her, on the erotic breathless sounds she made as she crested towards the release she needed, and prayed that he wouldn't lose himself in such torture.

She looked down at him, meeting his eyes just as she neared the peak.

'Come for me, Nora,' he growled against her, feeling heat pulse in his groin as she followed his command with a brutal arching of her back and a sound that sent him wild.

He was over her in seconds, readying himself at her entrance.

Nora took him into the cradle of her thighs, her heart on the verge of bursting open with pleasure and emotion sweeping through her body. The way he looked down at her as he braced his powerful arms either side of her head... She almost came all over again.

Neither of them spoke as he pressed the tip of himself against her, but his eyes remained focused on her face as he slowly joined them, inch by glorious inch.

She felt a delicious stretch that almost bordered on pain at his more than sizeable girth. She looked away, embarrassed that she was not used to the sensation, and her body seemed to clench momentarily against the invasion.

He frowned, one hand cupping her cheek, forcing her to look up and see the silent question in his golden eyes. She covered his hand with her own, moving slowly against him, testing the sensation and feeling her inner muscles relax and pulse against the heat of him. He followed her lead, withdrawing slowly, then angling himself to move back inside in a slow stroke.

The sudden pulse of electricity that tightened inside her made her gasp, then smile up at him. That was all the encouragement he needed and he slowly moved against her, closing his eyes and letting out a low growl of pure animal pleasure. She moved too, her nails digging into his shoulders as he kept his rhythm slow but firm.

Her body remembered what to do, her hips seeming to

arch against him of their own volition, her legs winding around him and pulling him closer. His thrusts became a delicious brutal force against her core, sending her towards a second release.

She didn't think her body could withstand any more pleasure, but she was wrong. This climax felt completely different from the first, so intense she felt a knot in her throat as he looked down at her and twined his fingers through hers. She had the strongest urge to close her eyes against the intimacy of the moment, fearing she might ruin everything by crying. But if this was the last time he would look at her this way, she didn't want to hide.

She watched him move, feeling him grind the pleasure between them higher than she'd even thought possible. Just as her pleasure broke, and she heard an earth-shattering moan escape her own lips, he kissed her. His mouth captured the sound as he shuddered, growling into the kiss as he finally gave in and found his own release.

Nora wished they could have stayed lying side by side on the beautiful antique yacht for hours. The gentle sway of the water beneath them made it feel even more like a dream, but like all fairy-tales the magic had a time limit.

When she reluctantly announced that it was time to get back to the house and relieve Inés of her duties, Duarte agreed, helping her to dress. But his attempts at help quickly turned into another frantic lovemaking session, with her pressed against the stern of the ship, looking out at the lights of the town glittering across the black glass of the Atlantic.

Breathless, and drunk on passion, she smiled for the entire drive back to the house.

Inés was waiting in the kitchen and chuckled knowingly

at Nora's rumpled dress, before quickly updating her on Liam's thoroughly uneventful sleep and leaving them alone.

Nora went upstairs, checking on her son and tucking his covers around him. When she turned around, Duarte was in the doorway of the balcony watching her.

She bit her lower lip, feeling the weight of the moment pressing down on her. She walked towards him, and once more the words she knew she needed to say stuck in her throat, choking her. When she finally reached his side, his fingers came up to her lips.

'I see that serious look creeping back in,' he whispered. 'But the night isn't over yet.'

He gathered her up against him, taking her across the balcony and through the doors to his bedroom.

Nora shut off her mind, focusing on showing him the love she felt with every touch of her lips and her body against his.

CHAPTER EIGHT

DUARTE AWOKE TO an empty bed.

Sunlight streamed in through the balcony doors and a single look at the time on his watch had his brows raising. He hadn't slept for this long or this peacefully... *ever.* Not a single nightmare had plagued his sleep and his dreams had been filled with Nora. Vivid depictions of them together that had been so realistic they'd almost seemed real.

He ignored the strain of his own desire against the sheets, showering and dressing in clothing fit for sailing. He had a mountain of emails that needed his attention before the Florida opening, but he felt a deep longing to get out on the waves. He felt an urge to grab his sketchbooks and disappear into his ideas—but, strangely, he didn't want to be alone.

His mind conjured up an image of red curls flowing in the sea breeze and sultry silver eyes watching him as he commanded the ship to move over the waves. No, he didn't want to be alone today. He'd take them all out on *O Dançarina* for the afternoon.

His light mood followed him downstairs, where he stopped in the doorway that led out onto the terrace and took in the simple sight of Nora below, dangling her legs in the water of the swimming pool, Liam in her arms. She looked beautiful, her glossy red waves seeming to glow around her face in the mid-morning sunlight.

He was hit with a sudden erotic image of wrapping her hair around his fist as he made love to her from behind—one of the moments in his strange dreams the night before. She'd been different in the dream…her hair shorter. They'd been in the back seat of a car, with mountains all around them. The image had been intense…

As though she sensed him, she turned—and the look on her face was not what he'd expected. She looked miserable.

Something heavy twisted within him as he moved to walk towards her, but the gentle clearing of a throat behind him stopped him in his tracks.

Angelus Fiero stood just inside the archway of the dining room, his expression sombre and agitated.

'Angelus. It's good to see you.'

Duarte tried and failed to keep the annoyance from his voice. For once he hadn't been thinking of his investigation. He hadn't been consumed with revenge. But Duarte shook his hand, dropping the customary two kisses on his cheeks.

His father's oldest friend was a thin man, but today he looked even thinner since the last time Duarte had seen him, a few weeks previously. He leaned heavily on his cane—a recent addition after the gunshot wound that had almost ended him.

'You've always been a terrible liar.' Angelus chuckled, a strange tightness in his gaze. 'I'm sorry to bother you here, with your lovely guest…'

In his peripheral vision Duarte saw Nora stand up next to the pool, Inés at her side, the two women chatting animatedly.

He guided Angelus away from the windows and down the long hall to his barely used study at the back of the house. It was a dark room, lined with dusty bookcases, and it had an air of bleakness about it. He'd always hated the room, even when his father had used it as his study during their long summers here.

He sat on one of the high-backed armchairs and motioned for Angelus to take the other, frowning when the man refused his offer of coffee or any other refreshment.

A tightness settled into his gut.

'I have news.' Angelus snapped open the slim file he carried, a look of mild discomfort on his face. 'The evidence on the thumb drive was…fruitful.'

'Excellent.' Duarte reached for the file, only to have Angelus pull it back, a look of warning in his eyes.

'It involves your parents.'

The older man's eyes shone suspiciously as he glanced away, out of the window, towards the view of the front courtyard beyond. When he finally met his eyes again, they were suspiciously misty.

'Their deaths were not an accident, Duarte.'

The world stopped for a moment.

Duarte felt himself stand up, felt his hand snatch the file from Angelus's fingers. He saw the old man's pained look as though through a fog.

His heartbeat pounded in his ears as he read the detailed report outlining the various anonymous hitmen on Lionel Cabo's payroll and the jobs they'd been paid to complete. One item had been highlighted, dated seven years previously in London, England. Targets: Guilhermo and Rose Avelar.

He closed his eyes against the awful truth, willing it to disappear.

His parents had been good people. His father had been sole heir to his family fortune and had made the difficult decision to risk it all on a better future for his home city. The Avelar Foundation's development projects and charity efforts in Rio were world-famous. To think that their vision and refusal to bow to corruption had led to their deaths, just as it had almost led to his own...

'This was on the thumb drive Nora gave me?' He heard himself speak.

Fiero let out a heaving sigh. 'That's the next thing.' He stood up, his mouth tightening into a line. 'We pulled in a few of Cabo's associates for questioning. It didn't take much for them to start talking once they saw how much evidence we had against them. And they seemed to know exactly who our informant was: the only person Lionel Cabo had ever allowed to leave his organisation alive—the only person who had access to such secure information because she lived under the same roof. Duarte, she's his daughter. He had her identity kept secret, but we found it all.'

Another file was shoved into his hands. Images of countless passports and identities on each page. A couple of arrests under fake names. But there was a name at the top, on an original birth certificate that had been hidden from public record: Eleanora Cabo.

Duarte felt the world tilt on its axis for a moment.

Eleanora Cabo.

That name...

He stared from his old friend to the serious, frowning photograph of the woman he'd just made love to for half the night, feeling shock turn him to stone. 'How can this be?'

'Her mother is an Irish ecologist, currently running a wildlife sanctuary in Manaus. She divorced Lionel Cabo after less than a year of marriage, a divorce most likely linked to severe injuries sustained by her at the hands of a male she refused to name. Her anonymity was part of a legal agreement. As was changing her daughter's name and barring him from all access to her until she was an adult.

It seems she reconnected with her father the moment she turned eighteen.'

Duarte felt nausea burn his gut.

Lionel Cabo's daughter.

Cabo. The man who had killed his parents. Who had tried to have him killed.

Disbelief and rage fought within him. His temples throbbed and he rubbed circles against his skin, trying to calm the rising sensation.

A flash of memory struck, the picture in his mind so clear it made him dizzy. He saw himself standing in the grand entrance hall of a house he'd only ever seen before in pictures from his investigations: the Cabo mansion. He was looking down at the woman in front of him, cruel words spilling from his lips.

Nora's hair was shorter, blow-dried into a perfect style. She grabbed his wrist as he walked past her. *'Duarte. Please...don't leave me with him.'*

It was definitely a memory... Dear God!

Suddenly all his vivid dreams made sense. They were *memories*. Memories of the weeks he'd spent falling for a mysterious redhead in Rio, only to have his life become a living nightmare.

He turned away from Angelus's worried face, striding to the window and bracing his hands on the cold marble ledge for support. He crushed his fist against his forehead as more memories came rushing back.

The first time he'd seen her...the way he'd been drawn to her like a moth to a flame across the dance floor in a crowded samba club.

He'd been taken from that first glance. She'd been sexy, yet shy, fiercely intelligent and adventurous. Only having her for stolen hours at a time had been a thrill. She'd been shockingly inexperienced, but eager and honest in her pleasure, and of course he'd risen to the delicious challenge of initiating her into the world of lovemaking in every way he'd been able to think of.

She'd become an obsession. He'd even thought himself halfway in love with her until Cabo had approached him and revealed everything.

It had all made terrible sense. He'd been her mark. She'd been playing the part of his perfect woman.

And when the opportunity had come to play her at her own game he'd taken it—meeting with Lionel Cabo right under her nose and letting him offer his own daughter as a reward, only to throw it back in the man's face.

Angelus's words rang in his ears. *A secret.*

On their last night together they'd fallen asleep and she'd awoken in a panic. He'd had to run after her and convince her to let him drive her home. She'd refused, saying her father was overprotective. Their hours together were stolen because she had to sneak out. She wasn't allowed to leave the house alone.

He'd thought perhaps it was a religious thing, but then he'd found out the truth.

To know that her mother had gone so far as to get a court order against her child's father suggested something more than normal marital discord.

That haunting image of Nora's face in her father's entrance hall replayed in his mind again.

'Please, don't leave me with him.'

The Nora he knew would never beg. Not unless she was desperate. She'd been a prisoner in her own home and he'd left her there. He'd used her just as badly as her own father had done.

The memory of it made him tense with guilt.

No, not guilt.

He stood up, fisting his hands through his hair. She'd

made a fool of him. She'd had the evidence that could prove her father's guilt all this time. She'd been a guest in his home, eaten meals with him, made love to him, and never once thought to reveal all this. She'd said she'd had that thumb drive for months, that it had been her insurance. Surely that meant she had read it? Had seen his parents' names on that hit list?

He closed his eyes against the thought, the pain in his temples almost unbearable. The resurgence of his buried memories was like being hit in the head with that bullet all over again. He felt unbalanced and nauseated.

'I understand that this is a lot to take in,' said Angelus, sighing and shaking his head solemnly. 'What do you plan to do with her?'

'What do you mean?' Duarte frowned.

'Well, I came here to talk to you first. To warn you that the police want to move to arrest both Cabo and his daughter immediately.'

'No.' The word emerged as little more than a growl from his lips.

Angelus pursed his lips, eyeing him speculatively. 'She was part of Cabo's mobster family, Duarte. Possibly she knew that your parents were murdered and kept it to herself.'

'She gave me that evidence willingly. Surely that is in her favour?'

'Are you involved with her?'

When Duarte merely scowled, the old man let out a harsh frustrated sigh.

'This could be another part of Cabo's plan. Slithering her in here unnoticed and getting her under your skin. As the saying goes, "The apple doesn't fall far from the tree."'

'Don't talk about her like that.' Duarte bared his teeth, shocking himself.

'She has been lying to you this whole time!'

'When I found her she was just about to give birth, and she is being hunted by men she fears,' Duarte gritted. 'I quickly figured out that she was part of the organisation. Her personal relationship to Cabo is her own business. She's done nothing to me.'

Except lie to me. Such convincing lies.

'She has a child?' Fiero frowned. 'There's nothing about that in there.'

'He was born the day I arrived in Rio.' Duarte stood, running a hand over his scar as his mind processed the information he'd recovered with his memory. 'That's why I've had her under my protection.'

He didn't mention the fact that he'd also kept her here longer because he'd been enjoying her company, slowly courting her. He felt the older man's eyes on him, could practically hear him silently screaming at him not to be such a fool.

'I'm going to need time to process this.'

Angelus nodded and left just as stealthily as he'd arrived, his cane clicking as he departed from the house.

Even when the sound of his car's wheels had long disappeared up the driveway Duarte stood frozen at his desk, his mind going over and over all the information and wondering what it was about it that felt so wrong.

Nora had just finished settling Liam for his morning nap and now stood frozen on the staircase as she watched Angelus Fiero emerge into the entrance hall at the front of the house. She froze, anxiety stealing her voice.

She'd already been on tenterhooks since slipping back into her own bed in the early hours of that morning. She'd wanted to wake Duarte before she left and just get it over with. Tell him everything. But he'd been sleeping so peacefully, and she'd known her son would wake for his usual feed at dawn, so she'd left.

No matter how hard she'd tried to hold on to the afterglow of their night together, she'd spent the morning with a steadily increasing sense of dread in her gut. And when Inés had told her that Angelus Fiero had arrived, and he and Duarte had disappeared to speak in private, she'd prayed she wasn't too late.

The older man paused for a split second when he saw her, and then looked back towards the open door of Duarte's study down the hall. When he spoke, his voice was low.

'Finally I get to meet our selfless informant.' He narrowed his eyes at her, not with cruelty but not entirely kindly either. 'Surely you must have known that giving us that information would reveal your identity… Eleanora?'

She heard her birth name and something within her shattered. He knew. That meant Duarte knew. She'd waited too long to tell him and now…

The older man must have seen something in her face because he shook his head sadly. 'Just so you know, I came here expecting to leave with you in a police car.'

Nora felt cold fear sink into her bones, freezing her where she stood on the last step of the marble staircase.

'But you can relax. Apparently you planned your seduction well. Clever girl.' Angelus Fiero tutted, brushing invisible dust from his lapel. 'He's a better man than most.'

'I did not plan for any of this,' she said. She heard the steel in her voice and wondered how on earth she'd managed it when her legs felt like jelly beneath her.

The older man raised one brow, surprised. 'It doesn't matter. The situation remains the same. Goodbye, Senhorita Cabo.'

Angelus Fiero's voice had been a thin rasp in the echoing entrance hall, and the weight of his words remained in the air long after his car had disappeared down the driveway. She wanted to scream after him that it was not her name. It had not been her name for eighteen years of her life. She might have been a naïve teenager when she had been drawn into her father's world, but she had never taken his name.

She took a few shaky steps towards the study, where her reckoning awaited her. She hesitated, and braced her hand on the wall for support as she fought to compose herself. She was angry at herself—at her own cowardice and selfishness. And angry at the history she and Duarte had shared and how they seemed destined to hurt one another over and over again.

She stood in the doorway of the study and took in the silhouette of Duarte's powerful frame against the light from the window. He faced away from her, both hands braced on the ledge as he stared out into nothingness.

She wasn't sure how long she stood in silence, just listening to the sound of her own heartbeat in her ears. But eventually she must have made some barely perceptible sound because he spoke, still with his back turned to her.

'I assume you met Angelus Fiero on your way here?'

His words were a slash of sound in the painful silence, devoid of any emotion or the kindness she'd come to know from him.

'Yes.'

Nora fought not to launch into her own defence—fought to give him time to speak. She let her eyes roam over him, already mourning the feeling of being in his arms. He wore sand-coloured chinos and a navy polo shirt—sailing clothes, she thought with a pang of remorse. He'd told her he planned to take them all out on *O Dançerina*…

Without warning, Duarte turned to face her, then leaned back against the window ledge and folded his arms over the wide muscled expanse of his chest as he surveyed her.

Nora felt as if all the air had been sucked from her chest. The look in his eyes was a mirror image of that day in Rio, when he had walked past her in her father's entrance hall. It was like a cruel joke, having to relive one of the most painful moments of her life.

'Nothing to say?' he prompted, his voice cold as ice.

'I wanted to tell you. Once I was sure you wouldn't turn me in to the police...' She inhaled deeply, biting her bottom lip hard to stop her voice from shaking. 'I promised myself I would tell you yesterday, but then you were so wonderful. I couldn't find the right words...the right moment. I was a coward.'

'Yes. You were.' He met her eyes for the first time, assessing her. 'Did you know about your father's connection to my parents' death?'

She felt her blood run cold. 'What do you mean?'

'He ordered their murder. Staged it to look like an accident.'

He slid a file across the desk between them and she saw the brief flash of pain on his face as he spoke the words. She felt them hit her somewhere squarely in her solar plexus. She picked up the file with shaking hands, noticing the highlighted dates and names, reading that further investigations by the police detective in charge of the case had shown the report to be true.

Each line brought to her a sense of horror she'd never felt, and her stomach seemed to join in, lurching painfully. 'I think I'm going to be sick,' she breathed, dropping the file to the floor and seeing the pages scatter in a blur of motion.

She heard Duarte move around the desk to her side, touching her elbow briefly to guide her into one of the armchairs beside the tall bookcases that lined the room. Nora took a deep breath, then another, until finally the nausea and dizziness passed.

When she looked up again he stood at the bookcase, watching her intently. 'I swear I didn't know.' She shook her head, fresh hatred burning within her for the man who had caused so many people pain. 'I hope he rots in hell.'

Duarte looked away from her. 'I plan to ensure he never sees another day of freedom for the rest of his miserable life.'

'Prison is too good for him.'

'And what about you?' He looked down at her. 'You handed me that thumb drive, knowing it held evidence that could put you away too.'

'I hoped you would understand. I chose to…to trust you.'

'Listen to yourself.' He raised his voice. '*You* chose to trust *me*? I have never lied to you once. I have given you nothing but time and patience.'

Nora felt his eyes on her, felt the question in his words, but her shame and regret was too much. She closed her eyes and pressed a hand across the frantic beating of her own heart, trying to gather her remaining strength and get through this.

When she opened her eyes, he had moved closer. She bit her lower lip, seeing the distaste in his gaze. Then took a deep breath, knowing the moment had come for her to give him the truth he deserved. She only prayed she would be able to take his reaction.

'Your parents were being honoured posthumously in the Dia da Patria festivities. You came to Rio to accept their honour. I was sent to find you—to get information from you that my father could use against you for blackmail, to make you sign over that land.'

She placed her hands on her knees, avoiding his face, but she heard his swift intake of breath.

'We danced, flirted, then we walked along the beach and talked. You told me many things I could have used against you. About your sister, about your plans for the future. You were as shocked as I was that you'd given so much away. After our first kiss, I decided to defy my father and pretend my recording equipment had failed. I liked you. I said I was going to the bathroom and disappeared. But the next day you found me at school. I'd mentioned where I went to college and you wanted to return my coat...'

She shivered, remembering the sheepish look on his face when she'd emerged from her lecture to see him leaning against the bonnet of his sportscar, her classmates gawking at such a beautiful specimen of a man.

'But that's not the end of it,' he prompted. 'I remember...more.'

'There was more. You stayed in town for a week and we became...intimate. You returned a few days later and we continued our affair. It carried on like that for a month—until my father found out what was going on.'

'He threatened to hurt you...' Duarte spoke slowly.

'He threatened me in order to force your hand but you walked away. He was bluffing.'

'But my passport records show I took one more trip to Brazil, two months after that.'

'You tracked me down again, all anger and imperiousness. Still, we never could keep our hands off each other for long. I walked away from you that time. Only...we didn't use protection.'

Nora watched the realisation enter his eyes, moving into shock and narrowing to a deathly glimmer. He swallowed a few times, his voice seeming to fail him before he spoke.

'Are you telling me... Liam...?' His voice was a rasped whisper.

'I didn't want to lie to you,' she breathed, feeling her throat catch.

She had no idea how to make him see why she'd waited.

To tell him if she could have gone back in time she'd have told him the moment he'd appeared on that street in the rain. But now it was such a mess…

The space between them seemed to shorten and the room felt too small. It felt as if minutes of silence passed as they simply looked at one another, Nora still frantically trying to voice the truth she waited to give him.

'You are sure I am his father?' Duarte's question was like a gunshot in the silence.

She closed her eyes against the tears that threatened to fall. She would not cry in front of him. She had done enough crying over Duarte Avelar and all the strange, dangerous turns her life had taken since she'd met him.

She had often wondered how an intelligent woman like her mother had ever allowed herself to be controlled by a wealthy man. Why she had feared him. But now, looking up at the cold golden glint of Duarte's eyes on hers, knowing the sheer power he had at his fingertips, she was afraid.

She felt utterly powerless as she spoke, as if she was putting herself entirely at his mercy. She silently prayed that she wouldn't regret it.

'Yes,' she whispered. 'Liam is your son.'

CHAPTER NINE

DUARTE DIDN'T KNOW how long he remained silent, her words repeating themselves over and over in his mind as he fought to process them.

His son. He had a son.

An infant he had protected from the moment he was born...

He closed his eyes and swallowed hard. When he opened them Nora was staring at him, her large eyes so innocent and filled with sadness. He felt anger burn in his gut.

'Were you ever going to tell me?'

He heard the coldness of his voice and saw the way she flinched as he took a step towards her, but he was past caring. His logical side had been overtaken by pure outrage in the wake of her deceit.

'You don't understand...' She frowned, standing and taking a few steps away from him.

Duarte closed the space between them easily. 'Explain it to me, then.' He loomed over her, seeing her shoulders curve and her face turn a little paler. He heard his voice explode from him in a guttural growl. 'Explain why—even after seeing I was still alive, even after I offered you my protection and proved I was not a danger to you—you still decided to keep the knowledge that Liam was my own child from me?'

'I wanted to tell you from the first moment, but I didn't trust you. I needed to be sure you weren't a danger. You know who my father is—you know what he would do if he knew that not only are you alive but I had also given birth to your *son*. I was protecting us both. Protecting Liam.'

Her voice cracked on the last word—the first genuine loss of control he'd seen in her. She bit down hard on her lower lip, holding back the obvious emotion welling in her eyes.

'My son is my first priority. He didn't ask to be born into a world of danger and constant threat. It's my duty to keep him safe.'

'You think I would allow any harm to come to my own child?' The words felt both strange and right as he spoke them aloud. *His* child. *His* son. 'I deserved to know. All this time we've spent together…'

She looked up at him, her face a mask of barely controlled pain. 'I'm so sorry. I never wanted to hurt you. I think that's why I was delaying the inevitable.'

'That was not your choice to make.'

'It was better than having no choice at all.'

She spoke quietly, but he heard a thin thread of steel as it wound into her voice.

'Duarte, I've handled this poorly, but you need to understand that I was the child of a wealthy man who believed he knew what was best. My mother almost died trying to protect me from my father's enemies. Trying to keep him from taking me away once she decided to leave him. I know all too well what it means to be beholden to a man with power.'

'Don't you *dare* compare me to him.' He breathed hard.

'I'm not.' She shook her head, briefly touching his sleeve. 'You are nothing like my father, and I know that now. But when you came back…' She shook her head and walked away a few steps. 'At the end of our month together, after my father found out about us, and he went to find you. You know he put my safety on the table. Threatened to punish me for defying him with you.'

'He offered you to me like a prize,' Duarte said, the memory as clear as day.

'And you made it quite clear you didn't feel anything for me. You said I was nothing to you.'

Duarte froze, watching her closely. 'Did he hurt you?'

She looked away. 'Not physically. He always preferred emotional torture. I had to watch them take you, Duarte. My father forced me to go to that Avelar Foundation dinner the night of your kidnapping. He made sure I saw them take you. I screamed and I fought, but I was restrained and taken back to my father's house. He locked me up so I couldn't get help.' She wrapped her arms around herself, looking away from him. 'It was there, during that week, that I felt so sick…so tired and so faint. I calculated my dates and realised that I was carrying your child.'

'Did he know?'

'He called a doctor, who confirmed it. He was furious, but then…' Nora shivered, her eyes haunted. 'Then he smiled. He said now he had another thing over you… That night, I knew my father was at an event with his politician friends. I knew my time was limited, so I demanded to be taken to hospital for fluids, because I couldn't keep anything down. At the hospital I managed to slip away from my guards, borrowed a phone and found out where they were keeping you and Valerio. I sent a message to Angelus Fiero, praying he would get there in time. But when I got there you had already been shot.'

'You told me…' Duarte heard himself speak as the dreams he'd had all those months during his recovery finally made sense. 'You told me to live for you both.'

She nodded.

Duarte felt emotion tighten his throat but he pushed it away, turning from her and trying to get a grip on his thoughts, on the memories that swirled around like loose waves, intensifying his aching temples. She sounded as if she was telling the truth, but something within him resisted her words—resisted the belief that she was a victim just like he was.

How could he believe what she said? She had planned to keep this from him; she had lied.

He steeled his voice. 'Does your father know about Liam?'

'When I believed you were dead, I told him I'd lost the baby. I think his guilt over that was the only reason he let me go, let me leave the organisation. I was afraid he would try to use an heir as leverage against your estate, somehow. I kept my pregnancy hidden while I tried my best to finish my final semester, and then I made my plan to leave Rio. You know the rest.'

'I'll need a paternity test.'

He heard himself speak and saw her flinch at the words before she nodded silently, but he didn't care. Not when the memory of how they'd conceived their child was playing in his mind and tying him up in knots.

She had lied to him. She'd had all these memories that he was only now getting back, and still she had been able to pretend they were strangers.

She had believed him to be cruel and controlling— perhaps it was time he showed her just how heartless he could be.

'If he's my son…' Duarte felt his jaw tighten at the words, at the emotions they evoked within him. 'I won't be kept from him, Nora.'

'I know.'

'Your actions say differently. How do I know this isn't

some kind of new play from Cabo's organisation? His blood runs in your veins.'

She flinched as though he'd struck her with his words. 'You could trust me.'

He laughed—a harsh, low sound in his throat. 'Like you have trusted *me* so far?'

'Liam has Cabo blood too. Will you hold that over him? Blood is not the making of a person.' Her eyes met his, fire burning in their grey depths.

'How do I know you won't disappear the moment I leave this house? Where did you plan to go?'

'I grew up in Manaus on a small wildlife sanctuary.' She shrugged. 'I didn't like being so secluded then. But I wanted to make a fresh start for Liam somewhere safe, far away from the reach of my father.'

'If I hadn't brought you here…if we hadn't got close… would you ever have told me?'

She pressed her lips together. 'I don't know.'

She met his eyes without hesitation, but he couldn't hold her gaze. He couldn't look at her without thinking of what she'd planned to do, without imagining her choosing to keep something so important from him.

The thought that she might even have left Brazil with his son made something roar within him. The anger he felt was too much; he needed to get away from here—from her. He felt as if he was walking a razor-thin edge between control and madness.

A small cry sounded from the monitor at her hip and Duarte felt his chest tighten as Nora met his eyes again. He gestured for her to go, turning away from her to pinch the bridge of his nose.

He hesitated for a moment, then found himself following her, unable to stop his feet from moving in the direction of the infant's cries.

The windows of the room were closed, the shutters keeping the heat of the day out. Nora stood there in the dim light, holding the child to her chest as his cries softened. Duarte took a step closer, looking at the tiny face and wondering how he had ever missed it. The child had Nora's wide eyes, but that was where the resemblance ended. Everything else, from the colour of his skin to the dimple in the centre of his chin…

He reached out, touching his pinkie finger to that miniature dimple, and remembered that first moment in the hospital room, when a tiny hand had reached out to grip his finger. He wondered if Liam had sensed that he was safe with his *papai*? Would he have any memory of his first couple of months of uncertainty?

Duarte knew there and then that he didn't need a paternity test to tell him what he felt.

This was his son.

He looked up to see Nora watching him, a suspicious sheen in her silver eyes.

Clearing his throat, he stepped back from the intimacy of the moment. 'The Fort Lauderdale opening is in a few days. I see no reason to delay travelling.' Duarte kept his voice low. 'Be ready to fly in the morning.'

'You want to take us with you?' Nora's voice was calm, but he saw the sudden flash of defiance in her eyes, a bristling at the authority in his tone.

'I don't want to leave either of you anywhere in Brazil while your father is being taken into custody.'

He fought the urge to reach out and touch the child again, to memorise each tiny detail of his face. Something within his chest tightened again, almost painfully.

'I said I would protect you and that has not changed.'

'Okay.' She breathed. 'Duarte, I'm so sorry.'

He pressed his lips together, unable to look at her without feeling that roar within him starting up all over again.

'I have phone calls to make.'

He ignored the pain in her eyes and forced himself to leave the room. To leave behind the sudden need within him for the child who was such an integral part of him. To leave the woman who had made him feel as if he was finally glued back together only to tear him apart all over again.

He kept walking even after he reached the ground floor and went outside, passing the pool and moving down the length of the garden towards the sea. When his feet hit the sand, he left his shoes and shirt by the trees and broke into a run, taking out all his anger and pain on his body and pushing himself to his limits.

Nora had barely slept all night, and spent the eight-hour flight to Fort Lauderdale on tenterhooks because of the complete silence of the man by her side.

He seemed flat, somehow, as if all the colour had faded from him. He was helpful, checking if there was anything he could do to help with Liam, but there was a tightness to his eyes when he held him.

Eventually she stopped trying to talk at all and quietly watched a movie on her screen while he worked on his computer. The result was that she was practically delirious with tiredness by the time the warm Florida sun kissed her face.

When she saw a private SUV awaiting them on the Tarmac, she inwardly groaned with relief. She had never been more grateful for Duarte's ridiculous wealth, even if every other passenger on their flight did gawk at them as they were guided off the aircraft first.

When their driver finally came to a stop at the marina, she stepped out into the warm, humid air with shaky legs. Fort Lauderdale was very different from Brazil. The air was almost as heavy as the Amazonian climate in Manaus, but without the sounds of nature, and there were people everywhere. Well-dressed, wealthy people, who drove expensive cars and dripped with luxury brands.

She fought the urge to look down at her own three-year-old sandals and well-worn blue jeans.

Duarte pushed the pram across the wooden promenade, oblivious to the hordes of women who followed him with their eyes. He looked effortlessly gorgeous, in simple charcoal-coloured chinos and a silver-grey polo shirt. Even without the expensive watch on his wrist and the designer labels of his clothes, his entire being just screamed wealth.

Now he was turning that devastating smile on a well-dressed woman who introduced herself as one of his employees, and instructing a young man to bring the rest of their things as he confidently strode ahead towards the gigantic ship at the end of the pier.

Onboard the *Sirinetta II* superyacht, the staff jumped to attention around him, greeting Nora with wide smiles and curiosity. She knew that the Avelar family were practically royalty in Brazil, because of all their charity work, but clearly he was adored among his staff here too.

She avoided their gazes, wondering what they thought of the shabbily dressed woman walking onboard with a man like him.

Duarte took the lead, placing Liam down in a crib that had been set up in one of the cabins and ordering dinner to be served in the spacious dining area. He told her he would go for a swim first—the daily physiotherapy that he needed to keep his injuries at bay.

Nora debated going to lie down in bed herself, exhaustion warring with her need to speak with him alone. But in the end, she poured herself a glass of wine and waited.

He walked into the dining room still wet from his

shower, his chest bare and wearing only a low-slung pair of jeans. Nora groaned under her breath.

Over dinner she made an effort to ask him about his company's expansion and how it had come to pass, but his answers were short and clipped, and eventually she let the silence sit between them, the food having lost its flavour.

'Are we done?' he asked roughly, once he'd finished his meal and excused the staff for the night.

'I thought we might talk,' she said.

'I have no interest in talking with you tonight.' He rubbed a hand over the growth on his face, and there was a coldness in his eyes that made her cringe inwardly.

'Duarte, I know I have made mistakes...' She steeled herself against the flash of anger on his face. 'But I won't be kept on this yacht alone and punished with your silence. I came with you to see if we could try to find common ground.'

'There is only one piece of common ground between us that we've shared without dishonesty.' He sat back in his seat, a cruel twist to his lips as he surveyed her with obvious interest. 'If you're interested in communicating again in that way, I won't protest.'

'Is this your plan?' Nora stood up from the table. 'You're going to toy with me and keep me on edge with every conversation?'

'Only if you beg me to, *querida*.'

Duarte felt himself reacting to the fire in her more than he'd have liked. She was furious, her cheeks turning pink once she'd gathered his meaning.

He could have groaned as she braced her hands on the table and glared down at him.

'Hell would freeze over before I beg you for anything.' She spoke with deliberate sweetness. 'But, please, feel free to continue using my mistakes to avoid admitting your own part in this.'

'What part is that, exactly.'

'You told me you had never felt anything like what we shared in Rio. I was a virgin, and you didn't treat it like something to shy away from. You made me feel like I owned my body and my choices for the first time in my life. And yet when you discovered the truth you discarded me like old trash and discussed my worth over *cachaça* at Lionel Cabo's dining table.'

'You might have been inexperienced, but you were not innocent,' he drawled, leaning back in his chair. 'You are just as wicked as I am—in every way.'

She licked her lower lip, her eyes darkening. He waited for her response, knowing it was cruel to spar with her this way, but helpless to stop.

But she only frowned, turning away from him with a sigh. 'Stop trying to punish me, Duarte.'

He was behind her in a moment, gripping her wrist and pulling her towards him. He waited for her to move, to bridge the gap between them. Sure enough, her lips sought his without hesitation, giving him permission. He growled low in his throat at the heat of her mouth on his, as if he'd been starving for it. As if it had been months rather than a mere day since he'd last held her.

They both felt it—the current between them that pulsed and demanded attention. He'd hardly been able to concentrate during his swim, with images of the night they'd spent together playing in his mind, torturing him. It infuriated him how much he thought of her, of how she'd felt in his arms. Despite the revelations of the past twenty-four hours, he could concentrate on little else.

He turned her around, pushing her against the wall of the dining room and removing her worn jeans with one ferocious swipe of his hands. He hiked one of her thighs up over his hip, so he could angle himself against her through her underwear. She shivered, her hand reaching up to cup his jaw, a sudden tenderness in her eyes.

He pushed her hand away, grasping her wrist as he deepened the kiss for a long moment and then pulled back. 'If I wanted to punish you I know exactly where I'd start.' He moved his mouth to her neck, nipping softly as his hand moved down to pull the hem of her T-shirt up with a sharp tug. 'And believe me, Nora, you'd beg.'

She froze, placing her hands on his shoulders. 'What are we doing,' she whispered.

'I'm about to take you, hard and fast, against this wall.' He nuzzled her neck.

'I can't do this.' She pushed against him and he pulled away from her instantly. He watched as she pulled at the hem of her T-shirt, studiously avoiding his eyes. 'I can't be this for you…for whatever anger you're feeling. I won't be used.'

'I'm not…'

He struggled to find words, knowing she wasn't wrong. He *was* angry. He was using her body because it was easier to lose himself in his physical attraction to her than it was to look at all the rest of the things he felt when he thought of her betrayal. When he tried to align the Nora he'd come to know in Paraty with the one he'd met all those months ago as part of her father's schemes.

She moved away from him, her eyes filled with sadness, and he let her go, knowing he needed to put some space between them.

He needed to get a handle on himself.

CHAPTER TEN

NORA AWOKE WITH a start, the light streaming through the open curtains showing it was well past dawn. She reached out to the crib by the side of her bed only to find it empty. In a blind panic, she rushed out into the main saloon, only to find it silent.

She looked around, eventually hearing a low snore coming from one of the larger cabins at the end of the corridor. What she found there made her freeze, rooted to the spot, afraid to breathe lest she disturb the unbelievable scene before her.

Duarte lay on his back, one arm flung over his head as he slept on the large bed of the master cabin. Liam lay asleep by his side, in an almost identical pose, safely guarded by a nest of pillows. Nora placed a hand on her chest, feeling as though her heart might break at the beauty and pain of what she was looking at.

She wasn't sure how long she watched, how long her mind fought between happiness and despair over their uncertain future, but when she looked back to the bed Duarte's eyes were open, watching her. She waited for another flash of anger or reproach, but his face was utterly unreadable.

He rose gently, pressing a finger to his lips and motioning for her to follow him from the cabin.

'I never even heard him cry during the night,' she spoke

quickly, once the door was closed between them and the sleeping infant.

'I was still awake when I heard him get restless and I wanted to let you sleep.'

He stretched both arms above his head, unintentionally showcasing his impressively naked torso. The jeans he wore were slung dangerously low on his hips and Nora felt a sudden swift kick of desire so hard she was forced to avert her eyes.

'I didn't expect you to be comfortable with him so soon,' she said without thinking, her rational mind seeming to have gone out of the window at the sight of this gorgeous half-naked man being so caring for a small child.

'I'm full of surprises.' There was no humour in his gaze.

Nora swallowed the lump in her throat, wishing she had a cup of coffee to busy her suddenly trembling hands. Suddenly she was painfully aware of the fact that she wore her comfortable old pyjamas and her hair was likely a tangled mess.

'He'll sleep for a while more, I think.' Duarte handed her the small digital baby monitor. 'I'll order breakfast to be served up on the top deck. I'd like to discuss some things with you.'

She felt her chest tighten at his words and tried not to conjure up every terrible scenario she'd already thought of. Instead, she nodded once. 'I just need to freshen up first. I don't think your fancy staff would appreciate being made to serve me looking like *this*.'

'On the contrary. I find this look to be one of my favourites.'

His eyes swept briefly downwards to take in her worn flannel pyjama bottoms and white tank top before he shrugged one bare shoulder and leaned lazily against the panelled wall of the narrow corridor.

'However, if you need some help showering I will gladly play the kind host.'

Nora's mind showed her an image of him helping her to shower, his hands sliding slowly over her body…

They both seemed frozen in time for a moment, and she wondered if he could hear her heartbeat thundering against her ribs. He waited a breath, then let out a low whistle of amused laughter as he walked away.

'Don't say I didn't offer.'

She went into the cabin she'd claimed for herself and leaned back heavily against the door, exhaling long and hard with frustration. Was this how it would be between them now? Barely veiled anger followed by meaningless flirtation? Would she ever be able to have a conversation with him without remembering everything they'd shared?

They hadn't spoken yet about any plans for the future, but she knew it was coming. She knew Duarte was already analysing every angle and coming up with a plan.

She pulled a crinkled shirt over her head and looked at herself in the mirror. Even with the sleep she'd had, her eyes were still bruised underneath. She looked as exhausted and weak as she felt inside. She knew that if she had any chance of standing her ground with Duarte Avelar and his powerful world, she had to get back in control of herself. The idea that she'd need to dress to fit in with her surroundings chafed, but she knew how these circles worked.

She looked at herself in the mirror, closing her eyes against the dream she'd harboured of a simple life in the quiet peace of her mother's animal sanctuary. A life free of ridiculous rules and unwanted attention. A life free of deception and threats.

The more she thought of her mother's choices, the more she understood. But she was not her mother. She knew what came from hiding your child away from the world. She would not make that same mistake.

Duarte was not going to allow his son to be raised away from the privileged life he led. So she would do well to stop fighting him. She would have to overcome her emotions and put them behind her so that they could find a way to co-exist.

They had to.

She would not fight, but she would still remind him that she was not weak. She was not going to be ordered around, held to ransom under the weight of his unending anger towards her. She would hold her head high and stand her ground. If there was one good thing she'd learned from living under the tyrannical rule of her despicable father it was how to put on a show of strength even when she felt like crumbling inside.

She would not crumble—not for anyone.

Duarte had just sat down at a table on the open-air deck to pour himself a cup of coffee when he heard heels on the steps. His hand froze on its way to his mouth as Nora emerged into the morning sunshine. She carried Liam in one arm and in the other one of the colourful cushioned mats Duarte had ordered. She unrolled the mat in a shaded corner near the seating area and laid the infant down gently. He immediately began kicking his legs.

She looked up and met Duarte's gaze, a polite smile on her lips as she stood to her full height and walked over to the breakfast table.

His eyes devoured the jade-green dress she wore. Her long red hair was twisted into a neat coil at the base of her neck and he spotted the glint of delicate pearl earrings in her ears as she moved towards a seat and glanced back at Liam.

The serving staff arrived just as he moved to pull out her seat and he felt himself annoyed by their presence, by the pomp and glamour of the entire set-up in comparison with the simple days they'd spent at the beach house. Ornate dishes were being set out between them: fresh fruit platters and warm bread rolls, along with perfectly poached eggs in a creamy hollandaise sauce.

He tried not to watch her as she ate, his thoughts going over and over the events of the past few days.

'You wanted to talk.' She interrupted his thoughts, sitting back to dab her mouth delicately with her napkin once they'd both finished.

'My sister and Valerio will be arriving today.' Duarte sat back too, folding his hands on the table in front of him. 'I haven't told them about Liam yet.'

'You want to keep us hidden?' She clasped her hands together, pursing her lips slightly. 'Until your paternity test comes back?'

'There won't be a test, Nora.' He sat forward, running a hand along the length of his scar. 'I was angry when I said I wanted proof. Anyone with eyes can see that he is my son.'

'Well, that's good, I suppose…' She shrugged.

Duarte felt a flare of annoyance at this change in her. 'You *suppose*?'

'I told you that you are his father, that there is no doubt. But I understand why you wouldn't accept my explanation.' She took the napkin from her lap and folded it delicately beside her plate. 'So—your sister and her fiancé…will they want to meet him today?'

'They will want to meet both of you, I would imagine.'

'Surely there is no need for them to meet *me*.'

Her shoulders immediately became tense, and Duarte fought the urge to stand up and knead her unease away with his hands.

'I disagree. You are my son's mother.' He sat back, pushing away his errant thoughts. 'I had a lot of time to think last night. And I realised a few things. The first one is that I do not want to miss a single moment of my son's life.'

'Duarte, you know that's unreasonable, considering our situation.'

'Is it unreasonable to want to give him the kind of upbringing he's entitled to?' He measured his words, keeping his tone light. 'I have a large empty house in a quiet English village. It's safe, and the area is filled with young families. He would have access to a great education and the freedom to become…whatever he wishes.'

'That sounds wonderful.' She swallowed hard. 'Of course I want all those things for him. But I can't be expected to drop everything and follow your demands.'

'I'm not demanding anything, Nora. I'm offering a solution that I think will suit us both. I'm making a proposal.' He leaned forward, looking at her until she finally met his eyes. 'I realised last night that we don't need to make this difficult. Despite my anger towards you, I still find you intensely attractive. The idea of marriage to you is not unpleasant.'

Her face was a cool unflinching mask. Her words were deathly calm. 'Am I supposed to be flattered by that romantic statement?'

'I don't believe in perfect fairy-tales, and I'm pretty sure you don't either. That doesn't mean we can't try to be a family together. It's the most logical path.'

'First of all, you have no idea what I believe in or what I want for myself.' She leaned forward slightly, taking a deep breath before her eyes met his. 'And, secondly, are you telling me that you now trust me? That you suddenly forgive me for the things I've done and who my father is?'

Duarte felt her words hit him square in the chest. He

hesitated, looking away from her for a moment to try to school his features, and apparently that was all the confirmation she needed.

Her harsh exhalation of breath held the smallest hint of sadness. But he wouldn't lie to her to make her accept his proposal. He wouldn't make promises and say things he didn't mean. He believed she would put their son first and come to realise that this was the best way forward for the three of them. Surely his honesty was better than empty words?

She turned herself away from his gaze. 'Don't do it, Duarte, whatever it is you're about to ask of me…'

'You know exactly what I'm asking.' He reached across the table for her hand.

She pulled it away, closing her eyes. 'And if I say no?'

Her voice was barely a whisper and he heard the fear in it. 'I won't force you, if that's what you're asking me.'

He sat back in his chair, furious at her and at the way she viewed him. He took a moment to compose himself, feeling the urge to reach across the table and haul her into his arms to dispel those shadows from her eyes. He knew he needed to go into this with a cool head, but his logic seemed to go out of the window when it came to this woman, time and time again.

'I cannot abide the idea of splitting my son's life across two countries on opposite sides of the world, Nora.'

'That is not fair…' Her voice broke slightly on the last word.

'I never promised to play fair.'

'Why marriage?'

Nora could feel hurt and anger warring within her at the knowledge that he could be so cold and calculating.

'Do you trust me so little that you think I won't agree to any reasonable terms for co-parenting?'

'Marriage makes sense.'

Duarte took a sip from his coffee mug, as though they were discussing the weather and not the future entwining of their lives.

'From a practical viewpoint, we live on different continents with very different legal systems. It would make my legal rights regarding my son unclear.'

'That's not an answer,' she challenged him. 'Nor was there an actual marriage proposal anywhere in that ridiculous statement.'

He stood up and took a step towards her. 'I grew up with two loving parents and had a very happy childhood. I'm not some eternal bachelor; I always planned to settle down and start my own family someday.'

'What about *my* plans?' she asked, trying to ignore the warm, needy feeling his words stirred up. That yearning she had always harboured to truly belong somewhere, to be a part of a steady, happy home.

To give that kind of life to her son...

It would be so easy to say yes—to become his wife and commit to live with him, raising their son together. She had a feeling he wasn't suggesting a cold marriage of convenience—he would want her back in his bed—but that was where it would end for him. She would always be the woman who had lied to him. She would always be the daughter of the man who had killed his parents.

She closed her eyes against that painful truth, preparing herself to reason with him as to why marriage was never going to work between them...

The noise of a loud whistling from the marina below jarred them both.

'Duarte Avelar—you'd better not be hiding from me on my own ship.'

The female voice was calling from a distance and Nora felt her brows rise into her hairline.

Duarte cursed under his breath, and a thoroughly apologetic look crossed his features as he raised a hand and motioned for her to stay where she was while he strode across to the top of the steps.

Nora waited a few minutes, trying and failing to hear more than the slight murmur of voices as Duarte stood halfway down the stairs and greeted whoever it was. She moved to check on Liam, scooping him up into her arms and breathing in his comforting baby smell.

When the voices came closer, she turned to see a woman emerging onto the deck. Her hair was a cloud of thick ebony curls, her skin the same dark caramel as Duarte's. Even her golden eyes were a mirror image of the man who stood by her side. Another man followed them, sallow-skinned and blue-eyed.

Nora recognised him from the night of the Avelar Foundation dinner. The night of the kidnapping.

She felt a slight wobble in her legs as Valerio Marchesi looked up at her and narrowed his eyes in a manner that suggested she wasn't the only one who remembered that painful day.

What followed was perhaps the most intense hour of Nora's life, with Daniela Avelar sobbing as she held her nephew for the first time while Valerio and Duarte watched in shock. Apparently the elegant businesswoman had never been a baby person, and nor was she prone to such displays of emotion.

At one point Nora was very aware of the two men speaking in low tones in a corner of the deck. Duarte's friend and business partner seemed to have some things he wanted to say out of earshot. She saw the man's eyes dart to her, filled with evident mistrust, but she tried to pretend it didn't bother her.

When Dani insisted that Nora and baby Liam come to the launch of the new headquarters that evening, she politely declined.

So far Duarte had managed to navigate their entire interaction without once mentioning their relationship status or any details of their history together. She was grateful, but one look in his eyes as he was leaving told her he wasn't finished with their conversation from earlier.

She found herself suddenly intensely grateful that he was a hotshot CEO and his presence at the event was necessary.

When she was finally alone in her luxurious cabin, she lay down on the bed with her son by her side and blew out a long, frustrated breath.

The look on Duarte's face when she had asked him whether he had considered her own plans had spoken volumes. He hadn't even thought of her career dreams, her aspirations. No, he'd weighed up the situation and how it affected him and come up with the perfect solution to fulfil his duty to his son and keep her around as a handy bonus.

Was this what life would be like if she accepted Duarte's proposal? Trailing after him from city to city and waiting around while he attended events? Or, worse, would she be forced to play the dutiful wife on his arm?

He'd said he had a home in the English countryside and he'd made it sound idyllic. But the reality was he was a global businessman; his success took him to every corner of the world and she didn't expect that would change.

The last time Duarte had seen the Fort Lauderdale headquarters of Velamar International, the entire building had been mid-construction. Now he stepped into the glass-walled lobby and was awestruck at the level of detail everywhere he looked.

One detail caught him by surprise. The wall of the corridor that led to the common areas, where the drinks were to be served, was lined with picture frames. Upon first glance, he almost just walked by them, but something caught his eye.

He stopped and took a step back, frozen at the sight of his own blueprints and sketches for the original *Sirinetta* superyacht. For a moment Duarte wondered if they had been framed and put on show in memoriam—if perhaps he should avoid looking too close lest he should be met with an epithet of some sort about his tragic demise. But there was no mention of his death, only a succinct note on each frame, giving the date of his first concept and each stage on the road to production.

'We wouldn't be here without your brilliant mind.' Valerio appeared by his side, sliding a glass of champagne into his hands. 'You have always been the brains.'

'The creative brains, perhaps.' Duarte raised his glass in toast and gestured to the amazing building around them. 'But you were the one to come up with this crazy venture and build it into the powerhouse it is today.'

'I can't take the credit for any of this particular venture. Your sister did most of the legwork.'

Valerio smiled and raised his glass to where Dani now stood, welcoming their guests into the large conference area at the end of the corridor. She walked towards them, beaming.

'I still can't get used to seeing you together,' she said, and smiled as Valerio wrapped his arm around her waist and looked down at her with obvious adoration.

'I could say the same.' Duarte smiled too, noting their

mild shock at his light words as they all began making their way towards the party.

Dani moved away to talk with some of their investors, and Duarte saw his best friend staring at him in silent question.

'What I mean is, it's strangely normal to see you this way. It's like it was always going to come to this.' He placed a hand on his friend's shoulder. 'You make her happy.'

'She is everything to me.' Valerio spoke with gruff sincerity. 'Once I accepted that, everything else just followed. I knew it might cause a strain between us, but I hoped you would understand eventually.'

'I was a bastard when I first came home.' Duarte shook his head. 'I'm sorry.'

'You're not a bastard.' Valerio laughed as they entered the fray. 'You're just brutally stubborn and despise change in all its forms.'

Valerio's words were repeated in his mind long after they had finished their private conversation and separated to move through the crowd. He *did* despise change; he always had. It made him irritable and hostile. And when he looked at the past few months of his life he realised it had been one brutal change after another. He'd felt completely drained of mental energy.

Except at the beach house in Paraty he hadn't felt drained. He'd felt calmer and more at ease than he had in years. Now, surrounded by a mix of elite international business associates and clientele, he felt wound up and stifled. But he knew his role—knew what was expected of him.

He smiled and shook hands and tried to pretend he cared, when really he wasn't sure why he'd ever cared for this world at all.

The ship was quiet when Duarte arrived back from the event. Most of the staff had finished for the day, in anticipation of an early start preparing for the glamorous party on board the next afternoon to mark the opening of their new routes.

He wandered along the rows of empty tables on the entertaining deck, surrounded by stacks of chairs and boxes of decorations. In his old life he would have stayed to the end of the party at the new headquarters and ensured there was an after party in a fancy hotel penthouse, where everyone would have gone wild and he'd have ended the night with a beautiful woman in his bed.

The thought of it now made his blood run cold. He'd barely managed to stay for a full two hours tonight—only until his disaster of a speech had been given and he'd been able to slip away.

He was so distracted as he made his way down to the private saloon that separated the guest cabins that he almost missed the subtle clearing of a throat. Nora sat cross-legged on a sofa, her hair once again loose and flowing over one shoulder. She wore her ridiculous pyjama pants and tiny tank top, and one of her giant architecture books was splayed across her lap.

She looked like *heaven*...

He would be content to just lie down alongside her and sink into her warmth while she continued to read and ignored him.

He shook his head to clear the ridiculous thought. If she evoked such intense feelings in him it was just because he was stressed and irritated after his first evening of being 'on' as CEO of Velamar for the first time in months.

'You're still awake,' he said, trying to mask his inner turmoil with a light tone.

'I was waiting for you.' She stood up, folding her arms across her chest. 'I assume you got the message from Angelus Fiero?'

Duarte shook his head. 'I haven't received anything.'

She frowned, picking up an unsealed brown envelope from the coffee table and extending it towards him. 'It arrived an hour ago by courier. It was addressed to both of us. I assumed he must have already spoken with you.'

Duarte shook out the contents and read through the police reports quickly. Angelus had worked quickly, and a warrant for Cabo's arrest had been issued within hours of his leaving Duarte's study. The police had hauled the crime boss out of his Rio mansion in broad daylight and questioned him for hours until he cracked.

He'd confessed to everything, including the false imprisonment of his own daughter and his coercion of her to blackmail and work on his behalf. Nora would be given immunity for supplying evidence.

He looked up at the woman before him, her eyes tight with strain.

'He's going away for this, Nora,' Duarte said gruffly. 'The trial may not happen for a few months, but thanks to your evidence he won't get bail.'

'He's confessed to what he did to me...' She pressed her lips firmly together. 'He didn't have to...there was never any hard evidence.'

Duarte took a step towards her, seeing the way her lips trembled as she shook her head in disbelief. 'It's over, *querida*. He has no power over you any more.'

Nora had dreamt of the day that her father would get the punishment he deserved for all his wrongdoings, but a part of her had always believed him when he said he was untouchable. Now, seeing the cold, hard evidence of his sorry end in black and white, she came undone.

She let herself break, unable to stop the tears falling or the messy sobs racking her chest. She sobbed with relief for herself and the terror she'd endured under his tyranny, but she also sobbed for Duarte's mother and father, who had never got to see their children's wonderful achievements or to meet their grandson.

Eventually she closed her eyes and felt warm arms envelop her. She didn't pull away and stiffen, even though she knew she should. She accepted his comfort and sank into his chest until she could breathe again, which wasn't for a long while.

He didn't complain. He simply held her, his face on the top of her head so she could feel his breath against her hair. When she had finally quietened down, he pulled back just enough to look down at her.

'You are more than just his daughter, Nora,' he said gruffly. 'I was wrong to say that to you...to compare you to him. I'm sorry.'

She nodded, taking a step backwards out of his arms. 'It's okay.'

He seemed almost to extend an arm towards her, as though he wished to pull her back, before thinking better of the movement. 'It's not okay. I know I can be harsh and judgemental. I've done it before to my sister and my best friend and now to you.'

Nora looked down as his index finger and thumb circled her wrist and his hand slid down to entwine with hers. She shivered at the contact, tightening her hold on him and feeling her body sway towards his.

CHAPTER ELEVEN

'I'VE WANTED TO kiss you all day,' he said quietly.

His golden eyes were filled with such sombre sincerity that she felt her throat catch as his lips gently brushed hers.

'I've thought of nothing else...'

She felt herself fight against the intimacy of the moment, taking into account her own vulnerable state and the memory of his earlier proposal. But she wanted to kiss him too. She wanted to sink into the comfort of his heat and his strength and harness it, to chase away the shadows that haunted her.

A small part of her cried out to stop, to keep talking about the deep, dark cavern of mistrust that still lay between them. But she shook it off, losing herself in the glorious sensation of his lips devouring hers and his arms holding her so tightly.

When he lifted her up and walked them over to one of the plush sofas, she lay back and offered herself to him. His eyes darkened with arousal and he wasted no time in removing her pyjama bottoms and running soft kisses along the bare skin of her thighs.

She stopped him as his mouth reached her centre, laying her palm against his cheek as he looked up at her. 'I need you now, Duarte.'

Her voice was a husky whisper and he reacted instantly, pulling himself up over her and covering her with his big body.

The first contact of his bare skin flush against hers was almost too much. She spread her palms over his powerful shoulder muscles and just looked up at him for a long moment. She knew that this was real, not an instrument of anger, control or manipulation. And he felt it too, this intense connection between them. She could see it in his eyes as he slid into her in one sharp thrust, his hand splaying roughly through her hair to hold her in place.

It felt far too intense, locking eyes this way as their bodies began to move in a rhythm that managed to be both frantic and heartbreakingly intimate. Nora felt words in her throat, the need to tell him what she felt. But she closed her eyes, burying her face into his shoulder and focusing on the pleasure he gave her. On the way he touched her, the care he took in ensuring she found her pleasure...

Maybe that was his way of showing love. Even if trust could never truly exist between them, perhaps she could be happy so long as they had beautiful moments like this. Maybe that would be enough for her.

They made love hard and fast, barely able to catch their breath by the time they both fell in a pile of limbs on the carpeted floor. Duarte gathered her against his chest and let out a sigh that she felt deep within herself. A sigh of relief, as if he were coming back into the warmth of home after battling through a freezing storm.

But as she lay in the silent afterglow of their passion the silence crept over them once more and reality flooded back in.

She excused herself to go to the bathroom and stared at her flushed face, wondering how something that felt so wonderful could make her feel so hollow inside afterwards. She closed her eyes, wishing that loving him didn't have to hurt quite this much.

Duarte had spent the night in her cabin, in her bed, his warm body curled around hers. Despite her sadness, she'd slept well in his arms and had awoken at dawn to find him sitting back on the pillows, feeding their son.

After breakfast, he'd said he needed to run some errands for the day before the event that evening. She'd already told him she wasn't sure about attending the event, using her lack of appropriate clothing as an excuse. But as he'd been about to leave he'd kissed her softly and said he had asked his sister to offer her services to help her get ready.

Nora had not been prepared for Daniela Avelar to arrive an hour later, with a full entourage in tow. Though Daniela had made sure to double-check that her presence was welcome before she'd ushered in the small team of stylists, with racks of dresses and cases of hair and make-up.

Now Nora felt overwhelmed, but excited at the prospect of being pampered for an hour. She had always enjoyed dressing up for her father's events—she just hadn't enjoyed his authority over her appearance.

This wasn't the same, she told herself sternly as she felt her anxiety rising. Duarte had done this *for* her, not *to* her. It was not the same.

Her inner turmoil must have been apparent, because Daniela gave her a moment to collect herself and asked if she could hold Liam. Duarte's sister seemed thoroughly enamoured by the tiny infant, and only reluctantly returned him when Nora said he needed to sleep.

She settled him near the open balcony doors in his crib and immersed herself in looking through the expensive gowns on the racks in the makeshift dressing area that had been set up on the opposite side of the saloon.

'If you don't want to attend the event, you can move to my yacht,' Daniela spoke quietly beside her.

Nora turned to the other woman, noting the question in her golden eyes. 'I wasn't sure if I wanted to attend,' she said, clenching her hands together. 'But now I think I do want to be here for the celebration. I just haven't been very sociable of late.'

'Because of the baby?' Daniela asked.

'Even before that. I've been hiding myself away for a long time. I'm not sure I know how to be the kind of woman who wears gowns like this anymore.' She gave a weak laugh.

Daniela seemed to measure her words for a moment, becoming serious. 'Valerio told me who you are. Who your father is.' Golden eyes met hers earnestly.

Nora stiffened, looking away towards where her son slept. She wondered if Duarte had told his sister what her father had done. Why their beloved parents were no longer alive. She felt shame creep into her, clogging her throat.

Daniela stood up and closed the space between them. 'He also told me that you risked your father's wrath to try to save his life on that terrible night, and most likely saved my own fiancé's skin too.' She reached out to take her hands. 'I want to thank you.'

Nora shook her head, finding herself unable to find the right words to protest at the other woman's gratitude. Clearly Daniela didn't know the full story, because if she did she'd bet that this would be a very different conversation.

'I'm sorry you had to go through all that,' Daniela continued. 'I just want you to know I don't judge you for who your father is.'

Nora pressed her lips together, hearing the kindness in the woman's words but hating that they had to be said at all. She felt the reminder of her father's influence like a weight in her chest.

'When my brother came back from that place...' Daniela sighed, reaching out to examine one of the dresses on the rack. 'He was like a shell of his former self. I've never felt so helpless. But now here he is with you...with a child.'

'It's a lot to take in,' said Nora, pursing her lips.

'He hasn't said exactly what you are to one another, but I can tell that he's different. He looks more...alive.'

Nora frowned, remembering that this woman had believed her brother dead for six months, just as she had. They had both experienced grief and mourning over him, only to have him reappear in their lives.

'He proposed to me,' Nora blurted out, feeling the sudden urge to confide her turmoil in someone. To try to sort through her own tangled mind.

'Of course he did.' Daniela rolled her eyes. 'I bet he told you it was a practical solution too. I often wonder how a man can manage to run a multi-billion-dollar empire, with all its intricacies, and yet be utterly clueless when it comes to the workings of his own brain.'

'It's a rather complicated situation...' Nora hedged.

'With the Avelar family, it always is.' Daniela laughed. 'But if you do decide to marry him, I would be honoured to have you as my sister-in-law.'

Nora smiled, feeling some of her misery lift a little, despite herself.

Daniela walked over and laid a hand on the crib where Liam slept peacefully, taking a moment to gaze down at her infant nephew. Nora felt her heart swell a little, watching the obvious love this woman already had for a child she'd just met.

And as she sorted through the beautiful gowns, feeling the silk and the embroidered tulle, she wondered... Would it be so bad to be a part of their family?

Nora stood in front of the full-length mirror in her cabin, taking in the wondrous transformation Daniela's styling team had achieved in just a few short hours. Her hair had been swept back from her face and made to sit in graceful waves over one shoulder. Smoky make-up had been expertly applied to enhance the colour of her eyes, and her lips had been painted a perfect nude pink that seemed to make the roses of her cheeks glow.

She'd selected a pale blue strapless gown that accentuated her narrow waist and skimmed over her stomach. The material was a gauzy silk, embroidered with tiny delicate flowers that had glittering diamonds in their centres. She hadn't been quite brave enough to choose anything tight fitted, even though, at only seven weeks post-partum, her body had begun to feel normal again—if perhaps a little wider and less solid. This gown was comfortable, and light enough for the warm Florida evening, and the colour was perfect for her pale complexion.

She'd enjoyed every moment with Daniela, from selecting the colour for the polish on her now perfectly manicured nails to stepping into the expensive diamond-encrusted heels on her feet. For the first time in years she felt ultra-feminine and glamorous and...*happy.*

She had a small smile on her lips when Duarte appeared in the mirror behind her. He was impossibly handsome, in a simple black tuxedo with a pale blue handkerchief tucked into his pocket in exactly the same shade as the dress she wore.

'You look amazing.' He moved behind her, watching her

in the mirror as he lowered his lips to press them lightly against her neck. 'But there is just one thing missing.'

Nora watched as he revealed the small black box in his hand and held it in front of her. His eyes flicked up to hers in the mirror as he opened the box to reveal a stunning square-cut diamond ring that sparkled and played in the light.

'Duarte…' she breathed, feeling time slow and then spin around her as she turned to face him.

Her eyes were glued to the ring as he took it from the box and slid it onto the third finger of her left hand. It was stunning. It was the kind of ring any rational woman would dream of… And yet, when he slid it on and released her hand it felt cold and heavy on her finger.

She had told him she needed time. She had asked him to wait. He hadn't answered when she'd asked if he'd considered *her* plans for the future.

When she forced herself to look up at him she saw his eyes glowed with triumph and happiness.

'It fits.' He smiled, pressing a kiss to her fingers.

She forced herself to smile back, not wanting to ruin the moment. They had made love last night and fallen asleep in one another's arms; she knew they had more than just a passing attraction. It was only natural that he would assume he could introduce her as his fiancée, wasn't it?

Unease swirled in her gut, ruining the easy delight she'd felt moments before.

But he was about to celebrate the biggest moment of his career, she rationalised. His sister was here, his best friend and other family members. She didn't want to ruin this night for him, to cause him more pain. She had already hurt him so much with her poor choices in the past. He had said he wanted to be a family…maybe she owed him the chance?

The idea of a night of glamour suddenly seemed less appealing. The prospect of walking onto the entertaining deck on his arm and being introduced as his future wife was more than she could handle. She felt her insides shake, but steeled herself against the panic, telling herself to be grateful. To accept what he was offering and not dwell on what was missing between them.

Like trust…and love…

She closed her eyes and reached up to kiss him, hoping she would be able to get through the rest of the night without losing her composure completely.

Duarte was on edge. Maybe it was the single glass of champagne he'd allowed himself, or maybe it was the effect of having Nora by his side in that showstopping dress with his ring on her finger.

Every man on the yacht had turned to watch her when she'd arrived at the top of the steps. She always glowed with natural beauty, but after the added pampering and styling she bordered on ethereal. And yet no matter how much he'd tried to relax and enjoy the celebrations he knew something wasn't right. On the surface Nora was calm, and gave him reassuring smiles in between shaking hands with the various acquaintances and business associates he introduced her to. But every now and then he caught her looking off into the distance, with the faintest glimmer of unhappiness in her eyes.

Daniela had looked after Liam while Nora was busy getting dressed and was yet to return him to his mother. Duarte met Valerio's eyes across the crowded deck of the yacht and gave him a silent salute, wondering how long it would be before he was gifted with little nephews and nieces of his own.

A flurry of movement nearby caught his eye and he

smiled as he saw Valerio's parents and older brother arrive. He gestured to Nora to join him and soon he was embraced in the warmth and smiling faces of people who had been part of his extended family since he was a teenager.

Valerio's mother Renata immediately took Liam in her arms and began crying, and when she saw the ring on Nora's finger the tears started anew. The rest of the Marchesi men were more stoic, clapping him on the back and quietly offering parenting and marriage advice to both Duarte and Valerio.

'He is very like Guilhermo,' said Renata. She smiled, her face relaxed and serene as she looked down at the infant in her arms. 'His name is fitting…'

'I chose it in memory of Duarte's father,' Nora said quietly. 'He hasn't been christened yet, but his name will be Liam Duarte… Avelar.'

Duarte looked at her, not missing the way she'd hesitated over the last name. He was surprised at this revelation of the connection of Liam's name to his father's. He'd never made it himself. Liam was short for the Irish for William, she'd said on that first day in hospital, what felt like a lifetime ago. Something softened within him, knowing that even then—even when she had been unsure of him—she had chosen to honour his father that way.

'Little boy, you will break hearts,' Dani chimed in from his side, and they all raised their glasses in a toast to the oblivious baby, who promptly fell asleep and was placed in his pram.

'Duarte, you must tell us the story behind this beautiful family who have appeared with you out of the blue!' Valerio's father boomed.

'How did you two meet?' asked his mother.

Renata had directed her question to Nora, who immediately began to worry at her lower lip.

'It's a…a long story…' Nora began uncomfortably.

'We met in a samba club.' Duarte spoke over her and fixed a smile on his face, tightening his grip on Nora's hand as he felt the sudden tension in her body beside him. 'Very stereotypical for Rio, but there it is. I spotted her across the dance floor and whisked her away before any other man could steal her.'

Nora looked up at him, a glimmer of surprise in her eyes.

'Sounds like it was love at first sight,' said Renata, and smiled as she reached out to place a hand on Nora's with a dreamy sigh.

Nora stiffened and recoiled, and Duarte winced as he watched the older woman's eyes flash with confusion.

'Were they with you while you recovered on the Island?' asked Rigo, Valerio's older brother.

'No… Nora was actually busy finishing the final year of her degree in architecture,' Duarte hedged, avoiding the way Nora's gaze had flashed up to him. 'She's hoping to find an internship when we move back to England.'

'Such a long way for you to move…' Renata's face softened as she clearly mistook Nora's hostility for sadness. 'Have you family in Brazil?'

'My mother runs an animal sanctuary in the north, near the Amazon. My father is…is in Rio at the moment.'

Across from him, Duarte saw Valerio and Dani watching with furrowed brows. He felt the need to end the conversation, to take Nora away and protect her from having to talk about what had passed between them.

If they ignored it for long enough, maybe it would become less of a looming presence in their lives. He saw the shadows in her eyes when they were together; he knew they had both said and done things to one another that would be hard to come back from. He hoped someday it would be easier. But right now things were fragile between them, too fresh.

'I look forward to meeting both your parents,' the older woman continued, oblivious to the tension surrounding her. 'I've always considered the twins to be part of our family. Now we have two weddings to look forward to.'

'You won't be meeting my father, unfortunately.' Nora straightened as she spoke, suddenly pulling her hand from Duarte's. 'He's a notorious crime boss who is about to be put in prison for corruption, blackmail and murder.'

Everyone fell silent. Everyone except Dani, who took a deep, whistling intake of breath and as usual did her best to try to lighten the mood. 'Murder too? He was a busy man.'

'Yes, he was.'

Nora's voice was rough with emotion as she looked from Dani to Duarte. She opened her mouth to speak again and Duarte found himself shaking his head, urging her to stop while he swiftly changed the subject.

As he launched into a description of their time in Paraty he felt Nora shrink beside him, the tension rolling off her in waves. After a few minutes she quietly excused herself and turned to move through the crowd away from them.

'Have I said something wrong?' Renata looked to Duarte for assurance. 'She seems upset.'

Duarte cursed under his breath and quickly asked Dani to watch Liam while he followed his runaway fiancée.

He tracked her down to the rear viewing deck of the ship, which was quiet and empty of any guests. She faced away from him, her arms braced on the rail as she looked out into the distance. He stood beside her, taking her chin between his fingertips to turn her face towards him. Tears streaked her cheeks.

'Is this because of your father?' he asked softly. 'I know it must be hard to think of him. To answer questions.'

She pulled her face free of his grip, folding her arms across her chest and shaking her head softly. 'I know who my father is. I've had a lot of practice in what it feels like to be Lionel Cabo's daughter.'

'Then what's wrong?' He frowned.

'You and me. That's what's wrong.' She took a deep breath, wiping the remaining tears from her cheeks before she turned back to face him. 'I can't marry you, Duarte. I can't be a wife you're ashamed of.'

'I'm not ashamed,' he growled.

'You're lying.' She threw the words at him. 'I'm not prepared to skim over the gritty details of my life just to avoid judgement. You can't avoid everyone's questions and hide our history for ever. Your family deserve the truth.'

'I will give it to them…eventually. I want them to get to know you first.'

'You're trying to control everything—to manipulate them into liking me just so they don't show the same bias you did when you found out the truth about me. The first time *and* the second.' She shook her head, turning away from him. 'I may have made mistakes, and I may be the daughter of a crime boss, but I refuse to live another day feeling ashamed and hoping that one day you might truly trust me or love me. I refuse to accept the scraps of your affection.'

'That's what you think of me proposing to you? Trying to create a life with you? That you're getting the scraps?'

'If Liam hadn't been a factor in all of this you never would have considered marrying me…' She spoke quietly, twirling the diamond ring on her finger.

'Of course I would have, eventually.' he said quickly, frowning at her words and at the dark cloud that seemed intent on pulling her away from him. 'In Paraty, I felt the connection between us.'

She shook her head. 'That was before you found out about everything that had passed between us.'

Duarte let out a sharp huff of breath, feeling the situation getting away from him. They were both aware that this marriage was to secure his rights over his son, but he knew that wasn't all. He knew he felt more for her than he allowed himself to admit. But the idea of laying himself bare…

It wasn't something that came easily to him. Not after all they'd been through, and not with the swirl of emotions he felt whenever he thought of how she might have left him.

'I know that what I feel for you is more than you're offering me,' she said sadly. 'When I'm with you, I can't think straight. I think I fell in love with you that first night on the beach in Rio and it terrifies me.'

'You make it sound so terrible.' He looked away and steeled his jaw against her words, against the bloom of pleasure and pain they created in his chest.

'It's unhealthy, Duarte.' She closed her eyes. 'It's like I have an illusion of you but you keep everything real locked away, out of my reach. It's hurting me.'

When he looked back at her she'd slid the ring off her finger. She took his hand and folded the diamond into his palm. 'You said you wouldn't force me.'

'I won't.' He heard himself speak as though from far away. He curled his hands into fists by his sides to stop himself reaching out and making her take back her words.

'I'm sorry, Duarte,' she said quietly, and she walked away, leaving him alone in the darkness of the empty deck with nothing but the sound of the waves lapping against the side of the ship to accompany his turbulent thoughts.

CHAPTER TWELVE

NORA STARED BLANKLY out of the open balcony doors of her cabin and watched as the first glimmers of dawn filtered across the waves. She had barely slept, and her tears had continued to flow long after she'd silently collected Liam and returned to her bedroom to hide for the remainder of the party.

Daniela had come to knock on her door at one point, asking if she needed to talk. She'd remained silent until the woman's footsteps had disappeared back along the passageway, then she'd let the tears continue to fall.

She forced herself to get up when the morning light was bright enough. She grabbed her suitcase and began packing her clothes and Liam's into her small suitcase, inwardly planning what she would say to Duarte when she told him she wanted to leave. She knew she was doing the right thing. She knew she couldn't live the life Duarte was offering her, no matter how much she wished she could.

It would only make her grow to resent him. They would hate each other, and she couldn't raise her son in a home without love and trust. They both deserved more.

A knock on her door startled her. It opened to reveal Duarte, still wearing his trousers and shirt from the night before. His eyes were haunted and grim as he took in the sight of her and the suitcase open on the bed. She held her breath as she waited for him to speak, her heart bursting at the sight of him, with the need to take everything back and fall into his arms.

But she stayed still, her hands still holding the clothes she'd been folding.

'You're leaving.' It was a statement rather than a question.

'I'm going to stay with my mother,' she said firmly, feeling her insides shake. 'She hasn't met Liam yet. After a week or two I'll get in touch and we can discuss how to manage things going forward as co-parents.'

'I'll take you there,' he said quickly, his eyes sliding to where Liam lay kicking his feet. 'I'll have the jet readied by lunch.'

'No,' she said resolutely. 'I meant what I said last night. I can't think straight when I'm here…when I'm with you. I need to do this alone.'

He was quiet for a long moment, his jaw as tight as steel as he ran a hand over the scar on the side of his head. Then he seemed to measure his words, looking at her with a silent question before slipping his gaze away to stare at the open sea behind her.

'If you need anything…' He spoke the words on a low exhalation of breath, as though he had just finished waging a silent battle within himself. 'Promise me you will call.'

She heard the words and knew what it must have taken for him to speak them. He was trusting her to take his son. She felt another pitiful bloom of love for him in that moment, for this broken, scarred man who was giving her such a simple gift and likely didn't even know how much it meant to her. The gift of freedom.

It was the first small moment of trust between them as parents.

'I promise.'

She spoke softly, meaning every syllable. She wouldn't keep Duarte from his son. She would find a way to make this work.

With one final kiss on Liam's forehead, Duarte nodded at her once and left, closing the door softly behind him.

The rain had finally stopped falling when Nora drove her rented Jeep through the gates of the wildlife sanctuary, her eyes strained from hours of concentrating on the dirt road that followed the bank of the Amazon. She took in the familiar sprawling fields and the tidy rows of fruit trees on the hills. To her, this place had always felt like a world of its own—probably because during the eighteen years she'd lived here she'd rarely left.

She'd spent years hating her mother for keeping her here, and the irony was not lost on Nora. She was now returning to beg her mother to let her stay.

Her mother's house was a beautiful wooden structure that fitted in perfectly with the tall trees that surrounded it. The architecture student in her took a moment to appreciate her surroundings, how utterly flawless it was in its design.

Dr Maureen Beckett was a fiercely intelligent woman who could talk for hours about the animals she rescued, studied and reintroduced to the jungle. Yet when it came to her only daughter Nora had always found her mother to be distant and far too heavy-handed with criticism. She was not an unkind woman—quite the opposite—but she was known for her matter-of-fact approach and the fierceness with which she protected the large sprawling animal sanctuary she had founded three decades before.

Nora knocked on the door, readying herself for a reunion she knew would be anything but joyous. Likely there would be shock, and judgement of her situation. There might even be anger or, worse, that same cool detachment her mother had shown the day she'd announced she was leaving to live with her father all those years ago.

But when the door opened her mother took one look at her, and the small baby she carried in her arms, and promptly burst into tears, embracing them both in a hug filled with nothing but love.

Once she was safely inside, Nora finally allowed herself to fall apart, telling her mother everything.

Maureen was silent, one hand cradling her tiny grandson in her sun-freckled arms as she listened.

When Nora had finally stopped crying her mother took the seat beside her and drew her into her arms too. Just being held as she cried...being allowed the space to *feel* everything and not run away...it seemed to make her feel better and worse all at the same time.

And the thing that finally broke her was her mother revealing the thick envelope that had been delivered there a week before.

Nora's results from university.

She had forgotten that she had given the address of the sanctuary once she'd known she needed to leave.

She opened the envelope with shaking fingers to see that she had passed. She had her degree.

Her tears began all over again, until she thought she might never stop crying.

They talked all night, about all the unspoken things that had stood between them for years. Her mother explained how she'd attempted to follow Nora to Rio, but her father had caught up with her and told her if she ever sent so much as a letter to her daughter she would wake up to her sanctuary in flames. She'd had no choice but to come back and wait, hoping that Nora would get away and come home, even as her absence tore her apart.

Nora felt a fresh wave of love and understanding for this woman who had raised her—along with enormous guilt that she had compared her situation with Duarte to that of her and her mother. Duarte would never threaten to hurt her that way.

She found herself telling her mother everything that had happened between her and Liam's handsome billionaire father, expecting her to be horrified and warn her off.

Instead, her mother was thoughtful for a long moment. Then, 'Do you love him?' she asked.

Nora shook her head sadly. 'I do, but he doesn't love me.'

'Men don't always know how to say what they feel.' Her mother pursed her lips. 'I find his actions are usually the best way to gauge a man's devotion.'

That night Nora lay in bed, listening to the gentle sounds of rain on the roof above her, and thought of Duarte. Had his actions shown that he felt love for her?

Memories of how he'd courted her at the beach house in Paraty made her insides feel warm. He might not have known the truth about Liam then, but he'd known virtually everything else. And even after her revelation, when he'd been consumed with hurt and anger, he'd still shown her small unconscious gestures of affection—making sure she slept well, ensuring she wasn't uncomfortable around his family. When he'd kissed her, she'd felt love.

She closed her eyes and sent up a silent prayer that she hadn't just made the biggest mistake of her life by walking away from him. She knew she was doing the right thing in taking time alone to figure out what she wanted, but it didn't make being away from Duarte hurt any less.

Birds sang overhead and the smell of moist earth hung in the air from yet another heavy morning rain. As the sun peeked through the clouds the rain turned to a gentle mist over the fields. Nora paced herself, feeling the burn in her shins and silently thanking her mother for lending her the sturdy walking boots she wore. Even in her white cotton T-shirt and cargo shorts she already felt the effects of the heat.

In the week since she'd arrived at the sanctuary she'd fallen easily back into the simple life there. Now she reached the office and set about using the computer there to send some more emails, as she had done every day since the first morning she'd woken here.

She already had some offers of internships in London, but one stood out more than the others. It was near to the town where Duarte's home was.

She'd told herself she was tempted to take it for Liam, to make it easier to co-parent. She'd ignored the sound of her foolish heart beating away in the background of her mind. Of course she missed him; she woke up every day and wished he was by her side, but she needed to think practically.

On her way back to the house, she stopped to talk with some of the staff and once again gently avoided the subject of where she'd been and how long she'd be staying. It was a small community, and she wasn't eager to become the local source of gossip.

She took her time, stepping off the track to pick some fresh acai berries. The noise of the animals around her was so loud that she almost missed the sound of car tyres, making their way along the road at a pace much faster than any local would dare to drive. She turned just in time to see a large black Jeep barrel past her, turning at the fork in the track in the direction of her mother's home.

Her berries were scattered on the jungle floor, abandoned as she began to walk and then run in the direction of the house. She reached the fence at the end of the driveway just as a tall, dark man stepped out of the Jeep and turned to face her.

'Duarte,' she breathed, shock clouding her thoughts and rendering her unable to say anything more.

He looked terrible: his eyes were dark-rimmed, his shirt was wrinkled, and the trousers of his suit had mud splatters on them. But even though he looked utterly out of place, she'd never seen anyone look more imperious as he stood to his full height, looking down at her.

She came to a stop a few steps away from him, wrapping her arms around herself to avoid jumping into his arms.

'What are you doing here?'

'Do you want the polite answer or the truth?'

His voice was a low rasp, his eyes haunted as he raked his gaze over her with burning intensity.

'I think we've moved past politeness, don't you?' Nora said quietly.

Duarte nodded, running a hand along the untrimmed growth on his jawline. 'I've been a mess since you left. I told myself I wouldn't try to push you, wouldn't try to force you to come back to me, and I won't.' He closed his eyes and shook his head. 'But I've missed you, Nora. I've missed you both so much it feels like I've lost a limb. I decided that even if I drove all this way and you told me to leave, it would be enough…and I was right. Because seeing you right now, I'm not sorry.'

Nora felt a blush creep up her cheeks at the heat in his gaze. She took a step towards him, like a magnet being pulled towards its true north.

He held out a hand to stop her. 'You said you can't think straight around me, and I know what you mean.' He shook his head. 'I promised myself I wouldn't start throwing my feelings around and negating the very real concerns you had. But we've always had this intense chemistry between us, right from the start. That was never the issue. You were right to leave me. I was… I was the world's biggest fool.'

He took a step away, clearing his throat before he looked back at her and went on.

'I can see now why you wanted to come back to this place.'

His voice was warm, caressing her skin.

'It really is a paradise.'

'I never appreciated it until I left.' She took in a deep fortifying breath. 'But I've figured out a lot of things since I came back. Reconnecting with my mother was easier than I expected.'

'I'm glad you got what you needed.' His voice was rough. 'I took some time to re-evaluate things too. You leaving gave me the push I needed to make some hard choices. I told Dani the truth about our parents. It was a difficult conversation, but necessary. She asked me to pass on a message to you, to say that she misses you and Liam and she will come and find you if you keep her from him for too long.'

Nora felt tears build behind her eyes, thinking of Daniela and her wry sense of humour. 'That must have been hard,' she said softly, turning to face him.

'I'm just sorry I'd avoided it.' Sincerity blazed in his golden eyes. 'I'm sorry for how I handled everything, really.' He bit his lower lip, shaking his head. 'I wanted to tell you in person before word spread that I've resigned as CEO of Velamar.'

Nora gasped. 'Why would you do that?'

'I want to be free to work remotely, with less travel and less of that life in the spotlight, so I can focus on being with Liam. So we can create a parenting plan that considers both our needs and not just mine. Valerio was very understanding; he suggested I become a silent partner so I can focus on my own design firm.'

'That's…that's amazing, Duarte.'

'I don't know if you've thought about where you plan to live…?'

'You're *asking* me?' she said dumbly, hardly believing that he was here, that he was offering her everything she'd never thought possible.

Everything except himself…

Suddenly, his earlier words struck her. 'You said you'd told yourself you wouldn't use your feelings to make me come back. What *are* your feelings, Duarte?'

'Apart from feeling like a fool for letting you go?' He shook his head softly. 'I realised that the anger I felt when I got my memory back was so strong because I was in love with you. I never stopped being in love with you— even when your father came to me, even when I lay on the ground with you holding me and begging me to live. And when I found you again those feelings were always there, drawing me back to you. Back to where I belonged. Once I'd worked past my own stubbornness, and once I'd realised how much I hurt you by telling your father you meant nothing to me, I saw that my anger was only towards myself, and I saw how blind I'd been to what I'd had. And I saw that I'd had the kind of second chance that most people can only dream of…'

Nora felt her breathing become shallow as she took a step towards him, flattening her hands against his chest and feeling the steady beat of his heart under her fingertips.

'I don't want you to jump back into my arms,' he said. 'I know you have every reason to wait and see if I can keep my promises. But if you give me another chance I will do everything right this time. I will show you every ounce of love I possess.'

Nora claimed his lips then, unable to wait another moment to be in the warmth of his embrace. They kissed for what felt like hours, her heart singing with joy at his words, at how his body moulded around hers in a mirror of the relief and longing she felt.

When they finally separated he still held her close and breathed in the scent of her hair. He laughed. 'I think I might have to go back on that promise to leave.'

'I think so.' She smiled. 'I know we have a lot of plans to discuss, but about your proposal—'

He cut across her. 'I was wrong to make that proposal. I wanted to force you to stay with me, to be mine. If we do this now I want you to be with me because you *want* to. I don't care if we never get married, as long as we're together.'

'And if I say I want to live here in the rainforest for ever…?' Nora breathed, keeping her expression deliberately serious.

His eyes widened slightly. 'Well, it would be a hell of a commute, but I would make it work somehow.'

She closed her eyes, laughter bubbling in her chest along with an intense euphoria such as she had never experienced before. 'Well, if that isn't love I don't know what is.'

He lowered his mouth, nipping at her neck with his teeth and making her shiver. 'You are a cruel negotiator, Nora Beckett.'

The kiss that followed was even steamier than the first, leaving both of them out of breath and her shirt wrapped around her waist by the time she had the sense to break away.

'I don't really want to live here,' she said quickly. 'I've spent all week applying for internships in London. I want a fresh start. I want to create a family with you and turn your big house into a home. *Our* home.'

Her hands travelled over his chest, feeling a bump under his shirt. He smiled self-consciously, revealing a chain around his neck and on the end of it…her diamond engagement ring.

'I spent hours that day, picking this out.' He pulled it over his head, placing it in her palm. 'It doesn't need to mean anything. It can just be a symbol.'

'You know, I always dreamt of having my wedding here, in the local chapel, surrounded by the friends of my youth, my mother and our little community.'

Nora held the ring in her palm for a moment, watching it glitter and sparkle in the light. When she finally met his eyes again she felt a wave of emotion so strong it took her breath away. She placed the ring back in his hand.

'I want it to mean something, Duarte. If you'll still have me.'

He needed no further encouragement, getting down on one knee right there in the rain-soaked mud and taking her hand in his.

'I didn't give you a proper proposal the first time and I won't make that mistake again.' He looked up at her, the ring glittering in the light between them. 'Will you marry me?'

'I thought you'd never ask,' she breathed, getting down on her knees with him as he slid the ring onto her finger.

'I never thought I'd be so grateful for almost dying,' he murmured against her lips. 'If that pain was what I needed to go through to bring us back together I'd go through it all again right now, just to have you here in my arms where you belong.'

'Please don't,' she said. 'I was quite looking forward to celebrating our engagement somewhere private before we're interrupted.'

He laughed, standing up and scooping her into his arms to carry her into the house in search of the nearest bed.

'Lead the way, my love.'

'I always will.'

EPILOGUE

As a young girl, Nora had dreamt of her wedding day. She'd imagined herself walking down the aisle in a flowing gown to the sounds of a classical melody. As an adult, once she'd learned the truth of her parents' history, she'd stopped seeing marriage as something to celebrate. But now, as she walked down the planks at the sanctuary's wooden dock, hand in hand with the man she'd just vowed to love and cherish for ever, she felt her heart swell with joy.

They'd spoken their vows in the old chapel in the village, taking Liam into their arms between them towards the end of the ceremony when he'd begun to fuss. Nora wore a simple white strapless dress, with flowers from her mother's garden woven through her hair. Duarte looked effortlessly handsome in a tux, the shirt collar unbuttoned. She'd chosen the colour scheme, even convincing him to tuck one of her favourite purple orchids into his lapel.

They reached the small speedboat at the end of the dock and Nora turned to her husband, looking over her shoulder at the small crowd of their loved ones, still enjoying the wedding reception and dancing on the bank of the Amazon behind them.

'What is this surprise you've kept so secret?' she murmured against his lips, smiling at the sound of cheers erupting behind them.

'It's not a surprise if I tell you first.' He took her hand, helping her into the boat and getting behind the wheel. 'We'll only be away for a bit.'

She smiled as he manoeuvred them away from the sanctuary and along the river at a gentle speed. She placed her hand over his on the wheel, looking at the matching rings on their fingers and feeling herself smile even wider as the sun danced through the trees.

When he began to slow, she looked around.

'I read about this place a long time ago.' Duarte turned to face her. 'Do you know where we are?'

She shook her head.

'We're at the meeting of the waters. It's where two separate rivers finally meet and become one after running side by side for miles. Look down.'

He pointed to the river around them and Nora blinked. Sure enough, ahead of them the water seemed to cleave into two different shades. The dark, almost black waters of the Rio Negro ran seamlessly alongside the coffee colour of the Amazon before blending into one behind them.

They stood in silence for a moment, taking in the remarkable feat of nature.

'I can't believe I've never seen this before,' she breathed.

'Today has been perfect.' Duarte turned and took her hands in his, gently sliding her wedding ring from her finger and holding it up to the light. 'But I have one last surprise.'

She frowned, looking down at the inner circle of the ring. A soft gasp escaped her lips. Despite them having barely a week to plan their small civil ceremony, he'd somehow managed to have the platinum band engraved with the date and time of when they'd first met. The moment he'd asked her to dance and she'd lost her heart to him.

'I wanted us to make our own vows here, because I feel like it symbolises everything I love about you. About us.'

'Darkness and light,' Nora murmured, smiling as tears filled her eyes.

'I love you, Nora Avelar.' He slid the ring slowly back onto her finger, his eyes never leaving hers. 'I love everything you have been through, and everything that makes you the woman you are today. I promise to love and honour you for the rest of our lives.'

Her hands shook as she removed Duarte's ring and pressed it gently to her lips. 'There's nowhere else I could imagine making my vows to you than here on the water. This is beyond perfect.'

She slid the ring back onto his finger, smiling as she looked up into his brilliant golden eyes. 'I promise to love and honour you, Duarte Avelar. *Para sempre.*'

'Para sempre,' he echoed, sweeping her into his arms to show her just how good for ever could feel.

* * * * *

THE CEO'S
IMPOSSIBLE HEIR

HEIDI RICE

To my dad, Peter Rice, where my love of
Ireland – and Irish heroes – began.

CHAPTER ONE

ROSS DE COURTNEY STRODE into the ancient chapel, having landed his helicopter five minutes ago on a clifftop on the west coast of Ireland.

The chapel was nestled in the grounds of his soon-to-be new brother-in-law's imposing estate—and currently decorated in glowing lights and scented winter blooms, and packed with a crowd full of people he did not know.

Soon-to-be, my arse.

A few of the assembled guests glanced his way as he headed down the aisle towards the happy couple who were in the midst of saying their vows—the groom dressed in a slate-grey designer suit and the bride, Ross's foolishly sweet and trusting sister, Katie, in a flowing white concoction of silk and lace.

His footsteps echoed on the old stone but were silenced by the thuds of his own heartbeat and the fury squeezing his chest.

Katie had asked him—very politely—in a message yesterday not to attend the ceremony. It was the first time she'd deigned to return any of his calls or messages for months. She had 'things to tell him' apparently—important things that needed tact and delicacy to convey—about her newly acquired fiancé, the Irish billionaire Conall O'Riordan who Ross had met exactly once, five months ago now, at the opera in London.

Tact and delicacy, my arse.

The man was a thug, a ruthless, controlling thug who, just like the first man Katie had married—when she was just nineteen and the boy had only a few weeks to live— was not nearly good enough for her.

He'd done the wrong thing, then. Objecting to Katie's foolish decision to marry Tom and then standing back and waiting for her to see reason. And of course she hadn't, because Katie was a romantic. So she'd gone ahead and married Tom. Tom had died, and Ross and Katie hadn't spoken for five years, until that fortuitous night at the opera in December. When her Irish fiancé—who Ross did not know from Adam—had all but attacked him.

Well, he wasn't making the same mistake twice. This time he refused to see his sister hitch herself to another man who might hurt her.

Maybe he had no right to intervene in her life. She was twenty-four now, not nineteen. And the truth was, he'd never been much of a brother to her... Mostly because he'd never even known of his half-sister's existence until she was fourteen and her mother—one of his father's many discarded mistresses—had died. He'd tried to do the right thing then, paying for expensive schools and then college and publicly acknowledging her connection to the De Courtney family. Something his father in his usual cruel and selfish way had resolutely refused to do while he was still alive.

Even though they'd never been close, he couldn't let her marry O'Riordan, without at least making his feelings known.

More heads turned towards him as he approached the altar, the words of the ceremony barely audible above the thunder in his ears.

Personally, he would not have chosen to do this on the day, at the ceremony, like some scene straight out of a gothic novel or a Hollywood movie. But Katie had left him with no choice. She hadn't replied in any detail to the texts and emails he'd sent her trying to re-establish contact after their disastrous reunion at the opera five months ago. Her insistence she was going ahead with this wedding because she was madly in love with O'Riordan hadn't reassured him in the least.

Had the man cast some kind of a spell over his sister, with his money and his looks—or worse, was he a man like their father, who exerted a ruthless control over the women in his life?

The ceremony was reaching its peak when a young woman caught his eye, standing to the right of the groom holding the hand of a little boy dressed in a miniature suit.

Her wild red hair was piled on top of her head and threaded through with wild flowers.

The shot of heat and adrenaline and recognition that blasted into him was so fierce his steps faltered—and for one hideous moment he was back at the Westmoreland Summer Ball four years ago, dancing with the beautiful woman who had enchanted and mesmerised him that night.

Is it her?

He couldn't see her face, just her back, her bare shoulders, the graceful line of her neck, the seductive curve of one breast, the slender waist and long legs. He dragged his gaze back up, and it snagged on her nape again, the pale skin accentuated by the tendrils curling down from her hairdo.

He shook his head, tried to focus, the heat so real and all-consuming it momentarily obliterated his common sense.

Don't be ridiculous. It can't be her. This is your memory playing nasty tricks on you at a time of heightened emotion, which is precisely why you avoid this kind of drama, wherever possible.

The girl, whose name he'd never even known, had captivated him that night. Her quick, caustic wit delivered in a musical Irish accent and her bright, ethereal beauty—all flowing russet hair, translucent skin and piercing blue eyes—had momentarily turned him into an intoxicated and rapacious fool.

The heat kicked him squarely in the crotch as he recalled what had happened later that night, in the estate's garden. The fairy lights had cast a twinkle of magic over her soft skin as he'd devoured her. The subtle scent of night jasmine and ripe apples had been overwhelmed by the potent scent of her arousal as he'd stroked the slick heart of her desire. Her shattered sobs of pleasure had driven him wild as he'd eventually plunged into her and ridden them both towards oblivion…

They'd ended up making love—or rather having raw, sweaty, no-holds-barred sex—against an apple tree, not thirty yards from the rest of the party.

But what had seemed hopelessly hot and even weirdly romantic—given that he was not a romantic man—had turned first into an embarrassing obsession… After she'd run off—deliberately creating some kind of hokey Cinderella fantasy, he'd realised later—and he'd searched for her like a madman… And had then hit the cold, hard wall of reality three weeks later, when she'd contacted him on a withheld number, believing she could extort money out of him with the calculated lie he had got her pregnant.

And thus had ended his hot Cinderella fantasy.

Except it hadn't quite, because he still thought about her far too much. And, damn it, still had this visceral reaction when he spotted random women in crowds who had similar colouring or tilted their heads in a similar way. It was mortifying and infuriating, and seriously inconvenient. How typical he should be struck down by that deranged response now, when it could cause him maximum damage.

'If any man or woman knows of any lawful impediment why these two should not be joined in holy matrimony, speak now or for ever hold your peace.'

The priest's voice rang out, jolting Ross out of the memories and slamming him back into reality.

He dragged his gaze away from the offending bridesmaid's neck and forced the heat in his groin into a box marked 'get over yourself'.

He stood for a second, suspended in time, furious at being forced into such a public display, but at the same time knowing he could not let this moment—however clichéd—pass. Katie had left him with no choice.

'I object,' he said. And watched Katie and the mad Irishman swing round.

Gasps echoed throughout the crowd. And Katie's eyes widened. 'Ross? What are you doing here?'

Her groom's brows drew down in a furious frown. One Ross recognised from five long months ago at the opera the first time the man had laid eyes on him. The concern for his sister's welfare, which had been twisting his gut in knots for seven hours during the flight across the Atlantic, turned to stone.

You think I give a damn about your temper, buddy? No way am I letting you marry her until I know for sure you're not going to hurt her.

'What am I doing here?' he said, as conversationally as he could while the concern and the fury began to strangle him. 'I'm stopping this wedding until I can be sure this is what you really want, Katie,' he said, glad clarity had returned to his thoughts after the nasty little trick his memory had played on him.

But then the strangest thing happened: instead of saying anything, both Katie and her Irish groom turned to their left—ignoring him.

'Carmel, I'm so sorry,' his sister whispered.

'Mel, take Mac out of here,' the madman said in a voice that brooked no argument.

But then Ross turned too, realising the comments were directed at the young woman he had spotted a few moments before.

Recognition slammed into him like a freight train.

Her fierce blue eyes sparkled like sapphires—sheened with astonishment. The vibrant red hair only accentuated the flush racing over her pale features... And stabbed him hard in the chest.

The heat raced back, swiftly followed by a wave of shock. The concern that had been building inside him for hours now, ever since he'd made the decision to fly across the Atlantic, then pilot a helicopter to this godforsaken estate in the middle of nowhere to protect his sister, turned to something raw and painful.

It is her.

'Mammy, who's yer man?'

Ross's gaze dipped to the little boy standing beside her. The childish voice, tinged with the soft lilt of the boy's homeland, cut through the adult storm gathering around them.

The shock twisted in his stomach and his heartbeat slowed, the emotions rising in his chest becoming strangely opaque—almost as if he had walked into a fog and couldn't find his way out again. He took in the child's striking blue-green eyes, round with curiosity, his perfect little features, and the short blond curls rioting around his head, but all he could see was himself, aged about four, in the only picture he'd ever seen of himself as a child with his mother. Before his hair had darkened. And she had died. A photo his father had taken great pleasure in burning in front of him, when he was being sent off to boarding school.

'Stop snivelling, boy. Your mother was weak. You don't want to be weak too, do you?'

'What…?' The word choked out, barely audible as his gaze rose back to the woman's face, the horror engulfing him. 'How…?'

No. No. No.

This could not be true. This could not be happening. This was a dream. Not a dream. A waking nightmare.

He pressed his fingers to his temples, his gaze jerking between her and the child.

This toddler could not be his… His mind screamed in denial. He had taken the ultimate precaution to prevent this eventuality. He would not believe it.

She wrapped her arm around the boy's shoulders, to edge the child behind her and shield him from Ross's view.

'It's okay, Mac,' she said, the smoky voice he recognised edged now with anger but no less seductive—her stance defiant and brave as she straightened to her full height, like a young Valkyrie protecting her offspring. 'This man is nobody.'

He stepped towards her, determined to do… Something!

Who the hell are you kidding?

He had no clue what to do! The shock was still reverberating through him with such force, his sense of time and place and his usual cast-iron control had completely deserted him.

A strong hand on his shoulder dragged him back a step. 'Get away from my sister, you bastard.'

He recognised the madman's voice, could hear Katie's straight afterwards, begging them both to calm down, but all he could do was stand and stare as his hot Cinderella lifted the child into her arms and headed towards the vestry.

She's running away from me again.

For a moment he was back in the orchard, still struggling to deal with the shattering orgasm as he watched her panicked figure disappear into the moonlight.

But instead of scrambling to throw off the drugging afterglow while zipping up his trousers so he could charge after her, this time, he stood frozen to the spot. The boy's gaze met his as the child clung to his mother's neck. The neck that had driven him wild all those years ago... And again just moments before.

'You need to leave.' The groom tugged him round. 'You weren't invited and no one wants you here.'

'Take your hands off me,' he managed as he broke the man's hold.

He swung back. He had to follow her, and the boy, but his movements were stiff and mechanical. His racing heart punched his chest wall, the residual surge of heat—always there when he thought of her—only disturbing him more.

O'Riordan grabbed his arm this time. 'Come back here, you son of a...'

Ross turned, his fist clenched, ready to swat the bastard like a fly, but he couldn't seem to think coherently, or coordinate his body, so when he aimed at the man's head, he missed.

The answering blow shot towards him so fast he had no chance to evade it. Pain exploded in his jaw, his head snapping back.

The fog darkened.

'That's an impressive right hook,' he murmured, holding his burning face, a metallic taste filling his mouth as he staggered backwards.

The cries of assorted guests and Katie's tear-streaked

face were the last things he was aware of as he collapsed into an oddly welcome oblivion.

But as he dropped into the abyss, one last coherent thought tortured him.

How can she have given me a child...when I can never be anyone's father?

CHAPTER TWO

'GET OUT OF my way. You said yourself there are no signs of a concussion, so I would like to leave now.'

'But Mr De Courtney, I think it's best if you rest a while. You're clearly exhausted.'

'I'm not staying.'

Carmel O'Riordan stood in the hallway of Kildaragh Castle's east wing, stricken by the buzz in her abdomen at the sound of that deep, authoritative voice as Ross De Courtney argued with the paramedic Con had called after their uninvited wedding guest had been carried to this bedroom on the second floor.

She sank back against the wall, eavesdropping on the conversation, and tried to get up the guts to walk into the room… And confront her past.

The wedding had gone ahead, and now the reception was in full swing downstairs. But she still hadn't got over the shock of seeing Ross De Courtney again. Or discovering that Mac's father—a man whose identity she had never revealed to anyone, least of all her brother Conall—was also her new sister-in-law's brother.

She pressed damp palms to the thin silk of her bridesmaid's dress. Her fingers were shaking, because she couldn't get the picture out of her head of Ross's face, those sharp iridescent blue-green eyes going wide with surprise then dazed with shock as he'd looked upon her son—*their* son—for the first time twenty minutes ago.

Would that memory be lodged in her brain now for all eternity? Like all the others that had derailed her so many times in the last four years?

The sight of Ross De Courtney—tall and debonair in a dark tuxedo illuminated by the soft glow of torch light in an apple orchard, his gaze locked on hers, his touch tender and yet insatiable. His scent musky and addictive. His voice low with command and thick with desire. Each recollection gilded by the devastating heat and the wayward emotions that had intoxicated her.

She'd been such a fool that night, having gatecrashed Westmoreland's famous ball on the outskirts of London with her college friend Cheryl. All the way there in the car Cheryl had borrowed, they'd been busy joking about finding a billionaire to marry.

But then the joke had turned on her.

Ross De Courtney had been so handsome, so hot, so sophisticated and so into her—enjoying her bolshy sense of humour, never taking his eyes off her... He'd made her feel special and so, so grown up. After years of being desperate to feel like a woman instead of a girl, and finally get away from her brother Conall's overprotective custody, it had been so easy to believe it had all been real... Instead of a trick of the sultry summer night, her idiotic naiveté and her hyperactive hormones, which had homed in on him the minute she'd walked into the party and seen him standing alone. Ross had been moody and intense and hopelessly exciting—like Heathcliff and Mr Darcy and that vampire fella from *Twilight* all rolled into one.

She could still feel his touch on her skin, that sure, urgent excitement that had flowed through her like an electric current and made her do stupid things.

But then she'd run away, like an immature little fool.

And hadn't even given a thought to protection until three weeks later, when her period had failed to arrive.

'Now where the hell are my shoes?'

The brittle words from inside the room cut through Carmel's brutal trip down memory lane.

She swallowed around the lump forming in her throat and curled her fingers into fists to stop them shaking. She couldn't stand in the hallway for ever. She needed to face this man. Truth was, she probably didn't have that long before Conall came barging up the stairs to 'protect' her. Katie might have an amazing effect on her brother, but even she wasn't going to be able to hold him back for ever when he was in 'mother bear' mode.

Her brother had crossed so many lines. He'd hired a damn private detective to discover the identity of the man she had always refused to name. When he'd discovered Ross De Courtney was Mac's daddy, he'd then hired Ross's sister Katie as an event planner for their sister Imelda's wedding to her childhood sweetheart, Donal, in December. But he'd never really intended for Katie to plan a wedding. What he'd *really* been about was finding a way to get vengeance on the man who had fathered her son. A vengeance Carmel had never asked for and Conall had no right to claim.

But then, instead of getting vengeance on Ross, Conall had fallen in love with Katie. And now Ross was integrated into her and Mac's lives—for ever—by virtue of his relationship to Conall's new wife.

The fact that neither Con nor Katie had thought to tell her any of this before *their* wedding had infuriated her downstairs. But now all she felt was numb. And scared.

Ross De Courtney had rejected Mac before he was even born. Had accused her of lying about the pregnancy in a single damning text—the shock of which had taken her years to overcome. But she'd never forgotten a single word of his cruel instant reply after she'd worked up the courage to inform him of her pregnancy.

If you're pregnant, the child isn't mine. So if this is an attempt to extort money from me you're all out of luck.

How was she going to protect Mac from that rejection now? When Ross De Courtney was so closely related to her brother's wife?

But he hadn't looked dismissive or angry twenty minutes ago when he'd first set eyes on Mac. He'd looked absolutely stunned.

She needed to get to the bottom of that look, because it made no sense. Not only that, but that devastating text didn't make quite so much sense now either.

He'd accused her of terrible things, it was true, things she hadn't done. But there was no mistaking, she had come on to him that night.

He hadn't stolen her innocence, as her brother Conall liked to assume. She'd offered it to him, willingly.

She'd flirted with him mercilessly. She'd revelled in the role of virgin temptress and the way he'd made her feel. But as soon as the afterglow had faded, and the emotional impact had come crashing in on her, she'd run— like the little girl she was.

Virgin temptress, my butt. Virgin eejit more like.

All of which left enough grey areas now to make her question the conclusions she'd drawn about her child's father. What if he wasn't the out-and-out villain she'd assumed him to be? Whatever way she looked at it, the man was Mac's father. Had she been a coward to avoid addressing that reality in the years since? Coasting along on the assumption he didn't want to know his son thanks to one text. What if he had genuinely believed Mac wasn't his? She hadn't even considered that possibility before.

Had simply assumed he'd wanted to be rid of her, hadn't wanted to live up to his responsibilities and had found the cruellest possible way to dump her and forget about that night.

But what if the truth were more complicated?

She tapped her clenched fist against the door. 'Can I come in?' she said, steeling herself against the inevitable reaction as she stepped into the room, without waiting for a reply.

She hadn't steeled herself enough.

Sensation blindsided her as Ross De Courtney's head turned, and those vivid eyes fixed on her face. She took in his dishevelled appearance—the half-open shirt speckled with blood revealing a tantalising glimpse of chest hair, the scuffed trousers, the shoeless feet, the roughened chestnut hair furrowed into haphazard rows, and the darkening bruise on his jaw.

She drew in a sharp breath to reinflate her lungs.

How could the man look even more gorgeous now than he had that night? How was that fair?

He didn't say anything, he simply stared at her, the harsh line of his lips flattening. There was no antagonism there, but neither was there welcome. And it occurred to her for the first time that, however incredible their one night together had been—and it *had* been incredible— Ross De Courtney had always been impossible to read.

He'd been focussed solely on her that night, but she'd never for a moment known what he was thinking. And that disturbed her even more now.

'Ms O'Riordan, perhaps you can talk some sense into my patient.' The middle-aged paramedic who stood beside Ross spoke and she noticed him for the first time. 'I believe Mr De Courtney should rest a bit...'

'It's okay...um... Joe, is it?' she said, gathering enough of her wits about her to read the poor harassed paramedic's name badge. 'You can leave us. If Mr De Courtney shows any signs of blacking out again, I'll call you immediately.'

The older man glanced at his reluctant patient, then nodded. 'Fine, I'll be leaving you to it, then.'

The door closed behind him with a dull thud, which reverberated in her chest.

Was she the only one who could feel the awareness crackling in the air like an electrical force field? The last time they'd been alone together, she'd still been struggling to cope with the after-effects of an orgasm so intense she was sure she must have passed out herself for a moment.

An orgasm from an encounter that had produced the most precious thing in her life.

The significance of that now though, and the fact she could still feel the residual heat from that encounter so long ago, only increased her fear. She clamped down on the agonising swell of sensation and the tangle of nerves in her gut as she held out her hand to indicate one of the suite's armchairs. A hand she was pleased to see trembled only slightly.

'Do you want to take a seat, Mr De Courtney?' she said, drawing on every last ounce of her composure to maintain some semblance of dignity.

'*Mr* De Courtney?' he said, his tone more sharp than surprised. '*Really?*'

'I'm trying to be polite,' she snapped as the strain took its toll.

Seriously? Did he want to make this even tougher than it was already?

'Why?' he asked, as if he really didn't know.

'Because my mammy insisted upon manners at all times, and I'm trying to live by her example,' she snapped back, because an inane question deserved an inane answer. 'Don't be an *eejit*. Why do you think?'

'I don't know,' he said, looking a lot more composed than she felt. 'That's why I asked.'

'Okay, then, if you want plain speaking it's because polite seemed preferable to punching you on the jaw again,' she said, even though it wasn't aggression she felt towards him but something much more confusing.

There were a myriad emotions running through her, and not one of them was as simple as anger. Unfortunately.

He looked away, then tugged his fingers through his hair. 'I wouldn't blame you if you did,' he murmured, the resignation as clear as the frustration.

'Why would you say that?' she asked, far too aware of the livid bruise spreading across his jaw. 'Con shouldn't have hit you. He had no right.'

However confusing her emotions were towards this man, she had a new appreciation of him now after asking his sister Katie downstairs if she thought her brother was a bad man… Because she had needed to know his sister's opinion before she confronted him.

And Katie's reply, while angering Conall—who had decided Ross De Courtney was a villain of the first order—had been a lot more nuanced. Apparently she and Ross had been estranged for five years—after her marriage to her first husband, which Ross hadn't approved of. But she had pointed out he had acknowledged her as a teenager as soon as he discovered her existence and paid for a string of expensive schools and governesses. So, although they had never been close, it had surprised Katie when Conall told her that Ross had refused to acknowledge Mac.

Ross had come to Kildaragh to stop the wedding. Carmel had no idea why exactly but, given the obvious animosity between him and Conall as soon as he had appeared, she suspected it stemmed from some misguided desire to protect his sister from a marriage to her brother. The man had no knowledge of why her brother had reacted so aggressively towards him all those months ago when they first met, so that much at least made some sort of sense.

'He had every right,' Ross said, as his gaze locked back on hers. He searched her face, sending that disconcerting heat through her again. 'He's your brother.'

'That's madness,' she said, suddenly a little tired of the big brothers' code of honour. What gave men the right to make decisions about the women in their lives? And wasn't it beyond ironic he should support Conall's Neanderthal behaviour—given that he appeared to have come to Ireland to protect his sister from the same. 'Con did not have the right to interfere in my—'

'Is the boy mine?' he cut into her diatribe, slicing right through her indignation to the tender heart of the matter.

It hurt her to realise he didn't sound happy at the prospect, merely resigned.

She straightened.

'Yes, Mac is your son,' she said, refusing to be cowed by his underwhelming reaction.

Mac was the best thing to have happened to her, ever. A sweet, kind, funny, brave and bold little fella who was so much more than just someone's son. Maybe this man didn't feel the same way about him. But then he didn't know him… And, she had realised in the last hour, she had to take some of the responsibility for that. 'We can do a DNA test if you still don't believe me,' she snapped.

'That won't be necessary,' he said, taking the offer at face value and apparently unconcerned by the caustic tone. 'He looks just as I did at that age.'

He sat down heavily in the chair she had indicated. Not sat, so much as collapsed, as if all the breath had been yanked out of his lungs. He ran his fingers through his hair again, scraping it back from his forehead.

She noticed the exhaustion for the first time, in the bruised smudges beneath his eyes, the slumped line of his broad shoulders. And despite the anger she wanted to feel towards him, all she could feel in that moment was pity.

Because he didn't look resigned any more, he looked shattered.

She took the seat across from him, her legs shaky now too. She thought she'd been prepared to deal with this rejection again. Might even have hoped for it, as she made her way up to the suite, with every possible outcome from this meeting bouncing through her brain. Did she really want to allow Ross De Courtney a role in Mac's life? Wouldn't it be better if he didn't want to be Mac's father? Had no interest in getting to know him? Then she wouldn't have to deal with all the messy emotions of forming a relationship with a man who had devastated her once already. Or figure out if he should be a part of Mac's life. Because no matter whether he was Mac's biological father, that didn't give him any rights, in her opinion, unless she decided he was worthy of that place.

Wouldn't it be much easier not to have to make any of those decisions? To just go on as before?

But somehow, seeing his reaction, all she felt was devastated that he had no concept of how precious Mac was.

'Why were you so convinced I was lying,' she asked, attempting to keep her thoughts on Mac—and what was best for him, 'when I texted you?'

His head rose and she saw something flash in his gaze before he masked it. Regret? Sadness? Pain? It was impossible to tell.

He stared back at his hands, now clasped in his lap. His shoulders tightened into a rigid line. And she sensed the battle being waged. He didn't want to answer her question. But then he scrubbed his open palms down his face, cursed softly under his breath and straightened. The look he sent her was both direct and dispassionate.

'I did not believe the boy could possibly be mine, because I had myself sterilised, a decade ago, when I was twenty-one years old to avoid this ever happening.'

'You... What? But... *Why?*'

Ross could see the horror on Carmel O'Riordan's face. A face that had haunted his dreams for years, but, now it was in front of him, caused so many mixed emotions. All of them so far outside his comfort zone he was struggling to think with any clarity whatsoever.

She looked radiant, he thought, grimly. That vibrant russet hair, lit by the sunlight coming through the castle's casement windows, which made the red and gold tones even more vivid than they had been that night. Her pale skin was sprinkled with freckles he hadn't noticed four years ago in the moonlight. Had she covered them with make-up?

'Why would you do such a thing at such a young age?' she asked again.

He dragged his gaze away from her beauty. He'd fallen under that spell once before, and it had led them both here.

'A lot of reasons,' he said. Reasons he had no intention of elaborating on. He hadn't even wanted to tell her of the procedure he'd had done as soon as he could convince a doctor he knew what he was doing. But he figured he owed her the truth, to explain—if not condone—the mistakes he'd made four years ago. 'Anyway, my reasons are irrelevant now, because the procedure obviously didn't work.'

Once he got back to New York, he would have himself properly checked out. He'd never done any of the follow-up appointments. At the time he'd told himself he was far too busy, dealing with taking over the reins of De Courtney's and trying to drag it into the twenty-first century after his father's death. But looking back now, he could admit he'd found the constant prodding and poking emasculating—which would be ironic if it weren't so pathetic. He'd made the decision he did not ever want to get a woman pregnant, but he'd seen no need to dwell on it. He'd been a young man after all, foolish and impulsive and arrogant. As long as he could still get an erection, he had been more than happy after the effects of the operation had worn off.

And now he was a father. Responsible for another human life, who shared his DNA, and who would carry on the De Courtney line whether he wished it to be carried on or not. Although even that seemed a total irrelevance now. The reasons he'd based his decision on so long ago were all completely beside the point now that a little boy existed with his face and his blood…

'You don't…' He looked up to see her already pale skin had become ashen. 'You don't have some kind of genetic disease, do you? That you didn't want to pass on?'

'No.' *At least, not a biological one.*

'Oh, thank goodness.' Her shoulders slumped with relief. And he realised she had been terrified for her son. He waited for her to repeat her question about why he'd done it, but she surprised him. 'Do you think you might have other children you don't know about?'

The tremulous question, delivered in a gentle whisper, forced him to engage again, and answer her, when the thing he most wanted to do was disengage.

It had always been so much easier to deny his demons even existed, and now he was going to be forced to face them by a woman who could turn his insides to molten lava with a single breathless look.

The heat swelled and glowed in his abdomen, as it had an hour ago, when he'd got fixated on the back of her neck.

What was that even about? How could he still want her, when she had just turned his life upside down and inside out?

Nice try, you bastard. It wasn't her that did this, you did it to yourself. By being an arrogant, careless, entitled idiot who thought he could control his own fate.

'No,' he murmured. 'There won't be any others. You're the only woman I've ever had unprotected sex with,' he added, then stared back at his hands, aware of the pulsing ache in his jaw from her brother's punch as he clenched his teeth against the tidal wave of shame.

Exactly how desperate had he been to have her that night? Why hadn't he observed any of the danger signs, when he'd become so enchanted, so mesmerised, so addicted to her sultry smoky laugh, her quick wit and irreverent humour, that soft melodic accent, the earthy scent of her arousal?

Carmel O'Riordan was a stunning woman. Even more beautiful now than she had been then—but what the heck had got into him that night to make him forget every one of his own rules? And so quickly? Why had he been focussed solely on the need to plunge into her, to claim her, brand her, make her his? Because his behaviour had been nothing short of deranged, and he was very much afraid he still hadn't got a good firm grip on his attraction to her even now.

'Well, I guess that's good to know,' she said.

She brushed the tendrils back from her face, the nervous gesture oddly endearing.

He unlocked his jaw, to say what he should have said as soon as she came in.

'I owe you an apology, for that text,' he said. 'It was

unforgivable.' He threaded his fingers through his hair for about the five thousandth time that day gathering the courage to get it all out. 'And I owe your brother an apology too.'

Her brows launched up her forehead. 'Why on earth would you owe Con an apology?'

'I came here today to talk some sense into my sister, convinced Conall O'Riordan was a violent, volatile, controlling man who might do her harm, based on our one chance meeting in London months ago. I'm guessing now that at the time we met at the opera he already knew my connection to you, and his nephew?'

She nodded. 'Yes, apparently he did, he hired a private detective to find out your identity after I refused to tell him who you were. The arrogant—'

'I see,' he said, to halt her insults, not sure why the fact she hadn't divulged his name all those years ago should make the ache in his jaw move into his ribcage.

Why hadn't she told O'Riordan who he was when she found herself pregnant and alone? And why hadn't she ever followed up that text to demand a DNA test? All this time she had been surviving without any support from him... And okay, perhaps she didn't need his financial support—after all, her brother was a wealthy man—but still, the child had always been his responsibility, not her brother's. No wonder the man had looked as if he wanted to castrate him all those months ago in London. He'd had good cause.

'It doesn't matter how your brother discovered my identity,' he continued, rubbing the spot on his chest where the ache had centred.

He'd spent his whole life, determined not to be like his father, not to be as cruel or callous or controlling. Ross had prided himself on always keeping things light and non-committal with women, which was why his reaction to Carmel O'Riordan had bothered him so much. But he could see now how low he'd set the bar for himself, and with that text to Carmel—when she had informed him of her pregnancy—he'd failed to rise even to that pitiful level.

'The way your brother spoke to me that evening was not unprovoked as I had assumed. Nor was it born of a desire to isolate or control my sister's associations with me. Instead, he was motivated by a desire to protect you from a man he knew had wronged you, terribly.' He cringed inwardly. Good lord, the ironies just kept piling up. 'Which makes my presence here—and my attempt to interfere in your brother's marriage to my sister—wrong on every level.'

He stood and grabbed his jacket off the bed, the battle to maintain a semblance of control and ignore the claustrophobic weight starting to crush his ribs all but impossible. He needed time and space to deal with the emotions still churning inside him. Only then would he be able to figure out the best way to make amends, to her and her family and the boy. 'Which is my cue to leave, hopefully with more dignity than when I arrived,' he said. 'Although that could be a problem as I can't locate my shoes,' he added, the pathetic attempt at humour falling flat when her huge blue eyes widened and her brows rose further up her forehead. 'Perhaps you could speak to the paramedic and find out where he put them?'

'Wait a minute...' Carmel leapt to her feet—and placed her hands on her hips in a stubborn stance that accentuated her stunning figure in the slinky bridesmaid's dress.

The ache sank into his abdomen. *Great.*

'You're leaving?' she demanded. 'Just like that? Are you mad?' she said, her accent thickening.

Why did that fiery outrage only make her more irresistible? When he'd never been a man to appreciate any form of discord. Especially not with women he was dating… Not that he was dating her, he reminded himself, forcefully.

'What about Cormac?' she said.

'Who's Cormac?' he asked.

'Your son,' she snapped back with all the passion he could see sparking in her eyes.

Yes, of course.

He frowned, wondering how he had managed to forget about the huge elephant in the room, which was now pressing down on his chest again like a ten-ton weight. Score two to the heat pulsing in his pants. Yet more reason to be exceptionally wary of it.

'My legal team will be in touch as soon as I return to New York,' he said, determined to be as fair as he could be.

There was no way to repay her for what he had done, but he wanted to be as generous as possible. In fact, he would have to insist on it.

'If you'd like to make an accounting of your expenditure up to now, I will pay you the full amount…as I consider the error that resulted in your pregnancy to be mine. You can rest assured the maintenance I will pay for you and the boy going forward—and the trust fund I will set up for him—should ensure you and he will never want for anything ever again.'

CHAPTER THREE

AN ACCOUNTING? THE ERROR? What the actual...?

Carmel could feel her head exploding. She was so furious with the man in front of her, talking in that crisp, clear, completely passionless tone about her beautiful little boy—*their* beautiful little boy. Did he believe making an accounting of profit and loss would absolve him of his responsibilities as Mac's father? *Really?*

The outrage queued up in her throat like a stick of dynamite, stopping any coherent words from coming out of her mouth. She glared at him as he spotted his shoes under a chair and slipped them on, obviously intending to simply walk out of the door.

As he stepped past her she threw up her hands and slammed them against his chest, knocking him back a step. The ripple of reaction shot down her spine, at the flex of muscle and sinew, the whiff of his familiar scent—woodsy aftershave and soap—that got caught in her throat right beside the dynamite.

'Where do you think you're going?' she growled as the outrage exploded out of her mouth.

'Manhattan,' he offered.

'But you can't just go, this isn't over. I don't want an accounting. When did I ever ask you for money?' she shouted as her outrage grew like a wild beast.

She gripped his shirt front, far too conscious of the

awareness in his eyes and the electric energy flowing between them as his muscles tensed.

'You didn't,' he said, still calm, still dispassionate, even though the fire in his gaze was telling her he was as affected by the contact as she was.

He gripped her wrists, disengaged her hands from his torn shirt, but the feel of his thumbs touching her thundering pulse points sent her senses into overdrive—only making her more mad.

'But that's hardly the point,' he added, letting her wrists go to step away from her, as if she were a bomb about to detonate. 'I owe you a considerable amount for the boy's upkeep.'

'The boy has a name. It's Mac, or Little Mac, or Cormac when he's being naughty and I have to get stern with him.' She was babbling, but it was the only way to keep the outrage and the hurt at bay.

He blinked, as if the information was a complete anathema to him. 'I see,' he said, but she knew he really didn't see. There was so much she wanted to tell him about his child. Did he really not want to know any of it?

'And he doesn't need your money. What he needs is a father.'

He stiffened then, and his jaw tensed, his expression guarded. But she could still see the fire in his eyes. 'I'm afraid I can't offer him that,' he said, still not saying their child's name. 'I'm not capable of being anyone's father, other than in a financial sense.'

Oh, for the love of...

She cursed under her breath, suddenly sick of his platitudes and evasions.

'How could you possibly know that if you've never even tried?' she asked, exasperated now as well as angry.

Why did he have himself sterilised as a young man?

He hadn't given her an explanation, clearly hadn't

wanted to. But she found it hard to believe such a momentous decision could have been a frivolous one.

But still, he hadn't said he didn't *want* to be a father, he'd said he wasn't *capable* of being one. Which were two very different things. Maybe she was clutching at straws here, wanting to see more in him than was there. But there was a definite disconnect between a man who would fly thousands of miles to disrupt a wedding to save his sister from a man he believed might abuse her and the man who had barely spoken to the same sister in years. It made no sense. And Carmel had always been someone who had looked for sense in everything... Ever since her mother had taken her own life and everyone—her brother included—had resolutely refused to talk about it.

She hated secrets. She had always believed that talking about stuff openly and honestly was the only way to get to the heart of the matter and fix what was broken. Which was precisely why being unable to talk openly and honestly to her family, and more importantly her son, about his father over the last four years had been so damaging.

That ended now.

She had made mistakes too. Instead of allowing his one brutal text to make her a coward, and shielding her heart from more pain, she should have followed it up. Demanded to know why he had reacted so callously...

Well, she wasn't running any more.

'I don't need to try, when I know I won't be any good at it,' he said, through gritted teeth now, clearly holding onto his temper with an effort.

Good. Temper was better than the calm, controlled mask she'd been treated to so far—with his brittle apologies and his complete failure to explain his motivations. He was going to have to do a lot better than that before he'd be rid of her.

'How do you know?' she tried again.

'Because I just do,' he said, as stubborn as ever.

'Well, I don't believe that.' He'd never even met Mac, so how could he possibly know whether they would bond or not? But she didn't say as much. Because she had no intention of letting him bond with her precious child before she knew a lot more about him. But one thing she did know was that she was not about to let him buy off his paternal responsibilities as Mac's father either. The way he had clearly done with his fraternal responsibilities when he found out about his sister's existence. According to Katie, Ross had paid for expensive schools, tutors, governesses, even college, but he had never given her much of his time.

'No one knows if they'll be any good at parenthood until they have to do it,' she added. If all he felt right now towards Mac was responsibility, that was at least a start. Something they could work with. 'You have to learn on the job. Do you really think I thought I could be a mother at nineteen?'

His eyes widened and he winced. 'You were *nineteen* that night?' He ran his fingers through his hair, the blood draining out of his face. 'Good God, you were a child.'

'Nonsense,' she shot back.

He's worse than Conall. Men and their white knight complexes!

'I was a woman fully grown, with a woman's wants and needs…' Maybe she'd been naïve and foolish, and more than a little starstruck by him. But she'd known full well what she was doing and she'd enjoyed every second of it. Until the emotional consequences had hit home. 'And I believe I proved it rather comprehensively. As I recall, you were as well satisfied as I was that night,' she added, something about his concern making her feel like that reckless girl again. 'In fact, I should probably thank you,' she added, unable to stop herself from rubbing it in. 'I've heard tell from friends that a woman's first time is rarely as good as you made mine.'

'You were a virgin as well?' He hissed the words, shock turning to horror.

'Not for long,' she said, feeling like the badass she was when he cursed and slumped back into the chair.

Holding his head in his hands, he groaned. 'I'm surprised your brother didn't take out a contract on me after he found out my identity,' he said. 'Right now, I'd like to take one out on myself.'

The abject regret in his voice, the flags of shameful colour on his tanned cheeks had her going with instinct and reaching out to touch his shoulder. 'There's no need to take on so over it,' she said. 'When I was the one who came on to you?'

Yes, she'd been a little younger than him and hopelessly inexperienced, but she'd wanted to lose her virginity that night. And it had been spectacular, so she had no regrets about that much.

'Did you?' he said, his brows flattening in a grim line.

The doubt in his tone should have annoyed her more. She'd known her own mind that night, and she refused to let him take that power away from her just because he'd been her first and she'd been younger than he thought. But his gallantry was also intriguing. For a man who professed to be incapable of parenthood, he seemed to have a strong moral code.

'I'm not sure you did,' he said. 'All I can remember is I wanted you more than I'd ever wanted any woman before as soon as I set eyes on you. Damn it, Carmel, I took you against a tree your first time. Without using protection and without properly checking how old you were. It sickens me to even think of it.'

'You asked me my age twice, and both times I lied,'

she supplied, her heart pulsing strangely alongside the heat that refused to dim at the force in his statement.

'I wanted you more than I'd ever wanted any woman before as soon as I set eyes on you.'

So she *had* been special to him, at least in one respect. Good to know she wasn't the only one who had been blindsided by their physical chemistry.

'You did everything short of asking me for my ID,' she continued. 'As I had a very good fake one on me, even if you had, it wouldn't have done any good.'

'If I asked you twice, I must have suspected you weren't telling me the truth,' he said. 'Can't you see how wrong that is?'

'No, I can't.' She stood and strode across the room, suddenly needing to move, the pulsing at her core threatening to become as distracting now as it had been then.

It didn't matter if their chemistry was still strong, indulging it again was not an option. Not when their son would be caught in the middle. All of which meant talking about the events of that night—however satisfying she found it to goad him—probably was not a good idea, because it brought those needs and desires back into sharp focus.

She had a vibrator to quench that thirst now. She didn't need him. Or any man, and it would be best if she remembered that.

'But anyway, we're getting off the point,' she said, suddenly desperate to turn the conversation back to the matter at hand.

'What *was* the point exactly?' he asked.

'That I'm not going to let you give me or Mac any of your money.'

'What? That's preposterous.' He stood and crossed the room towards her. She held her ground, determined not to be swayed—even though she didn't know another man who wore righteous indignation as well.

Really, had he ever looked hotter? With his torn shirt and the stormy expression in those vivid aquamarine eyes finally making him look how she had always remembered him. Gone was the dispassionate control of moments ago, the brittle apology and the chilling cruelty of that text. This was the man she had met that night—exciting, forthright, determined and, oh, so passionate.

Okay, passion is so not the issue here, Mel.

Getting past that chilling control was what mattered, because she wanted to know him, not the masks he wore.

'On the contrary, we've just established how much I owe you,' he said. 'Not just for the child but also for what I did to you that night.'

The child? Why couldn't he say their son's name?

'In fairness, we've established no such thing,' she pointed out. 'All we've established is that you have a white knight complex almost as overdeveloped as my brother's. And that you think you can rid yourself of your paternal responsibilities to Mac by putting them into a neat little box called expenses paid. Well, I'm telling you, you can't.'

'What the hell does that even mean? I'm the boy's father. I have a responsibility towards him. And to you for what I took from you that night.'

'And as I've told you just now, you took nothing from me that I was not willing to give. And you gave me the most precious thing in my life in return, so you can consider that column already paid off.'

'Stop being deliberately facetious.' He glared at her, his expression thunderous. 'That's not what I'm offering and you know it.'

Oh, yes, it is, Ross, why can't you see that?

She stifled the wave of sympathy at how emotionally obtuse he appeared to be. And went for the jugular.

'If you don't wish to have a relationship with Mac, I'll certainly not force you to have one. The last thing I want is a father for my son who isn't interested in being one.' She knew what that was like, because her own mother had struggled to bond with her and Imelda and even Con. It hadn't been her mother's fault. But that didn't alter the awful effect her mother's emotional neglect had had on her and her siblings.

Con had closed himself off to emotion, Imelda had become lost in her own fantasy world. And she'd become wild and difficult, and hopelessly self-destructive. Because buried deep in her subconscious had been the certainty there must have been something terribly wrong with her if her own mother couldn't love her. Of course, she had come to see more clearly, after becoming a mother herself, it was her mother's depression that had robbed them both of that crucial connection.

She would never willingly subject her son to the same neglect, if something similar afflicted Ross that he was unwilling or unable to address. But that said, there was enough that didn't add up to make her wonder if Ross *could* be a father despite his protestations...

'Then what are we even arguing about?' he asked, even more exasperated.

'Simply this. If you're not prepared to be a father to Cormac, you can leave now and never see or speak to him or me again. But if you do that, I will not allow you to give him money. No maintenance, no trust fund, no generous allowance. Mac needs a daddy, not a piggy bank. You can be both, or you can be neither. And that's my final word on it.'

'*Your* final word?' Ross had to clench his teeth to stop himself from yelling, so frustrated, and frankly furious, he would not have been surprised if actual steam had started pouring from his ears.

Good God, she was the most incorrigible, intractable and stubborn woman he'd ever met. So intractable she seemed determined to harm herself as well as her son's best interests simply to make some asinine point.

'Yes,' she said, her chin popping out as if she needed to reiterate said asinine point. 'Take it or leave it.'

Right now, what he'd like to do was kiss that stubborn pout off her lips until she…

He cut off the insane direction of his thoughts as the damning heat spread through his system like wildfire.

Great, he was actually losing his mind. It was official.

He turned his back on her and crossed the room to stare out of the window. The waves crashed onto the rocks below them, echoing his turbulent mood.

Terrific, even the damn landscape is mocking me now.

He dragged his fingers through his hair, trying to calm his breathing, and dowse the heat once and for all so he could think.

At this rate, I'll be lucky if I'm not bald by the end of today.

He shoved his hands into the pockets of his trousers, far too aware of her standing behind him, waiting for an answer.

Unfortunately, she had him over a barrel. Even if she didn't know it yet.

Because there was no way in hell he could simply walk away from this situation, now. Not with his sense of honour intact. Not after everything that had transpired four years ago—and his damning role in it. Because that really would make him as much of a monster as his father.

He'd destroyed Carmel O'Riordan's innocence four years ago.

Perhaps she had been willing and able to make her

own decisions despite her youth and lack of experience... But he had exploited the physical connection between them ruthlessly, kissing and caressing her fragrant flesh in every place he knew would stoke her desire to fever pitch. That her artless, eager response had managed to set fire to his own libido—until he'd lost every ounce of his usual caution—was ultimately his responsibility too, because she'd had no idea at the time what she was doing to him.

To compound his crimes, he had then treated her appallingly with that knee-jerk text and there was also the boy to consider. A helpless, innocent child who hadn't chosen this situation. The only way he could live with himself was if he provided the boy—his son—with all the support he could ever need. Financially, at least.

So how did he persuade her he was not capable of being a father, that her son would be much better off without him in his life? He supposed he could explain the truth about his legacy, the barren emotional landscape of his own childhood. But he had humiliated himself enough for one day already with the confidences he'd been forced to share. And he suspected even if he told her the truth about his upbringing and how unsuitable it made him for the role she wished him to consider, it wouldn't be enough. Because Carmel O'Riordan appeared to be as stubborn as her brother's right hook.

Not only that, but he had no desire to unearth memories he had buried a lifetime ago.

He blew out a breath, struggling to calm the wayward emotions churning in his gut and find a tangible solution to the impasse. His gaze focussed on the rhythm of the surf, as it crashed against the rocks below, then retreated down the beach of the small cove.

The spring sunshine glinted off the water, the vibrant green Ireland was famous for carpeting the cliffs and spreading over the castle's gardens. A few guests from the wedding were milling about near the entrance to the chapel. His gaze snagged on a small child with a couple, the woman noticeably pregnant. His heart stilled, his exhaustion and frustration momentarily forgotten as he watched the child, so active and carefree, dashing backwards and forwards as the man—a strapping redhead who looked uncomfortable in his suit—chased after him while the woman directed the action and appeared to be finding it extremely amusing. He squinted, the gritty fatigue making his eyes smart.

Wait a minute, is that boy...?

He turned swiftly away from the window, the pressure on his chest increasing, to find Carmel watching him with a disturbing intensity—almost as if she could see into his thoughts.

Good luck with that, he thought, careful to keep the turmoil of emotions off his face.

And suddenly, he knew the only solution to this impasse was to show her exactly what kind of emotional connections he was and was not capable of.

With her hip cocked and her arms crossed, her stance accentuated her lithe figure. The sun shone off her haphazard hairdo and gave her fair skin a lustrous glow. But this time, instead of steeling himself against the inevitable spike to his libido, he welcomed it.

He could do sex. He couldn't do commitment. He never had—which was why that energetic, carefree little boy was much better off without a man like him in his life. That was the truth of the matter, and the only truth Carmel O'Riordan needed to understand.

She was clearly a smart and forthright woman. It was one of the things he'd found so compelling about her that night, her ability to speak her mind with wit and courage and refreshingly little thought to the consequences.

It had amused him and intrigued him and aroused him immensely, perhaps because he had always been forced to guard his own emotions so carefully.

But—although she'd had to grow up far too fast in the years since—she still seemed to be hopelessly naïve about men.

'I think the problem we have, Carmel, is that you don't know me,' he ventured. 'We've had one...' *Exciting? Mind-blowing? Cataclysmic?* He cleared his throat, to give himself time to search for the appropriate adjective. 'Diverting night together. And not much else. Perhaps you should spend some time with me? Then you'd realise I'm not a man you would want in your life long-term.' He stepped closer and touched his thumb to her cheek. She sucked in a breath, her eyes darkening, as he hooked one errant tendril behind her ear, then forced himself to drop his hand. The contact had been electrifying, just as he had expected it would be, making his point for him admirably. 'Nor am I father material.'

It was a dare, pure and simple. A dare he doubted she would accept.

The spark was still there, waiting to explode all over again. And given what that had led to last time, how could she afford to risk reigniting the flame?

She gave her head a slight shake, as if she had gone into a trance and was waking up again. He watched the emotions flit across her face—surprise, confusion, yearning...and panic as the penny dropped.

Bingo.

However naïve she was, or inexperienced she had been then, she knew full well they would both be playing with fire if she accepted his offer.

He pressed his hands back into his pockets, to resist the powerful urge to touch her again. And ignored the strange ambivalence at the realisation she would not accept his impulsive offer.

But then her true-blue eyes sparkled with the same recklessness he had once admired so much and her lips pursed in a thin line of determination.

'I accept, I think that's a grand idea,' she said. 'Spending time with you in your home would be the best way to assess your lifestyle as well as your suitability to be a daddy to Mac. I can come with you today if you'd like as Mac is already supposed to be spending this week with my sister, Immy, and her husband, Donal, while I finish a commission. Would it be okay if I brought my paints with me, so I can work?'

'You want to come with me? Today?' he said, astonished not just by her reckless decision, but also by the brutal wave of arousal. 'And stay for a week?'

'Yes. Where do you live?' she asked.

'New York,' he croaked, the blood diving south as he envisioned her in his condo in Tribeca. It was a big space, but hardly big enough to house them both without him being far too aware of her presence. He'd never invited any woman into his home for any length of time. Sleepovers at his apartment and the occasional weekender at his estate in the Hamptons were fine, but nothing more than that. When it came to women, he preferred to hold all the cards. But it already felt as if he had somehow dropped the ace.

'Really? I've never been to New York before. I've heard it's glorious.' She pushed her hair back from her face, the flush lighting her cheeks and the nervous gesture suggesting she wasn't as composed as she was making out—which was some consolation, but not much.

'I'll need a bit of time to pack and square things with Mac and my family.' She huffed out a breath. 'Especially Conall. When do you want to leave?'

He stared at her. She was actually serious. She intended to come and spend a week with him in New York.

A part of him knew at this point he should call her bluff. Rescind the offer, because he had no real desire to open up his life or his motivations to her scrutiny, but something stopped him. Perhaps it was the emotional fatigue finally getting to him after the seven-hour overnight journey to Ireland on a mission to protect the sister he'd barely spoken to in years. Perhaps it was the shock of seeing the woman who had haunted his dreams for so long again and discovering he was a father, against all the odds. Or maybe it was the residual heat still humming in his groin. But whatever it was, he couldn't seem to think anything but... *To hell with it.* Perhaps this really was the best way to persuade her he could never be a father to her son.

'I'd like to leave as soon as possible,' he said. If she was coming, she needed to know her visit would be on his terms, not hers. 'Can you be ready in an hour?'

'Give me two,' she said. 'I'd like you to meet Mac before we leave. We won't tell him who you are. Not yet. But it should keep us both focussed on why we're doing this.'

Ya think?

Exactly how naïve was she? Did she really think him coming face to face with the boy would be enough to kill this incessant heat?

'Sure,' he said, deciding meeting the boy would be a good first step in persuading her he knew absolutely nothing about children.

But as she left the room, his gaze snagged on the subtle sway of her hips in the figure-hugging bridesmaid's gown and the heat swelled again.

Wonderful. The next week is going to be nothing short of torture and you have only yourself to blame.

CHAPTER FOUR

'YOU'RE NOT GOING. I won't allow it. Have you lost your mind?'

Mel glared at her older brother, feeling her hackles rising fast enough to break the land-speed record. If there was one thing Conall had always been an expert at, it was making her mad.

'Er...hello, Con? I'm a grown woman, and this is not your decision,' she replied, channelling a certainty about the trip she didn't remotely feel.

With Con's tie and tuxedo jacket gone and his skin slightly flushed from one too many toasts during the wedding feast, he should have looked more relaxed, but the muscle twitching in his jaw was suggesting the opposite. He'd stayed away from her meeting with Ross, given her the privacy she'd asked for. And she had to give him credit for that—or rather give Katie credit for it. Because she suspected Con's new wife had managed to drum some sense into him, and also provided a gorgeous distraction. Her new sister-in-law stood beside Con now, looking completely stunning in her wedding dress—and apparently not remotely concerned at the two of them for ruining even more of her special day with their family drama.

'You're also a mother,' her brother added, his tone darkening. 'Have you thought of that, now?' he finished, slicing right to the heart of her insecurities. Another of her brother's specialities.

She'd never left Mac for more than a night before. But they'd been building up to his week staying with Imelda and her husband Donal for weeks now—because her work had exploded in the last few months, and she had an important commission to finish. Conall was right, it would be impossibly hard to leave Mac for a week, but she also knew full well the separation was likely to be much harder for her than her son.

Mac had always been a supremely confident and outgoing child. And she had her family to thank for that. They'd always been close-knit as siblings, having been orphaned when she and her sister were only eight and six and Con a young man of eighteen. They'd had a fair few rocky moments and some major blow ups in the years after her mother's death—with Conall as their guardian giving up what was left of his youth to become a mother and father to both her and Immy. But when she'd come home from London pregnant and alone that summer— and broken by Ross De Courtney's rejection—Imelda and Con hadn't hesitated to step up and help her heal. Sure, they'd judged, especially Con, but they'd also offered their unconditional support. Because of them, and now Donal and Katie too, Mac understood he was part of a much bigger unit than just the two of them. Surely that explained why he was such a robust, well-adjusted little guy, despite being the son of a nineteen-year-old single mum who'd had no clue what to do when he'd first been put into her tired arms after six excruciating hours of labour.

She knew how lucky she was to have such a solid, unwavering support network—and she was grateful for it. But she also knew that if there was a chance Mac could have a father of his own, she wasn't wrong to explore that possibility. She'd already spoken to Imelda in detail about her plans to contact Mac every day over a video app—and if Imelda reported any signs of distress, she would come straight back to Ireland on the next flight.

But having Con look at her with that accusatory glare in his eye had her confidence wavering.

'Of course, I know that, Con,' she said with a firmness she didn't feel. 'But I'm doing this for Mac to see if there's a chance Ross can be a father to him,' she said, but she could hear the defensiveness. And the questions she hadn't wanted to address—ever since Ross had touched her and the yearning had exploded inside her—whispered across her consciousness.

What if spending time with Ross De Courtney made that hunger worse? A hunger she'd had no practice in controlling because, not only had she never felt such a thing for another man, she'd never had sexual relations with any other man either.

'Ah, so going off to spend a week with your ex-lover is in your son's best interests now, is it?' Conall said, scepticism dripping from every word. 'That sounds mighty convenient to me.'

She stared at him, wanting to be furious with his implication, but not quite able to be... Because, what if he was right? And that shocking blast of heat and yearning *was* the real reason she'd decided to accept Ross's invitation? An invitation that she was sure had been born of frustration rather than intent.

She'd hate herself if she was subconsciously harbouring some secret notion to get Ross De Courtney into her life, as well as her son's. It would make her sad and pathetic and weak. And totally misguided. Because if the man wasn't father material, he certainly wasn't cut out for any other form of committed relationship. But worst of all, it would remind her of the little girl she'd once been, wanting her mother to love her, even though she could not.

'Conall, stop,' Katie said gently but firmly, interrupting the panicked questions multiplying in Carmel's head. 'Carmel has every right to make decisions for herself and Mac without having to deal with the third degree from you.'

'For the love of…' Con swore under his breath. Katie barely blinked. 'Katherine, why are you siding with her now?' Conall asked, sounding aggrieved. 'Maybe your brother isn't the total gobshite I thought he was,' he added, because Carmel had shared with them Ross's reasons for thinking he couldn't possibly be Mac's father— the news of his vasectomy at the age of only twenty-one having stunned them both into silence. 'But he's still not a man I'd trust with my sister for a week in a foreign country,' he added, speaking to his wife as if Carmel weren't standing right there, before levelling her with a look that teetered uncomfortably between concern and condescension. 'The man's a player, Mel, and a billionaire one at that, who's never had a serious relationship with anyone in his life, not even with his own sister,' he added. 'On that evidence, I'm not convinced he could ever be a halfway decent parent to Mac…'

'Fair point,' she interrupted him. 'But I want a chance to find out for my—'

'I get that,' Con said, cutting off her explanation. 'You want Mac to have his daddy in his life if at all possible. And maybe De Courtney will surprise us on that score. But is jetting off to New York with him so you guys can spend a cosy week…' he lifted his fingers to do sarcastic air quotes '…"Getting to know each other" really the way to go? What does that even entail? Are you going to be sharing a bed with him now?'

'Conall!' Katie gasped.

At exactly the same moment Carmel shouted, 'That's none of your business, Con.'

Of all the pig-headed, intrusive... How dared he?

Outrage flooded through her system, pushing away her doubts—and the echoes of that sad little girl—to remind her of the woman she had become. 'But just so you know, the answer is no.'

She was being ridiculous, she decided. So *what* if she was still attracted to Ross De Courtney? Surely it was to be expected. After all, he was the only man she'd ever had sex with. And he was... She took a steadying breath, aware of the liquid weight that had been there ever since he'd walked back into her life two hours ago now. Well, the man was a total ride and he always had been.

But the important thing here wasn't Ross De Courtney's hotness, it was the fact that she wasn't that starstruck, needy, reckless nineteen-year-old any more—nor was she the little girl without a mother's love. She was a mother herself now, with her own thriving online business doing pet portraits—and she'd had her heart broken once before by Ross. In short, she was all grown up now. She'd worked hard to build a life for her and her son, and there was no way she'd throw it all away for some cheap thrills. However tempting.

'Fine, I'm sorry.' The muscle in Conall's jaw softened and he had the decency to look contrite. 'I overstepped with that remark,' he murmured. 'It's just...' He drew close and gathered her into a hug. 'I'm your big brother. And I don't want to see you hurt by him again.'

She softened against him, the comforting scent of his cologne and the peaty smell of good Irish single malt whiskey gathering in her throat. Banding her arms around his waist, she hugged him back, aware of how far they'd come since that miserable Christmas morning when Con had found their mother dead...

She'd pushed her brother away so many times in the years after that dreadful event, especially as a teenager, when she'd acted out at every opportunity—to test his commitment, she realised now. They'd had some epic shouting matches as a result, but he'd always stuck regardless. Because Con wasn't just pig-headed and arrogant with a fiery temper that matched her own, he was also loyal to a fault and more resilient and hard-wearing than the limestone of the cliffs outside.

Her eyes stung as she drew back to gaze up at his familiar face. 'You've been much more than just a big brother to me, Con. So much more. And I appreciate it. But you've got to trust me on this. I know what I'm doing, okay?'

He drew in a careful breath and let it out slowly, clearly waging a battle with himself not to say any more on the subject. But at last he nodded. 'Okay, Smelly,' he said, using the nickname he'd first coined when—according to family legend—he'd had to change one of her nappies.

She laughed, because he knew how much she'd always hated that fecking nickname. Trust Con to get the final word.

But then he cupped her shoulders and gave her a paternal kiss on the forehead. 'I do trust you,' he murmured. 'And anyhow, if he hurts you again, I'll murder him. So there's that,' he added, only half joking, she suspected.

She forced her lips to lift in what she hoped was a confident smile as her eyes misted.

Now all she needed to do was learn how to trust herself with Ross De Courtney.

Grand! No pressure, then.

CHAPTER FIVE

ROSS STOOD ON the grass near the Kildaragh heliport, next to the company Puma he'd piloted from the airport in Knock to get to Conall O'Riordan's estate without delay what felt like several lifetimes ago, and braced as the O'Riordans headed towards him, en masse.

Carmel had changed out of the silky bridesmaid's dress into a pair of skinny jeans and a sweater, which did nothing to hide the lush contours of her lean body.

He stiffened against the inevitable surge of lust and shifted his gaze to the child—whose hand was firmly clasped in hers. The boy was literally bouncing along beside her, apparently carrying on a never-ending conversation that was making his mother smile.

The pregnant lady and the man he had spotted earlier in the gardens—who Ross had been informed by Katie were the other O'Riordan sibling, Imelda, and her husband, Donal—followed behind them. Conall O'Riordan, Ross's sister, and two footmen carrying a suitcase and assorted other luggage, brought up the rear.

He nodded to Katie as the party approached. He'd spoken to his sister ten minutes ago—a stilted, uncomfortable conversation, in which he'd apologised for disturbing her wedding and she'd apologised for not telling him sooner about his son's existence.

His sister sent him a tentative smile back now, but as

Carmel approached him with the boy Katie held back with her husband and in-laws, making it clear they were a united front. United behind Carmel, and Ross was the outsider.

His ribs squeezed at the stark statement of his sister's defection. Even though he knew it was his own fault. He'd never been much of a brother to her, to be fair. He should have repaired the rift between them years ago. But thoughts of his sister disappeared, the pang in his chest sharpening, as Carmel reached him with the child.

'Hi, Ross. This is Cormac,' she said. She drew in a ragged breath. 'My son,' she added, her voice breaking slightly. 'He wanted to say hello to you before we left.'

'Hiya,' the little boy piped up, then waved. The sunny smile seemed to consume his whole face, his head tipped way back so he could see Ross properly.

Ross blinked, momentarily tongue-tied, as it occurred to him he had no idea how to even greet the boy.

Going with instinct, because the boy's neck position looked uncomfortable, he sank onto one knee, to bring his gaze level with the child's. 'Hello,' he said, then had to clear his throat when the word came out on a low growl.

But the boy's smile didn't falter as he raised one chubby finger to point past Ross's shoulder to the helicopter. 'Does the 'copter belong to yous?' he asked, the Irish accent only making him more beguiling.

Ross glanced behind him to buy himself some time and consider how to respond, surprised by the realisation that, even though this would most likely be the only time he would ever talk to his son, he wanted to leave a good impression... Or at least not a bad one. 'Yes, it belongs to my company,' he said, deciding to stick with the facts.

'It's bigger than my uncle Con's 'copter,' the little boy shot back.

Ross's lips quirked. 'Is it, now?' he replied, stupidly pleased with the comment.

At least I've managed to best Conall O'Riordan with the size of my helicopter.

The little boy nodded, then tipped his head to one side. 'Does it hurt?' he asked, his fingertip brushing across the swollen area on Ross's jaw.

Ross's throat thickened, the soft, fleeting touch significant in a way he did not understand. 'A bit.'

'It looks hurty,' the boy said. 'Mammy says it's naughty to hit people. Why did Uncle Con hit you?'

'Um, well…' He paused, completely lost for words. The tips of his ears burned as a wave of shame washed through him at the thought of how he and O'Riordan had behaved in front of this impressionable child. What an arse he'd been to take a swing at the man. 'Possibly he hit me because I tried to hit him first,' he offered, knowing the explanation was inadequate at best. 'And missed.'

'Cormac, remember Uncle Con told you it was a mistake and he's sorry.' Carmel knelt next to the boy. 'And I'm sure Ross is sorry too,' she added, sending him a pointed look.

Ross remembered how she'd mentioned she always addressed her son by his full name when he was being disciplined. But the child seemed unafraid at the firm tone she used, his expression merely curious as he wrapped an arm around his mother's neck and leaned into her body.

'I am sorry,' Ross said, because her stern look seemed to require that he answer.

'Yes, Mammy, but…' the little boy began, turning to his mother and tugging on her hair. 'Still it *was* naughty now…'

'Mr De Courtney, we'll need to leave soon if we're going to make our departure time from Knock,' his co-pilot interrupted them.

'Okay, Brian, thanks.' Ross rose back to his feet. 'If you wish to say your goodbyes, I'll wait in the cockpit,' he said to Carmel, suddenly eager to get away from the emotion pushing against his chest—and the child who could never be a part of his life.

'Okay, I'll only be a minute,' Carmel said, the sheen of emotion in her eyes only making the pressure on his ribcage worse.

He dismissed it. What good did it do? Being intrigued by the boy? Moved, even? When he wasn't capable of forming a relationship with him?

'Goodbye, Cormac,' he murmured to the child, ignoring the fierce pang stabbing under his breastbone.

'Goodbye, Mr Ross,' the boy replied, with remarkable gravity for a child of such tender years. But as Carmel took her son's hand, to direct him back towards her family and say her goodbyes, the little boy swung round and shouted. 'Next time yous come we can play tag. Like I do with Uncle Donal.'

'Of course,' he said, oddly torn at the thought he'd just made a promise he would be unable to keep... Because there would never be a next time.

'I think, in the circumstances, it would be best if we call a halt to this trip. I can have the helicopter take you back to Kildaragh.'

Carmel swung round to find Ross standing behind her in the private jet they'd just boarded at Knock airport. He looked tall and indomitable, and tired, she thought as she studied him. She waited for her heartbeat to stop fluttering—the way it had been for the last thirty minutes, ever since she had watched him speak to their son for the first time. She needed to get that reaction under control before they got to New York.

'Why would it be best?' she asked.

They'd travelled in silence after she'd bid goodbye to Mac and her family, the noise of the propellors too loud to talk as Ross had piloted the helicopter down the coast to Knock airport. She'd been grateful for the chance to collect her thoughts, still reeling from the double whammy of seeing Ross talk to Mac—and saying goodbye to her baby boy for seven whole nights.

She knew something about luxury travel—after all, her brother was a billionaire—but even so she'd been impressed by how quickly they'd been ushered aboard De Courtney's private jet, which had been waiting on the tarmac when they arrived. But she'd sensed Ross's growing reluctance as soon as they'd boarded the plane, the tension between them only increasing. The smell of new leather filled her senses now as she waited for Ross to reply.

His brow furrowed. 'Surely it's blatantly obvious after my brief conversation with the boy—this trip is pointless?'

'I disagree,' she said, surprised that had been his take away from the encounter.

Certainly, he'd been awkward and ill at ease meeting his son. That was to be expected, as she would hazard a guess he had very little experience of children. But she had also noticed how moved he'd been, even if he didn't want to admit it. And how careful.

'Mac likes you already,' she said, simply.

His frown deepened. 'Then he's not a very good judge of character.'

'On the contrary,' she said, 'he's actually pretty astute for a three-year-old.'

He shoved his hands into the pockets. 'So you still wish to accompany me?' he asked again.

'Yes, I do. If the offer is still open,' she said, suddenly knowing the conversation they were having wasn't just about their son. Because the air felt charged. On one level, that scared her. But on another, after seeing him make an effort to talk to his son openly and honestly, it didn't.

Perhaps he was right. Perhaps this trip was a lost cause. After all, a week was hardly long enough to get to know anyone. Especially someone who seemed so guarded. But she was still convinced she had to try… And she was also coming to realise that there was more at stake here than just her son's welfare.

Didn't she deserve to finally know what had made her act so rashly all those years ago? She'd thrown herself at this man that night, revelled in the connection they'd shared, and a part of her had always blamed herself for that. Maybe if she got to the bottom of why he had captivated her so, she might be able to forgive that impulsive teenager for her mistakes. And finally let go of the little girl she'd been too, who had looked for love in places where it would never exist.

She waited for him to reply, her breath backing up in her lungs at the thought she might have pushed too hard. It was one of her favourite flaws, after all. And knowing she would be gutted if he backed out now and told her the trip was off.

The moment seemed to last for ever, the awareness beginning to ripple and burn over her skin as he studied her.

His eyes darkened and narrowed. Could he see how he affected her? Why did that only make the kinetic energy more volatile?

'The offer is still open,' he said, at last, and her breath released, making her feel light-headed. But then he stepped closer and touched his thumb to her cheek. He slid it down, making the heat race south, then cupped her chin and raised her face. 'But I should warn you, Carmel. I still want you,' he said, his voice rough with arousal. 'And that could complicate things considerably.'

Her lips opened, her breath guttering out, the anticipation almost as painful as the need as her gaze locked on his and what she saw in it both terrified and excited her. It was the same way he had looked at her all those years ago—focussed, intense—as if she were the only woman in the whole universe and he the only man.

She licked arid lips, and the heat in his gaze flared.

'Do you understand?' he demanded.

She nodded. 'Yes, I feel it too,' she said, not ashamed to admit it. Why should she be? She wasn't a girl any more. 'It doesn't mean we need act on it.'

He gave a strained laugh—then dropped his hand. 'Perhaps.'

'Mr De Courtney, the plane is ready to depart in ten minutes if you and Ms O'Riordan would like to strap yourselves in,' the flight attendant said, having entered the compartment unnoticed by either of them.

Ross's gaze lifted from her face. 'Thank you, Graham. I'm going to crash in the back bedroom. Make sure Ms O'Riordan has everything she needs for the duration of the flight.'

The attendant nodded. 'Of course, sir.'

Without another word to her, Ross headed towards the back of the plane.

She gaped. Had she just been dismissed?

The attendant approached her. 'Would you like to strap yourself in here and then I can show you to the guest bedroom when we reach altitude?'

'Sure, but just a minute...' she said, then shot after her host.

She opened the door she had seen Ross go into moments before. And stopped dead on the threshold.

He turned sharply at her entry, holding his torn shirt in his hand.

Oh. My.

She devoured the sight of his naked chest, her gaze riveted to the masculine display as the heat blazed up from her core and exploded in her cheeks.

The bulge of his biceps, the ridged six-pack defined by the sprinkle of hair that arrowed down beneath the waistband of his trousers, the flex of his shoulder muscles—were all quite simply magnificent.

'Was there something you wanted?' he prompted.

'I… Yes.' She dragged her gaze to his face, the wry twist of his lips not helping with her breathing difficulties, or her burning face. She sucked in a lung full of air and forced herself to ask the question that had been bothering her for nearly an hour. 'I just wanted to ask you, what made you kneel when you met him? Mac, that is?' she managed, realising the sight of his chest had almost made her forget her own son's name.

He threw away his shirt, clearly unbothered by his nakedness. 'Why do you want to know that?'

'It's just… You say you don't know anything about children. But it was thoughtful and intuitive to talk to him eye to eye like that. I was impressed. And so was Mac.'

'Hmm,' he said, clearly not particularly pleased by the observation. 'And you think this makes me a natural with children, do you?' he said, the bitter cynicism in the tone making it clear he disagreed.

'I just wondered why you did it,' she said, letting her own impatience show. The jury was still out on his potential as a father, and she only had a week to decide if she wanted to let him get to know her son. But she didn't see how they could make any progress on that unless he was willing to answer a simple question. 'That's all.'

'I'm afraid the answer is rather basic and not quite as intuitive as you believe,' he said, still prevaricating.

'Okay?' she prompted.

He sighed. 'My father was a tall man. His height used

to intimidate me at that age. I didn't wish to terrify the boy, the way my father terrified me. Satisfied?'

'Yes,' she said, the wave of sympathy almost as strong as the spurt of hope.

Perhaps this didn't have to be a lost cause at all.

He began to unbuckle his belt, his gaze darkening. 'Now I suggest you leave, unless you want to join me in this bed for the duration of the flight.'

'Right.' She scrambled out of the room, slamming the door behind her.

It was only once she had snapped her seat belt into place that it occurred to her she was more excited by his threat than intimidated by it.

Uh-oh.

CHAPTER SIX

WHAT AM I even doing here?

Carmel stood at the floor-to-ceiling window of Ross De Courtney's luxury condo and stared through the glass panes of the former garment factory at the street life below as Tribeca woke up for another day.

The guest room she'd been given was a work of art—all dramatic bare brick walls and vaulted arches, steel columns, polished walnut wood flooring and minimalist furniture, which included a bed big enough for about six people, and an en suite bathroom designed in stone and glass brick. The room even had its own roof terrace, beautifully appointed with trailing vines, wrought-iron furniture and bespoke lighting to create an intimate and yet generous outdoor space.

The views were spectacular, too. At seven stories up she could see the tourist boats on the Hudson River a block away and the New Jersey waterfront beyond, to her left was the dramatic spear of the One World Trade Center building, and below her was the bustle and energy of everyday New Yorkers—dressed in their trademark uniform of business attire and trainers—flowing out of and into the subway station on the corner or dodging the bike couriers and honking traffic to get to work, most of them sporting go-cups of barista coffee.

She knew something about luxury living from the

glimpses she'd had of her brother's lifestyle. But Ross
De Courtney's loft space, situated in the heart of one
of Manhattan's coolest neighbourhoods, was something
else—everything she had thought high-end New York living would be and more. But the edgy energy and purpose
of all the people below hustling to get somewhere—and
the stark modernity of the exclusive space she was staying in—only made her feel more out of place. And alone.

She'd been here for over twenty-four hours already,
after arriving on the flight across the Atlantic. And while
she'd spent a productive day yesterday—in between several power naps—exploring Ross's enormous loft apartment, the local area, and setting up a workstation with
the art supplies she'd brought with her in the apartment's
atrium, she'd barely seen anything of the man she'd come
here to get to know.

She sighed, and took a sip of the coffee she'd spent
twenty minutes figuring out how to brew on his state-of-
the-art espresso machine after waking up before dawn.

Thank you, epic jet lag!

He'd dropped her off late at night after their flight and
a limo ride from the airport, during which he'd spent the
whole time on his phone. Once they'd arrived at the apartment, he'd told her to make herself at home, given her a
set of keys and a contact number for his executive assistant, and then headed straight into his offices because he
apparently had 'important business'.

And she hadn't seen him since.

She didn't even know if he was in residence this morning. She'd tried to stay up the previous evening, to catch
him when he returned from work, but had eventually
crashed out at around eight p.m., New York time. And
slept like the dead until four this morning. She hadn't
heard him come in the night before, and there had been

no sign he'd even been in the kitchen last night during her adventures with the espresso machine this morning.

Is he avoiding me?

She took another gulp of the coffee, the pulse of confusion and loneliness only exacerbated by the memory of her truncated conversation over her video messaging app with her baby boy five minutes before.

'Mammy, I can't talk to yous. Uncle Donal is taking me to see the horses.'

'Okay, fella, shall I call you tomorrow?'

'Yes, bye.'

And then he'd been gone, and Imelda had appeared, flushed and smiling. 'Thanks so much for letting us have him for the week, Mel,' she'd said as she cradled her bump. 'We need the practice for when this little one arrives and he's doing great so far. He went to bed without complaint last night.'

'Ah, that's grand, Immy,' she'd replied, stupidly tearful at the thought her little boy was doing so well. Even better than she had expected. And a whole lot better than her.

She missed him, so much.

Not seeing his face first thing when she woke up had been super weird. Especially now she was questioning why she'd flown all this way to get to know a man who didn't seem to want to know her. Or Mac.

'You must contact me if there's any problem at all,' she'd told her sister, almost hoping Imelda would give her the excuse she needed to abandon what already seemed to be a fool's quest. 'I can hop straight on a flight if need be.'

'Sure, of course, but Mac's grand at the moment, he hasn't mentioned missing you once,' Imelda had said, with typical bluntness. Then she had sent Carmel a cheeky grin. 'How's things going with Mac's uber-hot daddy?'

'I'm not here to notice how hot he is, Immy,' she'd replied sternly, aware of the flush hitting her own cheeks—at the recollection of Ross without his shirt on in the close confines of the jet's bedroom. 'I'm here to get to know him a bit better and discuss Mac with him, and his place in his son's life. That's all.'

'Of course you are, and that's important for sure,' her sister had said, not making much of an effort to keep the mischievous twinkle out of her eyes—which was even visible from three thousand miles away. 'But sure there's no reason now not to notice what a ride he is at the same time.'

Oh, yes, there is, Immy. Oh, yes, there is.

She pressed her hand to her stomach, recalling the spike of heat and adrenaline at her sister's teasing before she'd ended the call, which was still buzzing uncomfortably in her abdomen now. Trust Imelda to make it worse.

The loud ring of the apartment's doorbell jerked her out of her thoughts. And had hot coffee spilling over her fingers. She cursed, then listened intently as she cleaned up the mess and tiptoed to the door of her bedroom to peek out.

If Ross answered the door, she'd at least know if he was here. Then she could waylay him before he left again. Perhaps they could have breakfast together? Although the thought of Ross De Courtney in any kind of domestic setting only unsettled her more.

The bell rang a second time and then she heard something else… Was that a dog barking?

Surprise rushed through her, which turned to visceral heat as the man himself appeared on the mezzanine level above and padded down the circular iron staircase from the apartment's upstairs floor. In nothing but a pair of shorts and a T-shirt, with his hair sleep-roughened and his jaw covered in dark stubble, it was obvious the doorbell had woken him.

The buzz in Carmel's abdomen turned to a hum as he scrubbed his hands down his face before walking past her hiding place to the apartment's front door.

Her gaze fixed on his back as he began the process of unlocking the several different latches on the huge iron door and the dog's barks became frenzied.

The worn T-shirt stretched over defined muscles, accentuating the impressive breadth of his shoulders. Carmel's gaze followed the line of his spine to the tight muscles of his glutes, displayed to perfection in stretchy black boxers.

Then he opened the door and all hell broke loose.

Surprise turned to complete astonishment as a large, floppy dog bounded into the room, its toenails scratching on the expensive flooring, its barks turning to ecstatic yips.

'Hey, boy, you missed me?' Ross said, his deep voice rough as the animal jumped to place its gigantic paws on his chest. What breed was that exactly?

A smaller person would surely have been bowled over by the dog's enthusiastic greeting, but Ross braced against the onslaught, obviously used to the frenzied hello, and managed to hold his ground as the huge hound lavished him with slobbering affection.

Ross De Courtney has a dog? Seriously?

She waited, expecting him to discipline the dog, but instead he rubbed its ears and a deep rusty laugh could be heard under the dog's barking.

'Relax, Rocky,' he said, eventually grabbing the dog's collar and managing to wrestle it back onto all fours. 'Now, sit, boy,' he said, with all the strident authority of a Fortune 500 Company CEO. The dog gave him a goofy grin and ignored him, its whole body wagging backwards and forwards with the force of its joy.

'Rocky, sit!' The incisive command was delivered by

a small middle-aged woman dressed in dungarees and biker boots—her Afro hair expertly tied back in a multi-coloured scarf—who must have brought the dog and followed it into the apartment.

The dog instantly dropped its butt, although the goofy grin remained fixed on Ross as if he were the most wonderful person in the known universe.

'How the heck do you do that, Nina?' Ross murmured, sounding disgruntled as the woman produced a treat and patted the dog's head.

Carmel grinned, feeling almost as goofy as the dog, her astonishment at the animal's appearance turning into a warm glow.

Ross De Courtney has a dog who adores him.

'Practice,' the dog trainer said as she unloaded a bowl, a blanket and a lead from her backpack. After dropping them on the kitchen counter, she gave the dog a quick scratch behind the ears before heading back towards the door. 'You've gotta show him who's boss, Ross. Not just tell him.'

'Right,' Ross replied, still endearingly disgruntled. 'I thought I was.'

'Uh-huh.' The woman snorted, her knowing smile more than a little sceptical. 'Dogs are smart, they know when someone's just playing at being a badass.'

They had a brief conversation about plans for the coming week—Nina was obviously his regular dog walker and sitter and had been looking after Rocky while Ross was out of the country—before the woman left.

Carmel stood watching from behind the door to her room, aware she was eavesdropping again, but unable to stop herself. A bubble of hope swelled under her breastbone right next to the warm glow as she observed Ross interact with his devoted pet. Talking in a firm, steady voice, he calmed the animal down, rewarded him every time he did as he was told, and fed and watered him, before pouring himself a mug of coffee and tipping a large helping of psychedelic cereal into a bowl. The rapport between Ross and the animal—which Carmel eventually decided was some kind of haphazard cross between a wolfhound and a Labrador—was unmistakable once the dog stretched out its lumbering limbs over the expensive rug in the centre of the living area for a nap.

Questions bombarded her. How old was the dog? How long had it been his? Where had he got it? Because it looked like some kind of rescue dog. Definitely a mongrel crossbreed and not at all the sort of expensive pedigree status symbol she would expect a man in his position to own if he owned a pet at all. Especially a man who had insisted he didn't do emotional attachments.

The bubble of hope became painful.

Maybe it was the jet lag, or the emotional hit of her earlier conversation with Mac, or simply the weird disconnect of being so far away from home—and so far outside her comfort zone—with a man who still had the power to make her ache after all these years… But this discovery felt significant. And also strangely touching.

That Ross De Courtney not only had a softer side he hadn't told her about. But one he'd actively refused to acknowledge.

Ross gave a huge yawn, and raked his fingers through his hair, carving the thick chestnut mass into haphazard rows.

The swell of emotion sharpened into something much more immediate. And the hum in her abdomen returned, to go with the warm glow. She cleared her throat loudly, determined to ignore it.

Ross's head lifted, and his gaze locked on her.

The heat climbed into her cheeks and bottomed out in her stomach.

'You're up early,' he said, the curt, frustrated tone unmistakable. 'How long have you been standing there?'

The easy camaraderie he'd shown the dog had disappeared, along with his relaxed demeanour. He had morphed back into the brooding billionaire again—guarded and suspicious and watchful.

The only problem was, it was harder to pull off while he was seated on a bar stool in his shorts with a bowl of the sort of sugary cereal Mac would consider a major treat. She'd seen a glimpse of the man who existed behind the mask now and it had given her hope.

She walked into the room, brutally aware a second too late she hadn't changed out of her own sleep attire when his gaze skimmed over her bare legs—could he tell she wasn't wearing a bra? The visceral surge of heat soared.

But she forced herself to keep on walking. Not to back down, not to apologise, and most of all to keep the conversation where it needed to be.

'Long enough,' she said. 'So just answer me this, Ross. You have the capacity to love Rocky here.' The dog's ears pricked up at the sound of his name and he bounded towards her. She laughed at the animal's greeting, surprised but also pleased to see that up close he was an even uglier dog than she'd realised, one ear apparently chewed off, his snout scarred and his eyes two different colours—one murky brown, the other murky grey. 'But you don't have the capacity to love your own child? Is that the way of it?'

'It's hardly the same thing,' Ross managed, furious she had spied on him, but even more furious at the spike of arousal as his houseguest bent forward to give Rocky's stomach a generous rub and her breasts swayed under soft cotton. 'A dog is not a child,' he added, trying to keep his mind on the conversation, and his irritation. And not the surge of desire working its way south.

He'd stayed at work until late in the evening last night, catching up on emails and doing conference calls with some of De Courtney's Asian offices precisely so he could avoid this sort of scenario. He'd had plans to be out today as soon as Nina dropped off Rocky, but he'd overslept. And now here they were, both virtually naked with only a goofy dog to keep them sane. While he'd missed his pet, Rocky wasn't doing a damn thing to stop the heat swelling in his groin.

'I know, but surely the ability to care and nurture is not that different,' she said as he tried to keep track of the conversation and not the way her too short nightwear gave him a glimpse of her panties as she bent over—and made her bare, toned legs look about a mile long. 'All I'm saying is if you have the capacity to care for Rocky here, why wouldn't you have the capacity to care for Mac?' she said, scratching his dog's head vigorously and laughing when Rocky collapsed on the floor to display his stomach for a scratch—like the great big attention junkie he was.

Heck, Rocky, show a bit of restraint, why don't you?

'Hey, boy, you like that, don't you?' she said, still chuckling, the throaty sound playing havoc with his control. The dog's eyes became dazed with pleasure.

He knew how Rocky felt as he watched her breasts under the loose T-shirt—which shouldn't have looked seductive, but somehow was more tantalising than the most expensive lingerie.

Is she even wearing a bra?

The dog's tongue flopped out of the side of its mouth as it panted its approval, in seventh heaven now from the vigorous stomach rub.

Terrific, now he was jealous of his own dog.

He remained perched on the stool, grateful for the breakfast bar, which was hiding the strength of his own reaction.

She finished rubbing Rocky's belly, patted the animal and then rose, to fix that inquisitive gaze back on him. The forthright consideration in her bright blue eyes only made him more uncomfortable and on edge. Almost as if she could see inside him, to something that wasn't there… Or rather, something that he certainly did not intend to acknowledge.

'You didn't answer my question,' she said as she walked towards the breakfast bar.

He kept his gaze on her face, so as not to increase the torture by dwelling on the way the T-shirt barely skimmed her bottom.

When exactly had he become a leg man, as well as a breast man, by the way?

She perched on the stool opposite, hiding her legs at last.

This was precisely why he hadn't wanted to have her in his condo. Intrusive questions were bad enough, but the feel of his control slipping was far worse.

She cleared her throat.

'What was the question again?' he asked, because he'd totally lost the thread of the conversation.

'If you can form an attachment to Rocky, why would you think you can't form one to Mac?' she repeated, the flush on her cheeks suggesting she knew exactly where his mind had wandered. Why did that only make the insistent heat worse?

He took a mouthful of his Lucky Charms and chewed slowly, to give himself time to get his mind out of his shorts and form a coherent and persuasive argument.

He swallowed. 'A child requires a great deal more attention than a dog,' he murmured. 'And Nina spends almost as much time with Rocky as I do. Because I happen to be a workaholic.'

It was the truth.

He didn't have much of a social life, and that was the way he liked it. When he'd first taken over the reins of De Courtney's after his father's death he had resented the time and trouble it had taken to drag the ailing company into the twenty-first century, but he'd soon discovered he found the work rewarding. And he was good at it. Especially undoing all the harm his father had done with his autocratic and regressive approach to recruitment and training, not to mention innovation. The fact the bastard would be turning in his grave at all the changes Ross had made to De Courtney's archaic management structures was another fringe benefit. He'd never enjoyed socialising that much and had only attended those events where he needed to be seen. He had no family except Katie and he'd hardly spoken to her in years, and he had very few friends in New York—just a couple of guys he shared the occasional beer or squash game with. It was one of the reasons he'd moved to the US—he preferred his solitude and as much anonymity as he could have at the head of an international logistics conglomerate. And that just left his sex life, which he had always been careful to keep ruthlessly separate from other parts of his life.

All of which surely meant he wasn't cut out to be a father. No matter how easily he had bonded with Rocky, after finding the pup beaten and crying in a dumpster behind the apartment two summers ago. And he'd made a spur-of-the-moment decision to keep him.

But that hardly made him good parent material, not even close.

'That's true,' Carmel said, and nodded. 'A child does need your full attention at least some of the time. And I've already figured out how dedicated you are to your job.'

Something hollow pulsed in his chest, right alongside the surge of desire that would not die.

'I also live in New York, which would mean any time

I could give Mac would be limited,' he added, determined to press home the point—despite the hole forming in his chest.

Her pensive look faded, and her lips curved upward, the blue of her irises brightening to a rich sapphire. The hollow sensation turned to something raw and compelling.

'Do you know? That's the first time you've called Mac by his name,' she said, her voice fierce, and scarily rich with hope.

'Is it?' he said, staring back at her, absorbing the shock to his system as he struggled not to react to her smile.

Good grief, the woman was even more stunning when she smiled. That open and forthright expression of pure uninhibited joy was a lethal weapon... How could he have forgotten the devastating effect her spontaneous smile had had on him once before? The driving need to please her, to hear her laugh, something that had effectively derailed all his common sense four years ago.

He'd known it would be dangerous bringing her here. But the hit to his libido was nowhere near as concerning as the chasm opening up in his chest at the first sign of her approval.

'I think it's a very positive sign,' she said.

'I wouldn't read too much into it if I were you,' he said, trying to counter her excitement. But even he could hear the defensiveness in his voice.

Where was that coming from?

He didn't need her approval, or anyone's. He didn't need validation, or permission for the way he had chosen to live his life—avoiding forming the kind of emotional attachments she was speaking about. That hollow ache meant nothing. He'd stopped needing that kind of validation as a boy, when he'd discovered at a very young age his father didn't love him—and never would. That he was simply a means to an end. He didn't consider it a weakness, he considered it a strength. Because as soon as he'd finally accepted the truth, he'd worked on becoming emotionally self-sufficient.

And, okay, maybe Rocky had sneaked under his guard. But he didn't have room for any more emotional commitments. Why couldn't she accept that?

He opened his mouth to say exactly that, but before he could say any of it she said, 'You haven't said whether you want to be a father or not. Just that you can't be one.'

'I had a vasectomy when I was twenty-one,' he said, but even he could hear the cop-out in his answer. 'I think that speaks for itself.'

'Does it?' she said, far too astute for her own good, looking at him again with that forthright expression that suggested she could see right into his soul… A soul he'd spent a lifetime protecting from exactly this kind of examination, a soul that suddenly felt transparent and exposed. 'Because I'd say your reasons for having that vasectomy are what's really important, and you haven't explained them to me.'

'I didn't want to be a father,' he said flatly, but the lie felt heavy on his tongue, because she was right. It had never been about whether or not he *wanted* to be a father. He'd never even asked himself that question. It had always been much more basic than that. It had always been about not wanting to get a woman pregnant.

She crossed her arms over her chest, looking momentarily stricken by his answer. But then her gaze softened again. 'But now you are one, how do you feel about Mac?'

'Responsible. And terrified,' he said, surprising himself by blurting out the truth.

'Terrified? Why?' she pushed. The bright sheen of hope and excitement in her gaze—as if she'd made some important breakthrough, as if she had found something he knew wasn't there—only disturbing him more.

'That I'll do to him what my father did to me,' he said. 'And his father did to him. There's a legacy in the De Courtney family that no child should have to be any part of,' he said, determined to shut down the conversation.

But instead of her backing down, instead of her realising he was a lost cause—that he couldn't offer their son what didn't exist—the glow in her eyes only softened more.

'What did he do to you, Ross, that you would be terrified now to have a child of your own?' she asked.

The probing question, the glow of sympathy made the pain in his gut tangle with the need. And the hollow ache twisted—turning to impotent fury.

What right did she have to ask him questions he didn't want to answer? To probe and to push, to open the raw wound of his childhood and make that pain real again?

'He did nothing to me that I didn't get over a long time ago,' he said, his voice a husky growl, wanting to believe it.

'I don't believe you,' she said, her voice coming from miles away, through the buzzing in his ears. But then she reached across the breakfast bar and covered his hand with hers. Her touch—warm, deliberate, provocative, unashamed—ignited the desire like a lightning strike, turning the fury to fire.

He flipped his hand over and grasped her wrist before she could withdraw her hand. She jolted. Her pulse thundered under his thumb but her eyes darkened, the need there as visceral and volatile as his own.

He might have been embarrassed at how much he wanted her. But he could see she wanted him too. Why the hell had he worked so hard to ignore it? Giving into it again had seemed fraught with problems, but, frankly, how could this be any more problematic than it already was?

She was the mother of his son. And nothing was going to change that now. However much he might want to turn back the clock and take this commitment away—it was too damn late. Had been too damn late four years ago, when he'd plunged inside her without using protection and created a life.

She was right about that much at least. All his efforts to deny this connection weren't going to make it not so. That little boy *did* deserve a father. However inadequate he might be for the job, he would have to stop hiding. But he'd be damned if he'd bare his soul while he was at it. And he'd be damned if he'd deny the other connection they shared any longer—which had been taunting and tormenting them both as soon as he'd spotted her at the wedding.

Keeping hold of her wrist, he got off the stool and walked round the breakfast bar, not even sure what he planned to do any more, but feeling his emotions slipping out of his grasp again.

He stood in front of her, and tugged her off her stool, the force of his passion throbbing painfully in his boxers.

'I've got a child now and there's no changing that,' he admitted, knowing he'd been a coward not to acknowledge that before now. 'And you're right, whatever my misgivings, he deserves at least as much of my attention as Rocky. But right now, I don't want to talk about that.' And he certainly had no intention of ever sharing with her why he had struggled to come to terms with that truth. His childhood was ancient history. Unearthing it now would only make this transition more difficult.

Oddly the concession didn't fill him with panic as it had before. The child was bright, sweet, unbearably cute. He could never be a full-time father to the boy, and he would need to learn on the job, but maybe she was right about that too. She had been forced to figure it out. And if he could love Rocky, maybe he could find room in his heart to do a much better job than his father. Surely at the very least he couldn't possibly do as much harm. And he owed it to the lad to try. And to stop running.

'Because all I can think about is having you again.' He let his gaze roam over her face, then lifted one hand to cradle one heavy breast. He felt the nipple pebble into a hard peak beneath his thumb.

Yup, no bra.

'And tasting every damn inch of you that I didn't get to taste the first time,' he added, giving her fair warning.

He let her wrist go, giving her the choice.

But instead of pulling away, she looked him straight in the eye and then lifted up on tiptoes. She cupped his jaw, the trembling in her palm belied by the purpose in her eyes when she whispered against his lips, 'You don't scare me, Ross De Courtney.'

Then she clasped his face in her hands and pressed her lips to his.

He groaned as the fuse that had been lit long ago flared, sensation sparking through his body and turning the throbbing erection to iron. The need to claim her, to brand her as his, exploded along his nerve-endings, flooding his body like a river breaking its banks.

Grasping her waist, he lifted her into his arms, and carried her towards her guest bedroom, aware of the dog's playful barking through the pounding desperation.

His tongue thrust deep into the recesses of her mouth, gathering the sultry taste he remembered and taking control of the kiss.

He couldn't give her anything of real value. But he could give her this.

CHAPTER SEVEN

THE DOOR SLAMMED, cutting out the dog's bark. And Carmel found herself in her room alone with Ross, and the staggered sound of her breathing.

He let her go, her body sliding against the hard planes and angles of his, aware of the strident erection brushing her belly as she found her feet.

He kept his hand on her hip, holding her steady, her lips burning from the strength of his kiss.

This was madness. She knew that. But as she searched his face the pain she had glimpsed had been replaced with a fierce hunger. And the only way she could think of to free herself from that devastating feeling of connection was to feed it.

'Be sure,' he said, his voice as raw and desperate as she felt as his thumb brushed across her stinging lips with a tenderness, a patience she hadn't expected after that furious kiss.

'I am.' She nodded, struggling to speak around the lump jammed into her throat.

This was passion, desire, chemistry, part of a physical connection that had blindsided them both once before—it didn't need to mean more than that.

'Good,' he said, the word low with purpose.

But as his thumb trailed lower, slow, sure, steady, to

circle the nipple poking against the cotton, her breath released in a rush and her knees weakened.

Holding her waist, he bent his head to fasten his lips on the aching tip and suckle hard through the fabric.

She thrust her fingers into his hair as moisture flooded between her trembling thighs.

Don't think. Just feel.

Every sense went on high alert as he lifted the wet T-shirt over her head, threw it away.

He swore softly, seeing all of her for the first time.

She folded her arms over her naked breasts, the rush of shyness stupid but unavoidable. Her body wasn't as tight and toned as it had once been. Before Mac. And he was the first man now, the *only* man to ever see her naked.

'Don't…' He groaned, the rough tone part demand, part plea. 'Don't hide yourself from me,' he said, but made no move to touch her.

He wanted this to be her choice, she could see it in his eyes, the battle to hold himself back, to wait, as compelling as the need.

Don't think. Just feel. This is chemistry, basic and elemental, pure and simple.

She forced herself to unfold her arms and drop them to her sides. She arched her back, thrusting her breasts out, giving him the permission he sought. Refusing to be ashamed. Refusing to make this more than it was. Or ever could be.

This wasn't about the life they'd made together. She understood Mac had to be separate. Or she would be lost again, the way she had been once before. And she couldn't afford to be devastated again, by his rejection. She couldn't give him that power. Not now, not ever, when her little boy needed her whole. Always.

He scooped her up and placed her on the bed, then

hooked his thumbs in the waistband of her panties and drew them down her legs.

She lay fully naked now, panting, as his gaze roamed over her, burning each place it touched. She could hide nothing from him, the bright morning light through the windows showing every flaw and imperfection the pregnancy had wrought on her once perfect skin.

His fingertip touched the silvery scars on her belly, and she squirmed, feeling more exposed than she ever had before, the desire retreating to be replaced with something raw and disturbing.

But when his head rose and his eyes met hers, emotion swirled in the blue-green depths.

'I want… I want to see you naked too,' she managed, trying to find that assertive, rebellious girl again. The girl she'd been that night, bold and determined before the emotion had derailed her.

He let out a laugh, low and strained. Then levered himself off the bed and stripped off his T-shirt. The masculine beauty of his chest looked even more magnificent, if that were possible, than it had in the jet. The ripple of muscle and sinew, the defined lines of his hip flexors and the sprinkle of hair circling flat nipples and trailing through the ridged board of his abs were as breathtaking as they were intimidating. But then he dragged his shorts down.

The strident erection sprang out. And her breath backed up in her lungs.

How did I ever manage to fit that inside me?

The panicked thought only seemed to intensify the liquid fire at her core.

He climbed on the bed, clasped her chin in firm fingers to raise her gaze. 'What's wrong?'

The heat flooded her cheeks. She blinked and licked bone-dry lips, clearing the rubble in her throat.

'No...nothing. Everything's grand.'

A bit too grand really, she thought wryly. Not sure whether she wanted to laugh or cry at how gauche she felt.

He didn't know that he was the first—the only—man she had ever seen naked. That he was the only man who had ever been inside her. And she didn't want him to know, because that would only make her feel more vulnerable. And more like the frightened, overwhelmed girl she had been that night.

You're a woman now. Totally. Absolutely.

It didn't matter how little experience she still had of sex. She'd grown up in the years since that night in all the ways that mattered.

So stop blushing like a nun, you eejit.

'It's just... It's been a while now, since I've had sex,' she said, attempting to cover her gaffe. And feel less exposed to that penetrating, searching gaze. 'Being a mother is a full-time job.'

His lips crinkled in a rueful smile, only making her feel more gauche. The heat suffused her face like a forest fire.

'I can only imagine,' he murmured. 'Would you like me to slow down?'

She nodded, the emotion closing her throat and making her eyes burn, the comment reminding her of how he'd been that night. Passionate and provocative, yes, but also cautious and careful with her, until the need had overtaken them both.

Don't read too much into it. He's a pragmatic, methodical man. Why wouldn't he want to make it good for you?

'Tell me what you like,' he said.

She had no idea what she liked, but before she could come up with a creative lie he took the lead. His fingers skimmed down her body, circling her nipples.

Her back arched, the sensation shimmering again, the

mortification forgotten as he bent to lick at one turgid tip, then the other.

'That…' she choked out, bowing back, lifting her breasts to him, the need surging again—sure and relentless and uncomplicated. 'I like that a lot.'

The gruff laugh rumbled out of his chest and through her body. But before she had a moment to wonder what was so amusing, he captured the pebbled peak and suckled.

She launched off the bed, the sensation arrowing down to her core, making her writhe and squirm as he held her steady and played with the too sensitive peaks, nipping and sucking and licking until her tortured groans became sobs.

At last he lifted his head, to blow across her swollen breasts, the contact too much and yet not enough. Then he grasped her hips, and began to lick a trail down her torso heading towards…

Oh, God… Oh, no. Will he taste me there?

His tongue caressed, circling her belly button, trailing lower still.

'Ah… Oh, God… Yes…' Her sobs became moans, the need so intense now she could barely breathe, no longer think, the twisting deep in her belly tightening like a vice.

Holding her hips, he angled her pelvis. 'Open for me, Carmel. I need to taste all of you.'

Her thighs loosened as if by his command, and his tongue found the heart of her at last, licking at the bundle of frayed nerves, sending shockwaves through her body.

She sobbed, panted. One long finger entered her, stretching the tight, tender flesh. Then two, while his lips remained fastened on the core of her pleasure, the vice tightening to the verge of pain.

She bucked against him, riding those delving fingers, impaling herself, ignoring the pinch to let the pleasure build.

She cried out as his mouth suckled, the waves building and building, the vice cinching into one unbearable torment. Fire tore through her and she cried out as the wave crashed over her at last, blasting through every fibre of her being, sending her high, only to drop her down to earth, shattered and shaking, sweating and worn through.

Her eyelids fluttered open, to find him above her staring down, his eyes dark with a dangerous heat.

'You are so responsive,' he said. 'I adore watching you come.'

'I adore you making me come,' she said back, and was rewarded with a deep chuckle.

She hadn't meant to be funny, but somehow his amusement relaxed her. 'Do you have a condom?' she asked, desperate to feel him inside her now.

He nodded, the silent look reminding her of their aborted conversation about his vasectomy. The vasectomy that hadn't worked.

She'd touched a nerve there, she knew, asking him about his reasons for it. But when she'd reached for him a moment later, seeing the pain he'd been so determined to hide, it hadn't just been in sympathy. A part of her had wanted to ignite the heat, so she could forget that terrifying tug of connection.

He reached past her, delved in the bedside table, and found a foil packet. She watched, still shaky, still shattered, but oddly pleased to see how clumsy he was, how frantic he must be to have her too—to deny that connection as well—as he sheathed himself.

'I can't wait any longer,' he said.

She cupped his cheek, felt the stubble rasp against her palm, almost as raw as her emotions. 'Then don't,' she said, her voice sounding far away as the pounding in her ears became deafening.

Angling her hips, he notched himself at her entrance

and pressed inside, the slick heat from her orgasm easing his way despite the tightness.

At last, he was lodged deep, so deep she could feel him everywhere.

'Okay?' he asked.

'Yes,' she murmured.

And then he began to move. Slow at first, but so large, so overwhelming.

His harsh grunts met her broken sobs as the fire built again, even faster and hotter than before. She clung to his broad shoulders and focussed desperately on the sound of their sweat-slicked bodies.

The waves gathered again, like a storm now, sensation driving sensation, every nerve-ending raw and real and unprotected, the pleasure battering her.

He shouted out as she felt him grow even bigger inside her, touching every single part of her, but as she broke into a thousand tiny pieces she was very much afraid this time he had shattered more than just her body, because she could still feel the deep, elemental pulse of connection in her heart.

CHAPTER EIGHT

The afterglow did nothing to stop the thunderous pulsing in Carmel's ears as Ross rolled away from her, then
left the bed and walked into the en suite bathroom without a word.

The residual pulse of heat at the sight of his naked
backside, the defined muscles flexing, did nothing for her
galloping pulse. Or her shattered state of mind.

She dragged the bed's duvet up to cover herself.

Had she just done something phenomenally stupid,
because, despite two staggering orgasms in the space of
less than ten minutes, the emotions were still charging
through her system—too raw, too real—and the yearning hadn't diminished in the slightest.

She could hear the water running in the en suite bathroom. Should she get up? Get dressed? With her body still
humming from his caresses?

But worse than the physical impact on her body—
which felt a little bruised now, after the intensity of their
joining—was that devastating feeling of intimacy.

She had thought she wouldn't feel that again. Despite
her lack of experience she wasn't a virgin any more—
and she had new important priorities in her life now. But
somehow, where she had hoped for mindless pleasure,
what she'd got was far more dangerous. His care and attention had brought back so many memories from their

first night. He had been focussed on her pleasure first and foremost then too, and it had made her yearn for so much more. For things she couldn't have and shouldn't need any more.

He appeared in the doorway, a towel slung around his hips.

The inevitable blush spread across her chest and suffused her cheeks.

Wow, awkward, much? Perhaps she should have considered this before she had chosen to jump into bed with him. Because the easy out—to lose herself in sex—now appeared to be anything but.

Then again, she was fairly sure she'd stopped thinking all together the moment he'd grasped her wrist, the purpose and passion in his gaze searing her skin.

'How are you?' he asked.

'Grand.' She blinked, mortified by the foolish sting of tears. She kept the duvet clasped to her chest and struggled to sit up, feeling far too vulnerable in her prone position on the bed.

It was a bit late for regrets, but one thing she couldn't bear was for him to think this interlude had meant more to her than it should. She'd made a conscious decision to sleep with him again, and it had been mind-blowing. She refused to regret that decision now. She could handle the fallout now the afterglow had faded—because she wasn't that emotional wreck of a girl any more. She couldn't be.

'I should probably get to work on my commission,' she said, hoping he would take the hint and leave—so she could get what had happened into some kind of perspective. It was just a physical connection. No more, no less. Why should it interfere with their shared priorities now as parents?

After all, before they'd jumped each other, Ross had made a major concession there. By finally admitting he needed—even wanted—to have a relationship with his son. That was huge. And so much more important than anything else. She still didn't really understand why he had struggled so to accept his place in Mac's life, or indeed why he had wanted a vasectomy so young… What exactly had his father done to him, to make him so convinced he should never be a parent himself? But surely it was best she didn't know the whys and wherefores. Didn't probe into that lost look, which had resonated so strongly with the girl she'd been. She needed to protect herself now—couldn't let that needy girl back in. So all she really needed to know about that look was that he was prepared to move past it.

Instead of taking the hint, though, and leaving, Ross padded across the room's luxury carpeting and sat next to her on the bed. 'You're an artist, right?' he asked.

She swallowed, and nodded, surprised, not just by the intensity in his gaze, but the way it made her feel.

She'd told him about all her hopes and dreams that night—at the time, she'd been in her first term at art school with grand plans of becoming the next big thing on the Irish art scene—and he'd listened with the same intensity. In the years since—after she'd had to give up those dreams, or rather tailor them into something more useful—she'd dismissed his interest that night too. The thoughtful questions, the admiration in his gaze when she described her passions, had become just an effective means to get into her panties… And his technique had worked perfectly, because nothing could be more seductive to a girl who had lost her father at the age of six, and been at loggerheads with her brother ever since her mother's death two years later, than the wonder of uncritical male attention.

'So you found your dream?' he asked now, surprising her again. He remembered that too?

She gave a rough chuckle. 'Well, not precisely. I had to drop out of the Central Saint Martin's School of Art. And when I got back into the studio after Mac's birth, I had to make a living. But I like what I do.'

He frowned. 'What is it that you paint?'

'Portraiture. I specialise in dogs, actually. I love them and luckily for me so do my clientele. People are willing to pay quite a lot for a good likeness of their pet.'

His eyebrows rose but only a fraction. 'Do you and Mac have a dog?'

Her heartbeat clattered against her chest wall, her ribs squeezing. This was surely the first specific question he'd ever asked about their son. 'Mac adores dogs, but we can't afford one just yet. So he's happy hanging out with Imelda and Donal's two hounds when we need a doggie fix. I think he'd love to meet Rocky one day,' she ventured.

He nodded. 'I'm sure that can be arranged. Although I'd be concerned Rocky might knock him down. Rocky's quite big, Cormac is quite small and I'm still working on Rocky's manners.'

It was a thoughtful, considerate thing to say, so she couldn't resist asking.

'How did you end up picking him? He's a rescue dog, right?'

'Yeah. I didn't really pick him…he sort of picked me.'

'How so?' she asked, intrigued by the flags of colour on his cheeks. And trying not to let her gaze dip to his chest—which was having a far too predictable effect on her hormones again.

He sighed. And looked away.

'He was dumped in a trash can at the back of the apartment building as a puppy. Someone had beaten him quite severely. I heard his cries. Took him to the shelter. Two weeks later I rang to find out if he'd been successfully placed. And he hadn't. He's not the prettiest dog, as you probably noticed, but he's got a big heart.' He shrugged, as if his connection to his dog was a small thing, when she suspected it was massive. 'I'm not a sentimental man, but it seemed a shame to let him die after he'd fought so hard to stay alive.'

'I see,' she said, deeply touched by the story.

Ross De Courtney might believe he couldn't make emotional attachments, but Rocky proved otherwise.

'Is that why you called him Rocky? Because he's a fighter?'

'Yes,' he said, but then his intense gaze fixed back on her face. 'The marks, on your stomach, how did you get them?'

The blush reignited at the unexpected question—as she recalled how he'd trailed his fingers over the stretch marks while they were making love. Did he find them ugly?

'They're stretch marks. I got them when I was pregnant,' she said, bluntly, refusing to be embarrassed about the changes having his baby had made to her body—whatever he thought of them.

His Adam's apple bobbed as his throat contracted, and a muscle in his jaw hardened. He looked stricken, and she had no idea why.

'I was pretty huge when I got to the end of my pregnancy,' she offered, unable to read his reaction, suddenly needing to fill the silence—and take that stricken look out of his eyes. 'Mac was a big baby, nearly eleven pounds when he finally appeared. And, well, I slathered my belly in all sorts of concoctions, but it didn't…'

'Was it very painful?' he asked, interrupting the babbled stream of information with a direct look that could only be described as tortured.

'The stretch marks?' she asked.

'No, the birth.'

'Oh, yes, six hours of absolute agony,' she said with a small laugh, in a bid to lift the mood. But she realised her attempt at humour had backfired spectacularly when he paled.

She touched his arm, instinctively. 'Ross, what's wrong?'

'I'm sorry,' he said, the words brittle with self-loathing. A self-loathing she didn't understand.

'What for?' she asked.

'For putting you through that.' He stood, his whole body rigid with tension now.

'No need for an apology. I had a child I adore. The pain was totally worth it,' she said.

'That's not the point. I put your life at risk.'

'My...? *What?* No, you didn't.' She was so stumped now she didn't know what to say. He was totally over-reacting, but his face had become an implacable mask again, rigid and unrelenting.

'I was only joking when I said it was total agony.' She paused, needing to be forthright now in the face of his... Well, she wasn't even sure what this was, or where it was coming from. But the emotion had been wiped off his face, to be replaced by the same intransigence she'd seen before. She didn't like it. 'Okay, to be fair it hurt, a lot, but I had every pain relief known to woman by the end of it. And my life was never in danger.'

He rewrapped the towel around his waist, making her far too aware of his nakedness and hers—the ripple of sensation tearing through what was left of her composure.

'I need to get to work,' he said, abruptly changing the subject. 'We can discuss the details later, but compensating you for your pain and suffering because of my carelessness is non-negotiable.'

'But...that's madness.' She sputtered, but then he

grasped her chin, leaned down and pressed a kiss to her lips so possessive it cut off her thought processes entirely.

'We should probably also set some ground rules for the next week,' he added, letting her go. 'Sex-wise.'

The pragmatic comment had the blush firing into her cheeks.

How did he do that? Throw her completely for a loop without even trying? Because it was mortifying.

'What…what do you mean?' she said.

One dark eyebrow arched, and his gaze skimmed over her. She tightened her grip on the duvet—wondering for one panicked moment if he could see the hot weight lodged between her thighs that had started to pulse… *Again.*

'It's clear from what just happened that the exceptional chemistry between us is still very much there,' he said, the conversational, pragmatic tone belying the heat in his gaze and the brutal throbbing between her thighs. 'I figure we have two choices. We can either see that as a problem while you're here, in which case you should probably move into a hotel. Or we can enjoy it.'

'I…?' She stuttered, not sure what to say, or how to react. Was it really that easy for him to completely separate the sex from the emotion? 'You'd be okay with that?'

Was that possible? To treat this urge as purely biological? She'd wanted to believe she could be as pragmatic as he was about the sex, but could she? How would she even know if she was capable of that, when she'd never had a relationship with any man before now? Never even had a fling. Except for her one night with him—which was basically a micro-fling.

'Of course,' he said, as if there was no doubt in his mind whatsoever.

Had he ever had a committed relationship? Because from the insouciance in his tone now, it seemed doubtful.

'But it would be your choice, obviously,' he said. 'Why don't you think about how you want to proceed, and we can discuss it tonight? I'll make sure I'm back at a reasonable hour...' His gaze dipped again, making her ribs squeeze uncomfortably and her nipples tighten. 'And we can have dinner together.'

'Umm... Okay,' she managed as he strolled out of the room.

As the door closed behind him, the soft thud echoed in her chest.

She flopped back on the bed, her whole body humming again from just the thought of 'discussing' their options 'sex-wise' tonight.

She had no idea what to think any more, or feel. But as she turned her head to gaze out of the paned-glass window, one thing she did know for sure...

Thinking about him, and her choices, was going to keep her brain tied in knots, and her body alive with sensation, for the hours until she saw him again.

CHAPTER NINE

A car will be arriving at seven p.m. to pick you up. I thought it would be best if we discuss our options over dinner on neutral ground. Any problems text me.

CARMEL PLACED HER brush down on the paint table, wiped her hands on the cloth she kept tucked into the waistband of her jeans and picked up her phone as if it were loaded with nitroglycerine.

She reread the message from Ross. Then read it again, struggling to absorb the shot of heat and panic. And something else entirely. Something that felt disturbingly like exhilaration. Which could not be good.

Then she checked the time.

It was already five. She only had two hours before she would see him again…

Where was he taking her? Because he hadn't bothered to specify.

For goodness' sake, she didn't even have a single clue what to wear. Was he taking her to a restaurant? To talk about their sex life *in public*? Her cheeks burned… Was that the way of things in these situations? Did people do that in New York? Because they certainly didn't in rural Ireland.

She tapped out a reply as the panic—which she had

spent six solid hours immersed in her art to try and control—tightened around her ribs again…

Where are we going?

But as she went to press 'send', her thumb hovered
over the button.

She reread her reply, twice, and could hear her own
lack of social savvy and confidence revealed in the words.
Ross didn't know she'd been a virtual recluse since Mac
was born, rebuilding her life from the ground up.

And she didn't want him to know. Would he blame
himself for that too? And want to 'recompense' her for
the fact she'd chosen to spend the last four years living a
quiet life in County Galway learning how to be a mother?

She loved her quiet life. It worked for her, and Mac.
And she'd found an outlet for her art that she loved too,
she thought, glancing at the portrait she had lost herself
in as she attempted to capture the winsome intelligence
of a two-year-old cockapoo called Orwell.

She hadn't missed the social whirl she'd only glimpsed
in passing in the few weeks she'd been in London at art
school, and the night she'd first met Ross, once she'd returned home pregnant…

But somehow having him know how unsophisticated,
and unsure she was about going for dinner in a fancy restaurant in New York—where everyone seemed to ooze
confidence and style from every pore—would just add
to her feelings of inadequacy where he was concerned.
And make her feel as if she was at even more of a dis-
advantage when it came to discussing Mac's future relationship with his daddy… And what they were going to
do 'sex-wise' over the coming week.

So don't ask him where you're going tonight, you eejit.

After all, talking about Mac would not be hard. There

was so much she wanted to tell him about his son. And he seemed to have turned an important corner there this morning. When it came to the sex, all he was proposing was some fun while they got to know each other better and discussed their child's future. If they decided to go for it over the next week, to indulge themselves while she was here, it would be nothing more than a chance to blow off steam, to scratch an itch that had been there for four years—a quick fling with an end date already stamped on it. She needed to remember that above all else.

She deleted the reply and typed another.

Is there a dress code? What should I be wearing?

There now, that sounded less clueless, didn't it? Surely any woman would want to know that. But then the heavy weight sank into her sex and began to glow like a hot coal at the recollection of what she'd been wearing...or rather not wearing...when Ross had marched out of her room wearing nothing but a towel that morning.

And the innocent question suddenly seemed loaded with unintended innuendo.

'Oh, for the love of…'

She hissed, deleting the text. Then wrote another.

Cool, see you there.

She pressed 'send', before she could third-guess herself, and dumped the offending phone back on the paint table as if it were a grenade. Then she gathered up her brushes and palette so she could put aside her work for the day. She had two whole hours if she got a move on to scope out the cool little boutiques and vintage shops in the neighbourhood and find an outfit. Something that made her look and feel good, but which also suited her own sense of style.

She swallowed, convulsively. At the very least her quest should help distract her for the next two hours from the panic still closing her throat and the hot rock now pulsing in her panties at the thought of seeing him again.

Hallelujah for neutral ground!

'Would you like another beer, sir?'

'No, I'm good.' Ross glanced at the waiter who had been hovering for the last ten minutes in the private terrace he'd hired in the chic rooftop restaurant—which was one of Manhattan's most popular eateries, apparently, not that he'd ever dined here before.

He winced slightly at how stunning the space looked with the sun setting on the horizon, casting a reddish glow over the dramatic view of Manhattan's skyline through the terrace's tall brick arches.

Terrific, the wait staff probably thought he was about to propose. When all he had wanted to do was to make absolutely sure they didn't give into the chemistry again before they got a few important things straight about his responsibilities to his son, and what any liaison between them while Carmel was in New York would and would not entail.

He cleared his throat. 'By the way, once you've taken our drinks order, could you give us twenty minutes alone?'

'Absolutely, sir, and good luck,' the young man said, positively beaming. Ross bit back a groan.

But then Carmel appeared at the terrace entrance—and the groan got locked in his throat. The hum of arousal that had been tormenting him most of the day hit first, swiftly followed by what could only be described as awe.

He stood as she walked towards him.

Her vibrant red hair flowed out behind her in the light spring breeze, which also caught the floaty material of the short dress she wore, which was decorated with lavish red roses and clung to her torso, defining each and every one of the curves he had explored that morning.

A pair of combat boots and a leather jacket completed the original look. But as she approached his gaze rose to her face, and his pragmatism took another fatal hit. The make-up she wore—cherry-red lipstick to match the dress, smoky black eye liner and some kind of golden glitter on the lids, which sparkled in the light—made her look like a fairy queen, or a Valkyrie, stunningly beautiful, strikingly cool and so hot it hurt.

'Hi,' she said breathlessly as she reached him. 'Sorry I'm late. I wanted to walk the last couple of blocks.'

'Not a problem,' he murmured, trying to control the brutal reaction as he caught a lungful of her scent—something sultry and yet summery and as addictive as everything else about her.

'Wow, what a spectacular view,' she said, her voice rich with awe, the glittery eye shadow making her lids sparkle like rare gems.

There's only one spectacular view here, and it's not downtown Manhattan.

He swallowed round the lust swelling in his throat and held out her chair, silently cursing the decision to have this conversation in a restaurant.

Because the urge to lick every inch of her delicate flesh, taste the sweet sultry scent of her arousal, swallow the broken sobs of her pleasure again had already turned the hum of arousal into a roar.

'Is this a private space?' she said, glancing around.

He had to shake his head slightly, to unglue his gaze from her mouth and process the question.

Damn, De Courtney, get a grip.

'I thought you might prefer to talk without an audience,' he said.

Except talking is the last damn thing I want to do now.

He dragged his gaze away from those full lips.

Will her mouth taste like cherry?

'Really? That's so thoughtful of you,' she said, sounding as if she meant it as she seated herself. He walked back to his own chair and sat. He picked up his beer and finished it in one gulp to unstick his dry throat and give himself a moment to concentrate on easing the painful pulsing in his pants.

'More practical than thoughtful,' he said, desperately trying to regain his equilibrium and some semblance of control.

She blinked, the pure blue of her irises almost as breathtaking as the light blush on her pale skin.

'Thoughtful or not, I appreciate the privacy,' she said. 'I'm not gonna lie, I was nervous about meeting you here. I guess I'm too much of an unsophisticated Irish country lass to feel comfortable talking about my sex life over cocktails and cordon bleu cuisine with other people around.'

His gaze dipped of its own accord to the bodice of her dress, which cupped her breasts, the words 'sex life' delivered in that soft Irish burr detonating in his lap.

'You don't look unsophisticated,' he said. 'You look stunning.'

A bright smile curved her lips and lit her gaze, while the becoming blush spread across her collarbone. Something twisted deep inside him at the realisation of how much the offhand compliment had pleased her.

'Good to know the hour I spent scouring the vintage shops in Tribeca wasn't wasted,' she said as she shucked the leather jacket and handed it to the waiter, who had reappeared. The movement made the silky dress drift off her shoulder. The shot of adrenaline became turbo-charged as he glimpsed a purple lace bra strap before she tugged the dress back up.

Just kill me now.

'Hiya,' she said to the waiter, who Ross noticed was staring at his date with his tongue practically hanging out of his mouth.

Possessiveness shot through him and he glared at the kid. 'Perhaps you'd like to take our drinks order?'

The young man jerked. 'Umm, yes, of course. What can I get for you, ma'am?' he said, not taking his eyes off Carmel. Apparently Ross had become invisible.

'What's good here?' she asked, and the waiter proceeded to stammer his way through a complex list of cocktails.

Ross's irritation increased.

What could only have been a few minutes but felt like several hours later, Carmel's new number one fan had finally left them alone together, as Ross had requested.

'So I take it you had a productive day,' he said, struggling to make small talk—not his greatest strength at the best of times.

'Yes, very. Your apartment has so much light, it's a glorious place to paint,' she replied. 'And I'm particularly fond of my current subject. He's an adorable cockapoo with an abundance of personality. It's never hard to capture that on canvas. Plus, Nina dropped by to take Rocky out and we had a chat. She suggested introducing me to some of her other clients and their dogs while I'm here, which could be a great opportunity. She feels sure a lot of them would love a portrait of their pet.'

But I want you all to myself.

'I see,' he said, more curtly than he had intended, surprised by the strength of his disapproval. Where exactly was it coming from? Because it felt more than a little unreasonable… Just like the spike of possessiveness when he had caught the waiter staring at her. But he couldn't seem to shake it, even as the flushed excitement on her face dimmed.

'Do you have a problem with that?' she asked, the tone clipped as her smile died.

'Not precisely.' He shrugged, trying to make himself believe it. 'Obviously you're a free agent while you're here, and your career is your concern.' If painting pet portraits could really be called a career.

She'd had to drop out of art school to have his child. It seemed her brother hadn't stepped in to offer her any financial support—which seemed callous in the extreme, given that the guy was a billionaire—but ultimately, Ross knew, Conall O'Riordan wasn't the one responsible for supporting her and his son, he was.

Suddenly his knee-jerk reaction made perfect sense. This wasn't about some Neanderthal desire to keep her all to himself as 'his woman' while she was here, it was simply his desire to right the many wrongs he'd done her, with his thoughtless reply to that text.

'Just so you know, I've worked out a generous maintenance package for you and Cormac with my financial team today, which means you won't have to continue shouldering the financial burden of his care any longer. Or, I hope, making compromises with your art based on that burden.'

Instead of her looking pleased with the news though, her brows drew down and those lush lips tightened into a thin line of disapproval. The blue of her irises turned to flame as outrage sparked in her eyes.

He braced himself for what he suspected was going to be a fairly spectacular argument. Discord was not something he usually enjoyed in a relationship. But as he watched her anger build, the arousal became razor sharp.

And it occurred to him that, unlike any other woman he had ever dated, Carmel O'Riordan totally lived up to that age-old cliché, that she was even more stunningly beautiful when she was mad.

'Oh, have you now?' Carmel snapped, managing to temper her tone, just about.

But she could do absolutely nothing about the breathless rage threatening to blow her head off at his condescending and arrogant assumptions. And the prickle of fear beneath it. She'd spent the last four years refusing to take the many handouts Conall had offered her to help support her and Mac. So why should Ross's offer be any different?

His money didn't mean that he cared. She already knew that. So why should his persistence bother her so much? Or threaten to undermine the independence she'd worked so hard for?

'Since when has Mac become a burden to me?' she asked, because there were so many things wrong with his statement she didn't know where to start.

She knew she looked good in the fabulous vintage dress she'd found in a tiny shop off West Fourth Street, but still she'd been nervous at the thought of seeing him again, especially in the chic, uber-hip restaurant in the Murray Hill area of the city, which she'd immediately checked out on the Internet when the driver had told her of their destination. So nervous, in fact, she'd had to get out of the car a block early, even though she was already a few minutes late. Consequently, she'd been stunned... and moved...to find he'd booked this private space when she arrived, the view almost as staggeringly gorgeous as the sight of him in the twilight. His eyes had darkened, that searching gaze making bonfires ignite all over her skin, and the compliment had gone straight to her head.

The nerves hadn't died, exactly, but they'd shifted, making her focus on *them*—and the rare chemistry that she was becoming increasingly sure she wanted to indulge.

Where was the harm in taking him up on his offer? If he could be pragmatic, why couldn't she? Her life was in Ireland after all, and his in New York. And while they shared a child, apart from Mac they had nothing else in common, having never shared more than a few hot, stolen moments together. She wasn't the artless, foolish, lovestruck girl she'd once been. She had believed herself in love once and it had all been a lie, based on chemistry and heat and one enchanting night. She wouldn't fall for that romantic nonsense again—that little wobble after they'd made love again was just that, nothing more than a wobble, an echo, of a girl long gone. This man had captivated her four years ago. But she knew now he couldn't be further from her ideal partner...

Surely his insulting offer of 'compensation' for her pain and suffering only confirmed that? So why couldn't she control the stupid emotion pushing against her ribs?

'I didn't say that,' he said, even though he'd said exactly as much.

'And if you'll recall I have never asked you for money,' she said, reiterating the point yet again, annoyed the fury she wanted to feel had become something a great deal more disturbing.

How could she be moved by his desire to support her—when she didn't want or need his support?

He leaned back in his chair, the appreciation in his gaze unmistakable. The top buttons of his shirt were undone, and the movement drew her gaze down to where his chest hair peeked out.

Heat settled like a hot brick in her belly, tangling with the nerves and the fury and the unwanted emotion to create a cocktail of sensations she seemed unable to extinguish.

'I know,' he said, the calm tone only adding to her agitation. 'You've been consistently clear on that point. But that doesn't mean I don't owe you for the upkeep of my son. And the things you have clearly sacrificed in the last four years.'

'I've sacrificed nothing I did not wish to sacrifice. And I'm perfectly happy with the life I have now,' she said. 'Maybe doing pet portraits seems like a waste of my talent to you, but I like it and I'm good—'

'I didn't say it was,' he cut her off.

'Yes, but you implied it,' she said, because he totally had.

But then he leaned forward and covered the fist she had resting on the table with his hand. 'I didn't mean to,' he said. 'I'm proud of you, and everything you've done to make a life for our child. But I remember the smart, witty, brilliant girl I met that night who captivated me with her dreams. You had ambitions for your future, which I destroyed. I want to give them back to you.'

The statement—delivered in that deep husky, forceful voice—cut off the outrage at the knees, the hot brick in her belly rising up to pulse painfully in her chest.

She tugged her hand out from under his as the fury disappeared to be replaced by the deep yearning she knew had no place in this relationship.

He felt beholden to her. She had to make it very clear to him, he wasn't. But why did the thought he would even want to give her back dreams that had died long ago seem so dangerous?

She shook her head, stupidly close to tears. He didn't understand that those dreams didn't matter any more, because he had given her something far more precious.

Making him understand that was what she had to concentrate on now.

'I don't want those dreams back,' she said. 'And I don't want your money, Ross. I thought I made that clear when I came here.'

He settled back in his chair, his gaze studying her with an intensity she remembered from that night—as if she were a puzzle he was determined to solve.

She'd found it exhilarating then. It scared her that look could still trigger the giddy bumps in her heart rate now.

She placed her hand in her lap, her skin still burning from the touch of his palm.

'As I understood it, you wanted me to form a relationship with Mac,' he said. 'I've said I'm willing to do that. I doubt I'll be much of a father, but I'm willing to try.'

'Okay,' she said.

'But you have to meet me halfway, Carmel. You have to let me provide financial security for you both.'

'Why?'

'Because it's important to me.'

'But *why* is it so important?' she asked again, almost as tired of his evasions as she was of her own see-sawing emotions.

He simply stared at her, but then he looked away. And she knew he was debating whether to tell her more.

The waiter chose that precise moment to arrive with their drinks and the menus.

She spent several minutes checking the array of eclectic and delicious-sounding dishes, taking the opportunity to calm her racing heartbeat. But once they'd ordered and the waiter had left them alone again, she knew she had to find out why he was so obsessed with providing for her and Mac to stop herself from misconstruing his motivations again.

'You didn't answer my question,' she said.

He took a sip of the beer he'd ordered.

But just when she thought there was no way he would tell her more, he murmured, 'Because I spent my whole childhood watching my father exploit and abuse the women he slept with... And never live up to the responsibility of being a father to his own children. I vowed to myself then, I would be better than him.' He sighed, and for a moment she could see the turmoil in his eyes, devastating memories lurking there that she suspected he had no intention of sharing... 'What I did to you, and Mac, means I have broken that vow. Do you understand?'

Emotion pulsed hard in her chest at his forthright, honest answer. And the misery she glimpsed in his eyes.

It saddened her and moved her... But it also made the fear release its grip on her throat. His offer, his need to provide for her wasn't really about her, about *them*. This was about his past, his childhood, his dysfunctional relationship with his father.

'You didn't exploit me, Ross. Or abuse me,' she said, knowing she couldn't let him take responsibility for her choices. Because it would make her a victim, and she never had been one. 'And you've offered to try and be a father to Mac, even though you're not confident in the role...' A lack of confidence she was beginning to understand now stemmed from his unhappy relationship with his own father. 'So you certainly haven't abandoned your responsibility towards him. And while it's touching you would want to give my dreams back to me, only I can decide what my dreams are, and only I can make them come true. The girl you met that night doesn't exist any more. She's not who I am now. And I'm glad of that. Having Mac has turned me into a stronger, smarter, less impulsive person. I was forced to grow up, for sure, but I've no regrets about that. And neither should you.'

He stared at her for the longest time, the silence only

broken by the distant sound of sirens from the street below. She could feel her breath squeezing in her lungs, the moment somehow so significant—a battle of wills between his honour and her independence, which she knew she had to win.

But at last he broke eye contact and swore under his breath.

When his gaze met hers again, she saw rueful amusement, the feelings she had glimpsed earlier carefully masked again. But something had shifted between them, something important, because now she knew she had his respect.

'You're not going to accept the maintenance settlement, are you?' he said, giving it one last try, but he didn't seem surprised when she shook her head.

He thrust his fingers through his hair, which she had begun to recognise as a sign of his frustration, but then he let out a rough chuckle, which seemed to wrap around her heart. Why did she get the impression Ross De Courtney didn't laugh often enough?

'Do you have any idea how ironic it is that I wrote that unforgivable text four years ago convinced you were a conniving little gold-digger, and here I am now, frustrated beyond belief that you have point-blank refused—over and over again—to take the money I want to throw at you?'

She laughed, stupidly relieved they could finally share a joke about it. 'Actually, I'd call it poetic justice for that text, but then Conall has always said I've got a cruel sense of humour.'

'The fact I find myself agreeing with your brother only compounds the irony,' he said, the rueful tone intensified by the rich appreciation in his gaze.

Her heart bobbed into her throat. She swallowed it down ruthlessly, determined to concentrate on the pulse pounding in the sweet spot between her thighs, which he had exploited so comprehensively that morning—and nothing else.

'Doesn't it just?' she said, then wondered if she was enjoying the moment of connection a bit too much.

Whoa, girl. Don't go complicating this. Not again.

The sun had set on one of the most spectacular views she'd ever seen in her life, and it felt as if a huge hurdle to their future association as Mac's parents had been overcome. Plus she'd seen a crucial bit more about the man behind the mask. Maybe it had only been a glimpse, grudgingly given, but she could see now Ross's relationship with his father was the key to why he believed he would struggle to parent Mac, and she could give him some solace on that score at least, from her own experience. No need to make this new accord mean anything more.

'Would you let me at least set up a trust fund for Mac?' he said.

'I don't need your…' she began, but he held up his hand.

'I know you don't need my money,' he said. 'And I know now my money is no substitute for me attempting to be some kind of father to him. But it would make me feel a little bit better about abandoning him for the first three years of his life.'

She wanted to tell him no again. But she could see she needed to compromise now. Relinquishing even this much control over her son's life was hard, but how could she let Ross be a father to Mac, if she couldn't even allow him to set up a trust fund for his son?

'Okay, I can accept that,' she said. 'As long as you promise not to let him buy a motorcycle with the money when he's sixteen,' she added, desperately trying to make light of a difficult concession on her part.

She'd wanted Ross to consider being a real daddy to Mac. Why hadn't she realised, until this minute, everything that would entail?

He laughed. 'I'll tell my legal team to make his mother the primary trustee until he's thirty-five, how's that?'

'Perfect,' she said, just as the waiter arrived with the dishes they'd ordered.

The delicious aroma of grilled chicken and delicate spices filled her nostrils, and the tension that had been tying her gut in knots since getting his text that afternoon unravelled enough to make her realise she was absolutely ravenous.

Ross watched Carmel tuck into her food with the same take-no-prisoners gusto with which she appeared to tackle everything in her life—from motherhood, to art, to sex.

The woman certainly drove a hard bargain, he thought, as he sliced off a chunk of the succulent steak he'd ordered.

He let the juices melt on his tongue—while struggling to forget how much better she had tasted that morning. And how much he had been forced to reveal about his childhood, and his father.

He never talked about that time in his life. Or the man who had sired him. The flashbacks and nightmares he sometimes still suffered from were just one reason not to dwell on it. He'd had a disturbed night's sleep last night, thanks to the night terrors that had visited him in dreams and woken him up in a cold sweat—the shame of his own weakness almost as vivid as the brittle fear. But surely it was inevitable discovering he was a father would naturally bring the nightmares back again—at least for a little while.

Was that why he'd dived into a sexual relationship

this morning that could effectively blow up in his face? Perhaps. But he was past caring about the consequences now. All he knew was that he had to have her again. But that still didn't stop him hating the pity in her eyes when he'd been forced to tell her the real reason providing for her and her son's financial needs was so important to him.

He tried to shrug it off as they finished their meal and talked easily about the day's business. Or easily enough, if you didn't count the ticking bomb in his lap ready to explode every time she licked the dark chocolate and sea-salt mousse off her spoon. Or he noticed that vintage dress slipping off her shoulder again and he got another glimpse of that damn bra strap.

As soon as she had licked the final drops of chocolate off her spoon, the waiter arrived to whisk their dishes away and offer them coffee. Ross waited patiently, or patiently enough, but when the waiter began to walk away, he opened his mouth to bring up the subject of their sleeping arrangements for the rest of the week when she beat him to the punch.

'My mother died when I was eight years old,' she said, her gaze fixed on his face.

'I'm sorry,' he said automatically, nonplussed not just by the complete non-sequitur but also the wealth of emotion in those bottomless sapphire eyes. And the twist of anguish in his gut, at the thought of her, as such a young child, losing her mother.

He ought to know how that felt—after all he had lost his own mother when he was even younger... He tensed. Not true. Although his mother had died when he was five, he barely remembered her.

'It's okay, we weren't particularly close,' she said, still watching him with a disturbing level of intimacy.

'Are you sure?' he said, because he didn't believe her. He could hear the hollow tone of loss in her voice.

She gave him a weak smile. Then nodded. 'She suffered from depression. Had been battling it for all of my life—she had two miscarriages before I was born and that's when it struck. It got much worse when my daddy died in a farm accident. Then one Christmas morning, two years almost to the day of his death, she decided to end it. Con went to her room to wake her up... And found her dead.'

'Hell.' He whispered the word, shocked not just by the devastating picture she painted of her family's tragedy, but also the pragmatism with which she delivered the news. 'That's horrendous.'

'Yes...' She let out a small laugh completely devoid of humour. 'Yes, it is horrendous. For so many reasons. It's horrendous that my daddy died the way he did. It's horrendous that my mammy couldn't cope without him. It's horrendous she never got the help she needed. And that Conall had to live with the trauma of finding her like that. And then had to take on so much responsibility when he was little more than a lad himself.'

'I'd say it's also horrendous you had to grow up without a mother,' he murmured.

'Yes, that too,' she said, almost as if her own loss was an afterthought. 'I suppose,' she added. 'But I didn't tell you so you'd feel sorry for me. I told you because...' She paused, sighed. 'Here's the thing—when I got pregnant with Mac my biggest fear was that I wouldn't be able to be a mother to him, because my own mother had been...' She hesitated again, then took a breath, and let it out slowly. 'Well, not much of a mother to me. I had no frame of reference. She hadn't been able to show love or even affection towards the end. She was in far too much pain to focus on anything other than the big black hole she couldn't climb out of. I worried constantly, while I watched my belly getting bigger, that I would have the same trouble bonding with my baby she had had bonding with me. Con and Imelda tried to explain to me it wasn't the same thing at all. That mam had been ill. But I'd always been secretly, even subconsciously, convinced there was something very wrong with me. And that's why she couldn't bond with me. That somehow I wasn't worthy of love. And what if that same thing was going to stop me loving Mac?'

He frowned. 'But that's absurd. What does one thing have to do with the other?' And anyway, he'd seen how she interacted with the boy. She obviously adored the child and he adored her. If anything, the closeness of their relationship had only intimidated him more.

'Nothing,' she said. 'Just like your father's inadequacies as a husband and a parent and, by the sounds of it, a human being have nothing whatsoever to do with you.'

He stared at her, the statement delivered in such a firm, no-nonsense tone, it took him a moment to realise they weren't talking about her family and her relationship with Mac any more. They were talking about him.

'That's not what I said,' he murmured, annoyed she had turned the tables on him so neatly, and annoyed even more by the fact he hadn't seen it coming.

'It's what you were thinking though,' she said.

Damn, she had him there.

'All I'm saying,' she said, leaning across the table to cover his hand with hers, 'is that it's okay to be scared of becoming a parent. Believe me, I was terrified. But don't let whatever cruel things he did to you influence your relationship with Mac. Because it's not relevant, unless you let it be.'

He stiffened and drew his hand out from under hers. The empathy in her voice and the compassion in her gaze made his stomach flip.

'I never said he was cruel to *me*,' he murmured, even

as the brutal memories clawed at the edges of his consciousness.

She watched him, her expression doubtful, but just when he thought she would call him out on his lie, her lips curved in a sweet and unbearably sympathetic smile. 'Then I'm glad.'

But he suspected she knew he wasn't telling the truth.

Reaching back across the table, he grasped her hand, then threaded his fingers through hers, suddenly determined to get back to a connection he understood.

She didn't resist, looking him squarely in the eyes. Her heartbeat punched her wrist as he rubbed his thumb across the pulse point.

'How about we stop talking about our pasts and start talking about what we plan to do for the rest of the night?' he said.

Being a parent was a role he doubted he would excel at for a number of reasons, but he was prepared to take her lead on that and hope for the best. Sex, however, was simple and something they both appeared to excel at, with each other. And it would defuse the tension currently twisting his gut into hard, angry knots.

'You didn't give me an answer,' he added, seeing the indecision in her eyes, which he was beginning to realise was unlike her. The woman seemed to have a natural inclination to rush headlong into everything. But not this. He wondered why that only made him want to convince her more.

'Because I haven't made up my mind,' she said, the words delivered on a tortured breath.

Smiling, as the shot of arousal echoed sharply in his groin, he opened her hand and lifted her palm to his mouth.

'Then let's see if I can persuade you,' he said, before biting gently into the soft flesh beneath her thumb.

She let out a soft moan, her vicious shiver of reaction making his own pulse dance.

But then she tugged her hand free and buried her fist in her lap. 'I want to sleep with you again,' she said boldly, her gaze direct. 'That's pretty obvious.'

'Ditto,' he said, unable to hide his grin as the dress slipped off her shoulder again.

She yanked it back up.

'I can see there's a but coming,' he said, determined to persuade her.

'But I don't want this…' She paused, and chewed her bottom lip, turning the trickle of heat into a flood. She thrust her thumb backwards and forwards between them. 'This *thing* between us to impact on your relationship with Mac.'

'It won't,' he said. 'Just to be clear, Carmel,' he added, astonished to realise he had yet to give her the 'hooking up' speech he gave every woman—usually long before he slept with them. Why he hadn't got around to it until now with her was something he would have to analyse at a later date, but the first order of business was to remedy the situation.

'All we're talking about is a short-term arrangement for the duration of your stay. I don't do long-term, it's just not in my make-up.'

'I know,' she said, completely unfazed. 'Your sister said as much. Don't worry, I'm certainly not looking for long-term either. Especially not with a guy like you.'

He frowned, taken aback not just by her pragmatic reply but also by the spurt of annoyance. 'Katie said that?' he asked, not sure why his sister's candour felt like disloyalty.

Given the history of their sibling relationship, why would Katie say any different? And why should he care? But what the hell did Carmel mean by a 'guy like you'…

What *kind* of a guy was he? Because he'd always considered himself fairly unique.

'Yes,' she answered. Then added, 'It's okay. Just sex works best for me, too.'

'Well, good,' he said, not quite able to keep the snap out of his voice as the annoyance and indignation combined. 'I'd hate to think you were expecting more from me than just orgasms on demand.'

Her gaze narrowed slightly. 'What's the problem? Isn't that the only thing you're offering?'

He forced himself to breathe and control the urge to contradict her... After all, it *was* all he could offer her, he'd just said so himself. It was all he had ever wanted to offer any woman.

But that didn't stop the questions queuing up in his head. Inappropriate questions which, intellectually, he knew he shouldn't want to ask her, had no right to ask her, but...

Who exactly had she slept with after losing her virginity to him? How many other men had there been in the past four years? Had they ever met his son? Formed a relationship with the boy when he had not? And what *kind* of guys *did* she consider worthy of more than just orgasm-supply duty? Because all of a sudden he wanted to know.

'Yes, precisely,' he said, through gritted teeth, holding onto the questions with an effort.

He'd get over his curiosity. This was just some weird reaction to spending all evening enthralled by those tantalising glimpses of her bra strap, the intermittent whiffs of her scent—fresh and sultry—and the torturous sight of her licking chocolate mousse off her spoon. Not to mention a much more revealing conversation about his past—and hers—than he had anticipated or was comfortable with. That was all.

She was still frowning at him. As if she was somehow aware he was struggling to keep his cool—which made the fact he was even more infuriating. What was it about this woman? How did she manage to push all his buttons without even trying? Buttons he hadn't even known he possessed till now...

No, he thought, that wasn't strictly speaking true. Because she'd pushed quite a few of his buttons that night four years ago, when he'd found himself haring after her escaping figure through the crowd of partygoers like a man possessed.

'So if orgasms on demand is all you want, what exactly is the problem with us going for it?' he managed, trying to finally ask a question that mattered, instead of all the ones that did not.

She heaved a deep sigh, which naturally made that damn dress slip off her shoulder again. Then glanced away from him. The fairy lights reflected in the glittery make-up on her eyelids. And he found himself catching his breath again, to stem the sharp flow of heat. She really was exquisite. This was all this was, an overpowering attraction to an extremely beautiful woman. Why was he complicating it? When he didn't want to and neither did she?

But then she turned towards him and he got momentarily lost in her sapphire eyes.

'I don't want it to be awkward, that's all. After it's over. Mac has to be my priority. As long as you're sure that won't be a problem?'

'A problem how?' he asked, because he was genuinely confused now.

'You know, that you won't get too attached. To me. And the orgasms.'

He wanted to laugh. Was she actually serious? Hadn't he just told her he didn't get attached? But the laugh died on his tongue, her dewy skin and large blue eyes suddenly making her look impossibly young... And vulnerable. When she'd never seemed that vulnerable before.

What a fool he'd been. He had been her first lover. And she was the mother of his child. Of course, that made her unlike any of the other women he had slept with, whatever her dating history since that night.

Not only that, but if he was to keep the promise he had made to her, about their son, he would never be able to sever this relationship the way he had severed every other relationship in his life before her when the woman he was dating had threatened to get too close.

For a moment, he considered forgoing the pleasure they could have during the coming days, and nights. To protect her, as well as himself, from the awkwardness she was referring to. But the rush of need came from nowhere, and he couldn't seem to say the words. Because it wasn't just sex he wanted, he realised. He wanted to know more about her. So much more.

He frowned, disturbed at how fascinated he was with her.

But surely, as long as he was well aware of the pitfalls of deepening this relationship over the next few days, he should be able to avoid falling into any of them?

After all, while he knew very little about real intimacy, so was naturally cautious about encouraging too much of it, he happened to be an expert at avoiding it.

'I guarantee, I won't get too attached,' he said, sure of this much at least.

And neither will you. Not when you realise how little I have to offer.

'Okay, then,' she said. 'I'd like to stay at your apartment for the rest of the week. And take you up on your orgasms-on-demand service.'

He gave a gruff chuckle, the rush of need making him a little giddy. He called the waiter over. 'Cancel the coffee order,' he said. 'And get the lady's jacket. We're leaving.'

CHAPTER TEN

CARMEL SHIVERED VIOLENTLY, but the cool spring breeze wasn't the only thing making goosebumps riot over her skin as the chauffeur-driven car drew up to the kerb in front of the restaurant entrance.

'Are you cold?' Ross asked, his hand settling on her back and making the silk of her dress feel like sandpaper.

She shook her head, aware of the heat slickening the heavy weight between her thighs.

She felt like that reckless girl again—intoxicated by the adrenaline rush. But she couldn't seem to stop herself from taking this opportunity to feed the hunger.

The driver opened the passenger door for them and Ross directed her into the warm interior. The scent of garbage from the street was replaced by the aroma of new leather and sandalwood cologne as Ross folded his tall body into the seat next to her.

'Put the partition up and take the scenic route, Jerry, slowly,' he said.

The hum of the screen lifting cocooned them into the shadowy space. She reached for her seat belt as the car pulled away, aware of her hand trembling. But as she went to snap the buckle in place, he caught her wrist.

'How about we live dangerously?' he said, the purpose and determination in his gaze accelerating her heartbeat.

She let the belt go, aware of the tension drawing tight

in her abdomen, and the heat firing up a few thousand extra degrees.

She nodded, giving him permission to pull her up and over his lap.

Suddenly she was perched above him. Her hands on his shoulders, her legs spread wide, her knees digging into the soft leather on either side of him, the short silk dress riding up to her hips. Excitement rippled and glowed at her core, making the hot nub burn as his large hands captured her bottom to drag her down, until she settled onto the hard ridge in his pants. His fingers kneaded and caressed, as urgent, desperate desire pounded through her body. Every one of her pulse points throbbed in unison, the rhythm in sync with the painful ache at her centre. She rubbed herself against the thick ridge as he caught her neck, lifting the hair away to tug her face down to his.

He captured her moan, the kiss firm and demanding. Her lips opened instinctively, giving him greater access, letting his tongue drive into her mouth, exploring, exploiting.

A harsh groan rumbled up from his chest as he cradled her cheek and tugged her head back to stare into her eyes. 'Take off the jacket,' he said, or rather commanded.

She did as she was told, scrambling out of the garment. The dress fell off her shoulder, as it had done so many times during the evening, but when she went to yank it back up he murmured, 'Don't.'

His thumb trailed across her collarbone, rubbing over the frantic pulse, then slipped under her exposed bra strap to draw it off her shoulder with the dress. The material tightened, snagging on the stiff peaks of her nipples. He cursed softly and undid the buttons on the dress's bodice, his other hand still caressing her bottom, his thumb sliding across the seam of flesh at the top of her thigh.

She gasped, thrusting her hips forward, the contact

too much and yet not enough, as she struggled to ride the ridge in his pants and release the coil tightening in her abdomen.

'Shh,' he murmured, the hint of amusement as rough and raw as she felt. 'We'll get to that in a minute.'

Just when she was gathering the words to protest, the bodice of the dress fell open to her waist, revealing the purple lace bra. Then his devilish fingers delved behind her back. The sharp snap of the hook releasing moments later startled her.

'What the…?' she murmured, shocked by his dexterity, as she whipped her hands off his shoulders to catch her breasts before she exposed herself to the whole of Manhattan.

He chuckled again, the low sound more than a little arrogant. He ran his thumb under the heavy flesh, making her nipples tighten painfully. Then pressed his face into her neck, kissing, licking. With her hands trapped trying to preserve her modesty, she shuddered, forced to absorb the onslaught of sensation, his tongue and teeth cruising across her collarbone, his other thumb still gliding backwards and forwards across that over-sensitised seam—too close and yet not close enough to where she needed him.

'Let go of the bra, Carmel,' he murmured, his hot breath making her nipples hurt even more.

'I can't, I don't want everyone to see,' she managed, aware of the sparkle of lights outside as the car crossed the busy junction at Times Square and Broadway. 'We might get arrested.'

He laughed, apparently delighted by her gaucheness, the rat.

'The glass is treated. The only one who can see you is me.'

She shuddered again, his thumb dipping beneath

the leg of her panties now, inching closer and closer to heaven.

'Are you...?' She swallowed around the lump of radioactive fuel suddenly jammed into her throat and throbbing between her legs. 'Are you sure?'

'Positive,' he said. 'Let go,' he demanded again.

Her hands released and seconds later he had pulled her arms out of the dress's sleeves, tugged her bra free and flung it away. She sat perched on his lap, naked to the waist, panting with need, but instead of covering herself, she forced herself to let him look his fill.

He groaned again, his gaze scorching the turgid flesh, before his hand cradled one heavy breast and his mouth captured the aching peak.

He licked and nipped, hardening the swollen flesh even more, making it pound and throb, before switching to the other breast. She had never realised she was so sensitive there. Her breasts had always been nothing more than functional. She'd loved feeding Mac when he was a baby, but this was so different, the arrows of need firing down to the hot spot at her core, building the brutal ache there with startling speed.

She cried out, barely able to breathe now around the torturous sensations firing through her body. Cupping her bottom and lifting her slightly, he kept his mouth on her breasts, sucking, nipping, caressing, her sobs echoing round the car, and slipped his fingers inside her panties to find the slick seam of her sex.

She jolted, bowed back, as he touched the heart of her.

The moan built from her core, slamming through her as the orgasm ripped into her, firing up from her toes and cascading through her in undulating waves. She rode his fingers, panting, sobbing, every part of her obliterated in the storm of sensation.

At last the orgasm ebbed, releasing her from its grip.

She collapsed onto him, washed out, worn through, damp and sweaty, and shaking with the intensity of her pleasure, aware of her naked breasts pressed against the fabric of his suit jacket, the nipples wet and sore from his attention.

Damn, he was still fully clothed.

Perhaps she would have been embarrassed that she was virtually naked and draped over him like a limp dishrag, but she couldn't think about anything in the moment, her mind floating in a shiny haze somewhere between bliss and consternation.

The last throes of the orgasm rippled through her as he finally slid his fingers from her swollen flesh. His hand caressed her neck, pressing her face into his shoulder, murmuring something in that deep, husky voice that made her feel cherished, important to him, when she knew she wasn't.

She clung on, breathing in the subtle scent of sandalwood and clean pine soap, the huge wave of afterglow at odds with the heavy weight settling on her chest.

How did he know just how to touch her, to make her fly? And how was she going to separate that from the painful pressure making her heartbeat stutter and stumble, and her ribs contract around her lungs?

He drew her head back at last, ran his thumb down the side of her neck as the car drew to a stop outside his loft. 'Ready for round two?'

She forced her lips to curve into what she hoped was a cocky grin, to cover the empty space opening up in her heart, then wriggled against the hard ridge in his pants while she pulled her dress back up. 'Bring it on.'

He laughed, but the sound reverberated in her chest, and did nothing to release the brutal stranglehold on her heart.

CHAPTER ELEVEN

CARMEL DABBED THE brush over the canvas one last time, to add texture to the paint layers, then lifted it away.

Enough. The portrait is finished.

She dropped the brush in the turpentine and shifted to glance past the easel at her model, who had taken to flopping out on the atrium's stone floor every morning after his first walk of the day with Nina.

Maybe he wasn't the prettiest dog in the universe, but he had so much character and charisma she had been unable to resist painting him when she'd finished the portrait of Orwell three days ago.

And you want to give Ross something tangible to remember this week by.

She frowned, pushing aside the sentimental thought.

'Hey, boy, want to look at yourself?' she asked, the sadness—at the thought her time with Ross was nearly over—squeezing her chest as Rocky's ears popped up, then his whole body followed.

The dog lopped over to the easel and stuffed his snout into her belly. She rubbed his head, giving a soft laugh. 'Not interested, eh?'

She was going to miss Rocky almost as much as his master when she returned to Ireland tomorrow.

Almost.

Who was she kidding? As much as she adored the

dog, she was going to miss Ross, so much more. Too much more.

She glanced at the sun beginning to slide towards the New Jersey shoreline in the distance, the turmoil of her thoughts deepening.

This shouldn't have happened. How had she become so attached to a moment—and a man—which was only supposed to be fleeting?

Ross would be home soon from work—for their last night together.

Her body quickened. The last six days, ever since they'd made their devil's bargain at the hip Murray Hill restaurant, had gone by in a haze of confused emotions and insatiable desire.

They made love two or three times each night, but why did it never seem to be enough? He would even wake her each morning from dreams, the heady touches triggering an instant and unstoppable response. They'd got into the habit of showering and eating breakfast together in the mornings. And then he was gone for the day. The hours she spent without him seemed to stretch into an agony of panicked thoughts and painful longing, peppered with a ton of 'what ifs' which had become harder and harder to shut away when he returned from work each day. And then there was that brutal shot of exhilaration, excitement, when he came back—always with some delicious takeout food they could dive into before diving into each other— which had stopped being all about the sex days ago.

Why couldn't she stop thinking about him? Not just the things he could do to her body, but the way he looked at her when she spoke about her day, or about her latest video call with Mac, or about a thousand other minute details of her life—that look, as if he was truly interested in what she had to say about herself, about their son, had come to mean far too much too.

And that was before she even factored in all the questions she wanted answers to, but had become too afraid to ask. Because that would only increase the sense of intimacy—an intimacy she knew she shouldn't need, shouldn't encourage, but seemed unable to resist.

The truth was, the only thing anchoring her to reality for the last few days had been her work, and Mac. Her brave happy little boy still wasn't showing any signs of missing her much, Imelda insisting he went to bed without a problem each night and was having lots of fun not just on the farm but also at Kildaragh—with Katie and Con who, to everyone's astonishment given Con's love of a grand gesture, had decided to stay in Galway for the first couple of weeks of their honeymoon.

She would have to thank them both when she got home for allowing her three-year-old terminator to gatecrash their romantic break.

But even as she thought of Katie and Con, she felt the pang of jealousy too at the settled, happy, wonderful future they had ahead of them together.

What was that even about?

They deserved their happiness. And this interlude with Ross was never supposed to have a future, they'd agreed as much in the Murray Hill restaurant a week ago. She didn't even want a future with him. This stupid yearning was nothing more than fanciful nonsense... And probably way too much great sex. She'd become addicted to the endorphin rush, that had to be it.

She cleaned the brushes and draped a clean sheet over the portrait, which she had decided to present to Ross tonight as a parting gift.

Not a romantic gesture, simply an acknowledgement of the fun we've had over this past week.

She gulped down the raw spot in her throat, knowing it was past time to leave New York.

Mac had asked for the first time this morning when she was coming home, igniting the yearning she always felt when she was away from him. She needed to return to Ireland now—to her real life again. Her little boy missed her and she missed him. Desperately. He grounded her and gave her life strength and purpose.

The last week had been filled with the heady excitement she had craved as a girl—a conflagration of physical fireworks—which Ross seemed capable of igniting simply by looking at her a certain way—but with it had come the emotional roller coaster she remembered all too well.

She'd become way too invested in falling asleep each night in his arms, or sparring with him about everything from politics to rugby to the latest gala at the Met over a bowl of Lucky Charms in the morning, or their impromptu picnics on the roof terrace each evening—and that look, which made her feel special, cherished, important to him, when she knew she wasn't, not really.

The domesticity, the simplicity of their routine in the last week had given her a fake insight into what it might be like to live with this hot, charismatic and taciturn man for real—but he wasn't her man, and she didn't want him to be.

She huffed out a breath. As the week had worn on, and the evenings and the mornings they spent together had become more intense, she'd lost perspective, that was all, become that girl again, who wanted something she couldn't have. Just like the little girl before her, who had craved her mother's attention, her mother's love, precisely because it was unavailable. It was a self-destructive notion that she needed to get a handle on.

Even if this could have been more, she knew Ross wasn't right for her... He was still so guarded, so wary, so unwilling to open himself to her or anyone else, but it horrified her to think that might be why she was so attracted to him. He presented a challenge, and she'd always had a bad habit of taking on challenges she couldn't win.

Rocky barked and shot out into the living area. Her heart thundered into her throat at the sound of the apartment's door opening, and the excited yips as Rocky gave his master his customarily insane greeting.

He's back early.

She held her ground, swallowed past the ball of anguish in her throat and finished putting away her paints, holding back the foolish urge to run out and give Ross an equally enthusiastic greeting.

Don't go soft now. Be cool, be calm, be smart. Protect yourself. Tonight's your last night... This is the way it has to be...

But as she listened to Ross's low voice talking to his pet and then he shouted, 'Hey, Carmel, where are you?' her heart ricocheted against her chest wall like a cannonball and the surge of sensory excitement was followed by the deep-seated yearning she still had no clue how to ignore.

She walked out into the living area, her thundering heart lifting into her throat as she spotted him, tall and indomitable and so hot in his business suit, with one hand caressing the dog's head and the other ripping off his tie.

His gaze locked on hers, possessive and intense—as always. And the heady rush of adrenaline and need shot through her on cue.

'Hey, how are you?' she said, disconcerted when her voice broke.

'Good,' he said. 'Now I'm finally home.'

The word *home* echoed in her chest, with far more resonance than she knew it deserved.

This isn't your home, or Mac's, it's his—he doesn't want you here, not in the long term. Why can't you get that through your eejit head?

'Sit, Rocky,' he demanded in a voice that brooked no argument. The dog planted his butt on the floor, his tail swishing against the polished wood, as Ross marched past him towards her.

Grasping her chin, he lifted her gaze to his, and the need on his face stabbed into her gut.

'Let's go to bed.'

It wasn't really a question, but she nodded anyway, the sensation flooding her system helping her to ignore the pulse of longing beneath.

He boosted her into his arms and strode across the room towards the curving metal staircase in the middle of the large space. She wrapped her legs around his waist and kissed him hungrily, channelling all the yearning into the promise of release.

Sex will make this better. Sex will take this ache away. Because sex is all this was ever meant to be.

But as they crashed into his bedroom together, and began to rip off each other's clothes, the brutal pain in her chest—and the frantic feeling of desperation and confusion and need—refused to go away.

Ross drew out slowly, the last spasms of another titanic orgasm still pulsing through his system as her swollen flesh released him. He rolled off her, flopped down, exhausted, sated—or as sated as he could be when he didn't seem able to completely satisfy his endless craving for her. He covered his eyes with his arm, holding back a staggered groan.

He could hear her breathing beside him, her deep sighs as shattered as he felt.

He'd taken her like a madman. Again. Hadn't even had the decency to wait until they'd eaten. Hell, he hadn't even been able to stop on the way home tonight long enough to pick up takeout for their evening meal, the way he'd been forcing himself to do up to now—just to prove he could be civilised enough to feed her before jumping her.

Why did this hunger keep getting worse? More insistent? Why couldn't he stop thinking about her? All day. Every day.

He'd lost focus at work in the last week, stopped caring about most of it, had curtailed his standard fourteen-hour days to eight hours, because he couldn't bear to be away from her a minute longer.

Today he'd been caught daydreaming about the sound of her sobs in the shower that morning while doing a conference call about a container ship emergency in the Gulf of Mexico—and made a fool of himself in front of the head of De Courtney's South American division and her two assistants because he'd had absolutely no clue what they were discussing when she asked him a direct question.

But as his breathing finally evened out and his heart-beat slowed, he knew it wasn't just this insatiable hunger that was the problem. It was so much more.

It was the sight of her each morning, her long legs crossed as she perched on one of the stools at his breakfast bar and tucked into the cereal she'd become as addicted to as he was.

It was the soft glow that seemed to light up her face every time she told him some new story or detail about their son—a soft glow he had become addicted to as well. So addicted he wasn't even sure any more if it was the insights she was giving him about his son—such as his obsession with horses and dogs, his love of arranging his toys in long lines all over her living room, his hatred of eating anything green despite her attempts to hide it in everything she cooked for him—which fascinated and captivated him, or the joyous light in her eyes when she was talking about Cormac.

It was the feel of her—so warm and soft in his arms as he fell asleep each night—that had managed to chase away the nightmares.

It was the dabs of bright colour in her hair from her work, which he enjoyed washing out after they had made love, the smell of turpentine and oil paint that lingered on her, and around the apartment now.

It was even the thought of knowing she would be there in the evening, waiting with Rocky, when he got back from the office. Making him realise he'd never really considered his condo a home until this week—which was ludicrous, seeing as he had owned the duplex loft for over six years, ever since moving to Manhattan.

But worst of all, it was the knowledge of how much he was going to miss all those things when she left tomorrow morning.

She stirred beside him and sat up. 'Did you bring anything home for supper?' she asked.

He dropped his arm, the inevitable hunger resurfacing as he absorbed the sight of her naked back, his gaze drifting down to her buttocks. 'Not today,' he said, unable to stop himself reaching out to caress the soft swell. She shivered and he lifted his fingers, aware of the heat settling in his groin again. 'I've run out of ideas. We've tried out pretty much every place I usually use,' he lied to cover the truth—that he hadn't wanted to wait a moment longer than necessary to see her again. 'How about I take you out for supper?' he made himself ask, even though the last thing he wanted to do right now was leave the apartment. Or this bed.

The truth was, if he could, he would happily spend the next fourteen hours, before her flight home, buried deep inside her, losing himself in this incendiary physical connection so he wouldn't have to dwell on all the other things he was going to miss when she was gone.

And the powerful urge to ask her to stay a while longer. He'd even come up with a plan to make that happen. Had asked his assistant to rearrange his schedule and have the staff at his estate in Long Island open up the house, simply so he could take a whole week off for the first time since his father's death ten years ago.

But he'd nixed the idea on the way home.

When the hell had he become so obsessed with her? It would be laughable, if it weren't so damn disturbing. And would it really be wise to spend twenty-four hours a day with her, when he was already spending every waking minute thinking about her?

She glanced over her shoulder at him, holding the duvet up to cover her breasts, breasts he had just spent several insatiable minutes devouring because he knew exactly how sensitive they were—and how she loved his attention there. A warm flush highlighted the freckles that covered her nose. Funny how he found the surprising glimpses of modesty as captivating as everything else about her. It enchanted him, probably because it reminded him so forcefully of the girl he had met that first night. The girl she had insisted was long gone. The girl who had been bold and beautiful, brutally honest and artlessly arousing, and yet at the same time had an innocence, a fragility beneath the boldness that had captivated him then, and made him want to protect her now… Even though he was fairly sure the only person she needed protecting from was him.

She smiled, that quick, generous smile that always made his heartbeat bounce in his chest. 'Okay, that would be grand. I've not seen much these past few days except the inside of this apartment,' she said. The little dig made him laugh, but he could see something else in her eyes that had his bouncing heart swelling in his throat.

'But I've got something to show you first,' she added, then threw off the duvet and got off the bed.

She hunted around for her clothing as he watched her, unable to deny himself the simple pleasure of studying her as she dressed in quick, efficient movements. First her panties went on, then the bra, which she hooked in the front then swivelled round so she could loop the straps over her shoulders. She wiggled back into the faded jeans—speckled with paint—which he knew she wore while she worked, then threw on a baggy green T-shirt with the insignia of the Irish Rugby Union Team, which was speckled with even more paint.

He stretched, and adjusted himself, grateful the heavy duvet hid the insistent erection already making a second appearance.

Since when had he found watching a woman dress so hot?

She swept back her wild red hair and tied it into a knot behind her head, then looked over her shoulder. 'You'll have to get out of bed, you know, if you're to see your surprise… And we're to eat before midnight.'

He chuckled, her sharp tongue as alluring as the rest of her. And forced himself to sit up. 'I'm going to have a quick shower. Do you want to join me?'

Arousal darkened her eyes, but she shook her head. 'If I do that we'll never get out of the apartment and you know it.'

'True,' he said, trying to keep his voice light and un-concerned, despite the brutal pulse of disappointment and yearning. And the knowledge that he was even going to miss her attitude.

Time to back off, De Courtney. This obsession is getting out of hand.

He dropped his feet off the bed, keeping the duvet firmly over his lap.

'I'll shower downstairs and meet you in the atrium,' she said, rushing out of the room before he could change his mind, and attempt to seduce her back into his bed.

He took care of the insistent desire in the shower—while he tried not to dwell on the humiliating fact he hadn't had to resort to such antics since he was a desperate teenager in an all-boys boarding school in the Scottish Highlands and the chance to interact with girls had been rarer than the chance to interact with Martians.

He took his time shaving and getting dressed in more casual clothes, determined not to let the yearning get the better of him again. Perhaps it was a good thing Carmel was leaving tomorrow. He'd become fixated on her, that much was obvious. Establishing his relationship with his son was what mattered now. Avoiding hard conversations about that had been all too easy while he was focussed on feeding the hunger—perhaps that was why it had resolutely refused to be fed.

He finally made his way downstairs. Rocky greeted him with his usual over-the-top enthusiasm. 'Hey, fella,' he said, his voice strangely raw as he knelt down to give the hound a tummy rub.

Thank God for the dog. He'll keep me company when she's gone. I'll be fine.

He'd never had any trouble being alone before now. This was all in his head.

But then he walked into the atrium and saw her standing in front of her easel, the evening light turning her damp red hair to a burnished gold. And the yearning dropped into his stomach like a stone.

I don't want her to go. Not yet. I'm not ready. And there's the boy to consider, I need to meet him, but I need her help with that.

Then she turned and stepped aside. 'Here, what do you think?' she said, directing his gaze to the painting on the easel beside her. 'I thought you might like a portrait of Rocky.'

He stared, so stunned for a moment, he was utterly speechless. The portrait was exquisite of course, the likeness striking, the dopey adoration in the dog's expression so expertly captured, it was hard to believe his pet wasn't embedded in the canvas instead of by his side, busy licking the back of his hand.

But as his gaze met hers, again, it wasn't the exquisite artistry of the portrait—the evidence of her incredible talent—that had the stone in his stomach turning into a boulder the size of El Capitan.

'You painted that? For me?' he said, the boulder rising up to scratch against his larynx. So astonished, he could barely speak.

He couldn't remember the last time he had received a gift. His father had never been a gift giver—believing his son's birthdays were simply another chance to drum into him his responsibility to the De Courtney name, while his Christmases had always been spent at school as a child. He didn't currently have any friends close enough to know when his birthday was, let alone celebrate it with him. Plus he avoided dating over the holiday season simply to avoid the kind of sentimentality that was now all but choking him.

Not only was this gift rare, though, it was also so thoughtful.

How had she captured what he saw in his pet so perfectly? Did she know how much he relied on Rocky for the warmth and companionship he had convinced himself he didn't need?

And suddenly he knew. He couldn't let her go. Because he needed time to find a way back from the precipice he was standing on the edge of as she stared at him now with the same soft glow he had seen on her face when she talked about their son… And the yearning in his chest turned into a black hole.

'Ross? Is everything okay?' Carmel's heart slammed into her throat. He looked stricken, his gaze jerking to hers—the flash of panic in it disturbing her almost as much as the melting pain in her own heart as she absorbed his visceral and transparent reaction to her gift. One minute he'd been his usual guarded self, his defences very much back in place, as she knew they would be, because they always seemed to return after they made love. She would glimpse something in the throes of passion that she had become as addicted to as the endorphin rush of good, hard, sweaty sex. But as soon as they collapsed on top of each other, each joining more frantic and furious than the last, the mask would return, and she was sure she had imagined that intense moment of connection.

But as his gaze rose to hers now, and she watched the shutters go down again, she knew she hadn't imagined it this time. Because for one terrifying moment he had been totally transparent and what she'd seen had broken her heart—yearning, desperation, confusion and panic, but most of all need.

And in that split second, she had the devastating thought that she was falling in love with him. That this yearning wasn't about sex, or the unfulfilled needs of that emotionally abandoned little girl, it was so much more dangerous than that.

'Do you like it?' she asked, her voice raw, terrified that her heart was already lost to him and knowing that, even if it was, it didn't really change anything. Because he had given her no indication that his heart was available to her. Or would ever be. That he was even capable of ever letting down the guard he had built around it.

Maybe he could love his dog. A dog's love was unconditional, and uncomplicated. But what indication had he given her he could love her? Or that he was even willing to try? None whatsoever.

She'd spent her childhood beating her head against that brick wall—trying to make her mother love her—and it had made her into someone reckless and impulsive and ultimately afraid. She couldn't spend her adulthood doing the same with him. But even knowing that, she couldn't seem to stop the giddy rush of pleasure when he spoke again, his voice rich with awe.

'It's incredible.'

'I thought I could give it to you as a parting gift,' she said, determined to remember their time was nearly over. She couldn't give into this yearning, this hope, this foolish need. Not again.

'Don't go.'

'What?' she asked, sure she hadn't heard him correctly. Wishing she hadn't felt her heart jolt.

'Don't go back to Ireland tomorrow,' he said. 'I have an estate in Long Island, which I mostly use for occasional weekend breaks and business hospitality purposes. But I haven't taken a proper holiday in ten years. The forecast is for warm weather. I'd like to take you there.'

'I can't stay,' she said, upset that for a second she'd even considered accepting his invitation. How far gone was she, that she would even want to pursue a reckless pipe dream when she'd missed her little boy so much? 'I need to go home. Mac needs me. And I need him.'

To ground me again and make me realise this isn't real.

'I thought we could fly him over, so he could spend the time with us there.'

'Are you…? Are you serious?' she asked, so shocked by his suggestion she couldn't think over the pounding in her chest.

He'd listened when she'd regaled him with stories about Mac, had asked a lot of questions about their child, but she hadn't expected this.

'Absolutely. If I'm going to form a relationship with him, I think we both know I'm going to need your help. I know nothing about children. This is a big step for us all. I don't want to make a mistake.'

'That's... I'm overwhelmed,' she said, because she was. But she forced the foolish bubble of hope down— knew it had no place in this arrangement. She needed to be practical now... And most of all she needed to protect herself, not just from these foolish, fanciful notions about Ross and her, but from the devastating prospect of letting that insecure girl reappear again, who had thought she could make someone love her just by wanting it enough.

'I'd have to go back and get him,' she said. If they were going to do this thing, it had to be about Mac—not them. Because there was no them. 'He's only three, I couldn't send him over on his own.'

'How about I ask Katie if she will accompany him?' he said. 'I need to repair things with her anyway. It's been five years and, after my behaviour at the wedding, I think perhaps more than a ten-minute conversation is required.'

Again, she was surprised, at his willingness to consider such an option. And at how open he was being to having a proper conversation with his sister. Surely this was a huge sign he was willing to do much more than simply go through the motions in his relationship with Mac?

'Okay, that could work,' she said, not sure Katie would go for it—after all, she was on her honeymoon at the moment. If anything, she was fairly sure Conall would insist on using the Rio Corp jet and accompanying his wife to New York, but if Ross was serious about repairing this rift, he would eventually have to talk to Con too. And involving her brother and his wife would be a good way of helping her to keep things in perspective and focus on what mattered now—Ross forming a relationship with his son.

'Good, I'll make the arrangements,' he said, in his usual no-nonsense fashion. But then he stepped forward and cupped her cheek. 'How about we order takeout? I'm not sure I want to leave the apartment tonight.'

She made herself smile, but the gesture felt desperately bittersweet as her abdomen pulsed at the purpose in his gaze. She covered his hand with hers, to draw it away from her face. 'That would be good, but, Ross...' She swallowed, knowing she had to make a clean break from him and the intimacy they had shared, before their son arrived. The danger to her heart was all too apparent now. 'We can't continue sleeping together while Cormac is with us. It would confuse him.'

It was a cop-out. Cormac wouldn't be confused. He didn't need to know they were even sleeping together if they were discreet. A part of her hated the lie and using her son to reinforce that lie. But she had no choice. Not if she was to keep her heart secure for the week ahead. Watching Ross bond with his son would be hard enough, without introducing the intimacy they had already shared into the equation. An intimacy she hadn't been as good at dealing with as she had believed.

'Why?' he asked. 'Hasn't he seen you dating before?'

'No, there hasn't been anyone...' She stopped. But his eyes narrowed, his gaze seeing much more than she wanted him to see. The flush burned in her cheeks, but it was already too late to disguise the truth.

Damn my Irish colouring.

'There hasn't been anyone but me?' he asked.

She could lie again. She wanted to lie, only feeling more exposed and wary at what the truth revealed, aware of the sudden intensity in his gaze. But a bigger part of her knew lying would only give the truth—that he was the only man she had ever slept with—more power.

She shrugged, even though the movement felt stiff. 'Being a single mum is a full-time job. I haven't had the time,' she said, trying to make it seem less of a big deal. Knowing in her heart it was just more evidence of how careful she needed to be now.

She had expected him to look spooked by the admission. Would have welcomed that reaction—because it would have given her at least some of the distance she so desperately craved.

But instead of looking spooked, he just looked even more intense. So intense she could feel the adrenaline rush over her skin.

'I see,' he murmured, then framed her face and pulled her close.

He slanted his lips across hers, his tongue thrusting deep, demanding a response. A response she was powerless to stop. The kiss was raw and possessive, and heartbreakingly intense.

She held his waist and kissed him back, letting the fear go, to indulge in the moment.

She wasn't that reckless girl any more. She would never jeopardise Mac's happiness, or her own, on a pipe dream—which was why she couldn't sleep with him again after tonight.

But as he lifted her easily into his arms to carry her upstairs she groaned, and gave herself permission to indulge that reckless girl, one last time.

CHAPTER TWELVE

'THANK YOU FOR interrupting your honeymoon, Katie. And bringing Mac over,' Ross said as he headed towards the liquor cabinet, needing a stiff drink. The evening sunlight shone off the water in the distance, the scent of sea air helping to calm his racing heartbeat.

He'd held his son for the first time ten minutes ago. His hands shook as he lifted the whisky bottle and splashed a few fingers in his glass.

'You're welcome, Ross. He was extremely excited during the flight over. But I think it was all too much for him and he crashed out on the helicopter ride to the estate,' Katie said.

He'd forgotten how little his child was. When the helicopter had touched down at the Long Island estate's heliport twenty minutes ago and his brother-in-law had emerged from it with Ross's sister by his side, carrying the sleeping boy—the child had looked so small and defenceless Ross's ribs had tightened.

Cormac had woken up momentarily, and smiled sleepily at his mother, reaching out to be held. She had scooped him into her arms with practised ease—but then she'd turned to Ross and said, 'He's heavy. Do you want to hold him?'

He'd reached to take the boy, only realising as he lifted

the sleeping child into his arms that he had no idea what he was doing.

But Mac had settled his head against his shoulder without complaint, his small arms wrapping around Ross's neck—the sweet scent of talcum powder and kid sweat invading his senses as the child dropped back into sleep.

Ross's heartbeat had accelerated as a boulder formed in his throat. Part panic, part fear, but mostly a fierce determination that he would do anything to protect this child. It had reminded him a little of how he had felt when he had lifted Rocky as an injured and abused puppy out of that dumpster, but this time the feeling had been a thousand times more intense.

But that moment had also brought the reason why he had invited Mac…and Carmel to Long Island into sharp and damning focus.

He took a gulp of the fiery Scotch, let the liquor burn his throat to suppress the jolt of annoyance at the memory of the assessing look in Conall O'Riordan's eyes as he had lifted the boy back out of Ross's arms so he and Carmel could settle him in his new bed, while Ross and Katie talked.

The knowledge O'Riordan had effectively taken Ross's place in Cormac's life for the last three years had been a sobering thought. But what was worse was the knowledge he had no right—not yet—to stake any kind of claim to being the boy's father. And that his reasons for inviting the boy here—with his mother—had been far from altruistic.

He'd resented Carmel's suggestion they stop having sex yesterday evening, had been filled with an almost visceral urge to change her mind, especially when she had told him he was the only man she had ever slept with. That swift surge of possessiveness, of ownership almost, had made their joining even more intense, even more desperate, but this afternoon when they'd arrived at the estate—and this evening when they'd waited together for O'Riordan's helicopter to arrive—he'd forced himself to back off. To give her space. And now—after holding his son for the first time—he realised that attempting to seduce her back into his bed would be a mistake.

He'd waited far too long to take on the responsibility of parenthood. He could not afford to mess it up. But more than that, what more did he really have to offer Carmel?

He splashed another finger of Scotch into a tumbler. 'Would you like something to drink, Katie?'

'Nothing for me, thanks,' his sister said, but then he noticed the flush on her cheeks, and the way her hand swept down to cover her stomach.

He frowned, his gaze meeting hers. 'My God, you're pregnant.'

The colour intensified, and her eyes widened. 'How did you know?'

He choked out a laugh, the stunned surprise on her face somehow helping to break the tension gathering in his stomach.

It made him remember how transparent she'd always been. Even as a lonely, grief-stricken teenager, the first time he'd met her. She'd run up to him that day—a complete stranger—and wrapped her arms around him, her eyes flooding as she told him how grateful she was to have a brother.

He could remember at the time being extremely uncomfortable. Patting her stiffly on the shoulder and wondering what the hell he was supposed to do with a grieving teenage girl who he did not know from Adam.

In the end, he'd abrogated the responsibility to a series of expensive boarding schools. He'd failed Katie that day. He couldn't afford to fail Mac in the same way. Surely that was where he had to concentrate his energies, not on the kinetic sexual connection he shared with the boy's mother, however tempting.

'You're an open book, Katie,' he said.

The knots in his stomach tightened again as the news of her pregnancy echoed in his chest.

His baby sister was having a baby of her own. But how much better prepared for that role was she than he was? Katie, even as a girl, had always been open and compassionate and generous. All things he would have to learn, if he was going to have any hope of living up to the task of being a father.

'Or you're a mind reader,' she countered, sounding disgruntled.

He smiled and poured her a soda water, added ice and a slice of lime. He handed her the drink. 'I guess congratulations are in order. When is the baby due?'

She took the glass and grinned, all the love she already felt for this unborn life shining in her eyes. 'We had the dating scan two days ago and they basically put the due date on Christmas Eve,' she said, her excitement suffusing her whole face now. 'Dreadful timing really—who wants to be born on Christmas Eve? But we got pregnant quicker than we thought. Poor Con's still in shock, actually. He was convinced it would take several months— he had worked out a whole schedule for when exactly we should stop taking contraception so we'd have a spring baby, which he thought was the perfect time for a birthday.' She cradled her still flat belly, her grin widening. 'But apparently baby didn't get the memo.'

'Bummer,' he said, his smile becoming genuine at the thought of 'poor Con' having his carefully laid plans shot to hell.

Welcome to the chaos, bro.

But then the empty space opened up again.

When was his own son's birthday? How could he even

pretend to be a father when he didn't know something so fundamental...and had never thought to ask?

'You should have told me you were pregnant,' he said, as it occurred to him she hadn't just changed her honeymoon plans to make the trip to the US at such short notice. 'Carmel and I could have made other arrangements.'

'Don't be silly, I'm perfectly fine,' she said, touching his arm. 'And we were happy to do it. Con has a house in Maine he's been waiting to show off to me for a while and then we're heading to his place in Monterey.'

He very much doubted her husband had been quite as happy to accommodate him—as he recalled the frown on O'Riordan's face when he'd first spotted Carmel and him standing together at the heliport.

He suspected the guy was even now grilling Carmel about what exactly the two of them had been doing together in the last week, but he kept his opinion of O'Riordan's reaction to himself, the enthusiasm in Katie's eyes both humbling, and painfully bittersweet—because his affair with Carmel was now over.

'I'm so excited you've made the decision to be a part of Mac's life. He's an incredible little boy. You won't regret it,' she added.

'I just hope he doesn't,' he mumbled.

'He won't,' Katie said and touched his arm. 'I think you're going to make an incredible father.'

'Thanks,' he said, humbled all over again by her belief in him, as it occurred to him he'd done absolutely nothing to deserve it.

The truth was he'd been a piss-poor brother. And it was way past time to change that too. *Really* change it.

'I'm sorry, Katie,' he said, realising how long overdue the apology was when she tilted her head, her gaze puzzled, her smile fading.

'What for?' she asked softly.

'Everything.' He huffed out a breath, looked away, because he couldn't bear to see the scepticism he knew he *would* deserve.

His gaze tracked towards the horizon, across the manicured lawn, the tennis courts, the guest house where Carmel and Mac would be staying, the pool—surrounded now by new railings, which he'd had installed before Mac's arrival.

He'd spent a small fortune refurbishing the estate buildings three years ago—the mansion had originally been constructed by a railroad baron in the nineteen-tens but had fallen into disrepair since the eighties. But how much time had he spent here? Virtually none. In many ways, the lavish but unlived-in property was a symbol for his life. He'd worked so hard, spent so much time and effort building De Courtney's, but with every goal he had achieved his life had only become emptier as he'd shed all his personal responsibilities, and shunned companionship and love.

The L word made him shudder.

Did he love his son? Already? Was that possible? The thought had his heart rate ramping up again.

He breathed deeply, trying to counter his haphazard pulse.

Calm down. You can handle this.

The twinkle of lights from the pool house reflected off the surface of the water as the sun sank into the ripple of surf in the distance, casting a red glow over the wooden walkway that tracked past the tennis courts and into the dunes. Whatever happened now, whatever he was capable of feeling for the boy, he made a vow never to shirk his responsibilities again. He would learn to be a good father. And maybe finally fulfil the promise he had made all those years ago to be a better man than his own father.

And he would keep his hands off Carmel, even if it killed him.

He turned back to his sister. 'I'm sorry for treating you like an inconvenience, a debt to be paid, rather than a sister,' he said in reply to her question.

She stood, watching him. But, weirdly, he didn't see scepticism, all he saw was compassion.

'You deserved—needed—so much more than I was ever capable of giving you. So I'm sorry for that too,' he finished.

She shook her head. But the all-inclusive smile, the unconditional love he knew he did not deserve, still suffused her features—and tore a hole in his chest.

'You did the best you could, Ross. But I also think you're capable of much more than you think,' she said, so simply it had fear slicing into his heart.

No, he wasn't. He knew he wasn't. He was selfish and entitled and absolutely terrified of love... Or he would have been a much better brother to her all those years ago.

And he would never have asked his sister to bring his son all the way to America, primarily so he would have a chance to sleep with the boy's mother for another week.

'I think you're ready now to open your heart to Mac...' Her smile widened, her eyes twinkling with excitement. 'And maybe his mum too, because it's pretty obvious there's a lot more going on between you and Carmel than just figuring out your new parenting arrangements.' She laughed, the sound light and soft and devoid of judgement. 'And that makes me so happy. Carmel's an amazing woman, brave and honest and talented and...' Her smile widened. 'Well, I'll stop being a matchmaker, but I think you two could make a great couple—even without factoring in Mac.'

'I'm not sure your husband agrees,' he managed as the shaft of fear twisted and turned in his gut.

Maybe he could love his son. He already felt the fierce need to protect him. But Carmel? That wasn't going to happen. Ever.

'Ignore Conall,' Katie said, still beaming, still so sure he would make a good partner for Carmel… On no evidence whatsoever.

Katie wasn't just sweet, and generous and kind, he realised, she was also irrepressibly optimistic and hopelessly naïve. Why else would she have forgiven him so easily after the way he'd treated her?

'My husband has been known to be chronically wrong about affairs of the heart,' she continued, the secret smile tugging at her lips suggesting her courtship with O'Riordan hadn't been quite as blissful as Ross had assumed.

Yeah, but O'Riordan's dead right about this.

'And he's more like a father to Mel and Immy than a brother,' she added. 'So he has a tendency to be a tad overprotective. But, believe me, Carmel is her own woman. And if she trusts you enough to let you form a relationship with Mac, my guess is she's probably already halfway in love with you.'

The guilt plunged like a knife deep into his gut.

No way. She can't be in love with me.

'I see,' he said, taking another sip of his whisky as he hoped like hell Katie was wrong.

CHAPTER THIRTEEN

'MR ROSS, CAN WE play more?'

'No way, slugger, it's time to get out of the water before you turn into a fish.'

Carmel grinned as she listened to Ross and Mac in the pool. Her little boy giggled and she lowered her book to see Ross hoist Mac out of the water—where they'd been playing together all afternoon—and sling him over his shoulder to stride out of the pool.

Rocky joined in the fun, barking uproariously and dashing over from his spot beside Carmel's lounger. Ross stood on the pool tiles—the water running in distracting rivulets down his broad shoulders and making his swimming shorts cling to his backside.

The inevitable endorphin rush joined the painful pounding in her chest that was always there when she watched the two of them together.

She blinked, her skin heating—her heart hurting in ways she hadn't expected and couldn't afford to acknowledge.

Ross lowered the giggling, squirming Mac to his feet, and she found herself enchanted by the tableau they made together. He wrapped a towel around his son and began to dry him with a confidence she was sure would have surprised them both six days ago—when she had handed him their sleeping son at the heliport, and she had seen the stunned emotion as he'd held Mac for the first time.

Mac's giggles got considerably louder as the dog helped out with the drying routine using his tongue.

'Rocky, sit!' Ross said.

The dog stopped licking Mac's face and planted its butt on the tiles—having learned to obey his master's voice. Mac wrapped his arms round Rocky's neck, burying his face in his fur.

'I love Rocky,' he said.

The dog sat obediently. Any worries they'd had about introducing Rocky to their child had quickly been dispelled. The pressure on her chest increased. The rescue dog had turned out to be a natural with children—his usually excitable temperament placid and protective with Mac.

But Rocky was not as much of a natural with children as Ross had turned out to be.

'I know you do,' Ross replied. 'I think he loves you too,' he added, the roughness in his voice making Carmel's eyes sting.

Ross loved his son. And Mac absolutely adored his father.

The weight on her chest grew as she thought back over the events of the past week. Which had been easy in some ways and incredibly hard in others.

Ross had thrown himself into fatherhood with a determination and purpose—and a hands-on approach—she hadn't expected, but she realised now, she should have.

He was a pragmatic, goal-oriented man, who knew how to pay attention to details. From the moment they'd arrived at the estate, the morning before Conall and Katie were due to fly in to drop Mac off, Carmel had known she had made the right choice to take this extra week and the opportunities it held… To finally give her son a father, however painful this week had promised to be for her.

The estate itself had been the first surprise. She'd expected something sleek and stylish and glaringly modern.

Instead, what she'd found was a lovingly restored Italianate mansion—reminiscent of something straight out of *The Great Gatsby*—which had been meticulously prepared for their son's arrival. Not only had Ross had a room repainted next to hers in the large guest house by the pool, and fitted with everything a little boy could possibly want—including a bed shaped like a pirate ship and a box full of age-appropriate toys—he'd even thought to have the estate's pool fenced in.

The workmen had been finishing off the railings when they had arrived, and he'd simply said, 'I thought it would be best to make sure he couldn't hurt himself.'

At that moment, she'd had to force herself not to allow that foolish bubble of hope to get wedged in her throat again. Not to give into the emotions that had derailed her during their week together in New York.

The interrogation she'd had from Con during his flying visit had helped. Her brother had questioned her about whether there was 'something going on' between them as soon as they'd been alone together after putting Mac to bed. And she'd been able to tell him the truth, or as much of the truth as he deserved to know, that there was nothing going on between them, not any more.

He'd looked at her suspiciously, no doubt picking up on the qualification in the statement, but to her surprise, instead of giving her another earful about how wrong Ross De Courtney was for her—something she was already well aware of—her brother had simply sighed, then given her a hard hug and whispered:

'Be careful, Mel. You and Mac are precious to me—and I don't want to see either one of you hurt.'

Conall's capitulation had empowered her despite the pain. That her brother had finally accepted she had the right to make her own choices felt important, like a validation, that she was doing the right thing now by stepping back, taking stock, instead of rushing headlong into feelings that would never be reciprocated.

The only problem was, knowing she was doing the right thing hadn't made it any easier to deal with the news that Con was about to become a father himself.

She'd been overjoyed for him and Katie, of course she had. She knew he would make a magnificent father and Katie a wonderful mother. But a secret, shameful, mean-spirited part of her had also resented the fact her brother was going to have it all, when she could not.

And as she'd watched Ross begin to establish a strong, loving relationship with their son, that niggling, mean-spirited, resentful part of herself had refused to go away.

Which was of course ludicrous, because the man had surprised her in the best way possible.

He'd talked to Mac so carefully, so practically, and increasingly taken on the more difficult elements of childcare without hesitation—had even, she could admit now, established a rapport with their son that was very different from her own. Where she tended to baby Mac, to worry about the risks rather than see the reward of allowing her son more independence, Ross was firmer with him, but also bolder. He was protective but also pragmatic and she'd been forced to admit that it had allowed Mac to gain in confidence, particularly in the swimming pool, where he'd been tentative at the beginning of the week to put his head under the water, but was now happy to leap in and go under, as long as he knew Ross would be there to scoop him up if he struggled.

She hated that she'd even resented a little bit seeing Mac grow to rely on his father, but she had. Up till now it had only ever been her and Mac. She'd held all the cards, made all the decisions. And while on the one hand it had been good at the end of each day to have someone else to talk to about Mac, it had also been much harder than she had expected to let go of that control. To know that she wasn't the only one who would have a say in Mac's upbringing from now on.

They hadn't had any conversations about visitation rights, formal custody agreements—perhaps because she had been careful to keep the evening meals they shared to an absolute minimum, the torture of being alone with Ross, and knowing she had no right to touch him, to indulge the pulsing ache in her sex as well as her heart, quite hard enough without being forced to talk about the permanent relationship she was going to have to share with him now.

Unfortunately, she doubted Ross would let her get away with that again tonight. She was already dreading the thought of spending the evening talking about the legalities of their continued relationship—in sterile, unemotional detail, when unemotional was the last thing she felt.

'Okay, buster, how about we feed you and the dog?' Ross said as he lifted Mac back into his arms, and the boy wrapped his arm around his neck.

'I want pizza.'

'What? Again?' Ross did a comical double take.

Mac nodded enthusiastically.

Ross laughed. 'I guess we'll have to ask Ellie if she has any left,' he said, talking about the chef who Mac had charmed just like everyone else on the six-person staff.

'Yes, please, Mr Ross,' he said, playing with Ross's hair now, in the way he had always done with her when she held him like that.

Mr Ross.

The name echoed miserably in Carmel's heart. Like

a symbol of her cowardice and selfishness in the last six days. It was way past time Mac knew who Ross really was. Not just Mammy's friend, but his father.

They hadn't had a chance to discuss it in the last six days, like so much else about Ross's permanent relationship with his son, because she'd avoided it. The same way she'd avoided being alone with Mac's daddy.

She swallowed heavily as Ross walked towards her toting their son, the surge of desire at the sight of his long limbs and naked chest prickling across her skin like wildfire—and making her feel like even more of a failure. Even more of a fraud.

Ross had scrupulously observed her request to end their intimate relationship while Mac was here. He'd escorted her to the guest house, after they had their meal together on the nearby terrace each evening. And had made no move to even touch her, let alone kiss her, since they'd arrived at the mansion.

And in a weird way, she'd even resented that too—that it was so easy for him to end their physical relationship, when it was so hard for her.

Her gaze took in the toned skin glistening in the afternoon sunlight, the bunched muscles of his biceps as he held their son aloft, the rakish beard scruff shadowing his jaw, which she'd watched appear in the last few days and had been itching to run her nails through.

Each night she woke from dreams, sweaty and aroused, the longing so intense she'd often had to resort to finding her own release.

The demands of navigating the massive adjustments when it came to co-parenting their child had taken some of the edge off that insistent, endless yearning in the early days, but every time she was near Ross now, she felt the pull. And she knew he felt it too.

She'd seen him watching her, when he thought she wasn't looking.

But what was worse, she couldn't seem to separate the physical yearning from the emotional yearning any more. Instead of their enforced abstinence making it go away, it seemed to have made it gather and grow, to become this huge lump of need and longing.

'I'm going to take Mac in now. He wants pizza again, is that okay?' Ross stood before her in all his glory, the prickles of heat now both damning her and terrifying her.

'Please, Mammy, can I now?' Mac chimed in.

'I don't suppose another pizza night would do any harm,' she said.

Mac started cheering.

'Cool,' Ross said, his voice roughening as his gaze flicked to her cleavage and back up again. 'You want me to handle his bath and bedtime routine?' he asked.

'Why don't we do it together?' she said. She should tell Mac Ross was his daddy. What was she waiting for? This wasn't about her and Ross, and it never had been. Perhaps if she finally acknowledged that—told her little boy who Ross really was—it would make the craving shrink, instead of grow.

He nodded and headed off with their baby in his arms, Rocky following on their heels.

Her gaze dipped to admire his glutes in the wet shorts. She forced it back up.

Focus, Mel, on what's best for Mac. And only Mac.

'Mammy, Mammy, Mr Ross said if Rocky has a puppy we can have him. Can we?'

Ross watched Mac reach out from his bed as his mother walked into the little boy's bedroom.

'Oh, did he now?' she said as she perched on the edge of the bed and gave their son an easy hug. She sent Ross a tense smile, and he caught a whiff of her scent—earthy and hopelessly seductive—the surge of need shot through him, vicious, unstoppable and unrelenting.

Only one more night to keep your hands to yourself.

They'd managed to stick to their no-sex rule, had focussed on their son these past few days—he couldn't afford to give into the need now. He dragged his gaze away from her to concentrate on the boy.

'It's okay, I doubt Rocky will be having pups any time soon,' he said, determined to keep his mind on what mattered, instead of what shouldn't.

The last six days had been a revelation in so many ways. He had fallen completely and utterly under the spell of the little boy who he still couldn't quite believe was a part of him. And fatherhood, much to his astonishment, hadn't been nearly as much of a struggle as he'd assumed. It was intense and disturbing on one level, the emotional independence he'd clung to for so long now utterly shot to hell. Every time he held the child's soft, sturdy body in his arms, listened to him giggle, or even whine, watched his small round face light up with excitement or frown with intelligence, or breathed in the scent of talcum powder and bubblegum shampoo, the fierceness of what he felt still shocked him, but it didn't terrify him any more.

His feelings about Mac were surprisingly simple and straightforward and, once he'd let them in without hesitation, were much easier to handle than to deny… His feelings for the boy's mother, though, remained a minefield that had only got worse as the week wore on.

Especially as he watched her struggle with the new reality of letting him be a father to her son.

He wanted her incessantly, of course. The effort to stay away from her, not to let their quiet evening meals lead to more, had been pure torture. But far worse was the yearning, the desire to be with her constantly, the fascination of simply watching her. It made him feel like the small boy he'd once been, giving ownership of his happiness to someone else.

But it was that struggle to share her son, the moments when he could see the doubts and fears cross her face, and realised how hard she must have had to strive to do this all alone, that had really crucified him.

Because it had made him realise how strong and how brave she really was.

The nightmares, not surprisingly, now he could no longer hold her in his arms each night, had also come back with a vengeance. Haunting his dreams and waking him up, confused, alone and yet painfully aroused.

'Can we have a puppy, Mammy, please?' Mac held her cheeks, forcing her to look directly at him.

Ross huffed out a laugh, trying to ease the tension in his gut. And force the sweet, simple feelings for the child to the fore. Because they made so much more sense than his obsession with Carmel.

'Mr Ross said so. Can we?'

Carmel tugged her face away and laughed. The first real laugh he'd heard from her in days. The light musical sound arrowed into Ross's gut, as it always did.

'We'll see, but before you go to sleep, I have something important to tell you,' she said, deflecting the boy's attention with an ease that always impressed him. 'Or rather, *we* have something important to tell you,' she said, glancing his way and sending him a look that made his heart thunder even harder.

He frowned, confused by the direction of the conversation, and the fierce glow in her eyes… He'd seen it before, on the pool terrace that afternoon, and so many other times in the past few days, often when he was with Mac. It disturbed him how it only increased the yearning.

She's not yours…she can't be…you don't want her to be.

'What, Mammy?' Mac said at the exact same time as he asked.

'We do?'

She nodded at him, then turned back to their son, but her hand reached out and covered his on the bedspread. The touch was electric, sparking so many reactions, not one of them safe, or subtle, or secure.

'Do you remember, you once asked me why you didn't have a daddy, Mac?' she said.

Mac nodded as Ross's heart began to pound painfully. Was she about to tell the boy who he really was? Damn it, he wasn't prepared for this.

'You said I did, but he couldn't be with me,' the little boy said as the pain in Ross's chest twisted with guilt, his grip on his emotions slipping even further.

Carmel nodded. So calm, when he could feel himself falling apart inside.

'He's with us now. Mr Ross is your father, Mac. And he wants to be a part of your life now, very much.'

Mac blinked sleepily, then his eyes widened, the spark of joy and instant acceptance making Ross's heart slam against his rib in hard heavy thumps.

'*Really?*' he asked, his little brows launching up his forehead.

Ross leaned forward, his hand shaking as he cupped his son's cheek. The boy's skin felt warm and impossibly soft beneath his palm. 'Yes, really,' he confirmed, his words coming out on a husky breath, the emotion all but choking him now.

'I'm sorry I wasn't here sooner,' he said, trying to concentrate on the child, and not the fissure opening up in his chest.

The boy was a smart, sweet, bright, brilliant child—who loved dogs and playing in the pool, who could eat a whole slice of pizza without taking a breath, and charm the pants off everyone he met—and he couldn't have been prouder to be his father. So why did he feel as if the black hole were opening up to swallow him whole?

'Can I call you Daddy?' the little boy asked, looking hesitant for the first time since Ross had met him.

'Of course, I would love for you to call me Daddy,' he replied. 'If you want to,' he finished, as it occurred to him he'd never called his own father by such a familiar name.

As much as he hated to think of the man who had frightened him so much as a child, and whom he had despised as an adult, he clung to that distinction.

Carmel had told him once his own father's failings as a human being didn't have to be his failings, and she'd been right about that. He would strive now to earn this child's trust and respect, the way his own father had never earned his.

But as the little boy flung his arms around his neck and whispered into his ear, 'Daddy, don't forget now, I want a puppy,' the aching hole in his heart refused to go away.

He blinked, the stinging sensation in his eyes making the hole bigger as he lifted the child out of his arms and placed him back in the bed.

'We'll have to talk about that more with your mother, and Rocky, but your request has been duly noted,' he said, the words scraping against his larynx. 'I think it's time for you to go to sleep now. You have a long journey home tomorrow,' he added, the thought crucifying him even more.

But as he pulled away, to let Carmel finish tucking their son in, the word *home* echoed in his chest and seemed to scrape against his throat.

The thought of how much he was going to miss his son, how much he was going to miss them both once they were gone tomorrow, only compounded the sense of loss, of pain and confusion.

He'd thought about it, of course he had, but until this moment he hadn't realised that they had turned this huge, palatial estate into a home in the last week. The way Carmel had turned his loft in Tribeca into a home too. The thought terrified him.

How had he let that happen? When had he ever been anything but self-sufficient? How come it only made him feel emptier inside?

Ross lifted off the bed, his steps heavy as he walked to the door, to give Carmel time to settle the boy, but then he heard the small sleepy voice say, 'Goodnight, Daddy.'

'Goodnight, son,' he replied.

He left the guest house and walked out onto the lawn beside the pool terrace to relieve the choking sensation in his throat. He looked up at the stars, and felt the deep sense of loss at the thought of returning to the city tomorrow. Without them.

He had to get out of here, to get away, from the pain in his chest and the hole she had made in his heart.

Resentment flared. She shouldn't have told Mac like that. Without his input. Shouldn't have hijacked him.

He spotted Rocky sleeping on one of the loungers, headed towards the small gate into the pool area ready to take the dog back to the main house, when he heard the guest house's door open behind him.

Longing shot through him. Swiftly followed by anger. Because the black hole in his stomach remained, which he had no idea how to repair now.

He turned, to see her walking towards him, the summery dress she'd changed into fluttering around her legs in the evening breeze. She had the baby monitor in her hand, which she always brought with her when they ate out on the garden terrace in view of the guest house.

'Why did you tell him?' he said, making no effort to keep the brittle edge of anger out of his voice—to disguise all the other emotions churning in his gut, which he had no idea now how to control... Longing, need, desire and a fear so huge it all but consumed him.

'I thought it was past time,' she said, with a flippancy that infuriated him even more.

How was this so easy for her?

'You don't think we should have talked about it first?' he said, still trying to control the brutal turmoil she had triggered.

She tilted her head to one side, considering, her whole face suffused by that ethereal glow that had captivated him and terrified him. *Always.* Ever since that sultry summer night so long ago when she'd mesmerised him with her soft lilting accent, her smart, erudite and impulsive personality and the rich scent of her arousal. She was looking at him now the way she'd looked at him then, as if she saw right through him. Knew all the things about him he didn't want her to know. Could see the frightened boy he'd once been, inside the man.

Exposed was too small a word for how it made him feel.

Exposed, and wary and... Needy. Damn it.

'I suppose,' she said. 'But we've only this one more night together, so I saw no point in waiting.'

We've only this one more night together.

The yearning reverberated through him, twisting something deep inside. Yanking at that empty space that had been growing ever since he'd seen her again... And he was very much afraid only she would ever fill.

The desire surged through him again, but this time it was sure and solid and elemental. And simple, unlike all the thoughts and feelings queuing up in his throat.

He stepped towards her, not sure what he was doing any more, but knowing he needed to taste her again, just once more. This enforced celibacy had been her idea, but he'd embraced it after his conversation with Katie, believing it was the best way, hell, the only way, to create the distance he needed to let her go...

But somehow it had backfired on him—because not having her had only made him want her more.

'Don't tempt me, Carmel,' he murmured, seeing her ragged pulse punch her collarbone and hearing the shattered pants of her breathing. She felt it too, this hunger, this need. That was all this was, a physical connection so intense they'd only increased it by keeping their hands to themselves... 'I'm not in the mood,' he finished, the statement closer to the truth than he wanted it to be.

He was on edge, the emotions he didn't understand, for her as much as the child, too close to the surface, threatening to tip him over into the abyss.

He heard the shattered sigh, felt her hands brace against his waist, saw her gaze darken with awareness... He braced himself, expecting her to pull back, even as her spicy scent filled his nostrils and the desire, so fierce, so urgent, beat in his groin.

But instead, she lifted her chin, the challenge in her gaze unmistakable as her fingers fisted in his shirt, the stars reflected in her eyes bottomless enough to drown him as she leaned into him.

'Kiss me, Ross,' she whispered, bold, provocative and as tortured as he was. 'We've only this one night, why should we waste it?'

His control snapped, like a high-tension wire winched too tightly.

He thrust his fingers into her hair, tugged her head back and slanted his mouth across hers, capturing her sigh of surrender and plunging his tongue deep into her mouth.

He took command of the kiss, absorbing her sighs, dragging her into his arms, grinding the hard weight of his arousal against her sex. Forcing back the turmoil of emotions lodged in his gut at the thought that he had to let her go tomorrow.

With the knowledge that, tonight, she was all his.

Heat spread through her body like wildfire, but it was the emotion closing her throat that made her groan as Ross's tongue invaded her mouth, claiming her sighs for the first time in six days. She tried to focus on the need, that brutal endorphin rush, but the terrible truth kept echoing in her brain.

You're not just falling, you've fallen. This man is it for you. There's no going back now. There never was.

His hands cupped her bottom, pressing her against the prominent ridge of his arousal, letting her know how much he needed her, how much he wanted her too. Clasping her waist, he lifted her easily into his arms, and wrenched his mouth away. She missed it instantly, the longing already at fever pitch.

'Where?' he rasped.

'My room,' she gasped. 'But we'll have to be quiet.' She'd dropped the baby monitor in the grass. But they would hear Mac if he woke up.

'Quiet? Yeah…' he said, his lips doing diabolical things to her neck, and her heart rate.

'Mammy? I had a bad dream.'

Mac's cry didn't register at first through the fog of dazed heat and terrifying emotion, until Ross froze, his fingers digging into her hips. His head jerked up and she saw the stricken look in his eyes before he gasped. 'Oh, God.'

He put her down so suddenly she stumbled. Looking over her shoulder, she saw Mac standing in the doorway of the guest house, in his PJs, his hair rumpled, rubbing his eyes.

The flames that had been burning in her abdomen died

down as she tried to switch into mummy mode. The heat continued to burn in her cheeks, though, as she scooped up their son. 'It's okay, baby. Mammy's here.'

Her little boy wrapped his arms round her neck, snuggled his face into her shoulder, still mostly asleep, thank goodness. She couldn't help the pounding in her chest as she carted him back to bed and tucked him in—getting a sleepy rendition of his nightmare, which had involved an enormous pizza and a puppy who kept eating Mac's share.

After kissing him, and promising that when they got a puppy they'd make sure it didn't like pizza, she levered herself off the bed.

Mac was already asleep as she rechecked the room's monitor, giving herself time before she returned outside.

What had they just been about to do? Because it had been so much more than just the fever of desire.

'I love him.'

She whispered the words to herself, forcing herself to face them, knowing them to be true, despite the fear still gripping her chest.

She closed the door to her little boy's room, stood with her back to it and tried to focus. She'd tried to deny her feelings for Ross, for six days, maybe even longer than that. Tried to make this need, this connection, about nothing but sex and her own insecurities. She'd been so scared before, terrified even, of admitting the truth to herself.

But how could it be so wrong? He'd shown himself to be a good father, a good man in the last week. She'd come to know him for who he really was. He wasn't the man she'd fallen for that night four years ago. Not a romantic notion, but flesh and blood, with fears and insecurities just like hers. He could make mistakes, try and fail, just as she had, but she admired him for that now. And yes, there were many things he seemed incapable or unwilling to share, about his past, his childhood, but she knew he had struggled to overcome them. Surely that was what mattered now.

How could she know how Ross really felt about her, about them, about the chance for them to make a future together with their son, instead of apart, if she didn't tell him she loved him? Her fear of her feelings had never really been about Ross and her—it had simply been an echo of that little girl. Who had become so scared to fail she'd refused to try.

She took a deep breath, the fear still huge, but somehow not as black or impenetrable. Not as final. Because now, finally, she had a plan.

She walked back out of the guest house to see Ross standing with his back to her. Her heart did a giddy two-step, the emotion flooding her again.

God, he was so gorgeous, so hot, but he was also flawed, and human, just as she was.

He held the dropped monitor in his hand, the rigid set of his shoulders reminding her of the haunted, horrified look that had crossed his face when he had spotted Mac.

Her courage faltered a little as she approached him. With his head bowed, and his body radiating tension, he seemed a million miles away. What had caused that awful look? she wondered.

She touched his shoulder and he jerked. 'It's okay, Daddy,' she murmured as he turned towards her. 'We didn't scar him for life,' she added, trying to keep her voice light and even, and ignore the painful hope swelling in her chest.

'Ross, what's wrong?' she said when she got a look at his face.

Where was the man who had been devouring her moments ago with such urgency? The man she was finally ready to admit she loved? Because the man in front of her now looked like a ghost. The blank expression so rigid, it was starting to scare her.

'Nothing,' he murmured, his voice as controlled as the rest of him. 'I'm tired. And I'm sure you are too,' he said. 'I'll have the staff bring some food over for you. You've got a long day tomorrow—and I need to head back to Manhattan early. I'll be over in the morning to say goodbye to Mac.'

She'd barely absorbed the long list of details—which he must have been preparing while she was putting Mac back to bed—before he nodded and turned.

Everything inside her rebelled.

No.

She grasped his arm to stop him walking away. 'Wait. What? That's it?'

She could feel the frantic beat of her heart threatening to choke her. But ignored it. This couldn't be happening. How could he suddenly be so cold? When only moments before…?

His mildly puzzled frown—so distant, so vacant—made the pain in her chest increase. 'I think it's for the best we don't finish what we started—which would clearly have been a mistake.'

'A…a mistake?' she stuttered, still stunned by the sudden change in him from wild, passionate lover to cold robot. 'How can it be a mistake when I… I'm in love with you?'

The declaration burst out on a tortured breath. It wasn't how she'd planned to tell him. But that sudden dismissal had left her reeling. Frantic and scared and suddenly so unsure again.

She'd never been a person to temper her feelings. To judge and weigh all the pros and cons carefully, methodically, before making a move. She'd seen that impulsiveness as a weakness for so long. Something to be corrected and suppressed. But she didn't want to live like that any more. To try and deny rather than confront. She was sick of being a coward.

If she'd been wrong, about everything she thought had been happening between them, about where they might go from here, she needed to know now. She could deal with the worst, she told herself. She just couldn't deal with lying to herself any longer.

He blinked several times, clearly as shocked as she was by the whispered revelation. But then a muscle in his jaw tensed, and the first stirrings of nausea churned in her stomach, alongside a deep wave of sadness. The same sadness that had overwhelmed her once before, when she'd received that cold, cruel, cutting text. How could she have forgotten that feeling so easily? Enough to open herself to the same torment again?

'You don't love me, Carmel. What you feel for me is infatuation, believe me, it will pass.'

No, it won't, and I don't want it to. Why can't we be a family? Why can't you let me in?

It was what she wanted to say, what she wanted to shout at him so he would hear her. Her feelings were her own and he had no right to doubt them... But the sadness had spread like a black cloud, over the bright twinkle of hope, covering everything in a thick impenetrable shadow and she knew... This wasn't her decision, it was his. She couldn't make him love her, any more than she had been able to make her mother love her.

And it would only hurt her more to try.

When she fell in love it was fierce and true and she was very much afraid for ever. But she was also a realist. And what she had to do now was deal with the truth. Because if he couldn't love her back, couldn't even accept her feelings for him, what chance would they ever have?

So she said nothing, just stood dumbly, refusing to

fight, refusing to cry, but most of all refusing to beg, as he walked into the night.

And the next day, when he came to the guest house to say goodbye to his son, she applied her make-up carefully so he wouldn't see the tears she'd shed over him. And she forced herself to stay strong, to stay calm, to say nothing about the agony of longing and to focus on keeping things light and upbeat for their little boy.

She told herself she would get over it. And she forced herself to pack away all her half-formed dreams for them the same way she packed away her clothes.

But when they boarded the De Courtney Corp chopper at the estate's heliport and she watched Ross standing on the grass and waving goodbye, his dark hair flattened by the wind from the helicopter's blades, the beard scruff that had abraded her skin the night before during that ferocious kiss now shaved off, she held her little boy a bit too tightly, and knew it was going to take a lot more than expertly applied make-up to repair her shattered heart.

CHAPTER FOURTEEN

'MR DE COURTNEY, the conference video call with the European hub is due to start in five minutes.'

Ross stared aimlessly at the Manhattan skyline from his office at the top of De Courtney Corp's US headquarters, only vaguely aware of his assistant's voice, so exhausted he wasn't sure he even had the energy to switch on his computer, let alone conduct a two-hour video call. It was three days, three long days since he had left Long Island, since he had watched the chopper containing Carmel and his son disappear on the horizon, and he still couldn't get her face out of his mind. Or the words she'd whispered to him:

'I'm in love with you.'

But the surge of impossible hope that replaying those words in his mind over and over again brought with it faded into a morass of guilt and loathing, and horror, as he recalled the sight of his child, his son, so small, so vulnerable, witnessing that frantic kiss. And the terrible memories that sight had triggered, memories he had buried for so long, memories he had only ever grasped in nightmares until three days ago, had come slamming back into his consciousness ever since… And refused to leave him now.

The sick dread pressed against his throat again.

His father's voice cold, callous, cruel, his mother's pleading, the cries, the agony, the blood...

He thrust shaking fingers through his hair.

How could Carmel love him when he was only half a man? And that half was not that different from his own father after all...

'Would you like me to get you some coffee before you start, Mr De Courtney?'

'No,' he said, turning to see his personal assistant standing at the door, looking concerned. 'Actually, yes, but can you cancel the call, Daniel?' he said.

'Um...of course...certainly, sir,' the young man said, but he looked even more concerned and completely confused. Probably because Ross had never shirked a work responsibility in his life.

He turned back to the view he couldn't see as his PA left to get his coffee.

He couldn't go on like this. He needed help. He felt as if he were in a fog, a dark, cloying fog he would never find his way out of. Mostly, he needed Carmel. She was the light on the horizon, thoughts of her the only thing he seemed to be able to cling onto when those dark memories loomed.

But he also couldn't forget her shattered expression that night, and her listless behaviour the next morning. So calm, so controlled, so devoid of passion. And so unlike the woman he knew.

He'd done that to her. How could he ask her for help, when his knee-jerk reaction to her declaration of love had destroyed everything they might have had?

'Mr De Courtney, you have a video caller,' Daniel said, walking back into the office with a cup of coffee. 'A Mrs O'Riordan?'

Carmel? The brutal surge of adrenaline was painfully dispelled when Daniel added, 'She says she's your sister?'

Not Carmel, Katie.

But then a strange thing happened. The rush of need would have disturbed him three days ago, but he was too exhausted to resist it now. Or question it. 'Put her through to my mobile,' he said, his voice rough.

Maybe Katie would know what he could do, how to fix what was broken?

He scraped his fingers through his hair, sat down at his desk, and picked up his smartphone to click on the link his PA had sent through.

'Katie?' he said, shamed by the desperation in his own voice as her familiar face appeared on the screen.

'Ross, what on earth did you do?'

The forthright, even aggressive tone was so unlike his usually sweet and malleable sister, all he could do was blink. 'What?'

'To Carmel, you dolt?'

The mention of her name had the pain he had been keeping so carefully leashed charging through his system all over again.

'You've seen her? What's wrong with her? Is she sick?' he said, concern and panic taking hold and shaking him to his core.

'We spoke to her via video chat, last night. And yes, she's sick. Heartsick. Although…' Her eyes narrowed. 'Ross, you look even worse than she does. What happened between you two?' The soft concern in her voice made the guilt bloom like a mushroom cloud.

He swallowed convulsively, to control the new wave of nausea. 'She told me she loved me and I threw it back in her face,' he said, blurting out the truth. But he was past caring now, what Katie thought of him, what anyone thought of him. 'I want to fix it, but I don't know if I can.'

'Oh, Ross. Of course you can, if you want to enough,'

Katie said, the concern in her gaze turning to determination. 'Do you?' she asked.

'Yes, yes, I do,' he said—that much at least was simple. 'But I've made such a mess of everything.' He wanted to believe Katie, but how could he vanquish the demons from his childhood? After all this time? And how could he risk sullying Carmel with them? 'But I'm not sure it can be fixed. I'm not even sure I deserve to have it fixed. I certainly know I do not deserve Carmel.'

Katie stared at him. 'You do know that's nonsense, don't you?' she said, the matter-of-fact tone, and her undying faith in him, making him wonder why he had ever believed he didn't want a sister. Or need one.

Then she added with complete conviction. 'I'm sure between the two of us, we can figure out a way to fix it.'

He wasn't sure he believed her, but he knew that if nothing else Katie had given him the courage to try.

CHAPTER FIFTEEN

CARMEL STARED UP at the large detached mansion house tucked at the end of a blossom-strewn mews in London's Kensington as the chauffeur-driven limousine that had picked her up at Heathrow glided through iron gates and into a pebbled courtyard.

'Where are we?' she asked the driver as he opened the door, confused now as well as wary. But too tired to summon the anger that had fortified her during the flight from Galway in Ross's private jet, after the text she'd received two days ago. His personal assistant had requested that she attend a meeting with his legal team today in London—to discuss Mr De Courtney's visitation rights and other financial matters.

Ross hadn't contacted her himself, and that had hurt, at first. But then she had been grateful. Seeing him again would only draw out the agony, she thought miserably as she stepped out of the car. Was that why he hadn't mentioned this meeting when he was video calling Mac last Sunday from Manhattan? Their conversation had been short and stilted and… Well, agonising… Which surely proved it would have been too soon to see him again in the flesh.

'This is one of the De Courtneys' ancestral homes, I believe, Ms O'Riordan,' the chauffeur remarked, although he seemed unsure.

Strange. She had assumed she would meet with Ross's legal team in the company's London headquarters.

'Okay,' she said, forcing down the new wave of sadness. She didn't really want to spend time in his ancestral home, but she followed the driver up the steps to the imposing Georgian building without complaint.

She just wanted to get this over with.

She hadn't slept properly in close to two weeks. Ever since she and Mac had returned from New York. She'd been burying herself in work, and childcare, her go-to strategy when anything in her life was stressing her out. But it seemed this crisis was bigger than any she'd faced before.

Why couldn't she forget that last night, the hope she'd had—so quickly dashed—that she and Ross might build a family together? A future? It had always been a ludicrous pipe dream—one last hurrah for that starstruck girl who had fallen under his spell in an apple orchard a lifetime ago. She needed to pull herself together now and stop thinking about what might have been and instead face the reality... And concentrate on the callous ease with which he had rejected her again.

Mac was what mattered now, and on that subject at least, she knew they were in accord—because she'd heard her son's giggles from the other room as he had chatted with his father in Manhattan for over an hour on Sunday. There was no reason to believe the legal team were going to ambush her with any conditions she couldn't accept. And if they did, she had Con's number on speed dial.

She stepped into the musty interior of the house and shivered. The gloomy hallway, mostly devoid of furniture, was even more austere and forbidding than the outside, despite the sunlight coming in through the stained-glass window above the door and illuminating the dust motes in the stale air.

The chauffeur stood back to let her enter then pointed towards an open door at the end of the hallway. 'I was asked to direct you to the library, and then leave. But I will wait outside for you when you wish to depart.'

Huh?

'Okay.' Carmel frowned, the house's chilling stillness only broken by the loud ticking of an antique grandfather clock as the chauffeur closed the front door behind him.

She made her way down the hallway, the blip of irritation fortifying her. Seriously? Didn't they think she had better things to be doing than spending the day in an empty house?

She stepped into the library. And her heart stopped, then rammed into her throat. Instead of the team of solicitors she had been prepared for, there was only one man, silhouetted in the room's mullioned windows. A man who had delighted and devastated her in equal measure.

'Ross?' she whispered.

Was she dreaming now?

But then he turned from his contemplation of the house's overgrown gardens. And her battered heart threatened to choke her. Pain shot through her, as fresh and raw and real as it had been two weeks ago, and she recalled every single word of his rejection for the five thousandth time.

'You don't love me, Carmel. What you feel for me is infatuation, believe me, it will pass.'

If this was infatuation, she wanted no part of it any more.

'Carmel,' he said, his voice husky and strangely hesitant as he crossed the room's parquet flooring, his footsteps echoing in the empty room—the books that must once have been here long gone.

'What are you doing in London?' she asked, surprised her voice sounded so steady when her ribs had become a vice, squeezing her chest so tightly she was afraid her heart might burst.

She drank in the sight of him, but everything about him now seemed intimidating—his long legs, broad shoulders, that devastatingly handsome face, the planes and angles sharper than she remembered them, the waves of chestnut hair furrowed into haphazard rows, the dark business suit and white shirt, so unlike the man who had played with their son for hours in the pool.

She stepped back, and he stopped.

'Don't, don't come any closer,' she said, the inevitable surge of heat her enemy now, like the painful yearning in her heart. 'If you've brought me here just to tell me again you don't love me, I got the message the first time,' she said, brutally ashamed of the quiver in her voice.

Her eyes stung. She'd shed so many tears for him already, how could there still be more? God, could he not even leave her with this last scrap of dignity?

'I brought you here to show you the house where I grew up.' He glanced around the room, thrusting his hands into his pockets, the hunched shoulders matching the flash of pain and loathing she had seen that night.

She should tell him no, she wasn't interested any more. But she couldn't seem to get the words out, past the thunderous emotion still choking her.

'Why?' she managed to ask, suddenly unbearably weary. Unbearably tense. The struggle to hold onto her tears so hard.

'Because I want you to know everything. So you can understand what happened on our last night, when you told me you loved me.'

She frowned. What was this now? Did he want her to say it again? So he could reject her again? Why was he talking in riddles?

But even as the caustic thoughts assailed her, she could

see that wasn't it. He looked tormented, on edge—whatever ghosts had haunted him that night, this was where they dwelled. And suddenly she wanted to know—all those things he had been so unwilling to share with her. So all she said was, 'Okay.'

He gave a stiff nod, then glanced around the empty shelves. 'This is the room where my father destroyed the only photograph I had of my mother in front of me,' he said, his voice so flat and remote it was chilling. 'I was seven.'

She shuddered, reminded of how he had spoken to her two weeks ago in that same monotone.

'That's hideous,' she managed. 'Why would he do such a thing?'

He shrugged, the movement tense but somehow painfully resigned too, as if it didn't really matter, when it clearly still hurt.

'He was sending me to boarding school and he was furious that I was still wetting the bed at night, according to my governess. I'd been having night terrors ever since…' He hesitated, swallowed. 'Ever since her death, two years before. He was concerned I would embarrass the De Courtney name at school.' His lips lifted in a rueful smile, but there was no humour in it, only sadness. 'To be fair, it worked. I was more terrified of him than the nightmares.'

'I… I'm so sorry, Ross. He sounds like a terrible father.'

She wanted to go to him, to hold him, to console him, the way she would Mac when he had a nightmare, but she could see the brittle tension, and sense the struggle within him to hold the demons at bay so he could talk about them. So she kept her distance.

She had known his father had scarred him, but had she ever realised to what extent? She'd dismissed that haunted look two weeks ago when Mac had appeared so unexpectedly, too busy wallowing in the rejection that had followed, the desire to tell him how she felt… Why hadn't she asked questions, thought more about what he might be feeling, instead of focussing on her own?

'If it's hard for you to be here, we don't have to stay,' she added. Suddenly wanting to leave this place. Sure, if he was going to reject her again, to tell her this was why he could never love her, she didn't want it to be here.

But he shook his head slowly, the small quirk of his lips somehow devastatingly poignant. 'Don't let me off the hook so easily, Carmel.'

She nodded slowly, realising that, for whatever reason, she had to let him show her the rest.

He led her out of the library, and up the stairs, reaching a large landing, his movements stiff and mechanical and comprehensively lacking his usual grace. He stopped on the threshold of the first room on the left. A huge piece of furniture—from the shape of it under the dustsheet, probably a four-poster bed—stood in the middle of the room. He hesitated, took in a lungful of air, then stepped inside.

'This is where the night terrors came from. This is the room where I watched my mother and her baby die. And where, the therapist believes, nine months before I may have watched him assault her.'

'Oh, God.' Carmel gasped beside him, then pressed her fingers to her lips. Ross tucked his hands into his pockets to stop them shaking.

One lone tear skimmed down her cheek, crucifying him. He could see pity in her gaze as she turned towards him. But more than that he could see compassion.

The nausea in his gut rose in a wave to push into his throat.

The sick, weightless feeling in his stomach reminded

him of those moments—between sleep and waking—
when he could see it all again so clearly. But he knew he
had to keep talking. He owed her this. So he forced himself to channel the advice the therapist he had employed
a week ago at Katie's suggestion had given him.

*You're not responsible for her death, Ross. But what
you saw between your parents would cause a deep
trauma for anyone—let alone a five-year-old child—
and that's what we need to address.*

He needed to tell her the truth, about the baggage he
might well carry with him always—and the truth about
his heritage, and the legacy he was terribly afraid might
lurk inside him.

'She used to like me to sleep with her,' he said. 'I
suspect now to stop him visiting her at night. But I can
remember one night. I woke and he was there, beside
the bed, kissing her, hurting her, she was crying and he
wouldn't stop...' He couldn't say any more, the vision
terrifying him even now.

'Ross...' She reached out her hand, grasped his fingers,
held on. 'Is that why you freaked out, when Mac woke up
and saw us kissing that night?' she asked.

'I... I suppose yes. It brought it all back. But...' He hesitated, scared to say the truth out loud. She squeezed his
fingers, giving him the courage he so desperately needed
to continue. He forced himself to turn, to look at her, to
give it to her straight. 'I wanted you so damn much in
that moment. I'm not sure I could have stopped, if you'd
asked me. She begged him to stop and he wouldn't and
I can't bear the thought that I might... That Mac might
have witnessed the same depraved—'

'Ross...' She cut him off, pressed a gentle palm to his
cheek, to stop the rambling confession. A lone teardrop
fell from her lid. 'What Mac witnessed, if he witnessed
anything at all, was a kiss between two consenting adults.

It's not the same thing at all,' she said so simply it pierced through the fog at last. The feel of her palm stroking his face felt so soft, so warm, soothing the brutal knots in his belly. 'And anyway, you did stop, so fast you almost dropped me,' she said, the humorous quirk of her lips warming the brutal chill that had overcome him the moment he had walked into this room.

But then she added, 'Can you tell me what happened when she died?'

He dipped his head. He didn't want to talk about it. But somehow it was easier now, knowing she didn't blame him, the way he had blamed himself, for his father's sins.

'I wasn't supposed to be in here,' he said. 'No one saw me, they were too busy trying to save her... But her cries had woken me up,' he said, but then the words simply ground to a halt.

'You don't need to tell me,' she said softly beside him. Weirdly, the fact she would let him stop, if he needed to, gave him the courage to carry on.

'I do... I want to,' he said, knowing it wasn't pity he saw in those stunning blue eyes, but a fierce compassion. 'I want you to know what you'll be dealing with, because... I still have the nightmares. They came back, after I discovered I had a son. And once I couldn't hold you at night. And they've been much worse, since we left Long Island.'

'Why didn't you tell me, Ross?' Her voice broke on his name, another tear slipping down her cheek.

'Because I was so ashamed,' he said simply.

She shook her head, then gripped his wrist and tugged his hand out of his pocket. She threaded her fingers through his and held on. The contact was like a balm again, releasing the renewed pressure in his chest.

'Is that why you had the vasectomy?' she asked, with

an emotional intelligence that he now knew he found as captivating as the rest of her.

He nodded. Funny she should figure that out when he never had.

'Yes, I think it was. I guess it all got jumbled up in my mind. He was there, in the room, demanding they save the baby, no matter what. It was another boy, another male heir, and I expect that was why he had assaulted her in the first place. Because that was always his priority. Continuing the De Courtney legacy.' He gathered in a painful breath, let it out again. 'There was so much blood,' he murmured, seeing it all again. The private medical team rushing around, the metallic smell suffocating him, the silent scream tearing a hole in his chest.

His breathing became laboured, but her hand gripped his, reassuring, empowering, making the nightmare vision retreat.

'So you had yourself sterilised as a young man, so you would never put a woman through what he had put your mother through,' she said softly. 'Can't you see how different that makes you from him?'

'Yes,' he said, because finally he did see. But then he dropped his chin, swallowed round the rawness in his own throat. 'Although it's kind of screwed up, especially as I never properly checked to find out if the damn procedure had actually worked.'

'Well, thank goodness it didn't or we wouldn't have Mac,' she said.

He chuckled at the force of feeling in the remark, his relief almost as glorious as the sudden feeling of lightness. The realisation she had lifted a weight that had burdened him for far too long.

He dragged her out of the room, slammed the door. Feeling strangely empowered at the thought of shutting out that part of his past. It would always be there, he knew that, but there was no reason to believe it could control him any more. Not if he could do this next bit.

'I spoke to Katie ten days ago.' He clasped her cheeks, no longer able to deny the wealth of feeling moving through him. Desperation yes, but also determination, and a strange sort of acceptance. 'I told her everything, and she suggested I get a therapist. I've had a couple of sessions already, and…' He paused, swallowed. 'It may take me a long time to finally get the nightmares to stop.' Although oddly, after this conversation with Carmel, he already felt as if he had turned an important corner.

Identifying your demons was one thing, but defeating them was another, and she had already helped him with that. He'd managed to laugh in a room that had once filled him with terror. Until today, he would never have believed that was even possible.

'I'm so sorry, Ross,' she said. 'I didn't ask what had spooked you that night and I should have. Instead I burdened you with my feelings when you were struggling to handle your own. It was selfish and immature and—'

'Stop.' He pressed his finger to her lips. 'No, it wasn't, Carmel,' he said. 'You were honest with me.' God, how he hoped that was still how she felt about him. 'And instead of being honest with you, I protected myself. That's not okay.'

'But, Ross…' She began again, grasping his hands, and looking at him with the same glow in her eyes that had captivated and terrified him so much.

And suddenly he knew… She still loved him. She hadn't changed her mind, even knowing the darkness that lurked inside him and might never be vanquished.

He let go of her cheeks and dropped to one knee, taking her hands in his.

'Ross?' She looked stunned. 'What are you doing?'

'What I should have done two weeks ago,' he said,

then swallowed down the last of his fear. 'When you told me you loved me.'

'But—' she said.

'Shh, now,' he said, but he grinned. Damn, but he adored the way she always needed to have the last word. But not this time. This time it was his turn to bare his soul. And her turn to listen. 'What I should have said, what I know now was already in my heart, was that I love you, too. And I love our little boy. And I would really like to marry you.'

Her big blue eyes widened even further, her mouth opening, then closing again.

For the second time ever he'd left her speechless. But this time felt so much better than the last.

'I know you will probably want to wait, until I've had a lot more therapy,' he qualified. 'But I'm planning to relocate to Galway—to buy a house near you and Mac so we can begin to—'

'No,' she interrupted him.

No? His heart jumped, stuttered, but before the panic could set in, she continued.

'No, I don't want to wait,' she declared, tugging him up off his knees as his heart soared. 'We've waited long enough. And so has Mac. And no, you don't need to buy a house. Because we already have one that we can share. It's only two bedrooms, but perhaps, if it's too small, we can—'

'Shut up, Carmel,' he groaned, dragging her into his arms, the weight of emotion all but choking him, but in a good way. In the right way. 'I don't care about the house, as long as you and Mac are in it… And Rocky,' he said.

She chuckled. 'And all his puppies.'

'Because then it will be home,' he finished.

Grasping his shoulders, she boosted herself into his

arms. He caught her easily as she wrapped her legs around his waist and began kissing his face.

He kissed her back with all the love bursting in his heart, the heat pounding through his veins as fierce and strong as the happiness enveloping him.

She reared back and gripped his cheeks. 'Now please tell me there's another bedroom in this place so we don't have to seal this deal in the hallway.'

He was still laughing as he sank into her a minute later, on the floor.

EPILOGUE

One year later

ROSS HEARD THE crowd hush and then the strains of the wedding march build at the back of Kildaragh's chapel. He imagined the bridal procession beginning to make their way down the aisle, the very same aisle he had marched down twelve months ago to stop a wedding.

Not yet...don't look yet.

He smiled, appreciating the irony—and the glorious swell of anticipation—as the melodic Celtic tune Carmel had chosen for her entrance matched the heavy thuds of his heartbeat.

Twelve months. Twelve long, endless months it had taken to get to this day. Because apparently he and Carmel had very different opinions about what 'not waiting' a moment longer than necessary to get married actually meant. But in a few minutes the waiting would finally be over.

Carmel, of course, had insisted everything had to be just right. So there'd been the wait for Immy and Donal's baby boy, Ronan, to be born, then another longer wait for Katie and Conall's daughter, Caitlyn, to finally arrive on Christmas Day. Then there had been a new house to build—so he could move his business headquarters here, as well as having room for his family. He'd put up with all the delays with remarkable patience and fortitude. Given that he'd been desperate to make her his wife—legally, officially, in every way that was humanly possible—as soon as she agreed to marry him. In the end, he'd brought Katie in to help plan the wedding and speed things along. But still it had taken one never-ending year to finally get to this day.

'Daddy, Mammy's coming now,' his little boy and best man—who looked particularly grown up with his blond curls slicked back and wearing a miniature wedding suit—announced loudly beside him. Ross smiled despite the nerves and looked down at his son, who had his arm wrapped around the neck of Ross's other best man, or rather his best dog.

'She looks so pretty,' Mac murmured, the awe in his tone making Ross realise he couldn't wait one damn moment longer.

He shifted round. And his thundering heartbeat got wedged in his throat—virtually cutting off his air supply.

Mac is wrong.

With her russet hair perched precariously on her head and threaded through with wildflowers, the sleek fall of cream silk accentuating her slender curves as she headed down the aisle towards him on her brother's arm, and that stunning bone structure, fair skin and pure blue eyes— only made more bewitching by the wisp of lace covering her face—Mac's mammy wasn't just pretty, she was absolutely stunning.

He had to force himself to keep breathing. Stunning, both inside and out.

At last, his bride and her brother reached them.

Katie and Imelda arrived behind them in their maid-of-honour dresses. His sister and his soon-to-be sister-in-law positively beamed with pleasure while Donal looked on from his spot in the front row, holding little Ronan securely on his lap and guarding a bassinet with the sleeping Caitlyn in it.

Conall presented Carmel's hand to Ross, then stepped back, winking at him. Incredible to think Con and he had actually become friends over the last year—more than friends, brothers—bonding over the chaos of new fatherhood and their shared dismay at exactly how they were supposed to handle the two extremely strong-willed women they'd chosen to share their lives with.

He took Carmel's hand, felt her fingers tremble in his—and suddenly the only thing he could concentrate on was her. She grinned at him, but the power and poignancy of the moment was reflected in her misty sapphire eyes.

He stroked his thumb across the soft skin and grinned back at her as the powerful thought squeezed his chest too. Tonight, they would be a family, in every sense of the word, before God and man.

'About time you showed up,' he murmured.

She gave a low chuckle, which struck him deep in his abdomen. 'Don't you worry, you'll not be getting rid of me or Mac now.'

He smiled back at her, the elation making his heart swell against his ribs. 'Don't *you* worry, I intend to hold you both to that promise, for all eternity.'

She blinked, the happy sheen in her eyes making his own sting.

But then Mac squeezed himself between them both, holding up the band of white gold Ross had given him not ten minutes ago and shouted, 'Can Rocky and me give you the ring now, Daddy?'

And the whole assembly dissolved into laughter.

'I now declare you man and wife. You may kiss your bride, Ross,' Father Meehan finally announced.

Carmel couldn't stop grinning, her heart so buoyant it was all but flying as Ross finally got around to lifting her veil.

Spontaneous applause swelled under the roof of the old chapel. She could hear Mac cheering like a lunatic as his uncle Conall boosted him into his arms, Rocky's excited barking, and a baby wailing—probably poor Caitlyn woken by all the commotion—and feel the confetti fluttering onto her cheeks. But all she could see was the love dancing in Ross's eyes—pure, true, strong, for ever—exactly the way it was dancing in her heart.

He placed callused palms on her warm cheeks, lifted her face to his, and pressed his mouth to hers at last.

She let out a soft sob, the exquisite sensation gathering in her belly nothing compared to the storm of emotion singing in her heart. The kiss went from sweet to carnal as his tongue delved deep, exploring, exploiting and claiming every inch of her as his. She pressed her hands to his waist and kissed him back with the same force and fury, claiming him right back as hers.

The applause, the barking, the shouting and baby cries faded until all she could hear was the sure solid beat of her heart. But then as her brand-new husband pulled away—forced to come up for air—she leaned up on tiptoes, held him close and whispered in his ear. 'By the way, you should know, in about seven and a bit months' time, it'll not just be me and Mac and Rocky you're stuck with for all eternity.'

His eyes popped wide, his hands tightening on her waist as she watched the emotions—emotions he no longer felt the need to hide from her—flicker across his face. Confusion, surprise, shock, awe... And uninhibited joy.

Then he lifted her off her feet, spun her round and

threw his head back to add yet more noise to their wild Irish wedding commotion.

Needless to say it took close to another whole eternity to calm down the dog and their son again long enough to tell them the good news, too.

* * * * *

COMING SOON!

We really hope you enjoyed reading this book.
If you're looking for more romance
be sure to head to the shops when
new books are available on

Thursday 17th
July

To see which titles are coming soon, please visit
millsandboon.co.uk/nextmonth

MILLS & BOON

LET'S TALK
Romance

For exclusive extracts, competitions and special offers, find us online:

f MillsandBoon

X @MillsandBoon

O @MillsandBoonUK

♪ @MillsandBoonUK

Get in touch on 01413 063 232

FOUR BRAND NEW BOOKS FROM
MILLS & BOON MODERN

The same great stories you love, a stylish new look!

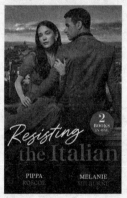

OUT NOW

Eight Modern stories published every month, find them all at:

millsandboon.co.uk

afterglow BOOKS

Afterglow Books is a trend-led, trope-filled list of books with diverse, authentic and relatable characters, a wide array of voices and representations, plus real world trials and tribulations. Featuring all the tropes you could possibly want (think small-town settings, fake relationships, grumpy vs sunshine, enemies to lovers) and all with a generous dose of spice in every story.

♪ @millsandboonuk

◎ @millsandboonuk

afterglowbooks.co.uk

#AfterglowBooks

For all the latest book news, exclusive content and giveaways scan the QR code below to sign up to the Afterglow newsletter:

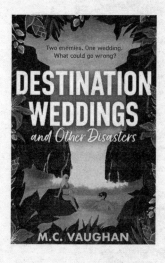
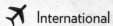